The Dark That Creates

The Light of Darkness Book Two

Steve Pantazis

SP Books

ISBN (paperback); 978-1-957921-03-7

ISBN (hardcover): 978-1-957921-02-0

Written by Steve Pantazis

Cover artwork by germancreative

Map design by Steve Pantazis

Interior artwork by Samsul Hidayat

Published by SP Books

To my wife, my love, my one and only
To my father, whose wisdom shaped my life
To my mother, who taught me to believe in myself

Contents

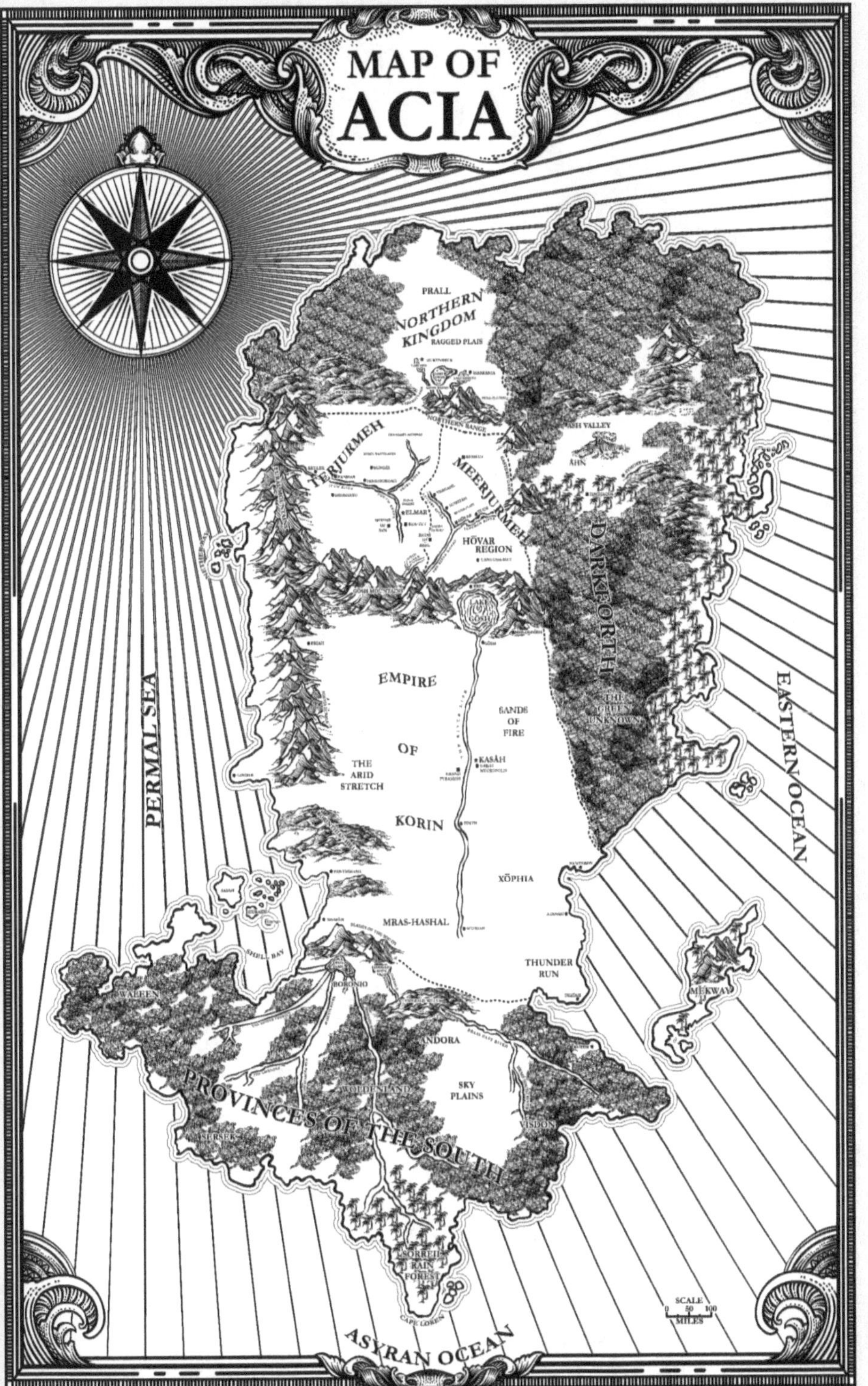

MAP OF ACIA
PRALL
NORTHERN KINGDOM
RAGGED PLAINS
NORTHERN RANGE
TERIURMEH
MEERJURMEH
HÖVAR REGION
DARKFORTH
VALLEY
ÄHN
THE GREEN UNKNOWN
EMPIRE OF KORIN
SANDS OF FIRE
THE ARID STRETCH
KASÄH
XÖPHIA
MRAS-HASHAL
THUNDER RUN
ELMAR
MEKWAY
PERMAL SEA
EASTERN OCEAN
SHELL BAY
BORONHO
ANDORA
SKY PLAINS
PROVINCES OF THE SOUTH
RAIN FOREST
CAPE LOREN
ASYRAN OCEAN
SCALE
0   50   100
MILES

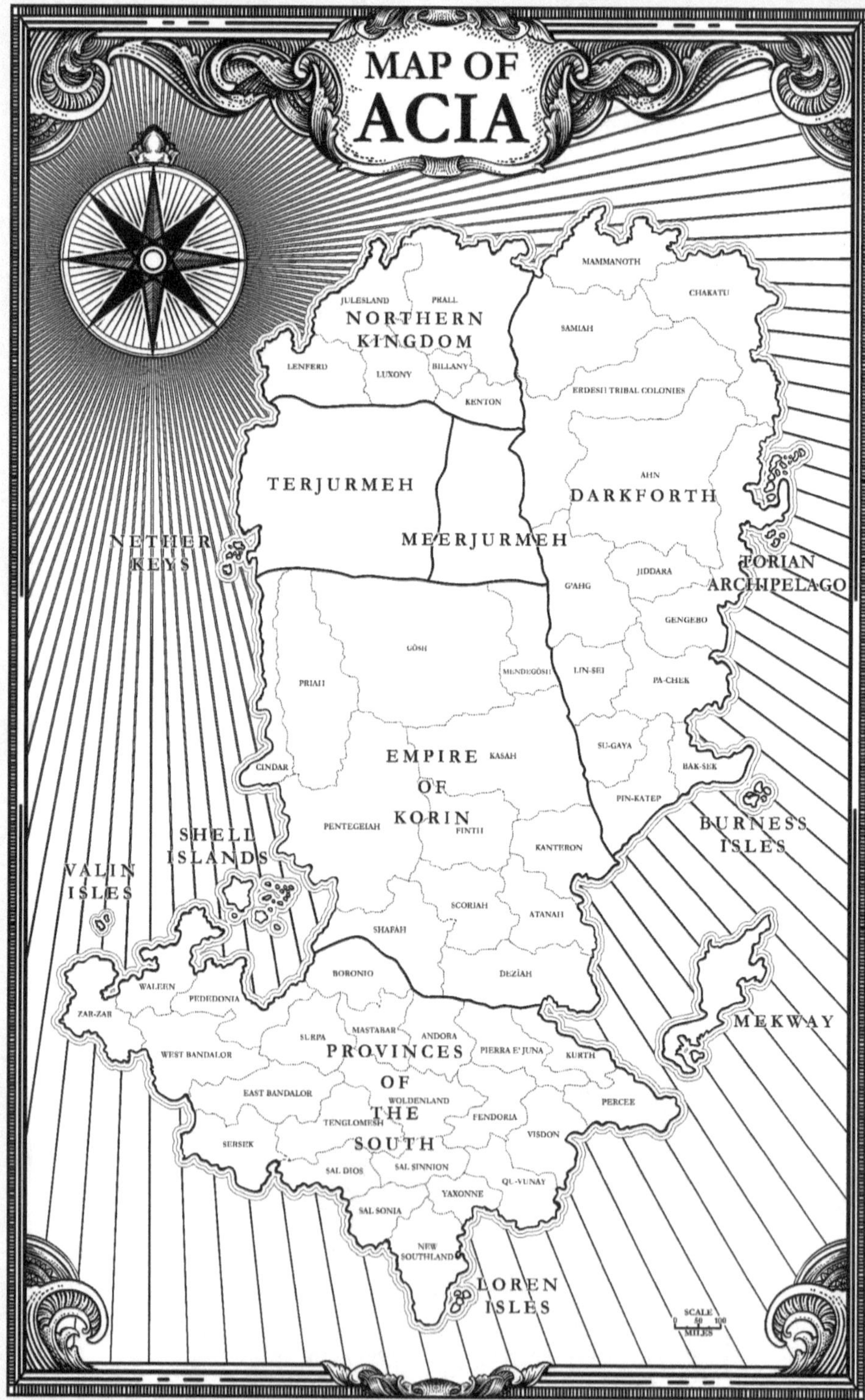

MAP OF ACIA
NORTHERN KINGDOM
JULESLAND
PRALL
LENFERD
LUXONY
BILLANY
KENTON
TERJURMEH
MEERJURMEH
NETHER KEYS
MAMMANOTH
CHAKATU
SAMIAH
ERDESH TRIBAL COLONIES
AHN
DARKFORTH
TORIAN ARCHIPELAGO
G'AHG
JIDDARA
GENGEBO
GÔSH
MENDEGÔSH
LIN-SEI
PA-CHEK
PRIAH
SU-GAYA
BÁK-SEK
EMPIRE
OF
KORIN
KASAH
CINDAR
PIN-KATEP
BURNESS ISLES
SHELL ISLANDS
PENTEGEIAH
FINTH
KANTERON
VALIN ISLES
SCORIAH
ATANAH
SHAFAH
BORONIO
DEZIAH
WALERN
MEKWAY
ZAR-ZAR
PEDEDONIA
MASTABAR
ANDORA
SURPA
PROVINCES
PIERRA E'JUNA
KURTH
WEST BANDALOR
OF
EAST BANDALOR
WOLDENLAND
PERCEE
THE
FENDORIA
TENGLOMESH
VISDON
SERSEK
SOUTH
SAL DIOS
SAL SINNION
QU-VUNAY
YAXONNE
SAL SONIA
NEW SOUTHLAND
LOREN ISLES
SCALE
0   50   100
MILES

Terjurmeh & Meerjurmeh

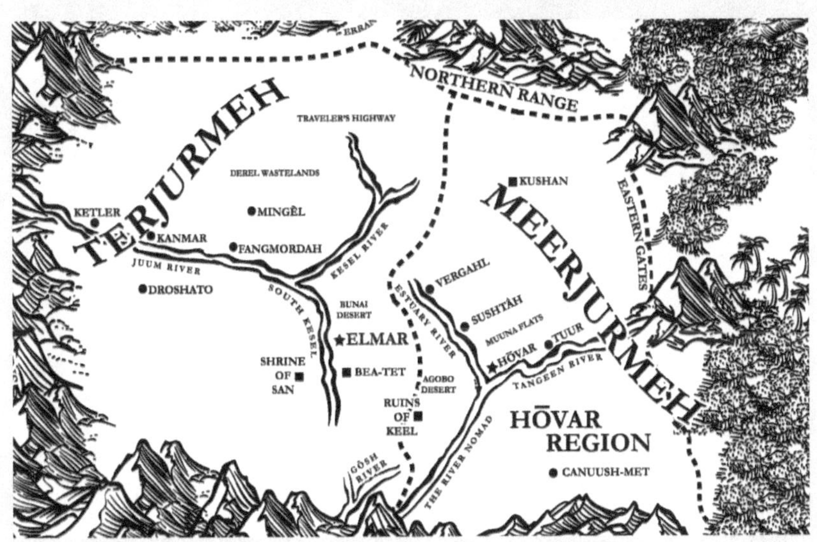

Northern Kingdom

DARKFORTH

DARKFORTH
SERPENT'S BELT
ASH VALLEY
VANYA
ÂHN
SYMORRAH
EASTERN GATES
HACHAQUA
URMEH
GION
JUSH-MET
MENDEGŌSH
SANDS OF FIRE
THE GREEN UNKNOWN

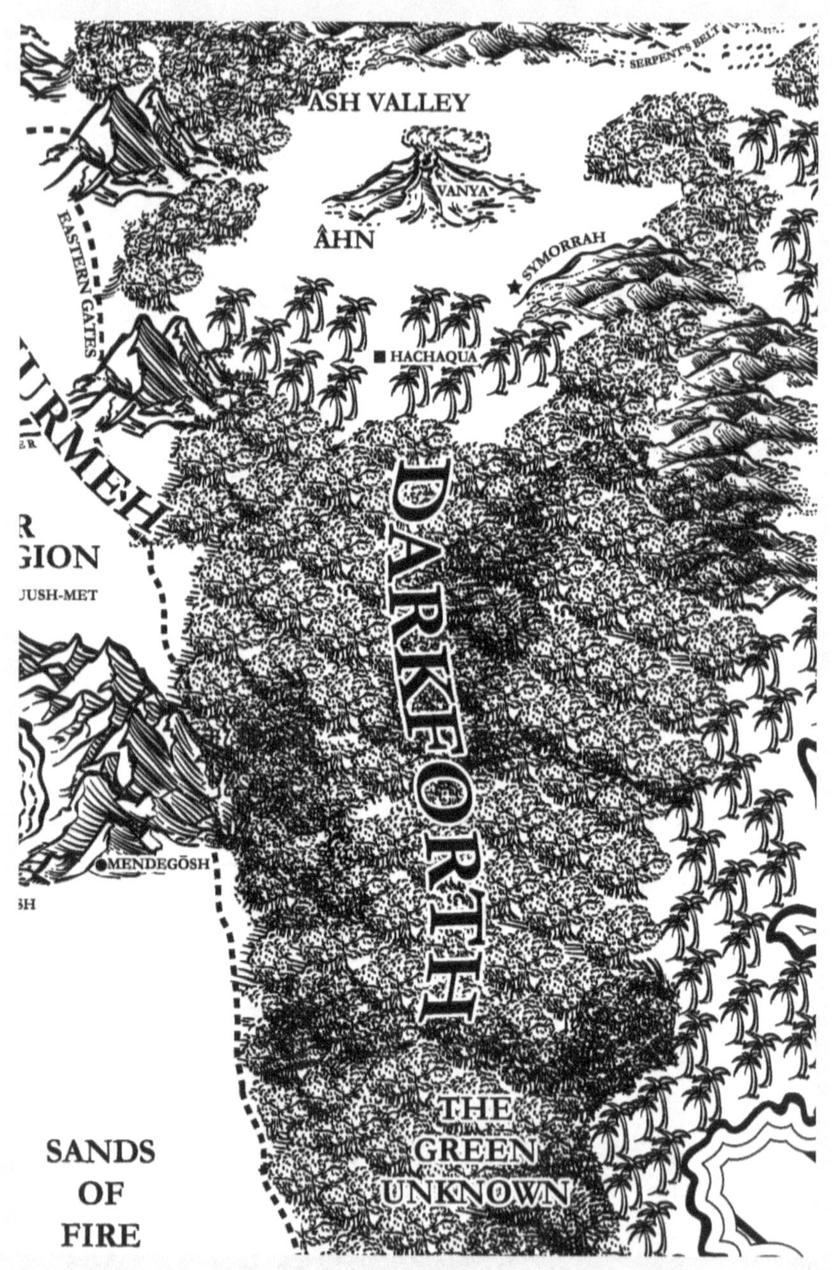

Empire of Korin

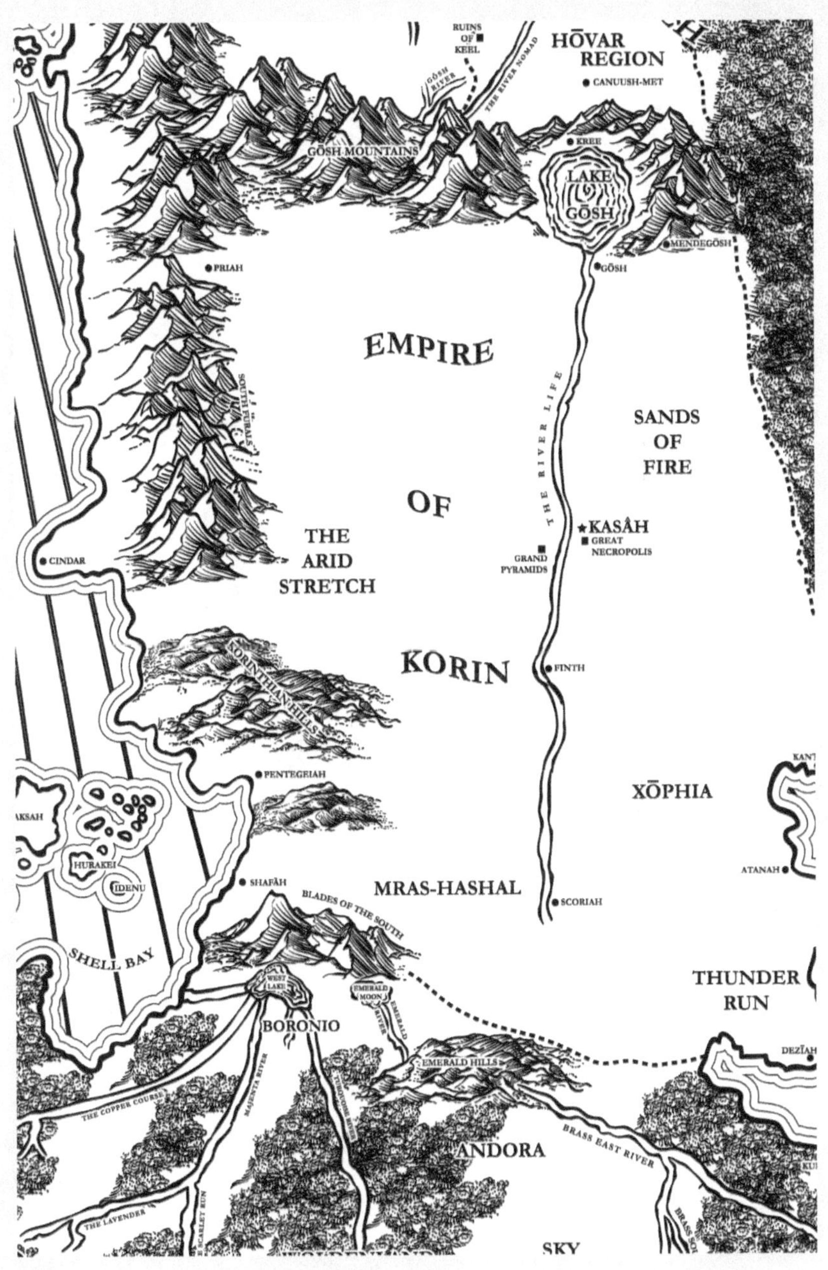

PROVINCES OF THE SOUTH

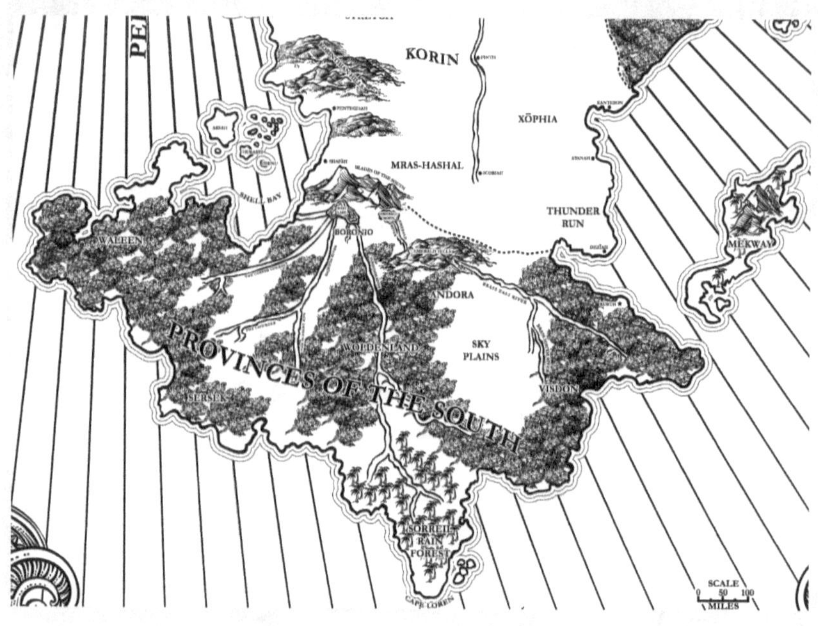

Chapter 1
Dark Prophecy

J ORIAH HURRIED DOWN THE winding stairs of the grand temple, sweat pouring from his brow, chest heaving to get enough of the stale air. He kept his left hand against the rough, stone wall to steady himself as he descended the precariously steep stairwell. One misstep, one false move, and he'd trip and tumble.

I'm always rushing, he thought, blinking the sting of perspiration from his eyes. *That's the crux of the problem.*

The temple, the Dome of San, crested the pinnacle of the capital city of Elmar as a beacon of faith. But it was larger than it appeared—much larger—plunging deep into the bedrock of the hill it sat upon. Torches danced in their sconces, casting mad shadows and releasing the smell of burning pitch.

Joriah slipped but caught himself, catching a crevice along the stone wall with fingers that clawed to find purchase. *Is there no end to this cursed spiral of stairs?*

There were few things Joriah despised more than being called to a meeting of the Temple elite. Not that he didn't appreciate their invitation. He was, after all, a mage of the Green Flame party, a layman in a country that bowed before the Temple's might. To be invited to a secret gathering of powerful clergy was deemed an honor of the highest level.

Yet I have no choice.

Joriah's duties seemed to grow by the day. As a senior mage of his party, he had the magi school at Maseah to run and new apprentices to recruit.

He also found himself pulled into an increasing number of meetings with top officials within his own party. And then there was today, a holiday of all occasions, where he dashed to rendezvous with Uhtah-Pei, the leader of his party, a man touted as one of the most controversial figures in the country.

Uhtah-Pei didn't just head up the Green Flame. He also served as a high-ranking official in the Temple, a member of the Sacred Nine. In a nation where the clergy were supposed to keep their noses out of secular affairs, Uhtah-Pei had boldly—and some would say recklessly—seized hold of the country's political apparatus and turned it on its head. Joriah believed in Uhtah-Pei, but the Articulate demanded too much of his time.

He taxes me without end, but what can I do?

There was nothing Joriah could do, not if he wanted his star to brighten among the constellation of magi in Terjurmeh.

Joriah reached the base of the stairs, winded, with hair matted to his forehead and sweat running from the back of his neck down his robe. He combed back his slick hair with his fingers, straightened his black robe, and entered the temple's antechamber as composed as possible, given the circumstances.

Two clerics stood guard before a sealed entryway, faces reflecting the sooty torchlight. One pulled down on a lever inset into the stone wall, and the round door rolled slowly to the side with a deep, grating sound. Joriah stepped across the grooved threshold and into the windowless, vaulted sanctum.

Four faces looked up from high-backed chairs around a circular table. None appeared happy at his tardy appearance.

"Apologies," he said, quickly taking the seat beside Uhtah-Pei.

The door closed with an unnerving boom, sealing the granite chamber from the outside, and Joriah along with it. Candles lit the room from a chandelier over the table. More along the wall gave off the pleasing scent of melting beeswax. A cool draft filtered down from a hidden gap somewhere in the ceiling.

Joriah noted he was the only layman among the small gathering, the others comprised of the Temple's upper echelon: three of Terjurmeh's five Articulates—Uhtah-Pei, Septamo, and Nisheppeh—and Baaka, Seer of Elmar, one of three Seers in the nation. Although uncomfortable sitting with such powerful individuals, it was Nisheppeh who made Joriah the most unsettled. She was the only woman among them, Third Articulate of the Temple but as dangerous as they came. Her heartless, dark eyes belied a sinister core as she looked at the newcomer, tracking his movement as a krell might track its prey. Even her short hair, black as crows' feathers, ended in a choppy sweep across her brow and to either side of her ears, like fangs.

Baaka wrinkled his nose from across the table. "You're late."

"My apologies, Holy One," Joriah said. "It took longer than expected to get through the crowds."

"It's a good thing it's a holiday," Baaka said, grinning. "Otherwise, we might have you stand naked in the corner, as we do with the clerics."

Joriah smiled politely. Baaka liked to poke fun, but in no way invited him to do the same. Joriah lifted the mug in front of him and gave it a sniff. There was an earthiness to it. A sip confirmed black tea, lukewarm from sitting there. He drank his fill.

Uhtah-Pei whispered into Joriah's ear. "Is your Gray Robe situated?" He was referring to Petrah, who'd left Maseah earlier in the morning.

"He is, Holy One."

Septamo, First Articulate of the Temple, frowned at the late arrival. He was second in line to the Mighty One, the Temple's papal head, and he liked to flaunt his authority. "Now that we're all here, I'd like to continue, if that's all right." He looked at Uhtah-Pei.

"Of course," Uhtah-Pei said with a noble bow of the head.

Joriah appreciated Uhtah-Pei's ability to defer to Septamo, even though the Articulates were equals. If there was one thing Joriah admired about the Temple's elite, it was their willingness to work together—and share power.

Septamo went on. "As I was saying, I spoke to the Mighty One yesterday after midnight service. He gave his blessing for phase one of our plan. We're to pass word to the senior members of the clergy right away."

"It's about time," Uhtah-Pei said. "What about the measures we proposed? Do we have the go-ahead to fortify our troop positions in the cities?"

"We do," Septamo said. "Triple the number of Temple troops over the next twenty-four months, sooner if possible."

Joriah could tell where this was going. Even though the Temple maintained its own force of troops for protecting its people, monuments, and temples, the numbers were negligible compared to the forces under the control of the parties. An increase in Temple troops meant the Temple was posturing to impose its will and—if Joriah was reading into this correctly—eventually seize power and abolish the political parties altogether.

It was an interesting play. The country of Terjurmeh was already a theocracy, but with dozens of parties vying for domination, it left Terjurmeh weak . . . and fractured. A unified Terjurmeh under the Temple's absolute rule, including control of her military, would make it a powerful adversary.

"And what about the *San-mahadi*?" Nisheppeh asked. Her voice, cold as her eyes, made Joriah shudder. He'd met her only twice, but it had been enough. In here, her skin took on a deep, shadowed tone against the flickering candles. In the daylight, Joriah recalled the unusual cobalt tint to her olive complexion, as if she'd battled demons in the underworld and absorbed their essence.

Septamo wrapped his thin fingers around his mug. "Your fellow Articulates helped me convince the Mighty One to reinstate the sacred order. He's appointing one of our senior priests to the top post as we speak. Effective tomorrow, the new head will have the authority to recruit mahadi and send them out to any secular organization or tribe at will."

Joriah knew of the mahadi only from historical texts. They were a volunteer force made up of clergy, anointed by the Temple to root out heretics in the name of San, used in the past as an extreme measure to purge threats to the Temple. This occurred whenever the balance of power favored the secular, as it was starting to with the Fist's rise in prominence among parties as of the most recent Great Council. Joriah hoped the mahadi could do their work before civil war broke out, pitting the parties against the Temple, an event that hadn't happened in a millennium.

Septamo continued. "I will announce His Holiness's edict to the masses, following my sermon at midnight. You all know what kind of response we're going to get, especially with every key politician within earshot. Baaka, we'll need a strong showing of Temple troops."

"Consider it done," Baaka said, flattening a wayward thread against the seam of his impeccable scarlet robe. "No party will even think to denounce the proclamation."

Septamo turned to Uhtah-Pei. "Speaking of parties, it sounds like yours is getting put to the test. Last I heard, you're being excluded from sanction talks with the Con-jurah. What's that about?"

Uhtah-Pei waved his hand dismissively. "It's nothing. The Fist and the Black Arrow are playing a silly game, that's all. They think if they shut us out of their talks, it will send a message to the other parties that we're no longer needed in the political community. No one will believe such a ruse."

"I'm not worried about ruses," Septamo said. "I'm worried about civil unrest turning into something disastrous. If the Green Flame alienates itself completely, we'll have an unstable situation. I need you to keep your party members under control. We can't afford any disruptions to our progress."

Uhtah-Pei scoffed. "Brother, you worry too much. I'll handle it. Just concentrate on our funding. The rest will take care of itself."

The First Articulate crossed his arms and sat back, his expression unpleasant.

Baaka tapped the tabletop with his knuckles. "While I enjoy hearing us squabble over political posturing, what I'd really like to know is what's going on with our An-jurahn brothers to the east."

Nisheppeh spoke up in an icy tone that made Joriah squirm in his seat like sharp nails raked across slate. "I met with members from the newly minted Warlord Council in Âhn. They're going to choose a War Chief once they have enough warlords on board. The An-jurah still struggle to annex the southern states. Octapia, who came to visit us a few months back, told me the priesthood is getting involved in the matter. They're sending their Su-yi to deal with the unwilling warlords. Everything should be cleared up by spring."

If Nisheppeh had been in Âhn, it meant she'd journeyed to Darkforth. Joriah began to understand this great plot being revealed and why the meeting had been called in secret. The An-jurah were allies of the Ter-jurah. Once, they were a single people. Now, they shared a common enemy: Meerjurmeh, the desert country that stood between Terjurmeh and the wilds of Darkforth. If the An-jurah were working to annex their warring states under one banner, as Nisheppeh suggested, it would be another step toward the prophecy of the An-jurah and Ter-jurah uniting to vanquish their enemy for good. Terjurmeh didn't have the strength to do it on its own. With Meerjurmeh's loose alliance with the Northern

Kingdom and the Empire of Korin, Terjurmeh would require the full strength of the An-jurah to wage war against Meerjurmeh.

Baaka gave an amused nod. "Those Su-yi are nasty bastards. I hear they skin their opponents and hang them upside down while they're still alive."

"I'm not swayed by your high priest's assertions," Septamo told Nisheppeh. "What assurance do we have that the An-jurah will bring us our frontline fodder when we need it?"

"I met with our *friend* in Darkforth before I left," Nisheppeh said, dark eyes dancing in the candlelight. "He insisted all the pieces will come together when the time comes. I consider that as good as San speaking directly into my ears. Wouldn't you agree?"

Septamo nodded, an odd look of satisfaction creeping onto his face. The "friend" Nisheppeh referred to was a divine agent of San's. He was called the Gatekeeper in the Holy Scriptures, a powerful being believed to have once been an angel, destined to set key events into motion to aid the children of San to defeat their enemies. If he assured certain events would happen, Joriah believed it.

Nisheppeh turned her haunting eyes toward the mage. "Our friend asked about a certain someone in your charge, a young man with a peculiar name."

"Petrah," Joriah said. "He's one of my journeymen."

"Our friend wants to know when Petrah will complete his mage training. I plan to speak to our friend on the morrow. What should I tell him?"

"Let me answer this," Uhtah-Pei said, patting Joriah's hand. "You can tell our friend the young man is well on his way to completing his training. He's leaving for Hōvar after the holiday. We've given him a mission. He's to spy for us in Hōvar. It'll be a good use of his talents, which Joriah believes are extraordinary for someone so new to the arcane arts. From there, he travels to Tuur to meet Anandawa, who is returning from Darkforth. Anandawa will speed up our journeyman's training.

Once his training is complete, we'll arrange for his travel to Darkforth. Petrah's abilities will be considerable by then. That's what our friend wants, isn't it?"

Nisheppeh pushed into the table with her long fingers. "Yes. Does your journeyman know of these illustrious plans?"

"No," Uhtah-Pei said. "Petrah knows only of his immediate task as a spy. He believes he's returning to Elmar to attend a journeyman school and resume his education. He doesn't know about Tuur or that our friend will send him home."

Baaka's eyes lit up. "Ah, so our young Petrah is going to have a family reunion."

Septamo frowned. "Why are we wasting time discussing this and why do we care if this journeyman reunites with his family? Aren't there more pressing matters than talking about some commoner under Joriah's charge?"

Baaka started laughing.

"You find that funny?"

"Not at all, Septamo," Baaka said. "I find it apropos. I'm sorry you've been kept in the dark, but our journeyman is San-Jahad's little brother. Hardly a commoner."

Looks of surprise filled the room. Even Nisheppeh arched an eyebrow. Joriah knew about Petrah's heritage from a previous conversation with Baaka. That Petrah and San-Jahad—the prophesied son of San, God of Darkness—shared the same father, making Petrah and San-Jahad brothers. Joriah would have thought Septamo would know of Petrah's divine blood and his relation to his brother.

Septamo came partway out of his seat. "That's quite the declaration. I know you have a fancy for prophecies, Baaka, but even this is a stretch, wouldn't you say?"

"You've seen his eyes," Baaka said. "The blue-eyed slave, if you recall? The one whose life you spared?"

"Him? He's the one?" Septamo furrowed his brow. "Manis-cor wanted him dead when I visited the slave works in Kanmar. It's rumored he burned a slave galley to ashes and helped the slaves aboard escape, costing the lives of the crew and her captain. You're telling me he's San-Jahad's brother because of the color of his eyes? He's just a slave. An escaped slave at that."

"*Was* a slave," Uhtah-Pei amended. "I released him from bondage."

"And he became one of your journeymen? How?"

Uhtah-Pei explained how Joriah recruited Petrah as a mage apprentice for the Green Flame, and Petrah's advancement to journeyman. "Imagine it, Septamo: our Gray Robe was a doomed slave when you first met him. Now, he's to serve a part in the greatest prophecy ever told. Have you ever heard of a slave rising to such prominence? It's unfathomable."

"Still," Septamo said, holding up a finger, "that doesn't make him the blood of the Great One. How would the son of a god become a slave, to begin with?"

"I've seen what Petrah sees," Baaka said. "Joriah brought him to me, and I looked into his mind. He's from San-Jahad's homeland, reborn here. His slavery is a matter of circumstance. He is without a doubt the blood of the Father, which makes him the blood of the Great One as well. His brother needs him. Fate calls and Petrah must answer. That's why our friend wants to send him home. If young Petrah can first conquer his channeling abilities and achieve magehood, imagine what a formidable warrior he will be by his brother's side when the Great One comes to Acia to help us defeat the Con-jurah and all the other believers of the false god."

Septamo seemed only slightly moved by the revelation. "San the Father begot many children over the ages, as we've all heard, although none among us today. Does the blue-eyed one share the same mother as the Great One?"

Baaka shrugged. "It's unimportant which vessel carried them into this world. Their mothers could have been whores for all we care. It's the children that are sacred and the ichor in their veins that matters. And, more importantly, it's their place in history that makes them who they are."

"What's your journeyman's place, then?" Septamo asked. "I've seen nothing in the Scriptures that speaks of a brother to San-Jahad. His part is apocryphal at best."

"Our friend is the Gatekeeper between the world of Acia and the Great One's, and Petrah is the Key," Baaka said. "He's the linchpin to San-Jahad's arrival. San-Jahad, who is the Great One, the Great Son, and also the Sword. You won't find the Key mentioned in the Scriptures, but you will find it written in the stars. I've seen it. Now that I have looked into Petrah's mind, I am certain of it." Baaka's lip curled into a contented smile.

Septamo nodded, finally giving in. "San indeed works in mysterious ways. We must recognize it when it presents itself in such a profound fashion. Your second sight is most welcome, Baaka."

"I agree," Nisheppeh said, teeth poking below her upper lip like a krell's. "We need to assure San-Jahad's brother is delivered safely to our friend. I suggest we keep him here in Elmar rather than send him off, at least until we can provide a proper escort after he's completed his training. I don't trust Anandawa. He's a loner and a renegade among magi, even if he's immensely talented in the arts."

Joriah waited for Uhtah-Pei to balk at the suggestion, which he did. "Petrah is *my* responsibility. He goes to Hōvar, as planned. Unless you can supply us with a spy unknown to the Meerjurmehan delegation. As for Anandawa, he's more than capable of keeping Petrah safe."

Nisheppeh folded her hands but didn't argue the point. Septamo abstained as well.

"Then it's settled," Uhtah-Pei said.

Joriah was thankful his leader stood up for their cause and pushed for Petrah to go to Hōvar, but the idea he might lose his Gray Robe didn't sit well with him. Still, the matter wasn't his to decide.

Quiet stole over the chamber, but only for a moment.

Baaka held out a finger and pointed it at each person at the table before hooking a thumb toward himself. "Every one of us has a purpose, a part in the Father's plan. Tonight, we proclaim it. Tomorrow, we set it into motion. We will cleanse our nation of heretics, and then we will go after the unbelievers who curse our god and make theirs supreme.

"This is a pivotal moment, brothers and sister. San is with us: his strength is in our hearts, his power in our souls, and soon, his vengeance at our fingertips. The Scriptures speak of the Great Reckoning—the end of days for the unworthy—as *his* time. It will be our time too."

The Seer stood and clasped his hands. "Pray with me."

Heads bowed.

"Father of Truth, hear our prayer. Guide us as we unfold your plan to purge the unbelievers from Acia. Enlighten us as we architect your mighty *Samath*. Strengthen us as we muster the courage to walk with you. Bless us as we sacrifice our captured enemies this holiday. Your divinity is ineffable, sacrosanct, and without measure. In your name, we ask these things. In the name of the Father, blood to spirit."

"Blood to spirit," repeated the group.

The Seer dabbed the air in the shape of the holy delta and sat down. The others remained quiet, absorbing the words with introspective devotion.

Samath.

Joriah knew the ancient word. It was the holiest of wars, whispered among soothsayers and zealots alike, the reclamation of the Truthful.

Armageddon.

Chapter 2
Feast of the Hammer

P ETRAH MOVED THROUGH THE packed streets of Elmar under the glare of the midday sun, squished together with hundreds of people. It seemed as if everyone in the country had descended on the capital to celebrate the holiday of Hah'xallah.

Petrah let his friend Kruush lead the way toward the city center. Stocky and sturdy, Kruush carved a path through the congestion, making room for Petrah and their other friends, Tan and Ahleen, who walked single file behind him.

Petrah didn't want to be here. The swell of people flocking to the streets, coupled with their shouts of jubilee, constant motion, and undesirable body odors, was too much for him. He'd gotten accustomed to the quiet and openness of Maseah during his time as a mage apprentice, the great estate that belonged to the Green Flame party. Just this morning, he'd left the estate, saying heartfelt goodbyes to friends like Taka and Ajoon. He hadn't expected Elmar to be so hectic on a holiday. Even on San's Day, when the crowds gathered for prayer in the city, there was room to breathe and some semblance of order. Today's crowds were pushy and suffocating. Maybe his friends would consider abandoning this madness and leaving the city ahead of the ambassador's schedule.

But first, he had to convince Kruush. "Can't we leave today?"

Kruush maneuvered around a donkey cart jutting out into the road. Like Petrah, he wore a simple beige tunic and sandals. The donkey brayed as Petrah passed, breath scented of hay, the bell around its throat ringing. "You know we can't do that," Kruush said.

The traffic eased for a few paces before forming another bottleneck. Tan and Ahleen were right behind them. Hawkers from vendor stalls tried to take advantage of the slowdown, competing for attention with wild hand waves and calls, adding to the chaotic jam of pedestrians. One old man with missing teeth dangled beaded necklaces with serak pendants in front of Ahleen, trying to negotiate with Tan to buy one for his "pretty lady."

Petrah pushed forward so Kruush could hear him. "But why can't we?"

Kruush cast dagger eyes at the hawker, who backed away. "Do you see all these people? It's a madhouse. We'd never make it out. Besides, I've already paid for a room for us, so that's that. And you forget, we're not traveling alone."

"But—"

"It's already decided. We leave tomorrow. Now let me concentrate on where we're going." Kruush squeezed past a pair of men who were standing in the middle of the street shouting at each other and pushed ahead.

Petrah knew better than to argue any further. And he knew Kruush was right and that Master Joriah would agree with him.

At first light on the morrow, Petrah and his friends would join the caravan of nomads and filter out the city gates. They'd trail the Terjurmehan ambassador's party and head across the desert to Hōvar, Meerjurmeh's capital, where Petrah would spy on behalf of the Green Flame—his first assignment as a mage journeyman. Master Joriah had coordinated with Kruush to ensure Petrah had a safe escort to Hōvar and would have everything he needed for his mission. Petrah didn't inquire how much Master Joriah had paid Kruush for this arrangement, but he'd asked Kruush if Ahleen and Tan knew about his mission.

"Of course they know," Kruush had said. "Did you think Tan and Ahleen thought you were traveling to Meerjurmeh on holiday? And before you get your head in a fuss about it, I told your master that I would tell them, but no others, and he agreed. To everyone else, you're a merchant's apprentice of the White Hand, working for me."

Petrah looked forward to proving himself to both Kruush and Master Joriah, but leaving Maseah—his home for the past year—left his stomach in knots. Was it because he'd be gone for almost two months, as Kruush had estimated? Was it the sheer responsibility of performing to Master Joriah's expectations? To Kruush's?

But as a young lady in a white tunic passed Petrah, with the same short hair and wide hips as Ajoon's, he knew. The young lady made eye contact with Petrah, furrowed her brow as Petrah's eyes lingered too long, and hurried along. Petrah's pulse quickened and his stomach clenched even tighter.

Ajoon's face remained etched in Petrah's mind. He remembered how her two-toned eyes had reflected the pain and confusion just a few hours earlier when he'd apologized to her. For the deadly incident involving Miko. For showing Ajoon his ugly side. For breaking their trust.

Her words came back to him with heaviness. *Petrah, I won't lie and say our friendship can be what it was. But my heart hurts.* His chest constricted, making each inhale more difficult than the last. *I forgive you*, she'd told him. He wanted to believe her. To believe he could repair their relationship. But to wait two months until he saw her again . . .

It's too long. Much too long.

Petrah practiced his mantra, Copper Still, to calm his runaway thoughts. With each step, the constriction in his chest eased; with each inhalation, the knots in his stomach loosened.

Being with his friends helped. Ahleen, like an older sister, shared a kind and comforting smile with him. Tan, acting his usual, playful self, flirted with not one but two ladies selling wares in stalls beside each other. Kruush, with a confident but comical flick of his wrist, fended off another hawker adamant about peddling his trinkets to Ahleen. Petrah loved his friends for who they were—and as they were. They were family, and they would always be his family.

The four arrived at their destination in the early afternoon: the top of an ancient quarry shaped into an amphitheater. It sloped down to a large oval arena buttressed by a sheer sandstone wall that enclosed it. Already, hundreds of bystanders had settled in among the many rows of stone seats, although none sat, as was the custom on Hah'xallah. Kruush led Petrah, Ahleen, and Tan a third of the way down to a vacant space that could accommodate them.

Ahleen said to Petrah, "It's quite something, isn't it?"

Petrah hadn't taken part in a gathering of this size since his visit to the Great Hall, the ten-story coliseum that served as the meeting center for the annual Terjurmehan Great Council. The noise and constant movement here were just as intense and no less grand.

"It is."

Petrah thought he spotted a couple of his classmates in the crowd, Nuk and Taline perhaps, but it was hard to tell with all the commotion. Everyone was here for the Reenactment, the centerpiece of the summer's-end holiday celebration. The magi who ran the school at Maseah encouraged their students to attend so they could learn the meaning of Hah'xallah firsthand.

"Hah'xallah reminds us of our heritage," Master Nole had said in class the week prior. "It reminds us we are Ter-jurah. Just as important, it reminds the Con-jurah who we are. We do that by reenacting the day they almost forgot."

It was a painful reminder, too, as Petrah understood it. Each year, the Ter-jurah reenacted the fourth-century Terjurmehan victory over the Con-jurah in a vivid portrayal of the famed battle, concluded by a ceremonial sacrifice of actual Con-jurahn captives done the "old way."

Hah'xallah had earned the name "Feast of the Hammer" because of how the Ter-jurahn actors would bludgeon their captives using war hammers. Petrah thought the act sadistic and reprehensible. What was the purpose of venerating a bunch of warriors who were dead for over two thousand years?

There is no purpose. It's just an excuse to carry on a meaningless tradition.

"Look at them," Kruush said, shaking his head. "They're like a sea of vultures. They can't wait for the blood."

"The good news is we leave tomorrow," Tan said.

Tomorrow, the city would empty, as Hah'xallah signaled the end of the hot season. The nomadic tribespeople of Terjurmeh would leave for the desert, where the cold season's more temperate weather would make their travel tolerable.

"Aye," Kruush said. "And not soon enough. I should have listened to Petrah and forsaken this insanity."

From where Petrah stood, the amphitheater eased down several dozen feet to a ring around the quarry floor, girded by a ten-foot vertical drop. Families crowded around him, talking excitedly among themselves, with anticipation of the day's main event taut on their eager faces. Up near the top, Petrah noticed a line of Temple soldiers with their customary squared, red linen headdresses and spears. They outnumbered the city troops two to one, which Petrah thought odd.

"Why do you suppose there are so many Temple troops?" Petrah asked above the din, gesturing to the soldiers. Petrah had gone into the city many times, both to attend Temple and to carry out tasks for his masters. He'd seen the Temple troops scattered about, only a handful at a time. He counted nearly thirty here.

"There must be a delegation from the Temple in town," Kruush said. "Someone important, I'm guessing."

"But so many soldiers? No, it must be something else."

Kruush shrugged.

Petrah changed the subject. "Where are the actors and slaves coming from?"

Kruush pointed at the far wall of the quarry. "See that opening? A tunnel leads from the slave barracks to the floor. They'll come through there."

Petrah spotted a shadowed entrance hewn into the blond-colored rock, covered by a metal grate. He pictured the wretched slaves huddled and then forced to walk out, only to meet a horrific ending. At least as a city slave in Kanmar, Petrah didn't have to worry about being executed, not without bringing it on himself.

These poor souls were doomed from the start.

A crying child drew Petrah's attention behind him. The boy was perhaps six or seven, with teary, red-rimmed eyes and a round face. An older man on his right—his father most likely—and a woman holding his hand on his left accompanied him. The woman shook a finger at the boy and then said something to the man, who slapped the child hard across the face. Petrah flinched as if his own face had been struck. The boy started to sob, but a threatening raise of the arm from his father reduced it to a whimper. When the father saw Petrah looking at him, he shrugged and said, "Boys."

Petrah turned back toward the quarry floor, teeth gritted and heat flushing through his body. The way the father hit the boy stirred the painful memories of the times Petrah had gotten flogged as a slave. The man's mannerisms reminded him of Meska, the Draad who had made Petrah's life miserable. *Meska got what he deserved.* The slave master had lost his life to the very slaves he'd oppressed, a fitting end.

Kruush picked up on Petrah's irritation. "Don't pay him any attention. It's not worth it."

Petrah folded his arms and tried to heed what Kruush said. Yet the situation chaffed Petrah the wrong way, and he couldn't shake it.

Actors dressed as Terjurmehan soldiers poured out onto the quarry floor. They trotted around the perimeter of the site, waving to the audience with mock swords, rousing cheers, and laughter. They wore red-dyed leather breastplates over camel-colored tunics and carried elongated shields embossed with flames. A second group of actors in ancient tan, Con-jurahn armor came out. The crowd booed them, cursing, shouting, and making derogatory motions with their hands.

The actors split up into Ter-jurahn and Con-jurahn camps on opposite sides of the arena floor. A red-robed priest, accompanied by two clerics, walked out into the center. He ascended a podium midfield and held up his hands. The crowd fell silent.

"Children of San," the priest cried. "Behold the battlefield of Andelah, the ancient site of the greatest victory in our history. The year is 394. Our ancient capital of Ekmed has fallen. The Con-jurah believe their lands unassailable, their borders impenetrable. But lo! Our warriors have crossed the great desert into their homeland. The Ter-jurah surprise the Con-jurah and take them by force. Behold the Reenactment!"

A cleric issued a battle cry, and the Ter-jurah charged across the field to the crowd's roar.

The actors engaged each other in a mock melee. They hacked and thrust dramatically with their blunt swords. The crowd hooted and jeered in response. One by one, the Con-jurah fell. Their leader, a man with a wing-tipped helm, lifted his shield in a yielding fashion and dropped to his knees. His soldiers followed suit and laid down their weapons. The battle was over.

The crowd chanted, "*Ufah! Ufah!*" Hammers! Hammers!

The priest and clerics on the podium waved their arms up and down, whipping the spectators into a frenzy. People stamped and shouted "ufah" in cadence. Petrah and his friends were among the minority who withheld from the fervor.

Petrah felt a tap on his shoulder. He glanced behind and saw the boy's father glaring at him. The man shook a fist at Petrah. "Say *Ufah*!" His son was next to him, half-heartedly doing his part, with a swollen face. It made Petrah want to punch the man.

"Mind your own business." Petrah turned around. How dare this man tell him what to do? The muscles in Petrah's shoulders quivered and a bloom of heat washed over his face.

Below, the actors waved goodbye to the crowd and left. Draadi came out, pulling a train of naked men and women shackled and chained to one another.

Slaves.

Real Con-jurahn slaves, shaking and terrified.

Petrah's throat tightened.

We shouldn't be here. This is wrong. Wrong!

Soldiers entered the field carrying heavy war hammers. As soon as they lifted the oversized weapons above their heads, the crowd went wild.

Ufah! Ufah!

Workers wheeled out long stone blocks and latched them to the end of the podium. The Draadi positioned the slaves in a single line. By fours, they dragged them over and chained them to the blocks, chin down. Petrah heard accusations of "murderers" and "bastards" and more sordid names from the crowd. The slaves whimpered and cried and begged, but the energized crowd overtook their pleas.

Petrah pulled on the collar of his tunic as if he couldn't breathe, couldn't swallow, as if he were himself shackled.

The presiding priest raised his hand, and the spectators quieted down.

Ahleen looked away. Petrah would have too, but the macabre display below drew his eyes, much the way one might watch a slave galley go up in flames.

The first round of hammers fell, and the crowd cheered.

The soldiers carted off the bludgeoned slaves and secured another group for execution. Parents and children alike shouted in glee around Petrah. *What's the matter with these people?* He wanted to claw his way to the front, jump down, and yank the hammers from the soldiers, perhaps use them on the soldiers instead. Behind him, the boy's father was lost in a fit of bloodlust. The smell was also getting to Petrah: sweat, stone, and gore reminiscent of the day Aggren died at the hands of Draadi.

Ahleen held Petrah's arm, firm but not too tight. It was exactly the support he needed. His eyes traveled to hers. They were shaped with concern.

Had they been alone somewhere quiet, he could have expressed to her how this place—these people—were affecting him. How they were dredging up terrible memories and squeezing the breath from his lungs. Ahleen was someone who would listen but never judge. She was as good a person as any he'd known. But there were things best kept to himself. Between Miko's death, leaving Maseah, and this depraved display of brutality, Petrah wanted to find a hole and vanish.

Petrah raised his voice over the cheering. "We shouldn't have come here."

"Try not to watch," Ahleen said. "It's better that way."

How could he turn away when everywhere he looked, lewdness ran rampant? These people were a sepsis with putrid hearts and misguided rapture. Petrah's face and arms tingled. It was the same sensation he'd felt when he faced off against Miko. He was ashamed to be among these animals.

Ufah! Ufah!

The blaring of the chanting assaulted his ears. Petrah looked over his shoulder at the father of the boy, who was shouting with all his worth. The boy's father was no different from the rest, perhaps the worst of them all.

He caught Petrah staring and motioned with his hand. "Turn around!"

Petrah continued to stare.

"What did I tell you?"

Petrah's masters taught him never to strike an unarmed man without cause. They taught him never to use divine power without necessitation. They taught him many things, but he forgot them all in that instant.

Petrah grabbed the man by his tunic and hauled him around. He uttered a single word of power and sent the shocked man cascading downward. People tumbled into one another, driven forward by invisible momentum, tangling together. The man landed a few rows down, his fall broken by spectators who shrieked and yelled.

Kruush snatched Petrah's arm. "What are you doing?"

Petrah yanked his arm away. His anger turned to humiliation as he noticed the stunned onlookers around him.

"We need to leave," Kruush said. "Right now."

Kruush led the way, shoving past irate bystanders. Ahleen and Tan went next, Petrah last. The boy's mother cursed after Petrah and even spat at him, but he kept his head down and moved forward. Along the top of the incline, he spotted a pair of Temple troops pointing at the chaotic disruption and laughing. Other troops seemed preoccupied or mildly amused. None left their posts. Petrah braced himself for one to reach out and grab him, but he made it past the exit and kept going.

He didn't look up until they were well clear of the quarry and the angry mob. When they had distanced themselves from the commotion, they stopped.

Petrah apologized to his friends. "I don't know what came over me. First the hammers, then what they did to the slaves, and then—" He was getting worked up again. At least the tingling was gone. He shuddered to imagine what might have happened if he'd had Jayeem's sword with him. "It's no excuse for my actions. I'm sorry."

"It's over now," Kruush said, as far from happy as Petrah had ever seen him. "You could have gotten yourself arrested and us with you."

"If we linger, that might still happen," Ahleen said. "We should head to our room."

Kruush bobbed his head. "Aye. Thank goodness we head out in the morning. We'll finally be away from this place."

Even at their distance from the amphitheater, the sickening cheer from the crowd carried into the streets.

Tan gave a vigorous nod. "Right. It's time to leave. And not a moment too soon."

Chapter 3
Desert Journey

P ETRAH BREATHED IN THE fresh air of the Bunai Desert. The tenseness in his back and neck, the grimace on his face, the strain of clenching his belly—all of it released as he took in the wide-open stretch of sandy soil and spiked shrubs warming under the morning sun. Not once had he experienced such freedom—even aboard Monta-por's barge, when he and his friends had traveled from port to port along the serene Juum and South Kesel rivers.

Petrah was glad to be freed of Elmar and its cloying tumult. The exodus from the city had taken many long hours. It wasn't until late in the day after Hah'xallah that they cleared its walls. No longer did the air carry the urban stink of food, trash, and industry. The desert air was clean, and its purity did wonders to tame Petrah's troubled thoughts.

Kruush's caravan headed east across the Bunai Desert. They would carve through the flats, stop at the oasis village of Bea-tet, which served as a major trading post, and then cross the great Adobo Desert, with its mountains of sand dunes, and end up in Hōvar, Meerjurmeh's capital.

One thing was certain to Petrah: walking the desert's harsh terrain entirely on foot would be an impossible task.

Fortunately, he had Chíla.

She was a gonatan, a pack animal with sturdy legs, short, beige hair, a long, flat head with large eyes, and a swooping neck. Humps of fat protruded from the sides of her hindquarters, which would help her endure the extremes of the desert journey.

It took some getting used to riding her, but Tan helped Petrah learn how to sit properly on the saddle, use the reins, guide Chíla, and relax his thigh muscles so he didn't squeeze too hard and cramp up. With practice, and by having Chíla follow Tan's gonatan, Petrah got the knack. After several hours, he stopped worrying about falling off his mount. The sway of Chíla's rhythm soothed him, allowing him to enjoy the tranquility of his desert surroundings.

The emptiness brings me peace.

One thing Petrah knew about himself was that he cherished the stillness of the world. He preferred the solitude of meditation over the excitement of city life. Even though meditation had proven difficult at first in his schooling as a mage apprentice, his instructor Master Maglo had tirelessly worked with him to block the distractions and help Petrah achieve a mental silence so complete, even the noise and motion around him couldn't penetrate its barrier.

Now, Petrah enjoyed tuning in to his surroundings: the light whistle of the wind, the rustle of dried thistle, the roll of a tumbleweed. Nature grounded him and hushed the calamity of his busy mind.

As Master Maglo had put it, *A quiet mind is a good home for the soul.*

Kruush's caravan trailed the Terjurmehan ambassador's convoy. Master Joriah had given specific instructions to Kruush to allow the delegation plenty of distance, but not so much as to be outpaced. They needed to follow the same schedule. Delegates from the Fist, Black Arrow, Silver Blade, and Copper Shield, and a few less prominent parties, made up the contingent. Green Flame members were absent and disallowed from attending, hence Petrah's role as the spy for his party. No one knew who lowly Petrah was. He'd only just earned the Gray. Before that, he was a Green Robe, a mage apprentice to whom nary a person paid attention to unless they caught sight of his brilliant blue eyes. It was the fundamental trait that distinguished him from other Ter-jurah. Not one individual he'd met had blue eyes.

But my brother has them, he thought as he rode Chíla through an expanse of desert shrubs.

The same brother who, like the Watcher, invaded his dreams. The masses had chanted his name.

Aman.

The Great One, according to the Holy Scriptures. San-Jahad too, and other appellatives of glorification.

Petrah had another name as well. Immael, the Watcher had said. His birth name.

Petrah had studied the prophecy that foretold the Great One's role in bringing victory to the Ter-jurah over their enemies. San-Jahad was the son of San, the God of Shadows.

And if he was San's son, and Petrah was his brother . . .

Then San is my father too.

Petrah laughed at the notion. The only divine thing about him was the arcane power he channeled. Any mortal with the right aptitude could learn to channel. Were they children of a god?

No, and I'm not either.

Yet the Watcher occupied his dreams with the same message, often upon his barren mountain under gray skies.

Your brother is the Sword, and you are the Key.

He was grooming Petrah for his eventual return to the homeland where he was born. The same homeland where his brother lived. A brother exalted because of his divine lineage to the dark god.

If he's really my brother.

Petrah doubted that too. In his dreams, Petrah's mother tried to hide him from Aman. Why would she do that? And why would she not claim Aman as her own son? If they were brothers, wouldn't she be his mother?

Petrah drowned in endless questions, weary from all the dreams he had to endure. His only rest came when he was awake.

And now he was on a desert journey with his friends, Kruush, Tan, and Ahleen.

But they were not alone.

Kruush's caravan comprised family members from the Goa tribe and two hired hands, Summi and Julan, to help with the sacks of salt to be delivered to Meerjurmeh. The agreement was to take the family to Bea-tet, where they would unite with the rest of their tribe.

"You're one of us on this trip," Kruush told Petrah on the first day. "Remember, you can't say a word about your party affiliation to anyone. I promised your master we'd sneak you in. That's my word, boy. Don't go embarrassing me."

Kruush introduced Petrah to the Goa tribe members and instructed him on their roles within the tribal hierarchy. Petrah committed their names and positions within the family to memory, using the methods learned in class at Maseah on how to memorize people, places, and terms—an important practice expected of him for the spy work he would do in Hōvar.

First came Jera, the eldest Goa male with the caravan—short and sturdy like Kruush, but with deeper-set eyes and grizzled hair. He appraised Petrah as if evaluating a gonatan on the market for sale. "You seem of good stock. A little lean, but hardy. Kruush said you're from Ketler. You're awfully tall for someone from those parts—unless my sister was japing when she complained about the men being too short in your village."

Petrah bowed under Kruush's watchful eye, careful as he said, "I suppose I'm the one weed that sprang from the earth before San could stifle my growth."

Jera laughed at that. "A weed you are then. Welcome, friend."

Jera had three sons: Nerod, his eldest, then Neru, and finally Anga. They were hard workers and enjoyed yelling at each other and boasting in good fun. Petrah liked Anga most of all, because of his jokes and the way he made Petrah feel like a cousin he'd not seen in years.

Anga rested a friendly hand on Petrah's shoulder as the unkind sun beat down on them. "I see Oma has taken a liking to you."

Petrah could hardly call Oma's frigid stare as "liking" him. Oma was the matriarch of the family, consummately serious and Petrah's least favorite, particularly with the way she drilled into him with her scrutinizing gaze. Like Ajoon, she had different colored eyes. Hers were brown and gray. Unlike Ajoon, her disposition was cold, even though she dressed it with wrinkled smiles.

She shuffled over to the pair.

Anga offered a smile and a warm, "Hello, Oma."

She brushed Anga's cheek with the back of her gnarled hand, loving and tender. "My favorite grandson." With Petrah, she shriveled her nose. "You smell like the city." She walked off.

Anga clapped Petrah on the back. "See? She likes you."

Petrah snorted. "If that's liking me, then I suppose standing here under the sweltering sun is pleasant."

Anga gave him a hearty pat on the chest. "It's quite pleasant, now that Oma has cast her shade upon you."

Jera's wife, Aelia, was the opposite of Oma: warm of heart and the soul of the family, who, with her daughters, Sinti and Khali, made sure everyone was fed, clothed, and healthy. Sinti was also skilled with the bow.

In the quiet of the evening, with the dreadful sun dipping below the earth and the heat shifting to a pleasing cool, Sinti practiced with the longbow. It was taller than her by a good six inches, but it bent as her silhouette did, graceful as the dappling shadows. She struck the red circle in the center of the wheel of hay with her arrow more often than not. Aelia and Khali clapped.

Tan, who was well versed in the bow as he was with the sword—back when he protected tribesmen for coin before enslavement—took the opportunity to demonstrate his skill while flirting with Sinti.

"If you don't mind," he said, placing a hand on the curve of Sinti's bow as if holding on to her hip, "I'd like to show you how it's done."

Sinti didn't let go when he tugged on the bow. "You assume you know something I don't."

He afforded her a confident grin. "I do."

She held firm. "What do I win when you lose?"

"When *I* win," he said with a straight face, "we take a quiet stroll and enjoy the sunset, away from everyone. But if you must insist on an alternative, then I will gladly take over your chores if I lose."

Sinti smirked. "I'll make you a list of things to do, then."

Anga gave Petrah a friendly jab with his elbow and whispered, "It'll be a long list too. I know from experience."

But when Tan took possession of the bow, it was as if he was a minstrel who'd taken to the stage, talented in a way that hushed the crowd, pulling them into the snare of his song as he weaved his lyrical enchantment. With Tan's treatment of the bow, each arrow, each release, struck true, piercing the oval of red with a snick of air and a slight twang of his bow—pure music.

Tan's marksmanship drew ululating praise from the tribesmen. Even Sinti afforded him a crescent of a smile.

Anga swiped a hand of relief across his forehead. "Close one, eh, Petrah?"

Petrah marveled at all of the arrow shafts protruding from the red circle. With Tan's precision, it was hardly a close contest. "He's a natural."

Tan held the bow out to Sinti. She tried to take it from him, but his grip was strong. "I believe you owe me a stroll, my lady."

She kept her hand firmly on the bow. "Is that the bargain I agreed to?"

His eyes lingered, holding her gaze. "Indeed."

Her lips tugged playfully into a smile. "I suppose a bargain is a bargain."

He let go of the bow. "I suppose it is. Shall we?"

Sinti set down her bow and walked east with Tan, past the edge of the encampment, toward the deepening shadows. Anga and the others dispersed, but Petrah continued to watch Tan and Sinti meander and banter. There was an ease to how they got along—one that reminded Petrah of Ajoon and him when they would go for walks.

Ahleen sidled up next to Petrah. "Tan has a way, doesn't he?"

"That's one way to describe it," Petrah said. "But I think he's met his match with Sinti. She's tenacious."

"Tenacious is exactly what Tan needs."

Ajoon was tenacious, too, Petrah noted, while Tan and Sinti maneuvered around a mound of cacti. *I bet Ajoon and Sinti would become fast friends.* Petrah exhaled the cooling air, forcing Ajoon from his thoughts.

Ahleen picked up on the shift in his demeanor, the droop of his bottom lip as if a fisherman had sunk hooks into it. "What's wrong?"

"It's—" What could he say? That he wondered if Ajoon was still having nightmares? That she was still traumatized over Miko's death? That she and Petrah could never go back to the friendship they had before? "It's nothing."

Besides Jera and his immediate family, Nerod and Neru had wives and children, and there was an assortment of cousins and other family members too. The children chased each other in circles, giggling and kicking up dust while the adults spoke lively, almost singsong, as they prepared supper.

"They're all so close-knit," Petrah said, admiring the simplicity, the beauty of these people. "Now I understand why there are so many nomads in our country. Look at them. They're free spirits." *They go where they want, and no one tells them what to do.*

"Then you can appreciate why Kruush, Tan, and I have stuck with the White Hand," Ahleen said. "It's not just about commerce, about trading, about making coin. It's about this." She stretched her arms wide, pointing her fingertips toward the vanishing horizons on either side. "I'm glad you're with us, Petrah." She leaned her head against the crook of his collarbone.

He wrapped a brotherly arm around her shoulder and gave it a squeeze. "Me too."

THE CARAVAN TRAVELED SLOWLY across the desert plains, stopping a few times to dig in during minor sandstorms.

Petrah spat sand from his mouth. "How can anyone stand traveling the desert with these storms?"

Kruush laughed. "You call that a storm? Wait until you've experienced a vaellra."

"That's still a sandstorm."

Kruush's brows lifted. "Is it now? Do you even know what vaellra is?"

Petrah wasn't going to allow Kruush to teach him a lesson. "It translates to 'vortex of the sands.' They educate us about these things in school, you know."

"Then tell me what this vortex is. Go on. I'm happy to learn from you."

Petrah huffed. "It's more severe than what we've experienced. Is that what you want to hear?"

Kruush's eyes darkened, becoming fierce. "Let me tell you what a vaellra is, lad. Imagine a wind so ferocious, you can't stand upright. Sand blasts your face as you kneel, chafing your skin, making it impossible to look—and that's with the vaellra miles away. But somehow you shield your eyes with your hands and glimpse the storm between your fingers as you resist being tossed. What you see isn't a severe whipping of sand, but a raging cyclone that blackens the sky, that screams so loud your ears bleed, that shrouds everything, and destroys all in its path. No man, no animal, no cart or wagon can withstand it. To face it is folly. It is a creature than cannot be reasoned with, cannot be stopped. To try is to imperil your life. That, my friend, is a vaellra. Pray to San you never get caught in such a monstrosity."

Petrah was mindful after that, noting every upshot of air, and glancing often behind him—trying to decide if the blur along the horizon was a mirage of whipped-up dust or the beginning of a deadly nightmare.

Petrah's challenges didn't end with that. Chíla was being difficult, falling behind Tan's gonatan, and for no obvious reason. "Come on, girl. Just a little faster." She ignored him.

The more Petrah rode her, the more he understood how feisty she was. If she didn't like his direction, she let him know by dragging down against her reins. He was no match for her stubbornness. The best he could do was compromise and give her a pat on the flank. She liked that, braying her approval.

Chíla took turns with the other gonatans, carrying sacks or pulling carts. When she wasn't burdened, Petrah could ride her for brief spurts. He enjoyed her spirit and affection, especially when she nuzzled him or ate cumpyia from his hand—hearty bars of oats, dried fruit, and nuts.

Day seven of travel came to a close, and the caravan rested for the evening on the lee of a barren hillock. The Terjurmehan envoy lay less than a mile ahead of them. Whenever the fifty-person contingent stopped, the Goa tribe would too.

Petrah offered to help set up camp, but Neru shooed him away. "You need rest," Neru said, observing Petrah's weariness. "Sit. Relax. You can help next time."

Petrah didn't want to relax, didn't want to wait until "next time," but he didn't want to offend the tribesman either. He took a seat at the edge of the camp as the sky turned from blue to orange and indigo and retrieved from his travel sack the two books he'd borrowed from the library at Maseah, *Channeling Linguistics* and *Orumen's Phrases*. The first was a guide to divine intonations, which he found utterly boring, and the second was a collection of artistic words and phrases for the creative mind. Petrah paged through the second book. It was a treatise that paid homage to the beauty of writing—something near and dear to Petrah's heart—filled with decadent lines of prose meant to inspire. Petrah's mind bloomed with ideas for songs and poems.

The sun had just begun to sink beneath the rocky horizon when Kruush walked up to him. "Reading, I see."

Petrah closed his book. "Just doing a little research."

"For?"

For things most people wouldn't understand, Petrah was tempted to say. He didn't want to imply Kruush was one of those people, so he simply said, "For my craft."

"I see. Mind if I join you?" Petrah patted the ground, and Kruush sat beside him. "You look like a tribesman."

Petrah fluffed the loose-fitting gebban he wore. It was a favorite of the nomadic peoples of Terjurmeh, an ankle-length garment made of cotton or sheep's wool, much like a tunic, that covered the arms and legs. The tribesmen wore earth-toned gebba, some with stripes or stitched patterns containing a fancy script that told of their family heritage—their ancestors and their deeds—the stories running around the hems and sleeves. Their bukara headdresses gave Petrah the impression of a cobra's hood—flaring cotton on either side of the face, trailing behind their necks in a variety of colors and decorations, and held in place by a circlet of reedwood or leather strap. The tribeswomen wore cotton headscarves and gebbettes, similar to the gebba, but with embroidered front panels and billowing backs.

"Just trying to act the part," Petrah said.

Kruush gave him an appraising look. "How are you holding up, lad?"

"Like I was made to travel the desert," Petrah said in a singsong voice. "Except for the blisters, achy joints, and sore muscles, of course." He had yet to get used to his own bukara, often fighting with the headdress when the wind gusted, although he learned to tie it in front of his mouth to shield himself from the updrafts of sand.

Kruush removed his sandal and lifted his foot. "See these?" He pointed at his calluses. "Get some of these and you won't feel a thing." He gave Petrah a friendly poke on the arm. He then drew in the air with a deep inhale. "Do you smell that? It's the scent of baked rocks and sand just beginning to cool. Something about the desert is calming at this time of day."

Petrah smelled it too, much to his delight.

Behind Kruush, workers secured the last of the haachi. The desert tents were made of durable canvas with wide, sweeping sides designed to withstand the wind. They set up camp in the shape of a ring: tents on the outside, and space for everything else, including the animals, on the inside. Tan was busy feeding a gonatan, accompanied by Sinti, who giggled at something he said.

"Those two are trouble," Kruush said, shaking his head, then laughing.

Petrah laughed too. "The worst." Seeing Sinti invoked thoughts of Ajoon. What was she doing now? Was she meditating, studying, wondering if Petrah was thinking about her? *She better not forget me.* "Do you suppose Tan will ever settle down?"

Kruush beamed. "Do you?"

Petrah doubted it.

"Tan pretends to be unattainable, but his heart is soft. Look at him. He's carrying on as if Sinti is but another lass under his spell, yet he's smitten. Look at his eyes. The eyes don't lie."

"Isn't he smitten with every lass he encounters?"

"True. He loves them all. That's his downfall, I suppose."

The gonatan Tan was feeding backed away. Another brayed. A third snorted. Tan grabbed their tethers while Sinti soothed them with brushes of her hands.

"Why are they so jittery?" Petrah asked.

"They smell something," Kruush said. "Probably krell. I wouldn't be surprised if there's a pack close by."

Petrah had never seen a krell, but he'd heard plenty of stories about them. They were the apex predators of the desert, cousins to the wolf but twice the size and cunning hunters. They were the anathema of the tribes. "Hopefully, we won't have to worry about that."

A whistle from the camp told them dinner was ready.

They gathered by the campfire, where strings of sizzling meat hung between Y-shaped rods, giving off a delicious aroma of charred fat with garlic and spices. Children giggled and chased one another while the adults sat cross-legged talking to each other, some preparing trays of nuts or unleavened bread, others telling jokes or listening intently, and a few praying. Ahleen sat in the corner of the group with Oma and a couple of Jera's daughters-in-law. Tan sat in the back with Summi and Julan, talking lively and flirting with Sinti.

Anga got Petrah's attention. "Kruush says you've never had lope before." He tore a strip of meat off the suspended twine, blew on it, and handed it to Petrah. "Taste this and tell me what you think."

Petrah put the entire piece in his mouth. It had the flavor of beef but was more tender. "This is amazing."

"Hah, told you!" Kruush said. "Anga, what do you need me to do?"

Anga waved Kruush away. "Sit down. Neru will help me. Neru! Come here."

Neru helped his brother unstring the cooked meat and place the pieces on a platter. He had the same brown, curly hair and full beard as his brother.

Kruush and Petrah sat down next to Jera and his eldest, Nerod. Petrah hadn't realized how long Kruush's beard had gotten until he saw him by the tribesmen. The younger men kept their beards trimmed, much like the way Master Joriah maintained his. The elders let theirs grow, Jera's running down to his chest. It was rude to grow your beard longer than your father's.

Petrah caught Oma looking at him. She had a small, round face, with fine lines creasing her skin like a pruned fig. She was skin-and-bones thin, her gebbette draping off her, too large for her person. Petrah swore she didn't blink. She smiled at him, her wrinkles stretching unnaturally in the firelight, teeth crooked and brown like bark. It wasn't just her fiendish smile or old age that abraded him like the bits of sand that nipped at his face. It was the unrestrained coldness of her stare—fixed on Petrah as if she was tracking him, hunting him, waiting to sink her fangs into his neck when he least expected it. That smile—that pretense—was a lure to get him to let down his guard and trap him. He shivered, drawing a singular conclusion.

She has no soul.

He turned away.

Anga and his brother piled steaming lope on a platter and passed it around while the women cut the bread.

"Your salt should fetch a good price this season," Jera said to Kruush as they ate.

Kruush bobbed his head. "Gods willing, it shall."

The flatbread was a wonderful compliment to the meat. There was fama too, the dip Petrah had tried in Fangmordah. He'd overheard a tribeswoman saying they made theirs with sesame paste instead of ground nuuma nuts. He sampled it. The earthy, salty smoothness and touch of natural oils blended to create a rich creaminess that danced on his tongue. He slathered a piece of flatbread and stuffed it into his mouth—which earned an approving nod from Jera—then washed it down with water from a skin being passed around.

"If the Con-jurah had a summer as brutal as ours, they'll pay well," Kruush said.

Petrah wondered about the sacks they were transporting. "Don't the Con-jurah have their own supply of salt?"

"They do," Kruush said, "but it's cheaper to get it from us. Big business in the desert."

"Like dusk," Jera said with a smile.

"Aye, like dusk," Kruush said, clapping Jera on the shoulder.

Petrah perked up at the mention of "dusk." It was the hallucinogenic spice Kruush had dreamed of trading back when he first made the deal to join the White Hand, when they were in Elmar. Petrah had never seen dusk, but he heard it turned the whites of the eyes different shades of purple.

He listened as the men speculated on future trade seasons. When dinner was finished, the women cleaned up and brought out water pipes, called jalibis, for the men to smoke. Petrah took a walk.

He headed toward the clearing where Jera's five grandchildren kicked around a swineskin—a gourd wrapped in the skin of a hog. There were two boys and three girls, all between the ages of six and eleven. Antiya, Neru's eight-year-old daughter, grabbed Petrah by the hem of his gebban. "Play with us!"

Petrah kicked the swineskin around with Antiya and her cousins. There wasn't any aim to the game, just fun. Petrah laughed as they tried to block him from passing the ball to the next person. After several minutes, he stepped back to watch them continue, reveling in their boundless energy and youth. He had let loose around a few friends, like Taka, but never to this extent. The rush and sweet ache in his muscles from playing made his head light and giddy.

After the game, Petrah whistled to himself as he made his way around the camp. But when he approached the gonatans, they seemed fidgety, snorting and bunching close, their tangled reins pulled taut against hitching posts. He went up to Chíla, but she made a grating sound and raised a hoof.

"Easy, girl. I was just trying to say hello."

Petrah strode past the ring of tents to the flat patch of ground beyond. The campfire cast the tents' shadows against the barren earth, and a waxing moon illuminated the distant landscape while jutting rock formations silhouetted against the darkness. Petrah let the whispering breeze caress his skin.

He was about to relax when he heard a howl. He caught the glint of something yellow. It was there for only a moment, a dot or pair of dots, and then gone again. He squinted. A pair of dots appeared, seemed to move, wink in, then out, then in, and then nothing again.

Petrah returned to camp. He was going to sit by the dying fire, but when he saw Oma grinning at him, he changed his mind and went to his tent.

THE CARAVAN TRAVELED FOR two days across the barren plains. Tan kept Petrah company much of the time, japing or speaking of his adventures with Kruush and of Meerjurmehan women. "They're lovely creatures. Not as stiff-laced as the women of Terjurmeh, with their pious attitudes or brothers always watching you." Tan laughed. "You'll get to see the beauts soon enough."

"My friend Taka would be jealous," Petrah said, leading Chíla by her reins. "He's much like you, with a penchant for the ladies, although he swears his heart belongs to one in particular. What's going on with you and Sinti?"

"She's too young for me, too inexperienced. We have fun, but that's all."

Petrah was hoping for a different answer. "Aren't you tired of being so . . . unattached?"

"As opposed to?"

"As opposed to having someone to call your own."

"*One* woman?"

"Yes, one. Acia is a big world, but even in such a large world, surely you can settle for just one woman. Isn't that enough?"

"Do you look at the night sky and say, I want just one star? There are thousands, Petrah. Each is different, each special. How can you choose just one?"

Petrah sighed. *He's impossible, far worse than Taka and his boasting.* Chíla slowed and Petrah had to tug at her to pick up the pace. "I would be happy with one, thank you very much."

"Would you now? I was wondering if you liked any at all."

Petrah made a face at Tan. "Not all of us are cut out to be philanderers like you. Take Kruush. He knew he wanted Ahleen back when such a thing was forbidden and seemed impossible. Yet he never gave up. I want to find someone. I want to marry and have children someday—lots and lots of children. Sons and daughters, born free and able to do what they want in life. Eventually, I'll be a mage and I'll be able to afford a piece of land to call my own. Nothing extravagant, just a humble dwelling with enough room for my family. That's not too much to ask for, is it?"

Tan gave it some thought, his ash-brown eyes fixed ahead to the wasteland as if he believed the dream was possible. He looked at Petrah with a twinkle of mischief. "I know how you'll find the one. I'll take you to a brothel when we reach Hōvar. Not just any brothel. The finest house of desire in all of Meerjurmeh. You've never seen such fair maidens. Trust me when I say you won't be disappointed."

"Now you really sound like Taka. I think you should reconsider Sinti. So what if she's young and inexperienced? You fancy her, and she fancies you. You have a connection."

Tan smiled, but there was a wistfulness to it. "What I fancy matters not in the way of the world. My road leads in a different direction than the road Sinti takes. She's a tribeswoman, and I'm a trader. Our destinations are not the same."

"But you can make them the same if you wanted. Life is about choices. We didn't have those choices not too long ago."

"Some things are beyond our control, Petrah. It's best to let them happen as they are supposed to."

It was as if the Watcher was speaking for Tan. *Well, he doesn't speak for me.* "You would rather go to a brothel than change course?"

Tan returned to being a scamp, and the seriousness of the conversation vanished as if it had been an illusion. "The brothel's not for me, young sir. It's for you. My treat. Unless you want to stay a virgin. You can always do that."

"You're an ass, you know that?"

Tan grinned. "Did you expect any less?"

They were a half day's travel from Bea-tet when they bedded down for the night. The full moon hung high in the northern sky, a bright circle of iridescence illuminating the flat surroundings. Petrah took off his sandals once he was finished helping with the camp's setup. The blisters hurt from the relentless march. He wiggled his toes.

Dinner was a scant offering of jerked meat, preserved fruit, and stale flatbread, and there was nothing to drink but stale water. No one was very talkative, and only a couple of the adults bothered to hang around the small, dung-fueled fire after dinner was done. Soon it was just Neru, who had the first watch.

Petrah left the fire and took a seat outside his tent. He closed his eyes and meditated. He tried to shut out his mother's voice. He clearly saw her face, the crow's feet sprouting from the corners of her eyes, the frown lines of her creased brow, her chapped lips forming the syllables of his birth name, Immael, over and over.

Petrah inhaled, slow and deep, and then let it all out. *The Watcher said she's alive. He said she misses me.*

Did she miss him?

Was she alive and well?

Did she even exist?

Petrah had asked himself the same questions many times. He was tired of asking.

He tried not to think about the dream-filled night ahead. Instead, he let his mind wander outward. He picked up the heartbeats of sleeping adults and children in the nearby tents, then the rodents scurrying hole-to-hole outside the camp. In the distance, a howl broke the stillness, followed by several responses and then silence. Petrah detected a new set of heartbeats, powerful, but far away—a thunderous rhythm, like the pounding of war drums. They throbbed in his mind and quickened his breathing. His heart pumped, accelerating until it matched theirs.

The adrenaline thrill disappeared as soon as he realized he was no longer alone.

Petrah opened his eyes to find Oma standing over him.

"May I sit?" she asked in her brittle voice.

Petrah wanted to say no, but he accepted her request.

Oma used her walking stick for support as she lowered herself to the ground. Her body shook as she attempted to sit. Petrah offered to help, but she batted him away.

"Oma's old, but not that old," she said, crossing her thin legs. The shadows made her wrinkles deep as water channels in an eroding hillside, far deeper than the ones Petrah pictured on his mother's face. "I love the smell of the desert at night. You notice every scent. You can even taste it. Not like the day. The sun ruins everything. It bakes the ground and clogs the nose. But the night is different. It's subtle. You have to pay close attention or you'll miss it."

Petrah took a whiff. It wasn't any more remarkable than the previous evening.

A faint howl broke somewhere east. Oma smiled. "They sing such beautiful songs, don't they? Like angels. Listen . . ."

Petrah waited a few seconds, and there was another howl, this one slower to crescendo and ending sharply. Definitely *not* the voice of an angel.

"Who would know from hearing them? They're such vicious hunters," Oma said. "Powerful bodies, legs made for sprinting, teeth for ripping—who would know? Would you?"

Petrah shrugged. "I just hope they go their own way."

"They're still out there. Watching. Waiting." Oma smiled, stretching her thin, wrinkled lips. "You feel them, don't you? With your mind. Like before, when you closed your eyes."

Petrah hesitated. "No, but I heard them."

Oma frowned. "Come now. You're not naïve and neither am I. You know things. Oma's not stupid. Do you think I'm stupid?"

"Of course not."

"I know you feel them. Before, when you were sitting here with your eyes shut, your breathing became heavier, faster. You were breathless by the time you opened your eyes."

There was a high-pitched bay, this one closer than the last. Neru lifted his head and rose. Oma waved him down, and he returned to tending the fire.

"He's a good boy," Oma said to Petrah. "Knows when to listen to his grandmother, when to trust her. I understand many things, boy. Don't let this wrinkled face fool you. Those krell—they do too. They smell Oma and know. They smell you and know."

"Know what?"

"That you're the reason they're here."

Petrah's brows puckered. "Me?"

Oma's eyes glinted coldly in the moonlight. "Yes, you. You didn't notice them the other night. You were standing close to where you are now, and I was watching. One called to you. I heard him. It was like a pack member calling to one of his own."

"That's ridiculous," Petrah said.

He didn't see it coming, but Oma reached over and slapped him across the face. "That's for disrespect! You need to mind your manners around the tribe, outsider. I'm not *your* oma, but you better treat me like I am."

Petrah rubbed the sting from his face. He was too shocked to be angry.

"They're waiting for you," she said. "They smell that blood of yours, and it drives them wild. Do you know why they followed us for miles across the desert? It's that demon inside you, aching to get out, dying to show itself." Oma examined him, her brown eye narrow, her gray one wide. "I see it—faint, like a ghost, but it's there. You're doing a lot of holding back, but the wall is going to break. You can't keep that thing bottled up inside forever. Those krell know it." She leaned in. "Oma knows it too."

Petrah got up and headed toward his tent. His face burned, but not from the slap.

"Go ahead," Oma called after him. "Walk away. Be rude to Oma." Her scowl became a wicked smile. "Have a good night, *demon*."

Chapter 4
Sandstorm

P ETRAH WAS COCOONED IN a wool blanket about ten feet from the sputtering fire when a noise jarred him from his sleep. Sometime after the unpleasant conversation with Oma, he had fetched his blanket, picked a spot away from everyone, and let the flames and glowing embers lull him to sleep. He didn't remember feeling tired or curling up.

Petrah lifted his stiff body and stretched. Neru was still sitting with his back to him, slouched. Above, the moon was a bright globe in the sky, washing the camp with soft, white light.

"Pssst," he called to Neru. The man didn't move.

The gonatans were agitated, bunched together and shivering, heads entwined. It was chilly, but Petrah doubted the animals were cold. He forewent the warmth of his blanket and investigated.

That was when he saw the frayed end of a rope. It dragged along the ground, the other end likely tied to one of the hitching posts hidden by flanks.

Chíla was gone!

It was evident she'd chewed through her rope. He'd seen her do it earlier, but it hadn't registered that she might succeed.

And now she's off, wandering who knows where!

Petrah darted a glance at Neru, but the man was unfazed, or asleep. No one else was outside.

A sharp draft made Petrah pull his gebban tightly about him. Then he heard something to the west.

He moved past stacks of salt at the perimeter of the encampment. Wind-smoothed boulders, strange, spiky plants, hillocks, and depressions comprised the moonlit landscape. The ground slanted downward into a wide-sweeping bowl. Between buffeting gusts and the sound of sand kicking up and shifting, Petrah heard something coming from that direction. It was hard to make out, but it sounded like chewing and grunting mixed with low growls. Against all warnings in his mind, he went toward it.

Petrah froze when he got to the edge of the descent.

About thirty feet downslope, six krell gorged on a bloodied corpse. Petrah knew well enough the krell were the top predator of the desert. Each was easily the body length of a gonatan, much larger than their forest-dwelling cousins, the wolf, and as ferocious a hunter as any big cat. It was the first time Petrah had a clear view of one. Yellow eyes gleamed, fangs shone white, and shaggy fur swept back in a tide of browns. Petrah didn't need anyone to tell him that poor Chíla was being devoured below, strings of her flesh distributed among hungry mouths. The air stank of blood and entrails.

The largest of the krell stopped eating, sniffed, and looked up. There was a black streak across its muzzle. It brandished its teeth and snarled. The others withdrew from their feast and followed the alpha male's gaze.

Petrah now had the attention of the entire pack.

Oh no!

He gauged how fast he could run back to camp.

Not fast enough.

They'd overtake him in a few bounds. But if he didn't try, he might give them a second, easy meal.

An alternative to running was backing up slowly to create distance without provoking the animals to attack. Perhaps they would lose interest in the skinny human who couldn't be more than a few morsels.

Petrah shifted his weight in his legs to begin his retreat, then stopped himself.

He recalled watching the wild dogs that occasioned the streets of Kanmar and how they'd dine on a carcass in plain sight of the marching column of slaves. The krell weren't so different in that way, were they? Maybe he was supposed to be here at this moment, observing these magnificent predators. Could this be what Oma was referring to?

Or maybe I'm being an idiot, and these will be my last thoughts.

He didn't move, not even when the alpha trotted around Chíla's body and approached the base of the slope. Two of the others came up to his side but hung back. One growled at Petrah, but the larger one snapped its jaws in the other's direction, and the growling ceased. Petrah held his breath. The muscles in his shoulders tightened, and the skin on the back of his neck prickled. Were these giant predators real? Or were his eyes deceiving him?

The leader moved up the incline cautiously, sniffing, then taking a couple more steps, then sniffing again. Petrah sensed the creature's heartbeat, the flow of blood, and the expanding and contracting of powerful lungs. This beast of the desert was very much real. Petrah never knew such a presence before. It inspired admiration.

You're beautiful, a hunter like no other. Come here. Come closer.

The words came unbidden, as if someone else was thinking them.

The thought tricked his body into relaxing. His shoulder muscles untensed, and he released his held breath. He softened his rigid, staggered stance and drew his legs together.

The alpha climbed the rest of the way until he was less than five feet from Petrah.

Petrah, against all reason, stretched out his hand, fingers cupped and wrist forward, as he would to a dog. The krell inched nearer and brought his muzzle within a foot of Petrah's exposed wrist. The krell exhaled hot, moist breath on his skin. He sniffed one more time, looked up at Petrah through huge yellow eyes, and took the final step.

Then it happened: contact.

The alpha male touched Petrah with the tip of his nose. The sensation was cool and wet, almost ticklish. Petrah slowly retracted his hand and felt the dark smear across the top. Chíla's blood.

The krell jerked his head. He growled and stepped back.

Neru shouted from behind Petrah. "Get away!"

Petrah looked over his shoulder to see Neru running toward the krell, waving a sword and making a ruckus as he ran. The krell bolted, taking the pack with him. Neru sprinted past Petrah, followed by Tan, Summi, and Julan. Nerod and two of his cousins blazed by next. They skidded down the short slope, spears, swords, and brands in hand. When the men came upon the mutilated gonatan, they stopped. The krell were gone. Petrah tried not to look at the remains of Chíla. He wiped the blood from his hand, repulsed by the sensation and smell, and waited for the men to come back up.

"Why were you just standing there?" Tan asked, huffing. "The damned beast was right in front of you!"

All eyes shifted to Petrah, who couldn't conjure a reasonable explanation. "He just came up to me."

"And bloody well could have killed you," Nerod said in an irritated tone. He turned to Neru and jabbed him in the chest with a finger. "The next time you fall asleep on watch, I'll throw you to the krell myself. Look at this." He pointed at Chíla. The smell of the gonatan's innards fouled the air. "This is your fault."

Neru said nothing. Kruush and Jera showed up a moment later. The rest of the tribe was awake, watching from within the safety of the ring of haachi.

"What happened?" Jera asked.

Tan explained.

"We need to burn the body and bury her in the sand," Jera said. "I'm not letting any krell or scavengers have seconds."

Petrah absently rubbed his wrist while Neru and his cousins went about the task.

They burned Chíla's body and buried what remained of her. Petrah couldn't stand to watch. He'd stood idly as she got feasted on. He tucked his hands under his arms and dipped his chin in shame.

What's wrong with me?

Everyone returned to camp, and the excitement died down. Oma was waiting with Ahleen and two of Jera's nephews. Oma's lip curled wickedly into a smile when Petrah looked at her. It sent a shiver down Petrah's neck. He grabbed his blanket and retired to his tent.

THE CARAVANS REACHED BEA-TET late morning.

The oasis village offered a remarkable departure from the barren desert surrounding it. Tall palms, lush shrubs, and an assortment of plants and birds occupied a ten-square-mile area with a lake at the center, fed by an underground spring. The village was strategic as a trading post for nomads during the cool season and a haven for a few permanent locals during the hot season. It sat thirty-five miles due east of the Shrine of San, the headquarters of the Temple and seat of the papacy for the Mighty One. Missionaries came to Bea-tet to rest before making the trek to the shrine. They'd have to cross the South Kesel river to get there, but there were ferrymen to aid in helping the missionaries get across.

Kruush and Jera greeted Moushet, Oma's brother, by the lake's edge. He was the Terad in charge of the Goa tribe, an elderly man of almost seventy. He was wiry and shriveled like his sister and seemed to have the same dark personality. Petrah stayed clear of him and spent his time helping Tan while Summi and Julan worked with Kruush to get the camp set up.

"Is that the ambassador?" Petrah asked Tan as they situated a large sack of salt atop a growing heap. An older man dressed in a red gebban with black trim sat on a chair beneath a palm in the middle of the Fist's camp, attended to by a skinny man in a loincloth with the mark of a slave on his ankle.

"That's him," Tan said. "He can be a beast, from what I've heard. Those poor Con-jurah are in for a real treat."

"That doesn't sound good for negotiations."

"Probably not. Worse, there's a priest in the ambassador's camp. I'm sure the Con-jurah will appreciate it when he shows up at the first meeting."

"I thought priests weren't allowed to get involved in political matters anymore."

Tan shrugged. "I don't know what's going on. The Temple announced an official inquisition on Hah'xallah. I overheard several people grumbling about it, but there's nothing anyone can do. If you denounce the Temple's edict or interfere in their business, you're a heretic. And we all know what the Temple does to heretics."

Petrah remembered the lesson from Master Nole's history class on the subject. "If you recant, maybe you're lucky and they just whip you. But if you don't—" His eyes stole to the shadows, to the memory of what the slavers had done to Meska. "You'll pray for a swift end."

The ambassador's party remained for two full days in Bea-tet. The morning of the third was brisk, a reminder of the encroaching winter. Kruush and his team assembled the train of animals and goods before sunrise. By the time the sun crested the horizon, they were ready to go. Kruush, Ahleen, and Tan said their goodbyes to Jera and his family. Petrah watched as Tan took Sinti aside. She wiped tears from her eyes, and his chin drooped. *He pretends his heart is invincible, but it's not. He's a big sap.*

Petrah locked forearms with Nerod, Neru, and Anga and was ready to head off when someone tugged on his sleeve.

It was Oma.

"No hug goodbye for Oma?" she said. She opened her skinny arms.

Despite his reluctance, Petrah hugged her. Her boniness and the greasy odor from her hair made him want to shove her away. But she gripped him with her fingers, digging into his back as if they were talons. She pulled him down and whispered into his ear. "The demon inside you made Oma proud the other night. If you were more like him, I might call you grandson. But you're not, are you?"

The heat of her breath sent a river of chills up his spine. He tried to pry himself free, but she clung to him like a desert vulture. Finally, she let go.

"Come back and visit Oma, you hear?"

Petrah couldn't shake her musty scent or the feel of her sharp nails digging into his skin. He nodded his reply and walked away. He hoped to never lay eyes on her again.

The dunes of the Agobo Desert were enormous. Petrah watched his footsteps disappear behind him as the wind drew and redrew the ripples of sand into a sea of ever-shifting patterns. It was as if there were no trace he had been here. How many travelers had passed this way and had their footprints erased, just as his were?

Petrah's calves ached from trudging through the difficult terrain. The sand was a golden hue in the sunlight and along the peaks of the dunes but was a reddish-brown on the slopes and troughs. He was glad the caravans traveled the pathways between the giant dunes. He couldn't imagine climbing up one hundred-foot inclines on a surface that constantly changed.

While meditating on the evening of the fourth night since leaving Bea-tet, Petrah felt a tingle in the back of his head. Master Joriah was attempting a mind link—*kandurata* in channeling terms. Master Maglo had trained Petrah to recognize the pattern. The link allowed magi to communicate over vast distances. Petrah wished he'd asked Master Maglo to teach Ajoon the method. Mind links were advanced techniques, often taught only to journeymen. Ajoon was smart. She could have picked it up. Then he could talk to her.

Maybe Master Maglo will show her, and she'll surprise me.

Petrah liked the thought of that.

Once he was linked with Master Joriah, Petrah heard his master's voice in his thoughts, and he could subvocalize his responses. It was perhaps the most important technique a mage could learn, as it made it possible for magi to coordinate in warfare and convey vital information to military leaders.

The conversation with Master Joriah lasted a few minutes, consisting mostly of questions: *How are you doing? Are you keeping pace with the ambassador's party? When will you reach Hōvar?* At the end of the mind link, Petrah was exhausted. Master Maglo said it would take some time to get used to. Eventually, it would become second nature. If Petrah had learned the technique as a Green Robe, he might have avoided the disaster with Miko. He could have contacted Master Joriah, and Miko would have been punished accordingly.

You have to live with your decisions.

Petrah grimaced. He could bury himself under a dune, and he'd still be stuck with these thoughts.

His encounter with the krell also prompted questions regarding his decisions. Oma had called him a demon. Was there one lurking inside? Is that why the krell had spared him, because the animals feared or respected the black spirit trapped inside his body? He knew there was an ugliness brewing within him. The question was, could he hold it back?

Evening descended, and Petrah helped set up camp for the night. When he was done, he sat down to rest on the cooling sand.

Ahleen wandered over to him. "Mind if I join you?" She wore a light-brown gebbette with a headscarf and sandals. She was lovely as always. He appreciated her offer to keep him company.

Petrah gestured an invitation with his hand. "Please."

"It's so beautiful at dusk," she said. In the west, the skyline was a blend of purples and reds, the horizon flat and featureless, as opposed to the east, where the land dipped into a depression dotted with cacti and brush.

"I can never tire of it," Petrah said. Was Ajoon looking at the same view right now, perhaps from one of their favorite benches facing the Kesel River?

"Kruush said your feet were hurting. I brought you some balm. It should help with the blisters." She held up a small tin.

"You're always fixing me."

"You're always breaking," she said with a smile. "Here, allow me." After examining the soles of his feet, she removed the lid from the tin and scooped out salve with her fingers. Mint and jasmine greeted him. The jasmine reminded him of Maseah and the sweet air at night.

"You know, I can do that myself."

"I know," she said. "But I'm better at it than you." He couldn't argue with that. "Try not to flinch."

Ahleen applied the salve to the blisters. As with the lacerations on his back from when he'd gotten whipped, Ahleen was gentle. He barely noticed her delicate touch, although the blisters were tender. When she finished, she handed him the tin. "In case you need it."

He accepted it. "Thank you."

"You should thank Summi. He made the salve himself."

"Then I shall thank him in earnest."

They sat together, watching the red swatch of sky turn maroon. After a time, Ahleen spoke.

"You've kept to yourself much of our trip. I was wondering if everything was all right."

If you only knew half the truth. "I don't mean to be so standoffish," Petrah said, "but I need to spend a lot of time meditating. It helps me focus. We magi—" Petrah smiled at his own slipup, eliciting a smile from Ahleen as well. "We *journeymen* need to practice our arts every day if we are to become proficient at our craft. Much of it involves quiet time, which seems counterintuitive, considering it looks like we're doing nothing at all."

"It's just that you seem—well—distant, perhaps."

Petrah scratched a line in the hard ground with a finger. He was always distracted, or more appropriately, preoccupied with things. *She's right. I am distant.* "It's not my intention. Truly. I've got a lot on my mind."

"I know. Kruush said there was an incident with one of your classmates and"—she paused a beat—"a fatality. I'm so sorry, Petrah."

Petrah dropped his gaze to the tiny pebbles scattered on the ground. "There's more to the story."

"I'm not trying to pry."

"I don't mind, really." He looked at her. Her large, brown eyes reflected sisterly concern. He took a deep breath and told her about Miko's deceit, his capture, captivity aboard the slave galley, and the melee that resulted in Miko's death. Then he spoke about Ajoon and how upset he was over almost destroying their friendship.

Ahleen remained quiet and attentive until he finished. Petrah swallowed several times in an attempt to tame his emotions, although his eyes got the better of him, growing damp.

Ajoon had said she'd accept Petrah's apology. She'd asked him if he was willing to take things slowly and start anew. When he agreed, he'd hoped to catch a smile, some semblance of the old Ajoon, the one who'd trusted him and smiled as bright as the sun. But she'd afforded him no smile or warmth, only clouds and shadows. Had she even forgiven him, or had he deluded himself into thinking she had?

"That's a lot to carry on your shoulders," Ahleen said. "Ajoon must be a special girl."

"She is. But I've made it hard on her. Does she even want to remain friends?" He drew in a sharp inhale of dry air. "I don't know." He rubbed granules of sand between his fingers. "I want to be friends. I want to—" He shook his head.

Ahleen placed a hand on his arm. "Do you wish it was more?"

I do. But—

But it was out of Petrah's control. He'd wounded Ajoon. Perhaps too deeply.

"I care for her, I won't deny that. We like the same things, we think the same way. She's smart and ambitious and very capable. But I'm afraid it will be a while before I see her again. A lot can happen in a short time. Look at you and Kruush. You're married! You both knew from the start that you were meant to be together and that it was more than friendship. I—" His stomach clenched. "I don't know, Ahleen." He rubbed his fingers back and forth across the sand, creating ripples. "She was there when I killed Miko. She saw me do it. If you saw how I acted that night, you wouldn't want to have anything to do with me."

Ahleen placed a hand over his. Her touch was soothing. "You need time, Petrah. You both do. Don't force things to happen and don't assume all is lost. It'll work out exactly as it should."

The wind picked up, tossing granules about. Petrah followed the swirl, the serpentine trails, and the shifting patterns of the shadowed landscape. His hair fluttered and his back straightened from the updraft as if the airiness made him buoyant. Ahleen's soothing words had that effect.

She gave his hand a squeeze and let go. "Whenever you want to talk, I'm here."

Ahleen left him and returned to the camp.

Petrah remained where he was, listening to the desert whisper in the twilight.

THE FOLLOWING DAY, THE travelers were making their way over a gently sloping dune when the wind picked up. Summi yelled frantically and started dragging his gonatan down the other side.

"Vaellra! Vaellra!"

"Quick!" Kruush called to everyone. "Get everything down."

Petrah and Tan were leading a train of gonatans pulling a pair of wains filled with sacks of salt while Ahleen and Julan trailed behind. They stopped.

Petrah shielded his eyes from the stinging sand and saw, to the eastern horizon, a black, billowing wall. Moments earlier, the air had been clear. Now, a great sandstorm was headed their way. Petrah was mesmerized by the beauty of vortices swirling madly, fading in and out of the dark curtain. Pillars of sand lifted into the heavens.

Tan grabbed his shoulder. "Move!"

Everyone scrambled to get the gonatans, carts, and goods downslope quickly and safely. There wasn't a safe hiding spot from vaellra, so the best anyone could do was dig in and pray.

The air grew thick and strangely orange. The approaching storm intensified, the wind coupled with a monstrous roar.

They hugged the lee of the dune at its base. Gonatans brayed and thrashed against their restraints, but Kruush and the others kept them from escaping. Above, sand cascaded down in sheets, swept over the top by gale-force winds.

Petrah couldn't imagine a mage in the world who could protect himself from such a storm. The rope slipped from his grasp. The gonatan he was holding pulled free.

"Hey!" he shouted, his voice lost in the wind.

Petrah started after the gonatan, but the animal continued to distance itself. A dark cloud swelled above and descended in a swirl. One second, the dune was visible; the next, it was gone. Petrah was blown backward and then sideways. He lost his bearing. He sank to his knees and used his arms to shield his eyes from the shredding force of the sand.

A sudden pressure drop made the sand fall from the sky as if poured from a pitcher. Down it rained, a massive dump. The sky cleared, the air calmed, and the whooshing sound abated. Petrah raised his arms and saw he was facing the wrong direction. He turned toward his companions. They were hunkered down against the bottom of the slope several dozen feet away, buried to the waist. Ahleen scooped sand away from her while Summi worked to pull Kruush free. Julan and Tan tried to keep the braying, thrashing gonatans from toppling the front cart, which leaned at a precarious angle to the tower of sand beside it.

"Over here!" Petrah yelled, waving his hands. Julan stopped to look up, but the gonatans bucked, demanding his attention.

A second later, the darkness returned, blacker, windier, and louder than ever.

A torrent of shifting forces toppled Petrah. He struck the sand face-first. Then it moved; or he did. He tried to construct an invisible shield about him, a simple defense technique Master Ecclesias had taught his class to protect against the elements, or from someone throwing a spear. The crude shielding worked well enough to keep the particulates from grating Petrah's skin. He became dizzy as his body rotated, despite the invisible barrier. He lost his concentration, and the shield dissipated.

One moment he was standing, the next flying through the dark maelstrom, ripped from the earth by cyclonic forces.

The tornado of sand and wind whipped him about its unseen axis. He tried to break loose, but it kept him prisoner. Black squeezed in from the sides of his vision as he felt a vacuum in his chest, then a burst of air slammed into him, ejecting him from the funnel.

Petrah struck the side of a dune hard, sending up a shower of sand. He rolled downward, tumbling until he hit a trough. Heaving, he flopped onto his back and coughed violently.

Petrah listened for the storm, dazed and unable to stop the world from spinning. The howl of the wind disappeared, replaced by his rapid breathing. Battered, bruised, and raw from the sand, he realized he couldn't move. After a fierce coughing fit, his breathing became less ragged and more regular.

Petrah rolled over onto his elbows to look around him. Nothing but sand as far as he could see. Endless dunes, all the same.

His heart raced and his senses grew sharp, drawing figures from the shadowed troughs—imagined people and gonatans. It was little more than the shifting sand and the illusion of familiar shapes.

Petrah turned north, south, east, and west, but everything looked the same. Peaks and valleys, browns and beiges, dunes and more dunes.

And the direst of conclusions: he was all alone.

Chapter 5
Lost

P ETRAH SPAT SAND FROM his dry mouth.

Caked in grit, he breathed in the desert's emptiness. The blue sky glared at him from between mountains of sand, unimpressed that he was still alive.

But I am alive.

Somewhere in the process of being thrown to where he lay, his headdress had been ripped from his person. His sandals were also gone. His only possession was his wrinkled gebban. All his belongings were with Kruush's caravan, and his friends could be anywhere by now. The most important resource was water, the next was protection from the merciless sun. While shaded at the moment by a large dune, he was still in deep trouble.

Unless I can locate a caravan.

Petrah assessed his surroundings.

He was in a trough. It was too close to midday to determine east from west, and he was alone.

Petrah could think of only two options: expose himself to the scorching sun by climbing to higher ground now, hoping to spot his friends' caravan, or wait until nightfall and risk his friends moving on.

The longer he waited, the drier his throat would become. Time was the enemy.

Option one it is.

Petrah trudged up the ridgeline of the largest dune he could find, a colossus that afforded a commanding view of the environs. He'd seen taller dunes over the past few days, the tallest Kruush estimated at almost a thousand feet at its pinnacle, maybe more.

This one would do just fine.

He shielded his eyes and tried to keep his bare soles from contacting the blistering sand on the sunny side of the ridge. He scanned the horizon, expecting to at least find some sign of the caravans, either tracks in the sand or items tossed by the storm, perhaps a reflection from a cook pot or a glint from a naked dagger. He saw neither, which sent tingles of apprehension down his neck and back.

Where are they? They have to be somewhere!

He searched again as the sun cooked his brow. Still nothing but untouched dunes and azure sky as far as he could see.

After minutes of enduring the sweltering heat, he slid partway down on the shaded side of the dune and rested his back against the cool sand. The dryness in his throat was unbearable, but he did his best not to think of it. He had a long wait ahead before he quenched his thirst.

The pang of fear returned as a gust swept sand over his head. *You're going to be buried out here.*

Petrah grabbed a fistful of sand and threw it in frustration. There was so much of it, everywhere. If he never saw sand again, he would be thankful.

You will not die.

One avenue was to attempt a mind link with Master Joriah. Maybe the mage could signal for help. The priest with the ambassador's contingent was the only person among both caravans who might have the ability to do a mind link. Would Master Joriah even try to contact the priest? Petrah hoped Master Joriah would choose his life over the possibility of giving away the Green Flame's surreptitious plans.

Petrah thought through the steps of a mind link when he realized he had never started one before. Even though he and Master Joriah had spoken mind-to-mind, it had been the mage who'd contacted him, not the other way around.

It couldn't be that hard to perform a mind link, could it?

Petrah worked through the process of constructing the link. What had Master Maglo said to do first?

Unclutter your thoughts.

And then?

Concentrate, the mage had told him. *Visualize me as your recipient. Hear the sound of my voice and follow the signature of my spirit. Every soul has a unique footprint, a way of being found. Picture knocking on the door of my soul and waiting for me to answer and invite you in. Even if I don't answer, it doesn't mean I'm not there. I could be asleep, distracted, meditating, or simply ignoring you. If you fail, try again. Eventually, you will succeed.*

Petrah wished the mage was with him right now, guiding him through the process. He'd practiced doing a mind link with Master Maglo, but it had been in a controlled environment, with the instructor behind a door, not across an entire desert.

Clear your mind.

Petrah slowed his breathing and dissolved his thoughts into nothingness.

Concentrate.

He did. First on Master Joriah's bearded face, then his deep voice. When he tried to remember the signature of the mage's spirit, the process fell apart. He had just spoken to Master Joriah. Why couldn't he recall the mage's telltale signature? Or Master Maglo's?

Petrah lost all semblance of concentration.

Salt from his cooling perspiration stung his eyes. He was losing precious water through his pores. He rested his head against the mountain of sand behind him.

I can't let this godforsaken wasteland be the end of me!

Maybe his friends were holding off until evening to look for him, perhaps hunkered down on the opposite side of a nearby dune, out of sight. They could very well be in the vicinity, waiting out the heat of the day.

Petrah closed his eyes. He would wait too.

Waiting turned into thinking of his life and future. What if he abandoned his magehood and joined the White Hand? Kruush, Tan, and Ahleen were his family, not the students at Maseah or his instructors or the members of the Magi Guild. Even Ajoon was just a friend. Petrah could become a hard worker for the White Hand, learn about trade and commerce from Kruush, and maybe find a tribeswoman along the way who would look past his foreign origins and accept him for who he was.

And who am I?

He thought back to his encounter with the krell. When the alpha male—with Chíla's blood still dripping from his jaws—had approached, Petrah's heartbeat had thrummed in cadence with the beast. Instead of fleeing, Petrah had allowed the animal to come up to him, to sniff his wrist. It could have ripped out his throat. It could have dragged him alive down that slope, to the rest of the hungry pack, but it didn't. Why? Was Oma right? Was there a demon inside Petrah? Was that what the alpha smelled? Petrah shivered at the thought?

Maybe I'm cursed.

The Watcher's metallic voice crept into his thoughts, like the shadow of a vaellra blackening all hope of escape.

I know your future. You'll see it yourself soon enough.

THE AIR COOLED CONSIDERABLY at twilight, but not as cold as it had been the past few evenings. Petrah dusted the granules from his body and ascended the tall dune again. He surveyed the unforgiving terrain, biting down on his chapped lips in the hope he would catch movement.

Bluish shadows and coppery ripples of sand shifted in the gentle breeze. No friends, no caravans, no signs of their animals, nor the bray of gonatans, or even a flicker from a campfire. No smells to account for other than the nondescript desert air. There was nothing but the soft shimmer of moonlight off the endless ridges spreading in all directions.

"Now what?" he shouted with outstretched arms.

Thinking about his dire situation stirred up a memory from school, from when he first met Hamma. Petrah remembered Hamma's tale of woe about how a vaellra had separated him and another boy from their tribe as a child. The boy had died, leaving Hamma to fend for himself. A Terad had saved Hamma's life at just the right time. The tribe leader had used his divine sight to find him.

Hamma was lucky. I need to be lucky, too.

A brisk upshot of air pelted his mouth with grains of sand. He spat them out. His throat was like the inner walls of a dry well, desperate for a single drop of water.

You're not dead yet, but you better get going.

From his vantage, it was hard to tell which way to head. Kruush had plotted their course, and Petrah vaguely recalled they were to go south from Bea-tet, then east. At what point one crossed over to the other, he wasn't sure, although he recalled the sun in his face at first light, which meant they were heading east. That was a good sign, he noted, since the caravans would continue in that general direction until they reached Hōvar.

Petrah set out. He hoped to go in the same direction as Kruush's caravan. If not that, then at least toward the ambassador's.

Petrah looked for the darkest section of the skyline. There was a midnight-blue gradient of sky near the horizon. That was east. He started toward it.

The waning moon neared its zenith. Petrah traveled as far as possible overnight. If his companions were ahead of him, perhaps he could catch up in the morning. The air grew cooler as the night went on. He shivered and rubbed his arms. Petrah preoccupied himself with his surroundings to keep his mind active and off his predicament.

The landscape, while bleak, held life. Tiny dimples in the sand revealed the passage of small animals or insects. At times, something would skitter by. Eventually, the moon sank to the horizon, and the stars became his only guide. Daylight followed not long after. In front of him, the sun crested the dunes and warmed the air. Petrah was thankful to stop shivering. But the temperature continued to climb, and soon it would be intolerable.

Where are they? he wondered sometime around midmorning. He'd hoped to have seen movement or familiar shapes by now. Petrah saw neither. By midday, his tongue was swollen and his thoughts disjointed. That he might be stranded permanently on this never-ending stretch of hell propelled him forward.

Then he saw something.

The dunes disappeared into a low-lying area, wide and level. The ground shimmered. Then he spotted a glorious sight in the distance.

Water!

Petrah hurried toward it. There were palms, too. He laughed. This was another oasis, just like Bea-tet!

But when he reached what he thought was the first of several palm trees, the illusion disintegrated. It wasn't a palm at all. It was a freestanding stone pillar. The shimmering also disappeared, replaced by desolation. What he assumed was water was cracked earth.

Petrah sank to his knees.

He clutched the broken ground and crushed it to a fine powder. This wasn't a desert oasis. It was the ruins of a deserted city.

Tall, monolithic columns, faceless and eroded by wind and time, stood in lines, supporting nothing but sky, or lay toppled whole or in sections. Chunks of pottery and shards of clayware lay scattered or jutting from the ground like teeth.

Petrah wobbled over to the nearest column. He pressed his palm against its faded, bone-colored surface. It wasn't wide enough to provide cover. He walked to a fallen section of a stone beam that had a crack running down its center. It provided much-needed shade. He leaned against it, noted the gritty texture, and considered hoisting himself up so he could lie down on top of it.

A hiss came from below. He looked down but saw nothing. Then he felt a sharp prick on his right ankle.

Petrah stumbled back. In the sand, he spotted a wavy trail disappear underneath the beam. His ankle throbbed. He looked at it and saw a pair of bite marks. The skin surrounding them reddened.

If you're bit, piss on it, Kruush once told him. A supposed nomad trick for handling a snakebite.

Assuming the venom didn't kill you first.

Petrah reached beneath his tunic so he could pee. He laughed when the folds of his gebban barred his way.

Petrah stumbled sideways, cackling as he groped. The whole thing was hilarious. He staggered several feet and tried not to fall. The world spun, and the pillars changed shape, melting into fractal blobs. "That's got to be the funniest—"

Vertigo struck. His body arched backward, and his legs gave out.

P ETRAH DREAMED.

He was standing in the rain, soaked and holding his mouth open to catch the drops. It spattered his chin, went up his nose, and made him cough. He shook his head to get the water out of his eyes.

When he opened them, he was dry and next to his mother, looking through the remnants of a giant metal building where several men had gathered. They wore the black outfits of his brother's army. They came to attention when his brother strode into the room. He was wearing his emblazoned dragon breastplate beneath his black cloak. He had on spiked greaves and chain mail gauntlets.

Petrah's mother's lips formed the name of his brother.

Aman.

His brother's dark brown, almost-black hair ran to the tops of his shoulders, framing tanned skin, stark blue eyes, and a prominent chin.

"He marshals his army," his mother told Petrah. "He will lead legions to victory. Fire will birth the great Dragon, and he will conquer the world under his child's shadowy wings. You will open the way for him. And then you will follow in the cinders and ash and bear witness to doom."

Petrah turned to say something to his mother, but when he did, he was standing atop a rocky peak overlooking a mountain range, battered by the frigid wind.

A man whispered into his ear. "Speak the Word. Use that secret of yours and hold nothing back."

Petrah's lips moved.

As soon as he uttered the final consonant, the mountaintops detonated in a cascade of avalanches, showering a torrent of ruination upon the forest below.

"Good," the man said. "Now feel it."

Petrah did, and it brought a desire for more. A bloodlust radiating from his core immediately overpowered the shame of committing such a vile act.

When he blinked, he was underground in a masonry cell where a girl with white hair cried.

"Why are you crying?" he asked.

She wiped the tears with a knuckle. "You can't stop him," she said. "You're not strong enough, because you're like him. You just don't know it yet."

"I'm nothing like him," Petrah said.

"No," she said, tears streaking her pale cheeks. "You're far, far worse. He only wants to enslave mankind, but you"—she pointed at him—"you want to destroy the heavens."

Petrah tried to say something, but he was whisked away to a barren hill under dismal skies. Hundreds of people surrounded him—men, women, and children—despondent and downtrodden, poorly armed survivors making their last stand against an army numbering in the tens of thousands in the valley that plunged below them. Black pennants snapped in the icy wind among the vast sea of soldiers stretching to the horizon. Aman rode his coal-colored stallion to the vanguard of his army. He thrust a mailed fist into the sky. A raucous cheer swept through his forces. With a thunderous start, he led them in a gallop that shook the plains. They charged the hill, a surging tide of death.

An elder among the survivors pleaded with Petrah. "Immael, we need you. Please stop him."

"I—I can't."

Petrah watched helplessly as the army engaged the survivors at the base of the ascent, felling them mercilessly with their swords and spears. Archers fired upward, sending a rain of arrows that blackened the sky. One arrow struck Petrah in the chest, penetrating his ribcage and knocking him onto his back.

When he looked up, he saw his brother crest the hill. All the survivors around Petrah were dead, save one, the girl with the white hair. A soldier handed off the frightened girl to Aman, who pulled her tightly against his body armor and set a knife to her throat.

"See what happens to the children?" Aman said. "See what you did?"

Petrah clutched the shaft of the arrow protruding from his chest and felt the wetness spreading through his gebban. He gulped air like a fish flopping on the ground.

"Father told you to do the right thing. He told you to help me. We are of the same blood, you and I. Yet you have forsaken our bond, and for what? Now look at yourself. You die in agony, as do the rest. Where is your faith now, Immael? Where?"

The girl trembled in Aman's grasp. Petrah tried to speak, but the blood in his lungs flooded his mouth.

"She chose you over me," Aman said, pulling the frightened girl's chin up. "Now watch what happens to those who betray me."

Petrah reached forward from the ground with an outstretched hand in a desperate plea to stop his brother.

Aman's eyes burned like blue fire. He yanked up on the girl's chin. She whimpered in his grasp, and for a moment, it looked as if he might let her go. Then, with a single draw of his blade, he slit her throat.

Warm blood sprayed Petrah's face, drowning his strangled cries.

"**O**VER HERE!" AHLEEN CALLED.

Kruush followed her as she ran over to Petrah, who lay unconscious and trembling, his body curled into a fetal position.

Kruush knelt by Petrah's side. "Julan, get me some water."

Julan handed him a water skin. Kruush pressed the nozzle to Petrah's blackened lips. They opened slightly, but the water dribbled onto the ground. Petrah wasn't responding.

"Let me look," Summi said. He felt Petrah's forehead, then his pulse. He tilted Petrah's head to the side and brought his ear close to his mouth. Ahleen watched with a strained face, bobbing up and down on her heels while Kruush held his breath.

"He's feverish," Summi said. "His breathing is shallow, and his heart rate is fast. And look at this." He pointed at Petrah's swollen right ankle. A pair of puncture wounds were inset on raised mounds of inflamed flesh. "Snakebite. Black rattler or copper bottom. Can't be sure from the fang marks. Either way, he's in terrible shape."

Kruush looked at Ahleen, then back at Summi. "Can you help him?"

"Let's move him to the shade. We'll cool him down and give him small amounts of water. We need to keep him here for the night. I'll grab some herbs for the poison, but it's mostly up to him to make it out of this. He doesn't have much time."

Summi and Julan moved the unconscious journeyman behind a crumbling wall. The triangular section of stone cast a generous shadow over his body.

Ahleen hooked her arm around Kruush's. Summi went to work, positioning Petrah on his back. "I'm so worried," she said.

Kruush rubbed her hand. "I know, my love. We'll pray for him."

"I can't believe we found him," Tan said. "It's a miracle."

"Don't jinx us," Kruush said with fierceness in his voice. "Just thank the stars we could find him. This is the only landmark in these parts. I don't even know where *this* is. It looks like the remains of a city."

"Ruins of Keel, I would guess," Tan said, looking around. "Which would put us farther south than we want."

Kruush tugged on his beard. "Gods. How far ahead do you suppose the ambassador's caravan is?"

"Half a day's march, maybe more. That sandstorm threw us off course."

Summi took dried herbs from a pouch, chewed them for a minute, and spat the chunk of pasty green onto his palm. He pressed it into the infected area on Petrah's ankle. The sharpness of camphor stung their eyes.

Tan pointed across the ruins. "We might be able to catch them if we head northeast in the morning and then due east in the afternoon, and keep going past sundown and repeat that the day after."

Ahleen doused a strip of cloth with water and daubed Petrah's sunburned forehead. She gently applied it to his lips and neck. "You're burning up," she whispered.

Summi cupped Petrah's chin and forced him to swallow a sip of water. He waited a few seconds, and then repeated the process. After a minute, he set Petrah's head down on a bedroll. Summi looked up at Kruush. "He needs rest."

"Summi, we are in your debt. Gratitude," Kruush said.

Summi smiled, poked the air in three places, and went to help Julan set up camp.

Ahleen leaned her head against Kruush's shoulder and entwined his fingers with hers. He rubbed his thumb over her knuckle and kissed her brow. They kept watch over Petrah, whose chest barely rose and fell. Ahleen began crying. She wiped the tears with her palm. "Sorry, I can't help myself."

"I know, my darling," Kruush said. "But he's a strong lad. He'll get through this."

BY NIGHTFALL, THE SWELLING was down and Petrah was sleeping peacefully. The next morning, his fever broke. He awoke of his own accord just after daybreak.

"Ahleen," he said weakly, reaching out.

"Easy," she said. "Don't force yourself." She offered him water, and he accepted.

"What happened?" he asked after a couple of swallows. "The last thing I remember was dreaming about this girl with white hair. She—" He stopped himself.

"It's not important," Ahleen said. "Your recovery is. You gave us quite the scare."

"You keep saving me, you know that?"

She smiled down at him. "Rest a little while longer."

Petrah fell back asleep. Ahleen left him alone so she could help the others pack. After an hour, the caravan was ready to go. Kruush and Summi made a makeshift litter to drag behind one of the gonatans and secured Petrah with ropes.

Tan walked over to Kruush. "All set?"

"Aye," Kruush said, looking around. "Let's get out of this blasted desert."

Chapter 6
The Unexpected

THEY REACHED HŌVAR EARLY on a clear morning. Petrah was well enough to ride a gonatan on his own. On the first day after his friends had found him unconscious at the Ruins of Keel, he'd been too weak to ride, beset by tremors and lightheadedness and prone to violent coughing fits that chafed his throat. The second day saw an end to the dizziness and shaking, and he could ride hunched over. By the third day, his strength had returned, and he no longer pitched forward in his saddle. Now, the coughing was infrequent, and the tenderness in the back of his throat was reduced to a slight tickle. He thanked the stars he'd mostly recovered from the venom of his snakebite.

The capital of Meerjurmeh sat nestled in a fertile river valley surrounded by plantations, farms, and vineyards. Petrah soaked in the sights, smells, and feel of this foreign city with the same vigor as the first time he'd laid eyes on Elmar.

She's beautiful, he thought. *More so than any city in Terjurmeh.*

It was the myriad colors, he decided, that distinguished her from the drab tones of the Terjurmehan cities. Sweeps of bright red, purple, and fuchsia blooms cascaded over Hōvar's tall, stone walls that formed a defensive perimeter, much the way the one in Kanmar did. Gentle slopes revealed paved streets, terraced gardens, villas, government buildings, churches, and a plenitude of monuments depicting heroes of yore. It was a crowded city, with many homes built upon one another in a variety of sandy hues and colorful pastel paints buttressing narrow and crooked streets, although some manses and parks occupied larger tracts of land.

The harbor boasted numerous watercraft for fishing and commerce and several warships that protected the waterways from invaders. Small fishing vessels slipped between massive cargo freighters, returning with their early morning catches. Three separate rivers converged in the delta, fed from the River Nomad to the south, which split northerly to form the Estuary River to the west and the Tangeen River to the east.

Then there was the famed University of Akan, where scholars from around the world flocked to and where gifted youths with a natural affinity for the arcane arts aspired to become expert channelers under the tutelage of renowned masters. The students there were said to practice the arts in the grand, mosaic-tiled courtyards. Or cluster among the stacks of the multi-leveled master library that formed a cylindrical well seven stories deep within the ground. Or focus the sun in spectacles of colorful splendor using the light-bending craft of Leventi. The school was said to rival—and even surpass—the Acadium of Korin.

Hōvar, Petrah had learned in school, was the nation's heart for trade but, more importantly, the worldwide center for Jahism, the country's dominant religion. Pilgrims from the Northern Kingdom, Korin, and even as far as the Provinces of the South flocked to the city each year to receive blessings from the Greater Light, the papal head of the Jahn Church.

Kruush led his party from the harbor on the South Estuary along the road leading to the plantations. The gonatans pulled twin wains of salt while Summi and Julan walked behind them and Ahleen, Tan, and Petrah rode in front. They passed pilgrims in white tunics heading toward the north gate of the city, who waved and voiced their blessings or patted the flanks of the beasts, drawing brays, or tossed bright red flower petals at Ahleen until she laughed. They chanted their daily prayers, forming a single chorus that stretched well over a mile.

Tan pulled up beside Petrah on his gonatan. "What do you think?"

Petrah glanced over his shoulder, watching the sandstone walls of the city retreat. A boy no older than five or six pointed at him and giggled before running ahead to chase a girl his age. "I think we're no longer in Elmar. These people, they're—"

"Happy?"

"I was going to say *different*. But, yes, happy."

"Can you believe some come hundreds of leagues to get here, a few as far as Cape Loram at the southern tip of Acia? I met a pretty lass from New Southland the last time I was here. She barely spoke Jurmehan, but we got along just fine." Tan's face bloomed into a devilish smile.

Petrah chuckled. "Of course you did. No woman is safe from you on this continent."

"I think by 'safe' you mean 'impervious to my charms.' But I'll take that as a compliment."

Kruush tossed a shriveled look over his shoulder. "From what I recall, she wasn't too fond of your brashness."

Tan lifted his chin in playful defiance. "Says you, soothsayer of love. Women love brashness. They equate it with bravery and boldness. Or have you been married so long, you forget your own courage in winning Ahleen's affections? Ahleen, am I wrong?"

Ahleen shook her head. "I'm staying out of this."

Tan winked at Petrah and whispered, "Don't worry, when we get the chance, I'll take you into the city where the beauties flock like pigeons."

Petrah looked forward to seeing the city up close in the days ahead. Kruush promised to show Petrah around to prepare for the Terjurmehan ambassador's visit with the Meerjurmehan leadership, which Master Joriah would approve of—not Tan's playful pursuits.

The road along the river took them past lush estates, with hedgerows and groves of palms serving as natural borders. An hour from the harbor, the road branched, taking them inland through the electrum-capped gates of Montabijon, the grand two-hundred-fifty-acre estate of affluent business mogul Mokan-lee. The welcome peacefulness reminded Petrah of Maseah.

Petrah fanned himself with the sleeve of his gebban. Although the slight humidity was a refreshing change from the stale desert, it made breathing more difficult. The venom from the snakebite had constricted his airways and given him the shakes for days. Thanks to Summi's herbs, he was faring much better. He hoped to be himself again by the next morning.

Petrah followed Kruush down the private dirt road. Estate workers greeted them. They carted the sacks of salt off to a storehouse and took the gonatans to a ranch to rest. Palm trees with bulbous clusters grew in abundance by the roadside, along with a profusion of tall plants with fragrant trumpet-like flowers and groves of orange, lemon, and avocado trees. Crows cawed among the manicured date palms.

The weary travelers walked up to an enormous three-story manor house named Bokania. Four servants awaited them by the double-doored main entrance, immaculately uniformed in white tunics, corded at the waist.

"We're staying here?" Petrah asked Tan, wide-eyed.

Tan clapped him on the back. "Now you know why I'm still in this business."

AFTER A PROPER BATH, courtesy of Mokan-lee's household staff, and outfitted in a fresh tunic, Petrah joined Tan and Kruush in the west wing tearoom on the second floor of the three-story manse. He'd not felt this clean since departing Maseah. Changing out of his gebban, which had stunk of gonatan and stone, was as liberating as his bath. The gebban, Petrah noted, was one of two possessions to survive the vaellra. The other was a satchel of paper and ink supplies. The sandstorm had taken Jayeem's sword from him, along with the books he'd borrowed from the library at Maseah.

No good had come from that sword. It's best lost among the sand dunes.

The books, though, were irreplaceable.

Kruush sat opposite Mokan-lee, separated from each other by a tiny, round table bearing saucers and cups brimming with hot tea. Clove incense burned, adding a sweet scent to the floral aromas. Tan and Petrah sat separately, joined by Mokan-lee's eldest son, Milio.

Both father and son presented themselves just as Petrah imagined aristocrats to be: stately, with regal movements of the hands and an air of confidence that reinforced their stature over the common class.

Mokan-lee was a finely groomed man, the light-tan skin on his long face clear, his beard trimmed with precision. Milio looked a lot like his father, right down to the square shape of his jaw. They both wore white, satin robes bearing the family crest: a flame surrounded by a wreath of j'boun, a flower with four pale, pink petals, a white center, and stamen tipped in lavender.

It surprised Petrah that the Con-jurah he'd seen so far were similar in physique to the Ter-jurah: squat mostly, round in the face, and skin the color of honey. Then he remembered they all shared the same lineage going back over three thousand years. They could trace their family trees to a time when they were all a single people, the An-jurah. Before the Great War tore them apart and religious differences divided them forever.

Kruush lifted his cup to his lips, and Mokan-lee's eyes followed. Kruush sniffed, sipped, and swished. He then slurped loudly. It was a Meer-jurmehan custom of respect. "This cha is exceptional."

"It's from my neighbor's tea gardens," Mokan-lee said. "His cha is renowned throughout Meerjurmeh. I'll have to get you some." Then, smiling, he added, "Perhaps on your next visit."

Petrah studied Mokan-lee. The mogul held his cup level and with care, mindful of how he picked it up and set it down. He wore silk that was free of wrinkles.

Petrah had seen such finery only worn by one man, Baaka, Seer of Elmar. He very much wanted to feel the material of Mokan-lee's garb, to see how it compared with the roughness of his journeyman's robe. The gray robe was back at Maseah, locked in his trunk. Petrah missed wearing the Gray. It too denoted a certain stature in the mage order's hierarchy, one that he would have been proud to wear had it not been for the way he'd earned it.

Kruush produced a devious smirk. "Trying to get me to come back, Mokan? While you're being generous, perhaps you could find me a fancy timekeeper like the one in the foyer downstairs."

"That 'timekeeper' you refer to is a *clock*, one of only three in all of Meerjurmeh. The wood alone costs more than a warship, and the mechanism inside is a masterful piece of art that no Con-jurahn artisan has yet to master. I bought it from the Valudin of Lenferd in the Northern Kingdom for a hefty sum I dare not repeat in present company. Gibbs Moraine is a distant cousin to the king, but his collection is kingly in its own right. Suffice it to say, master merchant, that you might want to amass a little wealth before you add one to your collection."

"I'm working on it," Kruush said with a smuggler's grin.

Petrah had seen the fabled timepiece upon entering the manor, prominently displayed downstairs between twin marble staircases, but didn't know what it was, until now. The clock was as tall as a man, the rich, burgundy wood finish polished to a sheen, the odd ticking from within a constant and steady confluence of working gears.

Master Nole had expounded on the subject of time, but he had condemned the mechanical keeping of it as a "gross offender of the natural order of things," citing that a mage truly came into his own when he was one with the movement of the sun, moon, and stars, requiring nothing but divine energy to guide the timeliness of one's actions. Still, Petrah agreed with Kruush: to possess such a timekeeper would be remarkable.

Petrah sipped his tea. The cha was bitter at first, like sprushah, but had a sweet, citrusy finish with a touch of pepper on the tongue.

Mokan-lee spoke to Petrah. "You drink like my grandmother. Are you an old widow?"

Petrah slurped. He looked up expectantly.

"Better."

Mokan-lee continued his talk with Kruush. "I hear your ambassador's in town. It'll be interesting to find out what he does about these trade sanctions your country has imposed. I lost a significant business interest when your countrymen ruined our lumber trade agreement with the Northerners. First rights are expensive, you know."

"The Iron Fist has a block for a brain," Kruush said. "He doesn't understand commerce, although he understands war aplenty. He didn't have to wreak havoc in Vergahl. He could have taken the city peacefully and left the farms and plantations intact instead of burning them. He should have made his point and left. But he didn't."

"He was sending a message—but more like a bull who charges into a pen without thinking, thrashing about and making an utter mess of things," Mokan-lee said. "Let's hope some good comes of this visit from your countrymen. I hear one of your major parties is absent from the talks. That tidbit of news doesn't sit well with me." The mogul swirled his cup, eyes fixed on Kruush, silent for a long moment. Petrah's ears perked up at the sound of ticking. Was it his imagination or could he hear the clock from all the way up here?

"Tell me," Mokan-lee said. "What's going on?"

Kruush brushed his large thumb over the gold rim of his cup. "It's that blasted alliance between the Fist and the Black Arrow. They're trying to squeeze out the Green Flame party from any political happenings of note. The Green Flame offended the Fist at the last Great Council, where the Articulate leading the Green Flame offended that peacock of an ass, Andus-nai and thus perpetuated a schism among top-ranking parties." Kruush shook his head. "The Silver Blade attempted to curry favor and save face by aligning the two parties. Then they convinced the Copper Shield to join in the fun. Don't even get me started on the Copper Shield and their conniving ways."

Kruush slurped a mouthful of tea and wiped his lips. "Now you have four parties working together—the Fist, Black Arrow, Silver Blade, and Copper Shield—whereas each party previously looked out for itself. Not only has this new alliance created a lopsided shift in the power balance among citizens and tribes, but it's causing friction with the Temple as well. The way things are going, we'll end up in a bloody civil war. Boils my balls just to think of it."

Mokan-lee aimed a pinky at him. "How does that affect us?"

Kruush swatted a hand in dismissal. "Nothing to worry about, my friend. Did that stunt up in Vergahl change anything? It didn't. Why? Because money's money. There's a lot of money to be made, and no one at the top with any sense is going to change that. Don't concern yourself over the squabbling parties. The White Hand will do its part, as promised. We're not stupid like the Green Flame."

Kruush's remark made Petrah flinch. Petrah's tea sloshed around his cup, but no one noticed. He'd been present at the Great Council and had witnessed Uhtah-Pei's bold move in rallying the tribes and declaring the Fist an enemy of the state. Perhaps it was stupid, or maybe it was brilliant. But Kruush was just being careful, drawing attention away from the White Hand.

"I hope you're right," Mokan-lee said. "I'd like to think I'm investing in the winning party."

Kruush raised his cup and smiled. "You are."

"Then let's drink to surviving a mock war and corrupt political system." Mokan-lee turned to Tan and Milio. "All of us."

Everyone grabbed a cup. Loud slurping noises filled the tearoom. A smattering of laughter filtered from the room next door where the women were having their tea.

They're having more fun than us. Anything was better than listening to boring politics.

But Petrah wasn't here to have fun. Master Joriah had assigned him a mission. Part of that mission was to understand the Con-jurahn way of life—their culture, their habits, their mannerisms, and yes, their politics.

Mokan-lee set his cup on the table. "Let's get down to business," he said to Kruush. "I like the way trade is going between us. You bring me salt; I give you dusk. I sell the salt to my suppliers for profit, you sell your product, and the cycle continues. It's a suitable arrangement. Despite any rumors of your country's instability, I'm pleased. But we need to progress. I want to step up operations and expand."

"What did you have in mind?" Kruush asked.

"I want you to get me an exclusive trade contract. All the salt import business. Every sack. Every grain. Everything."

Kruush glanced at Tan. "It's not so easy. There's a pecking order of sorts in my party. I've not quite 'earned my feathers,' as the Idarian adage goes, if you get my meaning."

"I do," Mokan-lee said. "There are obstacles on your side, but obstacles can be overcome. I trust you'll be able to do that."

"Of course. Give me another season and I'll get you that exclusive contract. Throw me a little extra this go-around and I'll grease every wheel I need to, just enough to do the job. And you *know* I'll do the job."

Mokan-lee smiled a politician's smile. "I know you will."

PETRAH WALKED ALONG THE terrace on Bokania's third floor the following morning. The terracotta patio faced the sloping gardens and vineyards in the cool air. His night's rest was the best he could remember. The bed was soft, the pillows filled with down. He was feeling himself again, and he was thankful for it. He fingered the supple material of his white robe.

Real silk.

He had found it draped over the chair in his room when he awoke. It was far more luxurious than his gebban or student robe, almost too luxurious.

Give it some time. I could get used to it.

He smiled as he tightened the sash on his robe. He leaned against the smooth, alabaster railing. It was peaceful here. Topiaries and palms formed mazelike patterns below, interspersed with small pools filled with koi. Bougainvillea spilled over whitewashed walls while yuccas sprouted in clusters. In the distance, he could barely make out the rectangular swaths of tilled soil where the fabled oplia plants grew in rows. He spotted armed soldiers from Mokan-lee's private militia guarding the precious farmland, as workers toiled, bent over among the waist-high plants.

The oplia would flower and produce bulbs. Kruush said the sap from the bulbs, once dried and ground into a fine powder, would produce the hallucinogenic spice called dusk—one of the most expensive commodities in the country.

Tomorrow was an important day, the first of the ambassador's meetings with the Con-jurahn leadership. Petrah had to be in position early, as close to the ambassador's location as possible. Kruush suggested they head into the city before dawn and find a spot near the assembly building where Petrah could conduct his mission.

Petrah closed his eyes, practicing the technique he would use to gather information at the assembly by picking up the vibrations of conversation through stone. Master Maglo's instructions came back to him.

Just block out the other sounds, Master Maglo had told him. *Then concentrate. The words will speak to you.*

Petrah concentrated on the gardens below. Instead of picking up conversations, he homed in on the twitter of songbirds. There were bluetails among the fruit trees. Thirty-five, he counted. Their songs were even more beautiful than the scarlet crescents of Terjurmeh. The birds sang to each other in a staccato pulse of calls and answers.

A bluetail swooped low and landed on the corner of the railing. It flicked its tail and trilled.

Well, hello there.

Petrah remained still. He didn't want to frighten it away. The bird had a white crest and feathers that changed from sky blue on the wings to deep blue on the tail. Petrah held out his finger and focused. He tried to perform a mind link with the bird.

Come to me, he projected.

The bluetail hopped a few inches closer.

It wiped its beak against the alabaster and kept hopping until it came within a foot of Petrah's finger.

That's it. Almost there.

It chirped a sonnet and bobbed its head. He whistled back, trying to mimic the song.

Another whistle came from behind.

The bluetail took flight and fluttered past him. Petrah turned to see the bird perch on a young woman's finger. She slowly lifted her hand until the bird was level with her eyes. She whistled softly, and the bluetail trilled back. She then thrust her hand out, and the bird flew off. When Petrah saw her face, the world stood still.

She was about his age, dressed in a white silk tunic that draped to the marble balcony floor. It was finely embroidered with long sleeves and lavender cuffs that flared out like satin plumes. He took in her large, brown eyes, then her small, pointed nose, and finally, her rosy full lips.

Petrah had never seen such beauty. Nor could he stop staring.

The girl smiled, but then frowned. "Well, are you going to say something?" Her long, brown hair was braided behind her with a j'boun flower over each ear. The sweet scent carried over to him.

"I, uh—" Petrah stammered.

"Never mind," she said, raising her nose. "I suppose the bird ate your tongue." She spun around and started to leave.

"Wait," he called.

She placed her hands on her hips. She was even more striking in this pose. "Yes?"

"I—uh—I didn't get your name." Petrah smiled, but it was as awkward as the squawk of his voice.

"And what makes you think you've earned the privilege?"

"I don't know. I . . ." He was at a loss for what to say.

"That's what I thought." She turned and left.

Petrah stood there for several seconds, heart pounding. Then he snapped out of his reverie and lost his smile.

I'm a fool.

PETRAH MADE THE MISTAKE of telling Kruush about his encounter. The older merchant laughed. "That's Mokan-lee's only daughter." Then, turning serious, he added, "I'd stay far away from her, my friend. We're guests here. The last thing you want to do is incur the wrath of a father mad about protecting his daughter's virtue."

Petrah blurted, "But I didn't do anything."

"No one said you did. I'm just imparting a little friendly advice."

To Petrah's disconcertment, he sat directly across from Mokan-lee's daughter at dinner. Petrah couldn't change seats either; the table was entirely occupied. Kruush and Tan sat next to Mokan-lee; Ahleen sat beside Mokan-lee's wife, Lila; Milio and his younger brother, Mikano, sat guardedly on either side of their sister; and a pair of senators and their wives sat by Petrah. Lila was an older replica of her daughter, with the same full lips and small nose, but the daughter's large eyes came from the father.

Senator Pallinne—whose granite features matched his strong tone—used his hands expressively as he spoke, commanding the attention of the entire table. Petrah examined his movements—the flick of a wrist, the jab of fingers, the wave of a hand. Petrah also committed the man's voice to memory after hearing he was to participate in the talks with the Ter-jurah.

"The question is," the senator said with a finger raised, "will their ambassador try to use Vergahl as leverage, or will he be smarter than that? What do you think, Mokan?"

Mokan-lee offered his own show of strength with an exaggerated lift of his right hand. "The last time their ambassador visited, he tried to parlay with the Lesser Light, but that was before the fiasco in Vergahl. If the ambassador is smart, he won't engage Kōs again. The attack on Vergahl bode poorly for Kōs in the eyes of the senate, making Kōs appear weak—especially being the son of a brilliant military strategist who actually won against the Ter-jurah in his day."

"An interesting point." Senator Pallinne shifted his granite chin to Kruush. "What do you think of your ambassador's mission here? Will he try to strongarm us and impose sanctions, or will he be more tactful and attempt a peace accord?"

Kruush, wise not to say anything that might offend the Con-jurah at the table, said, "I dare not venture a guess, Senator, for I am a simple businessman, not a statesman. I happily leave politicking to brilliant minds like yours. But I would hope our ambassador is tactful. I enjoy coming to Meerjurmeh. I'd hate to think he might instigate something that could close your borders to my people."

Senator Pallinne smiled at that. "That wouldn't be very good for trade, would it?"

"Not at all, Senator," Kruush said. With a sly curl of the lip, he added, "Nor for the export of certain spices."

"Perhaps you're more of a politician than you think."

Petrah observed the mannerisms of his hosts and tried to emulate their actions with similar movements of his hands under the table. They sipped wine in a civilized fashion—unlike tea—and one ate with their right hand and gestured with their left.

Dinner turned out to be an excruciatingly long event. There was course after course. Leafy greens with bright orange fruits, a soup with filets of trout, poultry kabobs with rice, and chilled mint water accompanied by spiced cookies.

Petrah found the constant staring of Mokan-lee's daughter unbearable. She watched him as he nibbled the meat off his skewer, sniffed and sipped his water, and dropped his spoon into his bowl, splashing soup everywhere. When their eyes met after he fumbled and fished his spoon out of his bowl, the corners of her lips lifted into a smile. Or was it a smirk? Her endless attention stole his appetite. Didn't her mother notice what her daughter was doing and how inappropriate it was?

She wasn't the only one Petrah had to worry about. Her brother, Milio, compounded the discomfort by catching Petrah every time he looked at his sister, and always with the same glare and grind of his square jaw.

He's just looking out for her, just being protective, Petrah told himself. Or perhaps Milio disliked Petrah.

Mikano wasn't as fierce-eyed as his older brother. He was curious, often watching Petrah's fingers as they shifted food around his plate. He was kind enough to smile with pity during Petrah's incident with the fish stew.

When the servant took the last plate away—the cookies Petrah had left untouched—Mokan-lee's daughter folded her hands and flattened her full lips into a thin line. Was it disappointment? Boredom, perhaps? Or was it something else?

Petrah was squirming in his seat by the time the men were told to retire to the smoke room.

She tortures me and enjoys it.

Ajoon had never done that to him. She'd always been honest and straightforward with Petrah.

And just a friend.

The "just" part lingered like the spice from the cookies that hung in the air.

Kruush excused Petrah, who couldn't wait to leave. Petrah walked through a dozen rooms and corridors before finding the exit to the gardens on the first floor. He planned to seek out an alcove to meditate and try again to contact Master Joriah.

It was cool outside, the nighttime air filled with the sounds of insects and birds. Petrah stood for a moment, peering into the dark. He could discern the details of the shrubbery and trees, despite the lack of light. He picked out the shapes of individual leaves, the distinct lines and twists of branches, the texture and shades of the bark.

The desert, with its long stretches of nondescript sand and rocky terrain, hadn't stood out as starkly as being here with so much foliage and variations in the terrain—fields, vineyards, and groves. They were as easy to see as in the daylight. Petrah's ability to perceive details in the dark had begun the night he'd fought Miko. Before that, objects had appeared as blends of shadows and silhouettes—the same as anyone he knew had experienced them. Now, he was nimble at night as an owl, mouse, or krell. Was this another manifestation of divine power? He never recalled Masters Nole or Maglo or any of the other instructors mentioning it. It wasn't in any book on channeling. Perhaps journeymen attained it before magehood. He would ask Master Maglo when he returned.

Petrah found a bench under a palm and sat. He closed his eyes, murmured a mantra, and slipped into a trance. A moment later, he attempted a mind link with his master. This time, he was rewarded with Master Joriah's voice.

Petrah, Master Joriah said. *I wasn't expecting to hear from you, but I'm glad you contacted me. Tell me everything.*

Petrah appraised his master on his arrival in Hōvar and that he would be Mokan-lee's guest until his mission was complete, thanks to Kruush.

Does anyone suspect you're with the Green Flame?

No, Master.

Good. Any trouble along the way? Anything I need to know?

Petrah rubbed his ankles together. He tried to decide if he should say anything about losing a day's journey because he'd gotten separated from his party. *No, Master. No trouble.*

There was a pause on the other end. Did Master Joriah suspect Petrah was holding back information? Petrah mashed his toes into his sandals, expecting the mage to question his comment, but Master Joriah switched to Petrah's spy mission, which was to begin in the morning.

Tell me your objective.

To report on the talks between the Terjurmehan and Meerjurmehan delegations, Petrah said. *And to note any decisions, agreements, terms, pushbacks, or concessions.*

I want facts, not opinions. His Holiness Uhtah-Pei and I can arrive at our own conclusions. Understood?

Yes, Master.

How do you plan to perform your task?

Petrah had spoken to Kruush about it, and both agreed Kruush would take him into the city to get close to the assembly building, where the delegations would hold their talks behind closed doors. Petrah relayed the information, and added, *I'll use the listening technique Master Maglo taught me. Master Maglo said it'll work in a range of up to one thousand feet before the quality attenuates.*

Make sure you find a spot where you can remain undisturbed and undistracted. And most importantly, undetected.

Kruush knows a café well within that range, close to the assembly building. That will allow me to stay put in one place.

Cafés are busy. What are your other options?

Petrah didn't have any other viable options. *There's the public square facing the building, but I don't think that would work. Kruush believes it's too noisy and crowded. He also believes the grounds around the government buildings will be cut off from public access.*

Agreed. Security increases with events like these. If the grounds next to the assembly building are off-limits to the public, then you won't be able to perform your work from any place around it. A slight pause, then, *Listen, Petrah. Assess the situation, use your wits, and find the right locale to do your work. Above all, do not abandon your mission. If you run into an issue, adapt accordingly. I'm counting on you.*

I will, Master, Petrah said.

I believe in you. The party believes in you. Good luck.

In other words, don't screw up.

Petrah disconnected, then slumped and placed his face in his hands. He released the tension in his chest. Mind links were tiring enough, but living up to Master Joriah's expectations was exhausting. *He expects perfection, nothing less.* Petrah imagined that if their roles were reversed, he'd expect it too.

Petrah propped his elbows on his knees and watched the fish dart in the dark water of the pool by his feet. This time, there was no Miko to ruin his evening.

"Are you all right?"

Petrah sat bolt upright. It was Mokan-lee's daughter again. She held a lantern in his face. "It's you." he said.

She frowned. "That's not a bad thing, is it?"

He uncrossed his ankles and shielded his eyes from the flickering light. "Well, no, I suppose not."

"You suppose not?"

Was this a continuation of supper where he had to second-guess everything he did? Or was it a valid question? He tripped over his words, confused. "I didn't mean that. I meant . . ."

"Yes?"

"I meant, no, it's not a bad thing. In fact, I'm glad to see you." He sat up tall. He'd finally said something right.

"You are? Well, that's a relief."

An awkward moment of silence followed, enough for Petrah to worry she might notice the flushness in his cheeks. Thankfully, it was dark out. She diverted to another topic.

"What kind of accent is that? It's not Terjurmehan, I don't think. I've been meaning to ask."

"It's complicated, really," Petrah said, not wanting to tell her he didn't know either. "I've been in Terjurmeh most of my life, though, so I consider it home." He hoped she wouldn't press him for more information.

"It's a nice accent, whatever it is."

There was a second beat of silence, but Petrah tried not to let it go too long. "Um, would you like to sit with me?" Petrah slid over to one end of the bench.

She set her lantern down, gathered the hem of her long skirt, and sat on the opposite side. Even on a two-person bench like this one, the gulf between them seemed vast. Petrah's heart thumped in his temples.

"So," she said, "why didn't you like your dinner?"

Because you watched me the entire time. But he didn't say that. "I wasn't all that hungry."

Her large, shapely eyes softened. "They told me you were terribly ill upon your arrival. Snakebite, I believe. My great-grandfather was bitten by a water rattler when he was twenty-six. They found him face down in the river, body swollen from the venom. A tragic way to pass. I saw you from my window when you arrived. You didn't look well. How did you survive?"

Had she really noticed him when he'd first gotten to the estate? A smile emerged on his lips, like the sun irresistibly rising toward the sky. "Quick thinking by my friends, actually. I had a fever and hallucinations. I would have died if not for them. I still have a cough, but it's going away."

"Is that why you're here by yourself? The men are inside drinking tea and smoking. Shouldn't you be in there with them?" It was a logical question, one any sensible person might ask.

Petrah didn't have a good answer, nor did he care. Her words drew him into the melody of her voice, like a hummingbird drawn to nectar. He found himself powerless from speaking his mind. "I suppose. But I'd rather be out here. I can think better apart from the smoke and the noise. You're lucky to have this. If I lived here, I'd be outside every night."

"You're a strange man."

"Why's that?"

"Men don't sit outside by themselves in the dark," she said. "They sit with each other and discuss manly things and smoke."

Another valid point, but the sweetness of her words was too intoxicating to resist. "Perhaps I'm strange then. I'd rather meditate than discuss manly things and breathe in someone else's smoke. Where I live, we have a place like Montabijon. Mine is called Maseah. It's in Elmar. I don't suppose you've ever been there."

"They don't like us over there. Papa says the people are evil, followers of the dark god. I hear they torture anyone who doesn't believe in San, forcing them to confess their sins. Is that true?"

Petrah didn't want to tell her about Hah'xallah, about the vile things he'd seen. But he couldn't deny what she said was true. "The Ter-jurah don't like the Con-jurah. Some are more tolerant than others, but yes, there is hate. Couldn't the same be said about the Con-jurah and how they view us?"

She gave it a moment's thought. "Yes. It's an ugly thing."

"Quite ugly. Wars have been fought between both sides. Great atrocities have been committed. Who is evil in that case, and who is good? People are people wherever they are. Just because a baby is born in a country where everybody prays to a different god doesn't make the baby evil, does it?"

"No, but—"

"Look at my friends. They're good people."

The girl smiled. "Yes, they're very nice. I think you're nice, too."

Petrah's cheeks warmed. He liked how she held his stare, how she made it seem as if they were the only ones in all of Meerjurmeh, and how she sweetened the very air he breathed.

A woman's voice came from the house. Thankfully, the girl turned toward the source before she could see Petrah blush.

"My mother's calling me," she said, rising abruptly. Petrah rose as well. She grabbed her lantern and started up the path.

Petrah followed her, heart racing again. "Wait!"

She spun, and he found himself almost on top of her. He could smell something sweet coming from her hair. Their eyes met, and his chest tightened.

"I have to go," she said softly. Reluctance carried in her voice.

"Before you go, please tell me your name." He hoped she wouldn't dash off as she had in their previous meeting.

Her brown eyes brightened. "It's Mina." She then trotted up to the manor.

Chapter 7
Spy

THE NEXT MORNING, KRUUSH and Petrah traveled alone into the city in one of Mokan-lee's covered horse-drawn coaches. They headed for the Copper District, the city center where all the government buildings were located, including the capitol and the assembly where the Ter-jurah and Con-jurah would have their talks.

Petrah did his best to keep his thoughts from drifting to Mina. Now that he knew her name, he had spoken it several times to himself, trying it on for size. He found he liked her name a lot. It was perfect, just like her.

You've already forgotten about Ajoon. Shame on you.

Petrah hung his head.

"Is something wrong?" Kruush asked.

"No." Petrah might as well had said yes by how Kruush raised an eyebrow.

"Come now, what's on your mind? Spit it out."

Petrah picked at the tufted, black leather of his seat. The coach creaked as the driver rounded a corner down a winding avenue, clattering over a rough patch of road before finding smooth flagstones. "I'd rather not talk about it."

"And I'd rather still be asleep. But we can't always have what we want, can we?"

Petrah didn't feel like talking about his woes of the heart, least of all to someone who had an opinion on everything. "If you don't mind, I'd prefer to keep it to myself."

Kruush shrugged. "Fine, be like that. It's none of my business anyway."

They rode in silence for a while. Petrah listened to the clop of hooves from the horse pulling their carriage and the jingle of its harness. Brooding about his dilemma wouldn't do Petrah any service, so he busied himself with the world outside his small, curtained window. He compared the architecture of Hōvar with Elmar, confirming in his mind how much more pleasing Hōvar was than Terjurmeh's capital. Here there were cobblestoned walkways, meditation gardens with decorative fountains, religious monuments of saints made of bronze, bathhouses for the clean-minded, and limestone buildings whitewashed and painted in bright colors along geometric patterns that followed their eaves. There were also museums, libraries, and plenty of markets where merchants sold fish, meat, cheeses, vegetables, and an assortment of pottery, cookware, and clothing.

"It's so much more beautiful here than home," Petrah said, drinking in everything with his eyes and breathing in the pleasing aromas from the cafes. "It even smells better."

"It *is* better," Kruush said. "Don't let Ahleen know I said that. She'd make us move here."

Petrah smiled at that. "I'd love to visit the University of Akan. They have an apprenticeship program for magi. My classmates and I spoke of it among ourselves, but we never discussed it in front of the masters. Perhaps you could take me to see it. I heard there's an arbor on the campus grounds where the magi meditate and listen to the wind to learn its secrets."

Kruush shook his big head. "Not a good idea, laddie. If the saying, 'takes one to know one' holds true, you'd be found out before you stepped ten feet onto the campus. Unless I'm mistaken about your craft and how 'sensitive' magi are to one another."

"No, you're right," Petrah said glumly. "Magi can pick up on each other's auras. I wouldn't want to bring any unnecessary attention to us."

Kruush's eyes softened. "It's not that I don't want to take you. Maybe we can see it from afar."

Petrah didn't want to see the university from afar. It was like being told you could see the most splendid work of art in the world, but you had to stand at a great distance, squint, and envision the details. "I suppose."

Kruush pinched his brow. "Come now, don't get all downtrodden. It's not like you want to attend the university, right?"

"What if I did?" Petrah and Ajoon would joke about it sometimes when they were alone at the library. The magi of Meerjurmeh wore white robes, as opposed to the Ter-jurah, who wore black. The idea of advocating an education in the arcane arts in an enemy country was not only taboo but could very well earn a mage apprentice—or journeyman—expulsion. But it was fun to pretend, even if it had to be done as whispers that ended up as laughs.

"Let's say you did," Kruush said. "What happens? You knock on the door at the university, announce you want to attend, and they put their arms around your shoulder and say, 'Gods, where have you been? We've been saving a place for you all year. Come in!'"

Petrah didn't like how Kruush poked fun at his expense. "You know they wouldn't do that."

"No, they wouldn't. Even if you renounced your affiliation with the school at Maseah, the Green Flame, and with Terjurmeh, they'd arrest you on the spot."

Petrah's foul mood deepened. "What you're saying then is that I should let all this silliness go. I guess I should. I'm here to perform a job, not be a tourist. Thank you for setting me straight."

Kruush's forehead crinkled like a piece of parchment squeezed into submission. "Don't get all high-and-mighty on me, boy. I'm just pointing out the reality of getting too close to people who would gladly do what the Draadi did to us. These Con-jurah—they're different from us, but not that different. They pray to one god, we pray to another. They protect their interests just as we do. And if you need a lesson on how stubborn a Meerjurmehan can get, just look at those old men over there."

Petrah saw elderly men sitting at the cafes, smoking from water pipes tipped in brass while drinking their cha. They faced each other in pairs along an entire set of tables with board games between the players. "They look harmless enough."

"Ah, but you're not really looking, are you? These crusty bastards smoke djap and play khet all day long. You'd think they were waging war by how they furrow their brows and curse at each other. You should hear them. I find it amusing, but I also find it telling. Sit across from one of them, and we'll see if you have all your limbs at the end of the day."

"They're playing games," Petrah said. "That's hardly threatening."

"Then you've never played khet."

"I've never even heard of it."

"It's a simple game to play, but it requires strategy . . . and ruthlessness. You can sit with one of these veterans, and they'll intimidate you into giving up your coin—and pride too."

Petrah forgot about his disagreement over the university, enraptured instead by this game he knew nothing about. "How does khet work?"

"Let me tell you." Kruush's eyes lit up like a pair of enchanted lamps. "There are always two players. The goal is to capture the pieces of your opponent, but you use your wits, your cunning, and lots of feints and misdirection. Think of it as a test of will, patience, skill, and subterfuge. You bluff when you're weak and appear despondent when you're strong. Your aim is to trick your opponent into losing the war. Using force isn't necessarily the best strategy, just like in any conflict. Often, politics wins the day. In the end, you declare victory by toppling your adversary's dynasty. Do that, and the cursing begins."

"Sounds Korinian, dynasties and all."

"It is. The Korinians invented it. They love their khet, but not as fiercely as the Con-jurah, especially the old men—although it's gaining favor with the young crows. They even have international tournaments these days, where professional players travel abroad to put their national pride on the line."

"People make money playing this?"

"Aye. Can you believe it? Mokan-lee's eldest boy, Milio, is both wily and tenacious. He's beaten me all three times I've played him. You'd think I'd spilled my entrails onto the desert sand after he eviscerated me."

Petrah tried to picture Kruush as a gamesman but failed to conjure an image without wanting to roll to the side and laugh. "Did you curse?"

"Did I curse?" Kruush looked at Petrah as if he'd asked the most pre-posterous question in the world. "Do sailors curse? Do drunken bastards curse? Of course I cursed! And Milio loved every moment."

That Petrah could picture. "I bet Milio got great satisfaction from his victories."

"Let's just say he'll make a fine old man someday." Kruush smiled slyly. "You should ask him to teach you to play. Who knows, maybe you'll have better luck than me."

And maybe he'll like me enough to not be so protective of his sister.

At least Mikano had been kind to him at dinner.

Petrah craned his neck to see the old men in action, now that he understood what khet was, but the coach had already moved on.

Women bustled about or occupied stalls selling their wares—all wearing variations of the gebbettes the Goa tribeswomen had worn in Petrah's caravan. Petrah noted the Meerjurmehan variant had brightly colored, threaded patterns over the backs of their shoulders, depicting songbirds, crests, or Jurmehan script.

"There seem to be a lot of businesswomen here in Hōvar," Petrah said.

"Yes, they're freer here than back home. Here, they're entitled to much the same rights as a man. You'll even find women in positions of government." Kruush looked thoughtful. "Maybe it's better that way."

Petrah could easily picture Ahleen running a kiosk that sold Terjurmehan goods like jewelry and headscarves. Or Ajoon taking a position with the senate, working under the tutelage of a senator like Pallinne.

The coach went around a donkey cart that had stopped in the middle of the avenue.

"I've heard the Prallites have powerful women too, especially their queen," Petrah said, recalling the rumors of the headstrong Northerners and how they embraced strength among both sexes. "It's all hush-hush, of course."

Kruush grinned. "They say Queen Elissa rules, and King Rengle is the one who bends the knee. I'd pay a few silvers to see that. Speaking of which, here." He handed Petrah a small leather purse. "You're going to need this over the next few days. Open it."

Petrah undid the thin cord wrapped around the brass button securing the flap and peered inside. It was filled with Meerjurmehan currency. He removed several disc-shaped coins of various sizes, each with a square notch in the center. Kruush explained the denominations: the smaller ones were copper desh and bronze urat, and the larger ones were silver loon. No gold tak though. The coins were embossed with different flowers, a theme that seemed to pervade Meerjurmehan culture as a reflection of its natural beauty. Petrah liked the silver the best because of the j'boun flower stamped on the front.

"Keep your money hidden," Kruush said. "Cities attract thieves."

Petrah secured the purse inside his robe. "I'll keep it safe."

The flagstone-paved avenue widened and got busier with coaches and city folk on foot. Awning-covered shops pressed together, and people milled about. Pungent cheese mixed with sweet spices and salted fish.

Kruush glanced out the window. "We just entered the Copper District. We're almost there."

Ahead, the avenue wound around a busy main square. Across the square, where the avenue looped, were limestone government buildings capped with copper roofs muddled with a patina of green along the fringes. The square teemed with people. Shoppers engaged with vendors selling goods at stalls around a central water fountain. A military presence at the far end had several buildings cordoned off from foot traffic. Soldiers with capes and plumed helms lined the steps of an elongated building with a marble colonnade that stretched at least thrice its height.

"That's the Ponia Tapa, the senate building," Kruush said. He pointed at a monolithic building near it, tall with nary any features. "The Vellum, the capitol where the Lesser Light and his cabinet sit."

A curved building next. "The Holy Court of the Ascended, where justice is served."

As the carriage grew closer, more buildings became visible. The most colorful one had stained glass windows and a sandstone exterior with bright buntings of red, yellow, green, and purple hanging over protruding panels of stone. "The arts center."

The last building sat atop a rise of sweeping steps. It had a fancy portico lined with statues holding up the pediment spanning across the entrance. Soldiers were stationed at the top and bottom of the stairs. "And, finally, the assembly building, where the delegations will meet."

The first meeting was scheduled to begin at midday. The sun was peeking above the tops of the easterly buildings, setting their rooftops ablaze in hues of rose.

Soldiers had the road blocked where the avenue looped around the square, preventing coaches and pedestrians from gaining access to the government buildings. Kruush and Petrah disembarked, and Kruush told their driver to take the coach the next avenue over, where he would meet him in an hour.

They entered the bustling square. Citizens dressed in a colorful assortment of robes, tunics, and togas—missionaries wore all white. Women had their hair twisted up into knots threaded with ribbons or braided into plaits over their shoulders. Most men had their hair trimmed short and were clean-shaven.

Kruush led Petrah to the burbling stone fountain. Pigeons congregated around it, cooing and pecking at the ground. Bordering the side and angled toward the assembly building were several eateries clustered together. They all had canvas awnings flecked with bird droppings. A few had tables outside, where a handful of diners gathered for their morning meal.

Petrah searched for the indoor café he and Kruush decided would give Petrah a superb view of the assembly building. "Which one is Jakk's?"

Kruush pointed at the far end, where a cat lazed in the center of a drooping brown awning. "It's good, eh? A nice, clear view for anyone sitting by a window. Tan and I ate there the last time we were here. The owner's a bit nosey, but don't mind him."

Petrah didn't like the sound of that, but Kruush said, "He just likes to make conversation. Jakk's all right. He doesn't mind our kind, which is good for us." It was good for Petrah too. "So, lad, what do you think of the place? Will it work?"

Petrah noted the close proximity to the assembly building and the open windows cut into the exterior wall. "It's perfect."

"Shall we head over?"

"Not yet. I want to wait for both delegations to arrive so I can see who is taking part in the talks. It's better if we're outside. But—" Petrah surveyed the square. He estimated their distance from the assembly building at around two hundred yards. "I need to get closer to pick up on their voices. I don't want to be obvious about what I'm doing."

Kruush placed a hand on Petrah's shoulder. "We'll pretend to shop, then."

They stopped by a covered stall. Its opening faced the line of government buildings. A short, older woman with thinning hair sold scrolls made of reed with decorative floral designs. She smiled at Kruush and Petrah. "Whatever you want, I can paint: poppy, lily, j'boun, iris, tulip—any flower, any design. A lovely gift for someone special." She pointed at the easel in the corner where she had a scroll stretched out with a half-painted rose in whimsical shades of maroon and scarlet. "Take your time." She left the men alone to browse.

Kruush pretended to be interested in a lively water lily arrangement mounted to the pole holding up one end of the tented stall. Petrah stood next to him to get a better look at the assembly building. The portico at the top served as the single point of entry. The entablature carried the motto, "Truth in law, truth in life," chiseled in Old Jurmehan. A soldier with a bright red crest atop his helm greeted a pair of men dressed in senatorial garb: wool tunics of off-white cinched about the waist with leather belts with red-and-gold striped sashes crosswise over their backs, fastened by brass buttons at the hip and breast.

More soldiers arrived, many serving as escorts to senators and their staff coming from the Ponia Tapa. Petrah recited Copper Still, dropped his mind into a meditative state, and tuned into the senators' voices using the listening technique Master Maglo had practiced with him. He committed the unique inflections of their voices to memory, picking up the tonal qualities that separated one from the other—specifically, the vibrations they produced with their speech. Master Maglo had referred to them as *signatures*, each unique to a person, no two alike.

A tug on the sleeve broke his concentration. It was the woman with the thinning hair. "You see anything you like? Something for your pretty lady, perhaps? Or your mother? I have many paintings to choose from, all with flowers painted from the heart." She rested a hand over her chest and smiled up at Petrah. Behind her, Kruush signaled for them to leave.

Petrah smiled warmly. "Not today, I'm afraid. But they're all beautiful." He followed Kruush to where spectators had gathered to watch the politicians wend their way up the broad steps of the assembly building.

A detachment of soldiers formed a perimeter along the edge of the square to keep the public from crossing the avenue. Unlike the senatorial escorts, these soldiers didn't have capes or plumes on their helms, but they were armed with short swords set in sheaths strapped to their belts.

"Look yonder," Petrah said. "The Ter-jurahn delegation has arrived."

The ambassador traveled on a palanquin while members of the Fist, Silver Blade, Black Arrow, and Copper Shield walked behind him. A contingent of six Terjurmehan soldiers provided protection. They wore burnished cuirasses and had arraks hanging by their sides. Armed Con-jurahn horsemen flanked them. Several Meerjurmehan politicians and a detail of caped guards met the group and exchanged pleasantries.

Petrah reentered a trance and focused on the sounds of their voices, projecting tethers of thought to latch on to one person before switching to the next. He memorized the signatures of the ambassador and one delegate from each Terjurmehan party. He hoped the Ter-jurahn priest would talk, but the man said nothing. If he didn't speak, Petrah couldn't get his signature. The Meerjurmehan guards were wary of the priest, perhaps because his scarlet robe was so different from everyone else's garb—or maybe it was the way he looked at them, as if peeling away their armor with his probing stare. Whispers and murmurs broke out among the spectators near Petrah. They pointed at the Ter-jurah as they spoke.

When the delegates and their entourages finally walked up the assembly steps, Petrah told Kruush he was ready to head inside Jakk's. The cat was still perched on the awning, asleep.

"I suppose now the real work begins," Kruush said. "Meet you at the other end of the square when you're done."

Petrah was about to lock forearms with his friend when he remembered it was a Terjurmehan custom and not something the locals appreciated. Con-jurahn men placed hands on each other's shoulders as a sign of friendly greeting and parting or touched fist to breast under more formal settings, such as with the Meerjurmehan senators. Petrah set his right hand on Kruush's shoulder, and Kruush did the same, giving him a squeeze.

"I'll leave you to it," Kruush said. "Good luck."

PETRAH SETTLED INTO AN acha wood chair at an open window in Jakk's café. Glazed tessellations of muted browns and reds adorned the archway of the window with a matching ceramic mosaic pattern on the tiny table butted up against the exterior wall.

Petrah welcomed the soothing feel of the breeze. The window provided an angled view of much of the assembly building, although the right third of the building was obstructed. Petrah leaned his head through the arched opening for a moment. He could see the entire portico atop the sweep of stairs.

Inside the café, Petrah counted five patrons, all at one table in the back, yammering and laughing. They drank tea and shared a water pipe that puffed clove-scented smoke into the air. A large piece of slate on the wall opposite the entrance had a list of food and drinks written in chalk.

The owner, Jakk, was wide-faced and heavy around the middle. He wore an apron dusted with flour. After checking on the table of five, he walked over to Petrah.

"Greetings, friend. What'll it be today—food, drink, or both?"

"Both." Petrah ordered a toasted cornmeal cake and a pot of black tea.

"An excellent choice, young man. Baked the cake myself this morning. I'll drizzle honey after I toast it, and you'll discover how tasty it is." Jakk studied Petrah's face with intense curiosity, quirking up a smile when he looked at Petrah's eyes. "First time here, I take it."

"First time, yes." Petrah squeezed the edge of the table and braced himself for questions on where he was from and what he was doing here.

Jakk kindly spared him the inquiry. He gave Petrah's shoulder a friendly pat instead and said, "Welcome," and headed to the kitchen.

Petrah let go of the table and eased back in his chair, relieved Jakk hadn't assailed him with questions. He returned his attention to the outside.

The soldiers forming a perimeter along the avenue by the assembly building split into two groups. One group remained to provide security while the second dispersed, heading in the Vellum's direction.

Petrah stilled his mind and calibrated the distance to the building—about two hundred fifty feet—and started feeling along the stone exterior with probing tendrils of thought. He needed to determine how best to penetrate the solid surface and tune into the delegates.

A young man brought Petrah his order, breaking his concentration. Warm wisps of toasted goodness rose from the cornmeal cake. Petrah used the distraction to taste it. The sweetness from the honey worked well with the saltiness of the cake. The tea had the same aroma as the cha he'd drunk at Bokania, but Mokan-lee's was far smoother than this brew.

Just as Petrah prepared to put himself into a meditative state, Jakk returned. *Gods, how am I supposed to get any work done?*

The big man peeked out the window, pressing his swooping gut against the sill. "Looks interesting, doesn't it? Lots of security today." He drew back, wiped his big paws of hands on his apron, and shook his head. "Politicians." To Petrah's surprise—and disappointment—he pulled out a chair and sat across from Petrah. "So, young man, what do you think of the cake? It's good with the honey, isn't it?"

"It's delicious." Petrah tried to be polite, but he also wanted the owner to leave him alone so he could resume his task. If Jakk dallied, Petrah could miss vital information being exchanged among the delegations. *Why didn't I listen to Master Joriah and pick somewhere quieter?*

Jakk went on as if Petrah had invited him to sit and chat. "It's a Con-jurahn specialty. This one is my grandmother's recipe. I was a wee lad when she taught me how to make it. 'Jakk,' she'd say, 'you have to stop eating the batter. You're going to get fat if you keep doing that.'" He patted his generous belly and chuckled. "She was right. I promised my grandmother I'd make her recipe when I opened my café. Sadly, she never got to see that day. But her recipes live on, here."

He presented the room with wide arms, then rested his forearms on the table and studied Petrah's eyes again. "We don't get many visitors from the North. Except for missionaries who want to visit the Mother Church. My brother traveled up Errant's Pass a few years back, decided it was too cold in the mountains, and came back." He lowered his voice and whispered, "I think he was afraid of the snow."

Then, in a louder voice, he said, "This must be hot weather for you. Although, looking at your face, you have quite the tan. Perhaps you grew up here." He shook his head. "No, you have an accent. Or am I wrong?"

Petrah had hoped to dodge questions of the sort, but Jakk wasn't going anywhere until Petrah answered him. *I could lie and say I'm from the North. Or . . .* "Actually, I'm visiting from Elmar."

Jakk laughed, a booming belly laugh that made his jowls jiggle. He waved a finger at Petrah. "Hah, you got me there. Ter-jurahn, eh?" He pushed away from the table, shaking the plate and teacup. "If you want to know anything about our beautiful city, let me know. In the meantime, enjoy the cake and the view." With that, he went to the front to greet another customer.

Petrah exhaled a relieved breath. He finished half his cake, washed it down with tea, and went back to work.

The day progressed at a miserable pace. Listening to conversations through stone was hard enough. From this distance, it was nigh impossible. Didn't Master Maglo's attenuation calculations factor in listening through solid materials? Petrah couldn't recall if stone diminished the effective range of his listening technique. But how could he get closer to the building with security being so tight?

While looking out the window in a trance state, Petrah tried different variations of the listening technique that had worked so well outside. *What am I doing wrong?* He was beginning to panic when he stumbled upon a string of words. He noticed he was running his finger over the rim of his teacup to calm his nerves. He lifted his finger, and the voice went away. When he began circling the rim again, it returned.

Well, I'll be!

Why the cup worked was beyond his ken, but he kept moving his finger in a slow circle. Petrah tuned in to the voice of the Terjurmehan ambassador, who was making what sounded like a prepared speech about existing trade sanctions. Petrah concentrated on the unique vibration of his voice. At one point, Petrah stopped moving his finger. He continued to hear the ambassador. The same when he lifted his finger: he sustained the connection. It was like picking up the resonation from a gong.

So that's the trick.

Master Ecclesias had used a hollowed bell during his exercises, where he'd created different notes with the edge of a baton. The students would harmonize their minds with the frequency, often chanting to emulate the sound. Acoustics, Petrah learned, was a key component of channeling. It was the foundation for words of power.

The ambassador's voice wasn't the only one Petrah heard. As he slowed his heart rate and deepened his meditative state, he heard other voices too, including the two senators from last night's dinner.

Jakk interrupted twice, once to get Petrah more tea and a second time to take a break while business was at a lull. A man and a woman enjoying a sweet treat replaced the table of five.

Jakk placed a friendly hand on Petrah's shoulder, weighing it down. "Can I get you anything else, young man?"

Petrah had been in the café for three hours. He couldn't expect Jakk to let him stay here indefinitely, even with a half pot of tea, now tepid. "No, thank you. I can leave if you like."

"Nonsense. Do you see any customers waiting in line?" Jakk appraised Petrah with his inquisitive eyes. "You look like a thinking man. Thinking men need a place to think. Stay, my friend. Leave when you want."

The assembly wrapped up for the day an hour later. Petrah was thoroughly fatigued. The two delegations had agreed to the standing trade arrangements and the promise of no further military action by either side. Concessions for giving up trade with the Northern Kingdom would be discussed in a subsequent meeting. Petrah was impressed by how cordial the Terjurmehan ambassador was. He'd expected the man to come in and assert his authority, like a tyrant, especially after what Tan had said in Bea-tet. The ambassador was anything but a tyrant, and the assemblage departed peacefully.

Petrah paid Jakk two urat for the food and drink plus a desh for letting him stay longer.

Jakk placed the desh back in Petrah's hand. "Keep your coin, young man. Save it for the next time you visit."

Petrah smiled. He appreciated the man's kindness. "Perhaps tomorrow."

Jakk laughed and clapped him on the back. "Tomorrow it is."

PETRAH RETURNED TO THE secluded garden at Montabijon that evening and reported his findings to Master Joriah. As requested, he presented facts, not opinions.

That's an interesting development, Master Joriah said. *Any mention of our party?*

None.

Continue your work. Keep me informed. Oh, and Petrah?

Yes, Master?

Nicely done today.

Petrah was beaming after they disconnected. It surprised him to see Mina standing in front of him when he opened his eyes.

"What were you doing?" she asked. "And why were you smiling like that?"

"Like what?"

"Like this." She mimicked his exaggerated smile, making it look ridiculous.

"If you must know, I was meditating."

"Oh." Mina sat down on the bench, this time right next to Petrah. Her flowery perfume was heady. "What do you meditate about?"

"Not much."

"Not much?"

Petrah sighed. "It helps me relax. The whole point is to block out the distractions around you and focus on your thoughts. From there, I explore ideas and determine what's going on around me, all without opening my eyes. I can even sense the heartbeats of animals and distinguish one kind from another. I'm getting pretty good at it, too."

Mina frowned. "You can communicate with animals?"

Petrah hadn't meant to tell her about his arcane abilities. *If she speaks to her father . . .*

He quickly backpedaled. "It's nothing, really."

Mina didn't probe any further. Petrah thought he was in the clear when she switched to another sensitive subject. "Where did you go today? You weren't with your master."

He looked at her strangely. "My master?"

"You know, Kruush. That's his name, right?"

"Oh, him. He wanted me to go into the city today."

"For . . . ?"

"For business," he said curtly. "*Our* business."

"You don't have to be so rude. I was just asking." She got up and stomped off.

Petrah sat dumbly. *Don't let her go, you dolt. Apologize!* He noticed Mina had forgotten her lantern. He snatched it up and ran after her. "Hey!"

She turned to him. "What?" Even angry, she appeared radiant, with brown eyes shaped as if an angel had come down to sculpt them.

"You forgot this." He held up her lantern.

"Oh." She took it from him and turned back to the path.

In a rash move that surprised even himself, Petrah caught the sleeve of her robe and tugged. She looked down at his hand in surprise. He withdrew it. "I'm sorry, I shouldn't have done that."

"Why did you?"

"I was hoping you could, you know, stay a little longer." It was as ridiculous as it sounded.

"I have to go." Her words came out soft, disinclined. "We can talk tomorrow. Maybe you can tell me more about your country."

"I'd like that. See you tomorrow then?"

She smiled and headed up the path.

Petrah watched her delicate footsteps as she walked toward the manor. She glanced his way once more and then disappeared inside the house.

WHEN PETRAH ARRIVED AT Jakk's the next morning, the owner greeted him with a wide grin. "The thinking man returns!
Come, come, sit wherever you like."

Petrah occupied the same seat by the open window. There were eight
patrons today, most engaged in lively conversation. Jakk's apron was
smeared with grease mixed with flour and scented with cinnamon.

"I'll bring you something I know you'll like," the big man said without
asking Petrah for his order.

Petrah wasn't hungry. His thoughts were on Mina and only her. He
could still smell the j'boun in her hair. He tried to subdue the twist
in his belly, the unfamiliar squeeze in his chest, and the inability to
think clearly. Each attempt to quiet his mind brought up an image of
Mina—tucking a lock of hair behind her ear, looking up at him, standing
close enough to feel her heartbeats through his skin.

Jakk returned with a puff pastry slathered in a glazed cream scented
sweet and peppery.

"You smell nutmeg," Jakk said, noting Petrah's sniffing. "Imported
from Sushtâh, just up the river. Have you visited there?"

Kruush and Ahleen had married in Sushtâh. The port city sat on the
Estuary River, north of Hōvar. "Not yet."

"It's quaint but busy, and filled with ancient history. Parpet is my
favorite—ruins centuries old. Some say they were built by the Korinians.
Others say the Con-jurah copied the Korinians. You should go sometime
and decide for yourself. It's an excellent place for a thinking man to
ponder the past." Jakk pointed at Petrah's plate. "I want your opinion
on my pastry. Be honest."

Petrah would have rather waited for his stomach—now in knots—to
settle. He pulled apart the flaky pastry and put a small piece in his mouth.

He wanted to enjoy the blend of caramel and sweet cream flavors but couldn't. "It's good."

Jakk cocked an eyebrow. "Good? Or passable? Come now, I asked for your honest opinion."

"No, really, it's good." Petrah forced the corners of his lips to lift.

Jakk gave him a questioning look, then tapped the table with his knuckles. "I'll check back later."

Petrah sipped his tea, wiped the flaky bits of pastry from his fingertips, and drew in a deep breath. He let it out slowly to make another attempt to clear his mind and put himself into a trance. He concentrated halfheartedly on the ambassador's presentation to the senate. When the back-and-forths between delegates turned bland, Petrah would slip out of his trance and think about Mina again—the delicate sway of her brown hair when she spoke; the way she bit one side of her lip when she listened; the subtle lift or dip of her shoulders when she reacted to something he said.

Petrah didn't notice Jakk was seated in front of him until the man cleared his throat and furrowed his bushy brow. "I've seen that look before. Yes, with my own son."

Petrah blinked. "What look?"

"Like this." The owner transformed his expression into one that was deadpan, almost miserable. "See? Even now, you're thinking of her, yes?"

"Her?" When Jakk rested his ox arms on the table and leaned forward, Petrah said, "Yes. But—" He couldn't figure out what to say next.

"How did I know?" Jakk pointed at Petrah's untouched food and grunted. "You stare out that window and then at the wall behind me. At first, I said to myself, 'Jakk, this young man is strange. He sits and sits and stares.' Then, I said, 'No, Jakk, he's not strange; he's a thinking man, imagining great things. You've seen this before with the university students who study philosophy and sit by the fountain for hours and then wander in for a bite before going back to their imagining.' But that look on your face—the same one I've seen on my son—it's apparent what the problem is. You're lost, my friend. Lost in love."

"But I—" Petrah forgot what he was going to say, as if someone had snatched the words from his mind. "Love?"

"Yes, my friend, you have the affliction. You might not know it, but *I* know it." Jakk patted Petrah on the hand and offered a charitable smile. "Stay for as long as you want."

Jakk went to the kitchen. Petrah stared after him, barely aware of what had happened. Then, with his stomach still in knots, he forced himself to get back to work.

"So," Ahleen said to Petrah, outside on Bokania's terrace before supper. There was a faint but inviting trail of spiced stew coming from within the manor. "I've seen little of you lately. How are you feeling?"

Petrah had tried to keep to himself, as Master Joriah requested. He was glad Ahleen had searched him out. He missed having her company.

"Healthier," he said. "No more coughing. My ankle's healing fine, thanks to you and Summi. You're my favorite nurse, you know."

Ahleen smiled and inclined her head. "At your service. Now try not to injure yourself again. How goes your work?"

"It's as interesting as a grain of sand. I've never cared for politics. Too many machinations. I'll be glad when it's over." *And glad to leave here.*

Ahleen picked up on his change of mood. "What's the matter?"

Petrah walked over to the balcony. He was thinking about Mina again and didn't want Ahleen to see the conflict in his eyes. Ajoon had taken a seat in the back of his mind, and he didn't like that. Why did Mina have such an effect on him? He didn't understand.

Ahleen came over to him, forcing him to make eye contact. "Petrah, you're avoiding the question. Please tell me what's going on. I only want to listen."

He tapped the tip of his sandal against one of the railing's balusters. "I'm—" he started. *Confused? Cursed? Mad? Irredeemable?* "It's nothing. I'll get over it."

"You can talk to me. It's just us, Petrah. Whatever you tell me stays with me."

"I know, but . . ." He grabbed the balustrade with both hands and squeezed. "I don't know how to say it."

"Would it have anything to do with a certain someone's daughter I've seen sneaking around late at night?"

Is it that obvious? Gods, save me from myself.

Petrah chewed his lip. He needed to talk to someone before he went crazy, and Ahleen was that someone.

"I can't stop thinking about her," he confessed. "I don't know why. I just can't! Back home, I had feelings for Ajoon. But this is different. I can't explain it. It . . . it hurts. Like physically hurts me right here." He patted his chest. "My heart's a mess. My head must be broken."

Ahleen reached over and took his hand. "Your head's not broken. You're in love."

Jakk had said the same thing. Why would Ahleen say it too? "But I just met her. I shouldn't feel like this now, should I? That kind of thing takes time, doesn't it?"

"That's what makes love so amazing," Ahleen said. "Kruush won't admit it, but he went through something similar when we met. He acted all brave in front of you and Tan, but he was just as thunderstruck in the heart."

"Then what about Ajoon? I feel something for her. She's funny, she's pretty—maybe not as pretty as Mina, but still. Why don't I feel as strongly about her? Why do I favor Mina? I barely know her."

"Love doesn't choose the person," Ahleen said, speaking as kindly and sisterly as she'd ever had. "Nor does it make sense. I can't say why you prefer Mina over Ajoon. Maybe Ajoon introduced you to love, but perhaps you couldn't unravel it. Or you hid your emotions from yourself. Perhaps when you met Mina, those emotions came to the surface, but stronger. It's hard to say. But I'll say this: your heart decides what it wants, not your mind. It rules over us, and there's nothing we can do to stop it."

"But Mina lives here, and I'm—" Petrah stammered, flustered. "I'm—"

"I know. She's the daughter of an aristocrat, which puts her in a distinct class, and you're a commoner from an enemy country, and so on. Love isn't fair, Petrah. Did you tell Mina how you feel?"

"I can't do *that*," he said. "I'm a nobody, a foreigner. You should have seen the way Milio looked at me at dinner the first night we were here. It was as if he wanted to cut off my head to protect his sister."

"He'd never do that. Milio's a big baby."

Petrah tilted his head back, afraid the wetness in his eyes would show. "I have to leave, Ahleen. I can't stay here any longer. I need to get out of this house before I lose my mind. Before *she* makes me lose my mind. I lie awake at night, wondering, what if? What if I were Con-jurahn? What if I came from a prominent family? What if I didn't have to go back to Terjurmeh? I need to get away from this place!"

Ahleen was tender with her response. "Do you want me to talk to Kruush? Maybe we can arrange for you to stay in one of the guest houses."

"What good would that do? I'd still see *her*."

"What about an inn? Or perhaps we should leave Hōvar. We can leave if you like."

"No, I can't do that to you and Kruush," Petrah said, squeezing one hand with the other. "Besides, my master wants me to finish my work. The council announced a recess for the rest of the week. They won't start again for another seven days." He took a deep breath. "Forget it. I'll be all right."

Ahleen nodded sympathetically. "Of course you will."

A pair of birds chirped among the trees beyond the terrace, singing to each other. Their tiny heartbeats danced in rhythm with each other. Is that what love was—two spirits as one, inseparable because of the bond between them?

"Supper is probably ready," Ahleen said, gathering her robe about her. "We should head in."

Petrah couldn't eat, not now. "I think I'll stay out here a little longer."

She left him on the terrace, alone to listen to the trill of songbirds as his chest tightened like a cage about his soul.

Chapter 8
Parting

WITH TALKS BETWEEN THE delegations suspended for a week, Petrah had nothing to do. Kruush wasn't happy about the delay. "We're going to outlast our welcome as guests. Mokan-lee is generous, but not *that* generous."

"What can *I* do about it?" Petrah said, helpless and hopeless in the same breath. "If you prefer, we can find lodging in the city. I'll contact Master Joriah to make sure he reimburses you for the inconvenience."

Kruush puffed out a cheek as if giving it some thought. "Let's hang onto that as an option. In the meantime, keep your nose clean."

Petrah honored Kruush's request and isolated himself, which meant avoiding Mina.

To pass the time, Petrah requested a visit to the small library at Bokania. The library, on the second floor, was a tiny, barrel-shaped room with a slit of a window unnecessarily covered by heavy velvet drapes, which Petrah tied back to let in the daylight. A wood bookcase followed the graceful curve of the room. Nestled between the bookcase and the window sat a worn, leather armchair with rolled arms and brass nails—a kingly throne for the learned reader.

Petrah browsed Mokan-lee's prized literary collection, which comprised books on history, architecture, politics, and rare biographies of famous Con-jurah.

But there was one book, a tiny, ancient, slender thing, that brought a smile to Petrah's face. The title read *Erun-lee's Diction for the Educated*

Mind. Could this have been written by one of Mokan-lee's forebears? It was different from the book Petrah had lost to the vaellra, *Orumen's Phrases*, but a welcome replacement. It contained a collection of scholarly words and examples of their use. Serious words like *promulgation*, *rectitude*, and *inviolability*. Lyrical ones like *puissant*, *saturnine*, and *gloaming*.

Petrah had worked tirelessly on his vocabulary at Maseah, but his thirst was unquenchable, his desire to portray himself beyond his years when speaking to his elders insatiable. He could speak the vernacular with friends, but with politicians, advisers, scribes, educators, and heads of state, he needed to transcend from Petrah the mage apprentice to Petrah the erudite. They might see a sixteen-year-old, but if they closed their eyes, they would hear a man twice or thrice that age. A man they would respect. At least that's what Petrah hoped.

Petrah devoured Erun-lee's book. He read it cover to cover, committed words to memory, and imagined fanciful but meaningful phrases he could use for his future—and for his poetry.

The next evening, Petrah chose a new garden to meditate in. This one had an old marble statue of a naked woman holding a pitcher that poured water into a pond. Petrah tried to shut out his worldly thoughts but had a difficult time doing so. First, it was Mina, then the conversation he'd had with Ahleen, then Ajoon. Petrah wished Master Joriah had sent Ajoon to accompany him.

If she'd been with me, none of this would be happening.

His sulking led him to darker pastures.

The Watcher and his rigid assertions, the brother he'd never met. His mother, whose sadness was perpetual. Choices and free will and fate. His fellow students and their time at school without him or Miko. Master Maglo and his cheerful disposition. Master Nole, the pragmatic instructor. Master Ecclesias and his endless exercises. Even Baaka, the Seer of Elmar, who had revealed Petrah's dark lineage.

I don't belong here. I belong in Elmar.

Petrah wanted to return to his training, to dedicate his waking hours to learning his craft, not thinking about the woes of love and the doom of dreams. Going back to Elmar was the only sensible choice.

Petrah was getting ready to turn in for the night when Mina appeared. He'd not heard her footfall over the pour of water.

She keeps finding me!

The moon shone above, giving her complexion a white sheen. The paleness was striking, like fine porcelain.

"I was wondering where you were," she said, as if they were playing a game of hide-and-go-seek. "I thought we could take a walk."

Part of him wanted to dismiss her and send her off, the other part was glad she came looking for him. "A walk sounds good."

Mina spoke colorfully of her life as they strolled. Petrah was content to listen to her talk, eager to learn all about her.

"It's good to get away from the manor," she said. "Don't get me wrong. My handmaid, Julette, is wonderful, but my mother is a little . . . much at times. Let's just say she prefers me to do needlework than unladylike things, like steal away to swim in the river or do something as crass as wrestle Mikano to the ground when he teases me."

"You wrestle with Mikano?"

"And win. I know his weak spots." She flashed a smirk. They walked along a path carved through fig trees. The leaves gave off a pleasant, grassy scent. Spots of moonlight dappled the winding trail. "My mother doesn't mind when I sit like a lady and read. She considers that *proper.* Do you know what she tells me?" Mina made herself sound older. "'A woman versed in the written word is one who avails herself to a higher station.'" Mina covered her mouth and giggled.

After reading Erun-lee's book, Petrah appreciated the idea of versing oneself in the written word to elevate their station.

Mina continued. "Mama doesn't really talk like that. Well, not unless she tries to teach me the proprieties of being a 'lady of the aristocracy.' As in reserved, demure, and deferential before one's husband. Ugh."

Petrah liked how expressive Mina was as she spoke; how she widened or narrowed her eyes, twisted or curled her lip, and lightened or deepened her voice. "What about your father?"

"Papa wants me to pursue a traditional role." Mina brushed a fig leaf with her fingertips as she passed. "He thinks he knows what's best for me. He'd rather I become a sow and suckle pigs until my hair turns gray. Can you imagine that, me a sow with a litter of piglets?" She giggled, which got Petrah laughing. "My father would have me wed by my eighteenth birthday, married to a senator's son if he had his way. Anything to advance our status in society."

Petrah enjoyed Mina's feistiness. She was a lot more energetic than Ajoon and outspoken too. "If you had your way, what would you do with your life?"

"Learn my father's business."

"Really!"

"Is that so hard to imagine? A woman getting involved in the affairs of men?"

"No, of course not. I was just surprised, that's all." Fig trees gave way to olive trees with gnarled trunks. Petrah picked up a light, woody scent.

"My father's grooming Milio to take over the business one day. He doesn't see my worth or value my interest. I want to work my way through the ranks of the Commerce Guild, and perhaps get involved with the senate. My father doesn't know it, but I pay attention to what the senators have to say when they visit. And, *if* I get married, my husband would have to be supportive, of course. He'd have to be open to the idea that a woman can rule a household and still be a productive member of society."

Petrah paused as they passed through a band of moonlight streaming between branches. Mina's eyes sparkled in the white light. "I've not spent much time here, but I've noticed Meerjurmeh is a better place for women. I've seen what Ahleen had to put up with back in Terjurmeh. It's wretched. But she's made something of herself. I'm proud of her."

"Ahleen is smart. She's kind and just as capable as the men. I like her."

They cleared the groves and came upon a vineyard with rows of grapevines as far as they could see. The soil was damper here, earthier. The moon bathed them in white as they started picking their way between the vines. "What about yourself?" Mina asked. "What are you looking for in your future?"

Petrah wished he could tell her about his aspirations for magehood. "Like you, I want to make something of myself. I'd like to settle down and find a place to call my own. And, *if* I marry, I'd want my wife to be happy and do whatever she wishes."

"Are you saying that to appease me? I won't be offended if you prefer a wife who bends the knee like a Prallite serf before her lord."

"Of course not! I meant what I said."

Mina giggled. "I was just teasing. You're sensitive. That's not a bad trait, mind you. You're a thinker too. And a meditator, which I find utterly intriguing."

"You do?"

"If you haven't noticed by now, I prefer the unconventional over the ordinary. If you told me you penned lyrics in your mind while you meditated and that you were aspiring to be a minstrel, I'd find that a lot more interesting than if you were daydreaming of swashbuckling as a hired hand. Are you secretly aspiring to become a minstrel, Petrah?"

"Hardly. I've handled a sword before, but I'd need ale to sing and plenty of it. If you must know, I've tried my hand at poetry, so you're not too far off the mark."

"And here I thought you were just another salt merchant apprentice. How silly of me." She plucked a vine leaf and pinched it between her fingers. She gave it a sniff and then let it twirl to the ground. "I like poetry too."

Petrah's heart swooned. "You do?"

"I love how lyrical it is. I love how it flows, especially when I read the verses aloud. I sometimes have Julette sit on my chair as I pace my room and read to her with a book of poems in hand. Or when she dresses me in the morning and I have a book propped up on my garment table. I've indoctrinated her into my madness." Her eyes flared with mischief.

Petrah had to ask, "Do you write poetry?"

"Write? No. I've dabbled. Scribbles here and there. Nothing cohesive or inspiring—just a line or two—and then I've lost the momentum. I might tuck the parchment away for another time. Or take a candle to it."

Petrah gasped. "You burn your poems? Why would you do that?"

"They're not poems as much as they are pieces of things. Someday I might finish one. Until then . . ." She shrugged. "And you? Have you completed any poems?"

"Nothing on par with what you've read, I'm afraid."

"You're too modest. I'd like to hear something you've written. If you don't mind, of course."

He'd written a couple of pieces, one for the taproom and the other a silly rhyme he was too embarrassed to recite. "I've got a better idea: I'll write you something new."

"You'd write something just for me?"

Petrah regretted committing himself to such a daunting task as soon as she asked the question. What could he possibly write that was suitable for an aristocrat's daughter?

"I'll need some time, of course." But he was armed now with a plethora of wonderful words and would "avail" himself, as Mina's mother put it, to applying those words to something beautiful and profound.

Mina smiled in earnest, her shapely eyes creasing delicately at the corners. A smile like hers could inspire many a sonnet or ballad. "Of course," she said.

THE NEXT MORNING, PETRAH was surprised to find a note slipped under his door.

Meet me by the arch at the orange grove – Mina, it read.

Petrah remembered seeing the manicured grove of orange trees but didn't recall any arch. He dressed quickly in his robe and skipped breakfast. No one was expecting him, so he was free to pass his time as he sought fit. Sure that not a soul was watching him, he slipped out of the manor and followed the trail to a secluded garden thick with the scent of honeysuckle. The sun kissed the fields, promising a warm, sticky day.

The arch turned out to be an old, curved trellis on the north side of the orange grove, taken over by climbing vines and delicate, purple blooms dangling like a hundred charms from a necklace. The blossoms gave off a honeyed fragrance.

Mina was waiting for him, but she wore a tunic with leggings and sandals with straps that were secured around her ankles. Her face was just as beautiful as it was in the moonlight. She curtsied. "I see you like my outfit, milord." She spoke with a funny accent when she said it, and he realized she was imitating a Northerner.

"You're dressed for . . . ?" He couldn't figure it out.

"Sport? Why yes, I am. Come, I want to show you something I think you'll like."

She led him behind the grove along a dirt path to the west end of the estate, where avocado trees grew in abundance.

"Where are we going?" His stomach grumbled, but he dismissed his hunger. He could be hungry for days, as long as he got to spend them with Mina.

"You said you could handle a sword."

"I did?"

"Forgetful, are we? You said so when you promised to write me a poem."

He'd forgotten his mention of the sword, fixated instead on the fact he'd have to write a poem that was better than a tavern sing-along. "I remember now."

"How good are you with the sword?"

Petrah looked down at the shadows of branches cast against the ground, trying not to let the memory of his encounter with Miko show on his face. "I can hold my own."

"You're being humble. Or are you pretending to know how to handle one?"

"Trust me," Petrah said, "I've had plenty of practice. I'd like to think I've retired."

Mina frowned but left the topic alone. Then she lightened up and clapped her hands. "We're here!"

"Here" equated to a long, level stretch of bare ground about two hundred feet in length, ending with three large discs of straw mounted to wooden stands, behind which stood a wall of mud bricks. The straw discs had centers painted in red. The aroma of freshly dug earth hung thickly in the morning air.

"What is this place?"

"It's a butt."

"A butt?"

She placed a hand over her mouth to keep from laughing. "An archery range, silly." When he didn't respond, she said, "I take it you've never used a bow."

Tan was good with the bow. He'd proven himself in his bet with Sinti, besting her with his archery skills. Petrah had never held an arrow, much less a bow. "I haven't."

"Then you're in for a real treat."

An older man approached, dressed in a leather hunting jacket, boots, and shin guards. He had white hair braided down his back and a long mustache that was waxed. "Good morning, fair Mina! I see you've brought a friend."

"Silas, this is Petrah, a houseguest of my father's. Petrah, Silas has been in my father's employ from before I was born."

"Pleased to make your acquaintance," Petrah said, unsure whether to place his hand on the man's shoulder in greeting, as Kruush had shown. He left his hands awkwardly by his side, and that seemed to go over well enough with Silas, whose leather perfumed the humid air.

"Silas has agreed to teach me archery in secret," Mina said. "We practice each week, whenever I can break away from Mama, who has made it her life to tether me to tedious lady crafts. If my father found out I was sneaking off to let loose arrows, he'd lock me up for good." She grinned.

Silas twisted the left end of his lengthy mustache into a point. "I doubt that, although I know your father's temper."

"It's you I worry about more. He'd dismiss you. Or worse."

Silas laughed. A long scar ran under his cleanly shaven jaw. "Your father might have a stern talk with me, but he values having a seasoned veteran like me watching over his oplia fields. What do you say, young lady? Shall we get to it?"

"Yes, please. But you should know Petrah's never handled a bow before."

"He hasn't?" Silas smiled boldly. "He won't be saying that on the morrow. Petrah, let's have a look at you. Stand where you are." He circled Petrah, his leather creaking as he appraised his subject. "You're built like a Northerner, tall and of nimble stock. The Prallites brag about having the best archers in the world. They claim it's their height and ability to handle the longbow better than anyone else and that their forests make for challenging terrain to hone their skills in hunting and battle. I don't doubt their ferocity on the battlefield, but I can tell you Con-jurahn archers are just as good, if not superior."

Mina pushed up on her tiptoes. "Tell him about 'splitting the wand.' Or better yet, show him."

Silas placed a friendly hand on Mina's shoulder. Petrah expected a lady of her station to rebuff the gesture, but she acted like it was an everyday thing. "What our aspiring archer speaks of is placing a stake downfield and then seeing who could split the wood with their arrow."

"I've seen him do it too," Mina said with a good dose of pride. "It's quite something. Perhaps I can become proficient well enough to split the wand someday."

"Someday," Silas said. "But not today. Today, we show our guest the basics with the short bow. Petrah, shall we begin?"

Petrah wasn't thrilled about learning how to use another weapon. He'd seen the consequences of wielding a sword. But with Mina clasping her hands in excitement, how could he refuse?

Silas fitted Petrah's left forearm with a leather bracer. "It's to keep the bowstring from whapping you and leaving a bruise," he said. "Now let's get you into a proper square stance. Remove your footwear. You want to go barefoot and feel the earth." He guided Petrah to the shooting line, which was marked by white powder. He pivoted Petrah about the waist, then kicked Petrah's bare feet apart shoulder width and had Petrah place his feet parallel to the line. "Just like that." He handed Petrah a bow and went over the mechanics of using it.

Mina watched with keen interest, already geared up with her own bow and quiver of arrows, which she held with ease, as if holding a dress. "You're doing great," she said.

I've not done anything yet, he would have liked to have replied, but Silas kept him busy, instructing him on how to hold the bow steady. He then gave a set of sequential commands: *ready your bow, nock, mark, draw,* and *loose*. He borrowed Mina's bow and one of her arrows and demonstrated how it was done. With a twang, Silas loosened an arrow that struck the straw target dead center with a neat thwap. "Now you try."

Petrah misjudged the tension of the bowstring and fired his first arrow at the ground. The second fared only slightly better, striking the bough of a neighboring tree. The third seemed to disappear as if eaten by the wind. Mina stifled a laugh.

"It's harder than I thought," Petrah admitted, baffled at his poor performance but also distracted by Mina.

"You're paying attention to the wrong target," Silas said with a wry smile. "The young lady is not your aim of this exercise."

Petrah shuffled his feet in embarrassment.

Silas handed him another arrow. "Let's try again. Might I suggest you pay attention to what's downrange?"

"I will," Petrah said, cheeks flushed.

"Ready your bow. Remember what I taught you."

Petrah managed a steadier hold on his bow. When he loosened the arrow, he nicked the next target over from the one he was supposed to hit.

"Better, but still off," Silas said. "You've wounded your enemy's comrade. Not a terrible mistake in a time of war, but it won't win you any victories. Let's give Mina her turn."

Petrah watched Mina take up her stance with practiced ease. She was a natural. She let loose her first arrow, which struck her target. Each subsequent arrow hit home as well. A couple even struck the red center. Mina smiled proudly after she emptied the quiver of her last arrow.

Silas congratulated her. "You've made a fine mess of your enemy, milady."

"Thank you, Silas." Mina curtsied, and then turned to Petrah. "All in a day's work, milord."

Petrah wished he was a lord, but Mina could have called him a peasant and he would have been good with it. Her spirit was as bright as the sunlight that cupped her face in its golden embrace.

"I'm afraid that's all the time we have today," Silas said. "You may fetch your arrows."

Mina waved at Petrah and started running. "Catch me if you can!"

Petrah chased her down the path. She maintained her lead, flying like the wind. She was a tiny thing but athletic, and from what he'd witnessed today, more than capable. They laughed as they hunted for his arrows, scattered among the brush on either side of the butt.

Once they retrieved the arrows and restocked their quivers, Silas took possession of the weapons.

Mina offered to carry her equipment and accompany Silas to the armory.

"Never mind that," he said. "Off with you. I've got it from here." He snuck Petrah a clever smile. Petrah reciprocated, but only when Mina wasn't looking.

Petrah and Mina took their time walking back to Bokania. Mina led them through the vineyard, along a patch of barren ground between rows of vines. Petrah found his hand drifting toward hers. She eased her pace and took his hand. Petrah's heart thumped as her skin touched his. It was smooth except for the pads on her fingers, which bore the wear from her archery pursuits. He looked down at her face, saw her smile, and interlaced his fingers with hers.

They continued through the vineyard, hand in hand.

ON THE FIFTH MORNING, the day before the council was to re-convene, Mokan-lee called Kruush into his private office. Kruush took a seat in a plush chair opposite a marble table with an engraved wood top. Mokan-lee paced the room.

"I'm concerned," Mokan-lee told him.

Kruush sat up straight in his chair. "What do you mean?"

"Your apprentice—he's spending a lot of time with my daughter. I don't like it."

"I know they talk after we sup in the evening, but that's all. I'm not aware of them spending time beyond that."

"Then you've been misinformed. Their time together has been pro-tracted. Hardly brief and hardly unnoticeable."

Before this moment, Kruush's relationship with Mokan-lee was iron-clad. But now . . .

"I'll talk to my apprentice right away," Kruush said. "We'll settle this. Don't you worry."

Mokan-lee quit pacing. "I'm not worried as much about your ap-prentice seeking my daughter as I am about my daughter seeking your apprentice. She keeps talking about him to her cousins."

"Do you want us to leave? We can check into an inn if the situation is intolerable. I have no problem doing that. Just give me the word."

Mokan-lee flicked his wrist. "Nonsense. You needn't do that. You're heading east to Tuur in a few days. I don't want to inconvenience you or your men over this or strain your finances. Besides, Lila wants Ahleen to stay with us while you're gone. She's desperate for good company. You wouldn't believe how she complains about her gossiping friends. No, I'll straighten the situation with my daughter personally."

Kruush smiled to mask his uneasiness. He needed to talk to Petrah before things got out of hand.

P ETRAH SAT AT HIS usual seat in Jakk's, face drawn and thoughts darkened. He had eaten almost nothing the previous day. Kruush's warning about staying away from Mina had stolen his appetite from him. He picked at his stack of fried potato cakes, recalling the conversation.

"Keep your distance," Kruush had told him. "You have to understand, it's his only daughter."

Petrah remembered the sinking feeling in his stomach. "I know. Don't worry, Kruush, I won't ruin things between you and Mokan-lee. I give you my word."

Petrah's heart was as heavy as a mountain. He had no right to jeopardize Tan and Kruush's business relationship. *What about* my *happiness? What about Mina's?* Maybe it was all a foolish dream, anyway. After all, their paths might be joined now, but they would diverge and grow separate. It wasn't fair for Petrah to give Mina false hope. *She's better off without me. She'll find someone else, someone her father will approve of.*

He pushed his platter away. He would return to Maseah. Ajoon would be there. Petrah wanted to think about Ajoon, but Mina kept his heart captive.

She's my jailor, and I'm her prisoner.

Did Mina have the same feelings for him? The way she looked at him with her large, brown eyes, the way she held his hand, the way she spoke to him—she had to.

Jakk sat down across from him. "Not going well, I take it?"

Petrah tried not to show his misery, but it was a losing battle. "I can't see her anymore. Or, I should say, her father forbids me from seeing her anymore."

"Ah, the father," Jakk said, whistling. "From the sound of your voice, I'd say he's the type who would cut you stem to stern to protect his daughter."

"Worse than that," Petrah said, grasping the full extent of his lousy predicament.

"My sympathy, friend. Perhaps there will be another lady sometime down the road, eh? Someone right for you. Someone who would appreciate a thinking man."

Petrah shook his head. "Not like her."

"I understand." Jakk gave him a friendly shake of the shoulder. "For what it's worth, you're a good lad. Never stop being who you are. Best of luck." He left Petrah to wallow in self-pity.

THE TALKS BETWEEN THE delegations ended on a neutral note. Neither side was satisfied with the other, but at least there would be no further military conflict. Petrah reported the results to Master Joriah. He was to depart early the next day.

Master Joriah praised him for his excellent spycraft and ability to remain undetected. *Uhtah-Pei is pleased with your performance. You are in San's grace.*

Thank you, Master. I look forward to going back to Maseah.

About that . . . I have a new assignment for you.

He informed Petrah he was to head to Tuur in the morning, the easternmost city of Meerjurmeh, where he would rendezvous with a Green Party mage named Anandawa who was returning from Darkforth with several An-jurahn officials. Together, they would head straight to Elmar. It was too dangerous for the delegation to step foot anywhere near the Meerjurmehan capital, which is why Tuur was chosen as the rally point.

Why can't I head home with Kruush? Petrah asked, frustrated that he had to travel to yet another city. *I'm eager to resume my studies.*

And you will. But Kruush isn't heading back. I paid him to take you to Tuur. Anandawa will continue your training. By the time you're home, you'll be miles ahead as a journeyman. This is important business, Petrah. I'm counting on you and so is His Holiness.

Petrah was furious to learn Kruush had known about this arrangement all along. He confronted his friend.

"Why didn't you tell me?"

"I was sworn to silence," Kruush said. "Now don't get that head of yours all up in a fuss. Business is business. You do what you have to do in Tuur, and I'll make sure you get there safely. That's what I promised your master, and I'm a man of my word."

I T WAS THE EARLY hours of the morning of their departure. Petrah gathered his belongings. He wasn't happy at all about traveling to Tuur. Master Joriah's praise should have given him a morale boost. Instead, it reminded him that duty would always come before his own happiness.

It's my fault. I tried to force something to happen beyond my control. Petrah had promised himself to defy the Watcher, to prove he could act of his own free will.

Who am I kidding? There is no free will.

The stubby candle flickered in his room. He didn't need the light—his enhanced eyesight allowed him to see in the dark—but the warm flame comforted him.

When he finished packing, he folded the white robe his host had given him. The silken material reminded him of Mina. She was forbidden from seeing him, just as he was from seeing her. Everyone was trying to govern him. He'd escaped slavery only to be subjected to the whims of others.

Stop thinking about her. You're heading east. Think about that.

There was a knock on the door.

"Come in," he said coldly.

The door opened, and Mina slipped inside, barefoot and with her nightgown drawn about her. She put a finger to her lips and closed the door. "We need to be quiet," she whispered.

Petrah looked at her, confused. "What are you doing here?"

"I had to see you one last time before you left."

Petrah found it difficult to control his emotions. He turned away, not wanting her to see his face.

"Look at me, Petrah."

He turned back to her, eyes brimming. "Why did you come to see me? It won't matter tomorrow or the next day. I'll be gone, and you . . . you'll just be a memory."

"How can you say that?"

"Because it's true."

"It's *not* true."

"It's not? Should we fetch your father and have him weigh in? He'll tell you to forget me. To forget us. That there never was an *us*. That I was infatuated with you. That I tried to take advantage of you. That I wanted to steal you from your family."

"He would never say that!"

"He wouldn't? Then why did he intervene?" Mina said nothing. "I'll tell you why. He wants to protect you from me, a lowly servant from an enemy country with nothing to offer. It doesn't matter what you want or what I want. All that matters is what your father wants. If you don't believe me, ask him. I don't blame him. If I were the head of a prominent family, I might feel the same. As I said, this will all be a memory. Maybe not tomorrow or a week from now, but give it some time. You'll see."

A tear streaked down Mina's left cheek. "No." She shook her head. "It can't be just a memory."

"It has to be! Can't you see? You're a silly girl."

"I'm not a silly girl! I know what I feel. I know what *you* feel."

"I feel nothing." It was a lie. "I—"

"Say it." She cried. "Say you feel nothing for me. I want you to look at me and say it!"

Petrah swallowed. He tried to stem his own tears, but they were pools, ready to cascade unbidden. "I can't."

"Say it, please . . ."

Petrah took her hand and held it up to his face. He averted his gaze from hers. He wanted to remember this moment, the feel of her skin, the scent of her hair, but he couldn't meet her eyes.

"Please, look at me," she pleaded.

He did, and the tears rolled down his face. He shook from the inside out. He couldn't stand to hold back his feelings any longer. "I love you," he said. The words sounded strange to his ears but also right. He'd never told anyone he'd loved them. "I know I shouldn't. But I do. I can't help myself, Mina. I can't sleep at night. I can't eat. I can't do anything without thinking about you."

Mina hugged him tight, molding herself into him. She fit just right. "Oh, Petrah." She pressed her warm face into his shoulder and clung to him. He didn't want to let go. He wanted to stay this way forever.

She wiped her tears. Her hair smelled of sweet blossoms catching the morning sun. "I know we've only known each other for the briefest time. I know I shouldn't feel like this. I know my father is just trying to protect me. But I can't help myself either. I love you too. I love you with all my heart."

Petrah caressed her face, feeling the tiny rivers over her supple skin. Her profession of love brought him happiness and elation beyond words. He drank her in with his eyes.

Then he kissed her.

It was a soft kiss. A perfect kiss.

Warm, wholesome, complete.

Petrah withdrew only to draw in breath. He kissed her again, even longer, pressing his lips to hers tenderly and then passionately.

It lasted minutes. It felt like an eternity.

Petrah traced the drying trail of tears on her face and marveled at the beauty of her brown eyes in the candlelight. *If I could but capture this moment and bottle it for the rest of time . . .*

They sat down on the edge of his bed and held each other's hands, peppering the long stares with kisses.

"Do you have to go?" Mina asked.

"I must. I have to travel to Tuur on business. Maybe on the way back . . ." Master Joriah wouldn't allow it. Or Kruush. Or the man he'd yet to meet, Anandawa.

Mina laid her head against his chest and wrapped her slender arms around him. Her body was light and supple, but her spirit was stronger than the steel of a sword. Behind her, the first light of day glowed through the window.

"I don't want you to go," she said. "I want you to stay here with me. Let me talk to Papa. He'll listen to me."

Petrah shook his head. "He won't listen. He's already decided about us. In fact, being here like this is dangerous. If he finds out, he'll—well, I committed to Kruush that I wouldn't push it that far. If I ruin things between Kruush and your father, I won't be able to forgive myself. I'm sure you understand that."

She gave a delicate nod. "Promise me you'll come back to me."

He brought her into the fold of his embrace. He wanted to promise her he would come back to her, but he couldn't say the words. Instead, he held her like he would never let go.

Chapter 9
Of Dreams and Sorrow

THE CLOSER PETRAH GOT to the City of Tuur, the stronger his desire to turn around.

He didn't want to leave Hōvar. Mina was there—and with her, all of his heart.

I should make Kruush take me back. The hell with his promise to Master Joriah.

If it were only that easy. The wills of both his friend and his master were unbendable. Master Joriah had paid Kruush to take Petrah east, and no amount of begging would make a difference.

Tuur paled compared to Hōvar. There were no terraced gardens, no magnificent manors, no lush plantations, no bright colors, and no high walls. The city was very much like an isolated outpost, even though it resided on the fertile north bank of the Tangeen River. Its drabness reflected Petrah's disinterest in breaching its walls.

Petrah watched the harbor come into view aboard the passenger barge he, Tan, Kruush, and Ahleen had taken from Hōvar. They'd left Summi and Julan back at Montabijon to manage their gonatans and equipment. Only a handful of ships were docked; most of them appeared to be fishing vessels. After two days on the water, Petrah was glad to go ashore, even to this dreadful place.

"Cheer up," Tan told him. "You're in Tuur. She's not so bad."

"If she has ale," Kruush said, "then she's a beauty in my eye."

Ahleen jabbed him playfully in the ribs. "You could have an alehouse in the middle of the desert, and you'd revel in the desolation's beauty."

Kruush's eyes gleamed. "Aye, I'll admit it: I'm a simple man with simple wants. But truth be told, my lady is all I need."

"Then I guess I'm a lucky gal." Ahleen leaned her head against his shoulder.

Petrah smiled at their affection for each other. They deserved to be happy.

If there was a bright spot in any of this, it was that his friends would return to Montabijon at some point. Perhaps Petrah could write Mina a letter—and a poem if he was bold—and they could take it to her. He would tell her of his adventures and his affections for her and that he missed her.

Petrah held on to the idea of it as he drew in the marshy air. The odor worsened the closer they got to the docks.

"Not exactly the welcome I was expecting," Kruush said, pinching his nose.

Tan chuckled. "It's probably why they say the catacombs are Tuur's most renowned feature."

"Do they now?"

"There's an extensive network of ancient tunnels running beneath the city, where the dead were once interred. Now it lies empty, the dead buried out in the desert as we do back home. The catacombs are nothing more than a tourist attraction. Charming, wouldn't you say?"

"If I'm a tourist, and I choose this place, then by all means, slit my throat."

Ahleen smacked him on the arm. "Kruush!"

"Apologies, my love. I was overcome by the moment."

Petrah was glad Ahleen was with them. She was supposed to have remained behind to keep Lila company, but she'd talked Kruush into letting her come.

I need all my friends with me, now more than ever.

HARDLY ANYONE OCCUPIED THE taproom of the Chaka Inn. Daylight filtered through dusty air from between slats in the roof. The inn came at the recommendation of Mokan-lee, who had stayed there while investigating a new venture. A few locals sat by the bar, hunched over their drinks or engaged in light conversation. They eyed the newcomers with sniffs and wrinkles of the nose and let their gazes linger before losing interest and going back to their business.

Kruush went up to the innkeeper, who was wiping down a table while his wife carried away empty bowls that smelled of a hearty, spiced stew. "We need two rooms for a couple of nights, someplace quiet and out of the way, if possible."

The innkeeper was an older man with a scarred face, lazy eye, and a limp. He didn't appear to be keen on the new arrivals.

"Our friend Mokan-lee recommended your fine inn. He's stayed here in the past and mentioned you personally. Dorgan, is it?" Kruush asked.

"Yes, Dorgan. Your friend stayed here, you say?" Dorgan swept the crumbs from the table onto the floor. "I'd have to check the ledger. The name doesn't ring a bell. Where's he from?"

"Hōvar. He owns a large plantation outside the city. He runs an import-export business and serves on the Lesser Light's Trade Council. I'm an associate."

"Might have heard of him," the innkeeper said. "We get all sorts of visitors from around the country. Although not your kind, typically, no offense."

"None taken."

"Two rooms, you say?" Dorgan gave Ahleen an appraising look and slung his cleaning rag over his shoulder. "I've got one available, far end of the inn, nice and quiet. It's got two beds, but I can get you an additional cot or two, depending on your sleeping arrangement." He eyed Ahleen again. "You'd have to pay for your stay upfront."

"I can do that," Kruush said. "We'll take the room . . . and another cot."

The innkeeper's wife, a plump, short woman with an off-kilter gait, led them to a small room on the far side of the inn, which she unlocked with a large brass key. She ushered them into a space barely big enough for two beds, let alone a cot. There was a slanted table with an oil lamp and a water basin, and a few shelves for storing clothing. The air was stifling with the window shut, but at least they had a window they could open.

The innkeeper's wife pointed the brass key at her guests. "This is a respectable inn. We want no trouble. We serve breakfast at dawn and supper at dusk and have ale on tap. The washroom is down the hall, the privy outside. I'll bring you another cot in a bit. Here's your key." She handed it to Ahleen and left.

"Not an admirer of us," Tan noted.

Kruush nodded. "And her husband doesn't like us either. Come on, let's get this blasted window open before we bake in here."

Kruush and Tan worked the window open while Petrah and Ahleen dropped off their packs, which contained an extra set of clothing. The innkeeper's wife returned as promised with a younger man carrying a spare cot. They situated it in the center, making it nearly impossible to step into the room without having to crawl over something.

Kruush spoke to Petrah after the workers left. "As soon as you receive word from your master, you meet your party and we're off. No complications, no problems. In and out." Once Petrah met up with Anandawa, Kruush, Tan, and Ahleen would return to Montabijon.

Petrah promised Kruush he'd blend in and remain invisible. Wearing a saba helped. It was the body-length shirt favored by the Con-jurah in this part of the country, with a breast pocket and a tassel dangling from the slit of the neck collar, much less conspicuous than the robe he'd worn in Hōvar.

Ahleen said she was tired and wanted to rest, so the men headed to the taproom to pass the remainder of the afternoon. Petrah shifted back and forth in the rickety chair and took another swig of ale. Curled up in the corner, a black cat with a tuft of white on its head lounged lazily. It yawned once and closed its eyes.

"You're a man with a heavy heart," Kruush said.

Petrah nodded gloomily.

"Mokan-lee is tough in business and even tougher with family. He might overlook your nationality if you forsake our god—a tall order for most Ter-jurah. He might even soften his position if you increase your stature—granted, you rid yourself of this mage enterprise and work with us. Mokan-lee's a businessman who respects like-minded individuals. Prove your worth to him and you'll earn his respect and possibly his approval."

"Even if I did all that," Petrah said, "I can't change my roots. I'm lowborn and his family is highborn. I can become the best businessman in the world, but I'll still be who I am. He wants a suitor of proper stature for Mina, someone with a title and land and someone from a prominent family. What do I have to offer?"

"I think you underestimate Mokan-lee. He's shrewd, not heartless. He'd be willing to invest in a future, but only if that future were pre-sented to him. I think he believes this is a passing fancy for his daughter. She's smitten, as are you. The question is will it last?"

Petrah's malaise turned to irritation. "What do you mean, 'will it last'? Why wouldn't it?"

"Now, don't get all defensive. I'm just pointing out the reality of the situation. She's young, and the longer you two are away from each other, the less shiny things will stay, if you catch my drift." Kruush tilted his mug to inspect it before setting it back down. "The thing is, you need to search your soul, not just your heart. Ask yourself if she is worth pursuing, worth waiting for, worth getting your hopes up for, only to perhaps have them dashed? If the answer is yes, find a way to persist and not give up."

"That could take years," Petrah said with an edge of desperation, realizing how much of a longshot his fleeting relationship had become. "By then, Mina will be married." *And my heart will be in tatters.*

"Mokan-lee wants what's best for the future of his family," Tan said. "That's the way fathers are. You can't let it defeat you. Love is tough. I've loved and lost aplenty. First love is the most difficult."

Kruush arched an eyebrow at Tan. "What do you know of the subject, other than visiting whorehouses?"

"I know enough," Tan said, straightening in his chair. "Now that the effects of that horrible sprushah have worn off, a lot of memories have returned."

Petrah shuddered, recalling that devil of a tea. His friends had suffered more than him, forgetting pieces of their past each day. The worst, however, came when they stopped drinking the tea—the shakes, dry mouth, and cravings that had lasted a torturous week.

"I've noticed details from my youth I'd not remembered in years. In fact, I was just thinking of my first love the other day," Tan said.

Kruush smirked. "And who is this kitten who stole your heart?"

"Her name is Aylea, and we met when I was fourteen. Petrah, you should have seen her: golden-brown hair, fairest eyes, just a waif of a thing. She was a year older than me, very sweet, very shy, from a tribe staying in Kanmar for the summer whose family name I've forgotten. Yes, quite sweet."

Tan closed his eyes as he reminisced, smiling. "She and I were thick as thieves, spending every waking moment with each other, sneaking out when the moon was full to go swimming in the Juum River. I thought that summer would last forever."

He looked at Petrah, smile lost. "As they say, all good things must end. Her tribe headed out into the desert, and I was left with a broken heart. I tried to run away, to chase after her, but I didn't make it past the city limits."

Tan took a large swallow of ale and wiped the dribble from his chin with the back of his hand. "I was a coward in a way, but deep down, I knew it was the proper thing to do. I never saw her again. The moral of the story is that sometimes you have to let go. When the right opportunity comes your way, you'll know."

Jakk had said the same thing.

Petrah peered into his mug of ale and swilled the contents, watching the foam break apart. "I know what I should do, and I appreciate you sharing your story. But I'm underwater, drowning like I'm at the bottom of a river. I don't know how to find the surface."

"'Time heals all,'" Tan said. "It's the oldest saying in the world, but it's true. Your wound is fresh, but it'll scab over and fade eventually. I know it's a cruel thing to say, since I'm me and not you. Still, I'll always love my Aylea, just as you will love your Mina, and our memories of these women will be some of the best we will ever have." Tan raised his mug. "To lost loves."

Petrah gave an unenthusiastic lift of his mug and drained it.

T HE NEXT DAY CAME and went. Master Joriah contacted Petrah,
letting him know Anandawa had been delayed but would arrive
by week's end at the latest, four days hence. Petrah shared the news with
Kruush and Tan.

Kruush didn't like it one bit. "Are you telling me we need to stay in this
flea-bitten hole for another four days?"

"We just need to be patient," Petrah said, propped up against the wall
on his cot. It was hot inside, and the air was thick with the odor of sweat.

"I've been patient. This sitting around business is tiring. How much
ale can one quaff in a day? And that innkeeper keeps looking at us funny. Four more days? It's unreasonable. Where's this mage, Anandawa,
coming from, anyway? Joriah never mentioned the particulars when we
made the arrangement to take you here."

"Darkforth."

"Darkforth? That awful place?" Kruush's eyes widened. Tan seemed
equally surprised, as did Ahleen. "Gods, why would the mage be coming
from there?"

"He's traveling with an An-jurahn delegation," Petrah said. "Something big is going on. That's the extent of what I know."

"I don't like it," Kruush said. "In fact, I don't like any part of this
deal your master has arranged. The An-jurah can't exactly come walking
into this city. Tuur's soldiers are always on the lookout for trouble. The
city might not be big, but they have a sizeable garrison, and they are
constantly fighting off marauders, Idarians in particular."

"The An-jurah will stay north of the city. Anandawa will come to fetch
me. I'll go with him, and you'll head back to Hōvar." *Without me.* Petrah
tried not to dwell on the thought.

Ahleen, who was squished next to Kruush on their bed, picked up on
his melancholy. "You don't have to go with them if you don't want. What
if you went back to Elmar with us? We'd take you."

Petrah pulled his knees up to his chest. "I know you would."

Ahleen shared a consoling smile. "You do whatever is right for you. We're here to support you."

"I appreciate that." Petrah wanted to tell her that he wished to leave and head back to Montabijon. That he didn't want to wait around for Anandawa.

But you can't. You made a promise to Master Joriah, and he's counting on you. Remember that.

"I'll be all right," he said and closed his eyes.

T HE DREAM WORLD WAS not kind to Petrah that night.

He sat in the saddle of a chestnut colt next to his brother, who was astride his giant black stallion. The stallion snorted and scraped his hoof against the barren ground. They were atop a barren hill under heavy, gray skies. The bodies of slaughtered defenders lay scattered about. Their haunting faces gazed at the austere sky with empty stares. Below, thousands of soldiers chanted the name of the man responsible for the brutal slaying.

Aman! Aman! Aman!

Petrah's brother raised a gauntleted fist, and the thunderous pulse of the army grew stronger. "They're ready," Aman said to Petrah over the clamor of the soldiers. He wheeled his stallion about. "It's time. Open the gate." He pointed across the barren hilltop.

Petrah tugged on the reins of his colt, turning his steed to face the direction Aman was pointing. The air shimmered ahead of them, taking up the space and shape of a cave entrance, blurring the landscape along its edges. Its center showed an entryway to a green valley, as if someone had carved out a window to another land. A hazy barrier swirled like a cloud over the opening.

"The way is barred," Aman said, "but you are the Key. All you have to do is step through, and we will follow." His deep-blue eyes brimmed with lust for wanton destruction. Heat emanated from his skin, and the aura around his body curved the space into a dark fold that defied the natural order of the world.

Petrah didn't want to go through the portal. "What are your intentions?"

"You know my intentions, little brother. Now do your part so we can go home."

"But *this* is our home," Petrah said. The foreign land was strange to him, yet it seemed as if he belonged here.

"This is our prison. Ahead lies our home. Take us there." Aman unsheathed his sword, its edges marred from the countless bones it had cleaved.

The portal beckoned, but Petrah refused his brother. "No."

"No?" Aman's intense blue eyes grew brighter. "*No?*"

Petrah's colt tugged restlessly at his reins. He fought to keep the horse under control. "I won't take you there. I won't let you lead your army through. I won't allow you to fulfill the prophecy of the Scriptures and unite the An-jurah and Ter-jurah against the world. This ends here."

Aman moved his horse forward, sword gripped lightly in his left hand. His eyes were transforming, losing their blue hue, becoming red like smelted ore. His breath stank of rotting carcasses, and his skin shrank back from his cheeks like the dead. "Fate is an interesting thing, Immael. You might refuse me, but you cannot stop the wheel of destiny." With that, he plunged the blade into Petrah's gut.

Petrah doubled over. He wheezed as he grasped the metal with both hands. His brother drove their horses toward the portal, Petrah still impaled. Blood poured from Petrah's mouth as he tried to halt his colt.

Then his body touched the portal.

A cold rippled through him as the hazy barrier disappeared.

Aman released the grip on his sword. The sudden weight pitched Petrah forward, twisting his innards.

Unable to hold himself up, Petrah fell to the ground.

His brother strode past him, through the portal, with his army at his back. Before his stallion passed through the other side, Aman gave Petrah one last look.

Then he disappeared.

PETRAH AWOKE CLUTCHING HIS stomach.

In a panic, he pulled up his saba and searched for blood. There wasn't any, just a phantom pain receding along with the nightmare that had engulfed his sleep.

He was alone in the room.

It was close to evening. The reddish hue of the sky pierced the window. Sweat made Petrah's saba cling to him. It was as if he were on the streets of Kanmar, perspiring as he marched back to the pits.

The door opened a moment later. It was Ahleen.

"Petrah—" she started, but faltered. Her eyes fell upon him, stricken with worry. "Are you ill?"

"I'm fine," he said, sitting up. "What is it?"

"It's Mina. She's here."

"Here, in Tuur?" The incredulity of it came out in his voice. He came to his feet. "How? Why?"

"I don't know, but she brought a bodyguard with her, one of Mokan-lee's men. Kruush is with her right now at the front of the inn. This isn't good, Petrah."

That foolish girl! Why didn't she listen to me and stay put?

Her father was going to kill him. He hastily laced up his sandals and followed Ahleen outside.

The cool evening air was the only good thing about leaving his room. The moisture from his scalp and brow evaporated as he walked beside Ahleen. Petrah wished he could have washed the salt and grime from his skin, but there wasn't any spare time. Kruush and Tan were off to the side of the inn in a heated discussion with a tall, young man Petrah presumed was Mina's bodyguard. He wore a breastplate with Montabijon's crest stamped onto it, and a scabbard hung from his belt. A few passersby on the street had stopped to take in the kerfuffle.

Petrah froze when he saw Mina standing behind her bodyguard, eyes fixed upon her feet as the argument ensued. She was wearing a simple, lavender dress whose hem brushed the tops of her sandals. She looked up, then over to Petrah. Immediately, her discomfort transformed into a smile. "Petrah!"

She rushed over and nearly jumped into his arms. She gave him the biggest squeeze. "Gods, I've missed you!"

The arguing stopped, and everyone looked at them. Kruush shook his head, then threw his hands up in the air and stormed off.

"You shouldn't have come here," Petrah told Mina, even though he didn't mean it.

"But I had to!" She clung to him as if they were standing on the edge of the world.

"This is"—how could he phrase it without sounding ungrateful—"quite the surprise."

She pulled back and looked up at him. "You're not happy to see me?"

"Of course I am. It's just that—" He glanced at Ahleen, who stood alongside Tan and Mina's bodyguard. Ahleen encouraged him with a nod. "It's that we'd already said our goodbyes in Hōvar. Does your father know you're here?"

Her brown eyes fell to his chest, where she picked at the tassel hanging from the collar of his saba. "No."

"Why did you let her take you here?" Petrah asked the bodyguard.

The guard's face flushed. "She told me she was coming here to visit her cousin and that her father gave her permission. My captain didn't say otherwise, so I assumed once we were aboard the barge"—he hesitated—"that our trip was sanctioned." He shook his head. "My lord will put me in chains for this."

"He might," Ahleen said. "But there's a way to fix the situation. We get Mina onboard a ship back to Hōvar right away."

"But I just got here!" Mina protested.

Ahleen gave her a long, hard look. "Do you want to get"—she turned to the guard—"what's your name?"

"Edden," he said.

"Do you want to get Edden hanged for kidnapping you?" The guard's eyes widened at the mention of the word.

Mina let go of Petrah. "He didn't kidnap me. It was my idea!"

"What do you think your father will do when he finds out Edden absconded with his only daughter? You'll receive a small punishment and Edden will receive a hefty one," Ahleen said. "Now listen to me. We're going right back to the docks. You're getting on the first available ship, and I'm coming with you. I'll talk to your father and smooth things out."

"But I don't want to go!"

"Mina—" Ahleen started.

"I don't!"

Petrah exchanged worried glances with Tan. He wished Kruush hadn't left in the middle of this, but Ahleen was well suited to handle the matter.

"If there isn't a ship ready to leave port tonight," she said, "we're going to talk to every captain we find and get one to change his mind. Got it?" Mina started to protest again, but Ahleen raised a firm finger. "Got it, young lady?"

Mina looked up at Petrah, on the verge of tears. "I'm not leaving. I'm staying with you."

Before Ahleen could interject, Petrah said, "Let me talk to Mina. Alone, please."

He walked with Mina around the inn to an alleyway. A cat skulking behind a bin stinking of rotten fish hissed at them, then took off. Once they were out of earshot and away from the foul smell, Petrah nestled the back of Mina's hand against his face. "You have no idea how good my heart feels to see you. I've missed you day and night."

"I've missed you, too, Petrah. We should be together. Who cares what Ahleen says about Papa? Papa will spare Edden. I'll gladly accept responsibility for my own actions."

"You're the one who will be spared. Edden will take the blame." Petrah didn't want to speak the words, but he did: "You have to go back."

"But I love you," she said. "With every fiber of my being."

"And I love you just the same."

"So then . . . ?"

"We're cut from a different cloth. Yours is finely spun, mine coarse like burlap. How do we mesh the two in your father's eyes? How do we get your father to accept us? The answer is, we can't."

She looked at him as if he had slapped her. "What does that have to do with how I feel? Do you think because you're a merchant's apprentice I care any less for you? I want to be with you. I don't care if my father disowns me. It's what I want." She crossed her arms.

Petrah let her pout. No matter how Mina felt for him or how he felt for her, she needed to know that now wasn't the time for them to be together. The voice of an old man, a slave who helped a naked, lost stranger. *Destiny. It's like an arrow in flight. The bowstring is pulled at birth; you hit your mark at death; and in between, the arc tells the story of where you're going.* If it was meant to be, his arrow's path would merge again with hers. Until then, he would hope for something more and let his dream of finding love and happiness fuel him until it happened . . . or came crashing down.

"I'll find a way to prove myself to your father," he said. "I swear it."

"When?"

It was a question he couldn't answer. "I don't know." It was the truth.

She dropped her chin, disappointed. He lifted it delicately with his finger. "I do love you, Mina. With my heart of hearts, as deep as my soul will go."

She gazed into his eyes, as if hoping he would change his mind and beg her to stay with him. Her eyes dimmed after a time, reverting to sadness. "I understand," she said with reluctance.

He pulled her close and kissed her tenderly.

P ETRAH WENT TO THE docks to see Mina off. It added to the pain of saying goodbye, but he needed to do it.

"I want you to have this." Mina placed a lock of her hair in his palm and closed his fingers over it. "So you can remember me."

Petrah lifted her hand to his lips and imparted a gentle kiss. "I will." He tried to hold back the torrent of emotions, but his eyes had grown damp, like hers.

It wasn't until she was aboard the barge that Petrah slipped the lock of hair into the breast pocket of his saba for safekeeping. His hand smelled like j'boun. He watched as she waved to him from the stern.

Kruush wasn't happy paying the ship's captain extra coin to leave port right away and was even less happy to see his wife leave. Ahleen refused to allow Mina to go home without her, and Kruush had promised Master Joriah to wait with Petrah until Anandawa arrived.

I've made a mess of everything.

Petrah's heart sank as the barge drifted from view in the dark, its solitary lantern dimming until he could no longer make out Mina's slender form, even with his enhanced eyesight. The water lapped the dock in the ship's wake, then went still. Although the river smelled a touch rank, Petrah thought he caught the faint fragrance of j'boun in the air.

Tan hung a brotherly hand on Petrah's shoulder. "It's better this way. If she'd stayed, you would have been put in an impossible position. I'm sorry this happened."

"Me too," Petrah said. "I never thought Mina would do something so impetuous."

Kruush sighed. "It is what it is. There's no limit to a woman's love. Mina would follow her heart to the ends of the earth if she could. She's young, spirited, and I daresay, bold and perhaps a bit rash, but a fine lass, with the dignity of a nobleman's daughter and the spunk of a hellion. She needs to mature some, is all. I have no qualms paying for her safe passage back to her father, even if it means missing my wife sorely."

"Even so," Petrah said, "I don't feel right about this. At least allow me to pay you back."

"Keep your coin. My fist weighs more than your purse." Kruush turned away from the docks, toward the road. "But if you insist on making things right, then I will allow you to buy me and Tan a fine draught of ale."

Petrah eked out a smile. "It's a deal then."

Kruush bowed, presenting the road. "After you, sir."

Chapter 10
Fork in the Road

PETRAH AWOKE THE NEXT morning as if a herd of wild horses had trampled his head. The heavy imbibing from the evening before left him with a headache that persisted throughout the afternoon. He retired early, hoping to escape the monotony of being awake, only to be saddled with endless visions of warfare and darkness in his sleep. It was one last dream, one final encounter with Aman that shook Petrah to the core, that made him question his future, his choices, and his decision to return to Terjurmeh.

Petrah and his brother were together, each astride their horses, facing Hōvar from the east under skies so gray they were almost black. An icy wind gripped the land, and from behind, Petrah saw an army so vast it blotted the horizon. Aman gave the command, and his army attacked the Meerjurmehan capital. First came a hail of giant stone missiles that pummeled the city's great outer wall, knocking loose sections until the wall was riddled with gaping holes. Then came fire from the sky that scorched the battlements and the troops defending them. Aman's soldiers climbed over the tumbledown of ruin like a massive colony of armored desert ants and overran the city. Hōvar didn't have a chance.

Petrah tried to steer his horse away from the devastation, but his grip froze. His arms, legs, and head too. Aman led a cavalry force west, and Petrah's horse followed, taking its paralyzed rider along. They went past the carnage, the smoke and flames, past the long outer wall, along the plantations, to Montabijon. Aman's sizeable force overwhelmed Mokan-lee's small militia and overtook Bokania. Soldiers dragged out the household staff and had them down on their knees. They forced Mokan-lee, his wife, and his sons to do the same. Mina ran out of the manor toward Petrah. She sidestepped one soldier, but a second tackled her. She fell to the ground. The soldier pinned her in place. Petrah couldn't move, couldn't speak.

Aman turned to Petrah. "She is pretty, isn't she? Such a shame."

Petrah pleaded, but his lips were stuck together as if sewn shut.

"I know, Immael, I know. We don't choose how we love, do we? The heart desires what it wants. It's inescapable, just like the future."

Aman dismounted and went over to Mina, his black cape flowing behind him. His soldiers had their swords ready to slay anyone who interfered. Mina called to Petrah, begged him to do something. Petrah's voice caught in his throat, failing him.

Aman towered over Mina, menacing in his black armor and piercing fire-blue eyes. She looked up at him, eyes wide and tear-filled. "So beautiful," he said to her. "But you believe in the wrong god, don't you? You and your family. You and your people. You all chose the wrong side, didn't you?" He gestured, and a soldier gripped Mina by the shoulders, trapping her. Aman drew his dagger.

Petrah screamed through pressed lips. Fire-blue eyes fell on him as his brother kneeled beside Mina.

"You chose wrong as well, Immael." Aman rested the blade against Mina's throat. "And now you learn the price you pay for your choices."

Petrah awoke before Aman could harm Mina, before he could do to her what he'd done to the white-haired girl.

Petrah shuddered in the dark of the wee hours. His entire body shook, tremors rising from his clenched gut. Then his stomach released itself, and he wept quietly as Kruush and Tan slumbered on. Aman had gone too far this time, had gotten too close to Petrah's heart.

He won't stop until he hurts everyone I care about.

Petrah sat up in his cot. He wiped his eyes, then brought his knees to his chest and wrapped his arms around them. He couldn't shake the image of Mina's frightened look, her helplessness, her desperation. He couldn't save her in his dream.

What if this wasn't a dream? What if it was a glimpse of the future?

I can't let him hurt her. I can't!

Petrah wrung his hands. He rested his head against the wall and considered his options.

If he went with Anandawa, he'd return to Terjurmeh. He'd never see Mina again. Aman would come to Acia with his black army. He'd march on Hōvar, destroy the city, and everything around it. No one would be safe. No one would survive.

He'll slaughter them all.

Unless someone stopped him.

In his dreams, the Watcher had told Petrah of a portal, a gateway between worlds. It lay atop a pyramid in a jungle in the northern part of Darkforth. *Hachaqua,* the Watcher had called the pyramid—translated by the indigenous tribesmen as the "beacon of stone." If Petrah *didn't* go with Anandawa—if he went east instead and found the portal the Watcher spoke of and entered the land where Aman hailed from—could *he* stop his brother?

"I have to," he whispered in the dark. "I have to save Mina. And her family. And everyone I care about." He might never be this far east again. He might never get an opportunity to find the portal.

Petrah looked at his sleeping companions. They knew nothing of his plight, his dreams, the prophecy in the Scriptures, or his blood ties to San-Jahad, as Baaka had revealed.

I must tell them. I can't keep this to myself any longer. They're my friends, the closest thing I have to family. They deserve to know.

But would they believe him? Or would they think of him as a madman?

One thing was certain. Petrah would not go with Anandawa. He would not return home.

KRUUSH AND TAN REMAINED quiet, seated upright in their beds as Petrah spoke to them about Aman, Petrah's link to him, and the terrible future Acia faced. They listened respectfully to Petrah's narrative.

Kruush gave a ponderous stroking of his beard before responding. "That's quite the tale. If I didn't know you, I'd say it was a pile of krell dung. But I know you, so I'm willing to give it my full consideration. That doesn't mean I believe it; it just means I'm considering it."

"I appreciate that, Kruush," Petrah said, not knowing whether to convince him further or let him mull it over. *Gods, he thinks I'm delusional. Maybe I am delusional.*

"We've all heard the prophecy at Temple," Tan said. "The priests love to talk about the Great Reckoning. San-Jahad is their hero, the avenger of the Ter-jurah. They call him the Sword, for he will 'smite his enemies and bring Truth to the world.' It's poetic and all, but it was never worth its salt, in my opinion."

Tan pressed his fingers into his bed, creating dimples. "Like Kruush, I'm having a tough time believing you're the brother of this mythical figure, or that such a figure even exists." He shaped the air with his hands, as if creating a giant statue of a man. "True, you have blue eyes. But you were a slave, Petrah! If you were so instrumental in San-Jahad's plans, why were you a slave? I could understand if you were one of the Articulates and you claimed divine lineage. But to have been beaten like a dog like the rest of us . . ." Tan leaned forward as if he wanted to lift

Petrah's saba and reveal the scars on his back to reinforce his point. "Why would San allow that?"

"You're right. It's a ludicrous claim. I'm an escapee, marked for life"—Petrah pointed at the faded triangle on his ankle—"and a mage journeyman, not even a real mage and certainly not an Articulate. I have nothing to prove I might be San-Jahad's brother, except perhaps the color of my eyes."

"It's not that we don't want to believe you," Kruush said. "It's that we're overwhelmed by your claim. Let me ask you: why do you believe it's true?"

Petrah had awoken each morning after his visit to Baaka asking the same question: how was this not a fabrication of the mind? How could he believe there really was a Watcher, a portal to another world? How could he believe he was related to a man who was touted in the Scriptures as San-Jahad—the Great One, the Great Son, and the Sword?

Because I know. In the depths of my soul, I know!

A smile planted itself on Petrah's face, one he couldn't erase because the answer was right in front of him. "I can prove it. If I show you what I've seen, you'd believe me, wouldn't you?"

Kruush cocked a suspicious eyebrow. "What do you have in mind?"

Petrah had Kruush sit still, just as Master Maglo had done with him back when the mage wanted to know why Petrah was having such a difficult time at school. In this case, Petrah reversed the technique, projecting thoughts rather than reading them. He remembered when Master Ecclesias had the students practice on each other as one of their exercises, pairing them off and making it a game of "what am I thinking?" Master Ecclesias called it *endurata*—the melding of minds. Petrah had been paired off with Ajoon, who projected thoughts of food—fish stew, pheasant pie, and sweet cakes—which got them both in trouble when they started laughing uncontrollably. There was no room for joviality here. What Petrah was about to do was deadly serious and required the most delicate of handling.

Kruush was shaking by the time Petrah was through sharing his dreams and waking thoughts. Everything he had held secret was bared, like walking naked through the streets of Kanmar. He held his breath, hoping Kruush wouldn't dismiss him outright.

Tan examined Kruush with a shrewd eye. "Are you all right?"

"Give me a minute." Kruush waved him off and massaged his temples. Petrah was weary too, holding himself upright, desperate to lay his head down on his bed, but more desperate to hear what Kruush had to say.

Kruush looked at Tan, then Petrah, and stared off at the wall. "I've seen darkness in my life," he said, "but nothing like this. As black as pitch and as cold as a river on a winter morning. You've been having these visions since you were in the pits?"

"Yes." The dreams carried back to Petrah's first memories when he was captured and enslaved at the age of eleven.

"Gods, what a burden. Even if you were delusional—and I'm not saying you are—it would be enough to drive a man mad. But you've held it in all this time. I would say that's a miracle in itself."

Tan seemed doubtful. "You're saying it's true? Everything Petrah suggested?"

"Aye, as true as witnessing it with my own eyes." Kruush made the sign of the holy delta. "He is as he claims he is: brother to the Great One himself. They were both born in a dying land, a treacherous place where only the strongest survive. Something went terribly wrong there, but these survivors have rallied behind their hero, and San-Jahad has built himself an army, thousands upon thousands of loyal followers. He plans to bring them here."

"For what purpose?" Tan glanced warily at Petrah.

"For what purpose?" Kruush repeated, as if the question were absurd. "Why to fulfill the prophecy written in those blasted Scriptures!" Kruush raised his hands ceremoniously. "Picture this: you've got an army at your back and your allies think you're the greatest hero the world has ever seen. The Ter-jurah and An-jurah pledge themselves. They join forces with the Great One and fight the Con-jurah until the Church has fallen. The Con-jurah will never stand a chance against that. Not that I love these people, mind you. Still, they will be attacked and slaughtered. You've seen what we did to Vergahl. We sacked the city. The rest of Meerjurmeh will fall. They'll come for Hōvar, the holy capital of Jahism, and burn it to the ground."

"The Northerners and Korinians won't let the Ter-jurah burn down their Church," Tan said. "They'll fight the Ter-jurah."

Kruush snorted. "And when has that happened before? In what history book has the Empire come to aid their beloved Church, hmmm?"

"The Korinians were pagans before," Tan said. "Now they're Jahnists. They recognize the authority of the Church. Prall will recognize it too. Hōvar is the center of Jahism. They won't let it fall. They'll heed Meerjurmeh's call if San-Jahad attacks."

"Says you, the Oracle of Tuur." Kruush bowed his head irreverently.

"Poke all the fun you want," Tan said. "I know what I'm talking about. But we're getting off course. We still haven't spoken about Petrah's role in this."

Kruush nodded slowly and then looked at Petrah, as did Tan.

It was Petrah's turn to speak, and he was realizing what he needed to say, cursed as it seemed. "I know what I have to do. It's not easy, but it's simple. Well, not simple. Not simple at all. But it's the right thing to do, even if it doesn't seem that way." The idea was so outrageous, Petrah was afraid to say it. "I have to stop him. I have to stop San-Jahad."

Kruush covered his mouth as if he might roll on the floor and snort like a pig. "Now *that* is the funniest thing I've heard in some time."

"I wasn't joking," Petrah said, crossing his arms.

"You're serious then."

"Absolutely serious. It's the only way, Kruush. Can't you see?"

"Not particularly. What I see is a valiant idea with a fool's thinking. No." Kruush shook his head. "The better solution is that you stay away from San-Jahad. He can't get here without you. If you don't go to him, he doesn't get through. This Watcher fellow said you're the Key, didn't he? Well, I might be a little slow, but even I know you can't open a door without a key."

"Kruush makes a good argument," Tan said. "If you stay away, the Great One can't get here. He'll be trapped in—well, wherever you would call it."

"What if he can still get through?" Petrah said. "There's no mention of a Key in any of the writings I've come across. However, the Scriptures are very clear in saying San-Jahad is coming here, not *how* he's coming here. If we assume for a moment they're true, who can stop him?"

"It would take an army, all of Meerjurmeh's forces, the Prallites' too," Tan said. "If you add Terjurmeh into the equation, then Korin would have to send their legions to keep Hōvar from falling. That doesn't even account for the An-jurah."

Kruush scoffed. "The An-jurah are scattered across the forests of Darkforth, like leaves in the wind. They haven't been a threat to the west in over two thousand years."

"And you know this for certain how?" Tan asked. "That mage Anandawa is arriving here with an An-jurahn party in the next day. I'd say the Ter-jurah and An-jurah are working together. Remember that our people were one with the An-jurah three thousand years ago, before the Con-jurah defeated us. The Great War might have split us into two people, but our belief in San is stronger than any gulf that separates us. Unless the mage's trip to Darkforth was for pleasure, and the An-jurah are here on holiday. There's always that."

Kruush puffed out his chest. "You're mocking me now?"

"I'm just pointing out the obvious."

"It's a foolish argument anyway," Kruush said. "Look at us, sitting in this flea-bitten inn, roasting in an oven of a room, trying to decide the fate of the world. Let the Con-jurah fight their own battle. It's not our fault their god can't protect them." Kruush gave a satisfactory nod and leaned his back against the plaster wall, dismissing the matter. Tan seemed to give up as well.

"That's it?" Petrah threw up his hands. "You don't have an army at your disposal, so you're going to pretend this isn't your concern?"

Kruush pushed himself off the wall. "What would you have us do, knock on the chamber of the Prime Manifest and tell him his Church is in danger of getting burned to the ground?"

"But someone has to stop my brother! Don't you see? If he leads his army to Hōvar, he'll destroy it. He'll kill everyone who believes in Jah or anyone who's allied with them. People like Mokan-lee and Lila, Milio, and Mikano." Petrah drew in a frightful breath and a horrible remembrance of the morning's dream. "People like Mina. You, Tan, and Ahleen too. Everyone I love, everyone I care about. He'll kill them all!"

Petrah hadn't meant to get so worked up, but when he realized what was at stake, he couldn't help himself. He glared at Tan, who looked down at his hands, and at Kruush, who twisted his beard's knot into a point.

Kruush let go of his beard. "Even so, who would believe us? If I told this to Mokan-lee, he'd laugh me out of his estate and never speak to me again. We have no one we can trust, no one to listen to us. We're on our own."

"Someone would have to talk to the Church," Tan said. "An official high up the order of priests. Or to the senate, or even the Lesser Light. But like Kruush said, who would listen to us?"

"Not just that," Kruush said. "We're Ter-jurah, not welcome as it is. There's not one person who would believe us. That means this argument is moot. Even if we bent an ear, what would we tell them? That there is the slightest chance their sworn enemy will attack them, led by a hero that only the Ter-jurah believe exists? The Con-jurah don't recognize our holy books, nor our religion. It's a waste of time thinking anyone at all in Meerjurmeh, even a street sweeper, would believe the end of the world has come."

If Aman breached the portal, no one would be safe, least of all Mina and her family, just as in Petrah's dream. Yet for such an obvious outcome in Petrah's mind, there wasn't a soul who would believe him. Kruush was right. "It's just us then, isn't it?"

"It looks like we're it," Tan said, confirming the futility of their argument.

Petrah wouldn't let the argument go so easily. Every problem, Master Nole asserted, had a solution, no matter how terrible the plight or how few the resources. "There's another way. I don't have to wait for my brother to come here." He hoped he wouldn't sound any crazier than he had the past few minutes. "I will go to him and stop him before he crosses over."

Kruush let out a hearty laugh. "Sure, why not! Go ahead and round up the ole chap and hang him from a tree while his soldiers cheer you on. Did that snake in the desert poison your brain, boy, or are you just plain delusional?"

"I'm not delusional," Petrah said defiantly. "The Watcher said the portal is in Âhn, the northern part of Darkforth. He showed it to me in my dream. I've seen the maps of the East. There's an ancient city called Symorrah, which is the capital of the An-jurah. There's a pyramid in its center. I travel there, climb to the top, and go through that portal. The way is already open. If I'm the Key, I'll be able to get through."

"And then what?" Tan asked.

"Then I find my brother. He won't harm me because he needs me. I'll earn his trust, and then . . ." Petrah let the silence speak for itself.

Kruush harrumphed. "I've seen what happens to you in your dreams. This isn't some mule waiting to be slaughtered by a krell. This is the Great One, and he's wicked and powerful."

"I've learned plenty of things at school," Petrah said, trying to sound confident, but knowing he wasn't doing a very good job at it. "I'm not exactly defenseless."

"You haven't even completed your training," Kruush said. "You can't face an enemy like this half-baked, Petrah. You need to finish your schooling and go from journeyman to master and become a mage, and not just any mage. A mage with true divine power, mightier than all of your masters. You have years ahead of you."

"There's no time for that," Petrah countered. "I'm here in Tuur, as far to the east as we can go in the civilized world. I may never have the opportunity to travel this way again. It's now or never, Kruush."

Kruush wasn't having it. "You're rushing things. Your brother will make mincemeat out of you. Think about it. The world won't end tomorrow. The Great Reckoning might come, but there's enough time left for you to complete the mastery of your craft, so you'll be prepared. Only then might you be ready to face him. And that's quite a stretch, you must admit."

Petrah's face was hot from how flushed it had become. Why couldn't Kruush get it? After what Petrah had shown him, he still was blind to the impending threat. "There's no time, I'm telling you! I have to go."

"There's always time," Kruush said. "Go back to your master and finish what you've learned. If that doesn't suit you, return to Hōvar and apply to their university. You can always renounce your affiliation with Terjurmeh, as you put it, and offer yourself as a student."

Petrah squeezed his raggedy pillow. If he smashed it into the side of Kruush's head, would it smack any sense into him? "You already told me they'd never accept me, and that they'd arrest me on the spot. Or did you forget?"

Kruush looked ready to swing his own pillow. "Then you have other choices. Korin has the Acadium, and the Provinces of the South have the College of Andora. Pick a place and finish learning your craft. But finish, for San's sake!"

Petrah tried to hold his tongue, to keep from lashing out. Kruush made it nigh impossible to hold a rational, calm conversation. "If it were that easy, I would. You don't understand. I have to strike first. Even if there is time, as you say, time is not in our favor. If I don't act while my brother least expects it, we're doomed, regardless of how well-prepared I am."

"And what I'm telling you, you stone-headed whelp," Kruush said, "is that if you attack early, it won't matter. You won't be prepared, and your brother will kill you. It's as simple as that." He folded his arms.

Petrah looked to Tan for support, but he wouldn't agree either. "I know a thing or two about fighting, Petrah, and this is definitely not a fair fight. Finish your schooling. Master the arts. You'll never survive otherwise."

Petrah wanted to smack both of them across the faces to wake them up. *Why can't they see? They're blind!* "So, that's it? I should study and bide my time? I should go back to school for several more years, while my brother amasses thousands to cross into our lands and butcher innocent people? Is that how I should go about it?"

"Given the options," Tan said, "I'd say yes."

Kruush kept his arms crossed. "Bloody hell, yes, if you ask me."

Petrah hated they were right about his schooling, about how he had so much more to learn before he was ready. He needed to stop his brother. He needed to keep Mina safe. He needed to protect Milio and Mikano and their parents. He needed to prevent the killing before it started. "Well, I disagree. If I go back with Anandawa, I won't get another chance like this." They continued to look at him as if he was out of his mind. "It's not like I'm asking you to go. The decision is mine."

"Why don't you ask us to go?" Tan said.

"Because," Petrah said, flustered. "Because you'll say no. And why should you risk your lives?"

Tan tutted. "You won't survive Darkforth alone. You can't go by yourself."

"So you're offering to go, then?"

Tan glanced at Kruush, who knotted his brow fiercely in protest.

"Even if you offered, I'd say no," Petrah said, trying to sound as if he didn't need them. "This is my decision. But I'm telling you right now: I'm not going with Anandawa. I'm heading east."

Kruush got off his bed and bristled like a river beast. "This is foolery, and you know it. You're a stubborn mule. If you go to Darkforth, you'll never return." He motioned to Tan. "Come on, Tan. Let's get ourselves a drink."

Tan got up, mumbled an apology, and left the room with Kruush, leaving Petrah to wallow in the despair clamping down on him like a noose around his throat.

PETRAH IGNORED MASTER JORIAH's call. He didn't have the will or strength to perform the mind link with his master. And he didn't like the fact Master Joriah had arranged for him to go with Anandawa. Master Joriah, Anandawa, Baaka, and Uhtah-Pei—they were one and the same—worshippers of San and believers of his favored son, Aman. They wanted Aman to succeed. They wanted him to invade Acia and crush *his* enemies—the Con-jurah, Prallites, and Korinians—which were *their* enemies. Even kindly Master Maglo would likely side with darkness if put to the test; Master Nole and Ecclesias too.

Petrah dug deeper, uncovering direr thoughts. Would Nuk and Taline take part in a war against the Con-jurah? What about Ajoon, who never once spoke ill against the good people of Meerjurmeh? How far would the Ter-jurah go to support the Temple in its mission and their god? Who would rally to Aman's cause? Who would defy him?

Night fell, and Petrah was alone in his room. No supper, no light, just the gloom and his troubled thoughts, although there was nowhere to hide in the dark anymore. All the details of the room were visible, an amalgamation of sharp corners, chipped walls, and wool blankets that needed the stink washed out of them.

By now, Mina would be home, facing a furious father. Edden would most likely be relieved of duty, maybe put under arrest for dereliction of his post, or worse. Petrah didn't pretend to know the laws of Meerjurmeh or the sovereignty of a landowner as powerful as Mokan-lee. In Terjurmeh, a soldier might get flogged or even put to death for risking the life of a person in their charge. What would Mokan-lee do about his rebellious daughter? Would he punish her for her sneaking off to Tuur?

Petrah could only imagine what Kruush and Tan were doing at this very moment.

Drinking, probably.

And speaking quietly so no one else could hear them, discussing how ridiculous Petrah's idea was. Even Petrah admitted to himself the irrationality of the idea.

I'll leave in the morning. Say my goodbyes and head east.

Kruush and Tan would return to Hōvar. As much as Petrah wanted them with him, they had to go back. His friends had a respectable, fledgling business. Kruush had a wife. They had responsibilities and obligations. Besides, Ahleen would never agree to them journeying to Darkforth. The only thing that ever came out of there, aside from death, was disease, starvation, and madness.

Or an arrow in the back.

The lands were wild, filled with Idarian hillmen. Then there were the Machoo, savages known for skinning their enemies. If Petrah traveled to Darkforth, could he survive the journey? And if he did, could he find the portal? And if he found it, could he stop his brother?

A lot of *ifs*, he conceded.

Petrah had dreamed of Aman skewering him, opening the portal, and pouring through with his army. Was that Petrah's future? Was he so willing to go there and make it come true? If Petrah was the Key, he'd be opening the door for his brother, as Kruush had pointed out. Free entry into Acia, thanks to a brash young fool.

In a different dream, Petrah had encountered a white-haired girl, whom his brother had slain. Petrah had died miserably as well. In a third dream, Petrah had been with Aman when he came after Mina and her family. Three dreams, three possible outcomes. Any one of them could come true. And if they were possible, then it meant other things were—such as putting a knife to Aman's throat and slitting it.

I'm a killer. I've killed before.

Petrah kicked his bedding with a bare foot, disgusted at himself for using Miko's death as an excuse to proclaim himself capable of doing the deed again. On Hah'xallah, Petrah had exhibited the same dark nature, where he'd thrust the crying boy's father into the crowd. What if Petrah had been armed? What would he have done in that fit of unbridled fury? What if he had used Kantaka, as Miko had?

Terrible things.

Petrah waited up for Tan and Kruush to return, but the hours passed, and sleep tugged at him, even though his stomach growled in protest. They were avoiding him. One moment he was sulking, the next asleep, cast into dreams as black as night.

A TAP ON THE foot roused him.

Petrah stirred to see Kruush and Tan dressed and standing over him. They looked worse for wear, with deep rings under the eyes and breath stinking of ale. Judging from the light through the window, it was midmorning. Petrah had slept a lot longer than he should have.

"What's going on?" he asked them, his throat dry and scratchy.

"We've made a decision," Kruush said in a voice of utter seriousness. "We've tossed it back and forth all evening long, but in the end, we both agreed on what we need to do. The question we have for you is, have you reconsidered your decision?"

Petrah had done nothing but question his decision. Every answer came back the same. "I have, but I'm still going."

"That's what we thought." Kruush ran a hand over the top of his unkempt hair. "Gods, you've put us in a tough spot. If we leave you, you'll head off into the wild unknown and likely end up dead. If we try to stop you, you'll escape. It's a damned situation, that's what it is."

Kruush looked at Tan, who spoke for both of them. "Kruush and I deliberated until we couldn't think clearly, but we've made our decision. We're going with you to Darkforth."

Petrah blinked the sleep from his eyes. Did he hear Tan correctly? "But why?"

"Because we won't let you go by yourself, that's why," Kruush said. "I don't care if San's blood runs through your veins; you'll die out there alone."

"You and Tan can die too. Isn't that enough of a reason not to go?"

Kruush's face bloomed a deep shade of red. "I'll tell you my reason I want to go: that brother of yours. I can't get his face out of my mind, what he did in your visions, what he plans to do. He's evil. And maybe I've drunk too much ale and got too little sleep, but I know what evil does. And what it will do to good people. People you care about. People

Tan and I care about, too. And, yes, it's risky, perhaps suicidal. But I won't let you handle this burden yourself. I won't."

Tan lifted his chin and pinned back his shoulders. "I won't, either. And that's a promise."

Petrah nodded, fully aware—and appreciative—of what his friends were willing to do for him. The enormity of it robbed the air from his lungs for a few seconds. When he spoke, he did so with gratitude and weight to his words. "You're right. I can't handle the burden alone. I want you both to know how much this means to me."

Kruush gave him a good pat on the leg. "Then it's settled. We're going. I know how to handle a horse and Tan knows how to handle a sword and bow, and you . . . Well, I'm sure you know a thing or two." He shared a crafty grin. "We've already arranged our travel east by hiring a guide, and I've dispatched a courier to send notice to Ahleen that our return will be delayed. She might be upset, but she'll understand. And Mokan-lee will just have to put up with my men for a little while longer."

Petrah hadn't expected his friends to go as far as hiring a guide and sending word back to Montabijon. "It could take weeks to get to Darkforth. Did you say in your letter where we're going?"

"Not exactly." Before Petrah could voice his dissent, Kruush added, "It's better she not know. I embellished, saying we were assisting you with your master's business. But it's for her peace of mind we keep buttoned up about the actual nature of our journey and, of course, our destination."

Petrah let out a laugh. Were they really going to Darkforth together? "This is madness, Kruush. You realize that, don't you?"

"Aye, it's a half grain short of lunacy, I agree."

Petrah rubbed his hands. They were slick with sweat. "And you hired a guide while I was asleep?"

"We went out at first light, nosed around, and got a couple of recommendations," Tan said. "We met with one named Sooka. The locals say he's a skilled tracker and outdoorsman and knows the lay of the land to the east better than anyone else."

The news lifted Petrah's hopes. Not only did his friends agree to accompany him to Darkforth, but they had a guide too. He tried to hold back his smile, but it shined through. "Thank you, Kruush. You too, Tan." He was weak in the limbs, the letdown from their intense conversation soaking into his body. "So when do we leave?"

Tan jabbed a thumb toward the door. "Right now."

Chapter 11
Sky Country

THEY ARRIVED AT A large farmstead on the outskirts of Hōvar in the late morning. The air was cool and clear and thick with the scent of hay. They had to leave today if they were to depart before Anandawa and the An-jurah showed up.

"Oy, Sooka," Kruush called.

The guide waved a hand. He was a short, wiry fellow, not quite what Petrah expected, with a ragged whirlwind of reddish-brown hair atop a thin face with an old Y-shaped scar running down the length of his left cheek, partially obscured by a tangled beard. He wore a battered cloak over stained pants that had seen better days and had on boots that looked as if a dog had chewed on them.

"This is Sooka," Kruush said, introducing him to Petrah. "So," he said to Sooka, "we're all set. Which way?"

Their new guide pointed at a paddock and a set of stables on the west end of the property. A barn, mill, and farmhouse sat off to the side. "The stable master said he'd meet us over there. You have the money, right?"

"Aye, it's all here," Kruush said, patting a bulge in his cargo pocket.

Sooka's eyes darted left and right suspiciously, as if he were afraid others were watching or listening in. Petrah didn't care for his nervous energy.

"We have a long first day's ride ahead of us," Sooka said, "and the area surrounding the city isn't exactly friendly territory. You can find cutthroats, brigands, and marauders on the loose. I'd like to make it to Crest's Mark by nightfall and stay clear of any travelers. How many An-jurah are you expecting in the caravan heading west?"

Kruush looked at Petrah, who said, "I don't know for sure, but somewhere around eight to ten. They're scheduled to arrive tomorrow. We want to avoid them at all costs. They'll have a mage with them. He has a particular interest in me because I'm supposed to accompany him to Elmar. He thinks I'm waiting for him in Tuur."

"I see." Sooka placed a hand behind his head and looked past the paddock toward the line of trees at the edge of the property. "A group that size will make it easy to spot from a distance. Would your mage suspect you're headed east?"

"Not at all," Petrah said. "If anything, he'll believe I took a barge back to Hōvar. By the time he finds out I haven't, we'll be long gone."

Sooka seemed content with the explanation. "Then we better get going."

IT WAS JUST PAST midday when they reached the city's north gate, all four on horseback. Petrah's gelding, Pepper, hadn't cooperated at first. It took Sooka several tries to get the journeyman to mount and stay put on his horse.

"Place your foot in the stirrup," Sooka told him with a scowl. "Now grab the horn. Lean forward and swing your other leg over."

Pepper was strong-willed. He backed up when he wasn't supposed to, turned left when he needed to go right, and stopped and thrashed his head when Petrah pulled too hard on the reins.

"Stop yanking," Sooka said, seated next to him on his black colt. "He's not a gonatan and certainly not a dinner bell. Keep your hands still and pulled taut, but not too taut. Just pretend you're trying to make him smile."

The north gate comprised twin stone turrets facing the Tangeen River and a low wall running to either side. Soldiers atop one turret, busy talking among themselves, gave the travelers only a passing glance. Petrah figured the soldiers were mainly interested in people attempting to enter the city, not the other way around.

By the time the gate faded from view, Petrah got used to his horse's rhythm, although Pepper was trying at times, pulling against his reins to snag a branch of climbing vine or break into a trot without provocation. Pepper was much more energetic than Petrah's old gonatan, Chíla, who'd given him far less trouble.

Sooka led them east, along the Tangeen. It was a half-mile to the opposite shore, the water too deep for their horses to ford. They traveled across the dry, level ground, away from the riverbank's fertile, wet soil, and kept an eye out for anyone heading west. The river's current continued to speed up the farther they went. They came upon a hilly area in the midafternoon populated by brush and lots of boulders, some as tall as Petrah.

"Stop!" Sooka said. They reined in their horses. "Look. Riders." Petrah saw a tiny dust cloud a couple of miles upriver. "Quick, we need to head into the hills." He spurred his horse, and the others did the same. Sooka took them through a shallow pass between rising slopes. They climbed the pass until they reached higher ground, shielded from the river by a hillside.

Sooka dismounted and had everyone else do the same.

He handed Kruush the reins to his horse and crept up a larger hill. He lay flat at the top for some time. Then he came sprinting down. "There are about a dozen of them, eight on horseback, the rest in a horse-drawn cart with camping equipment. Most of them are armed. The lead riders are wearing robes, black and red."

Kruush nodded. "Magi and priests. And the rest?"

"Soldiers or officers, An-jurahn for sure, judging by their clothing and armor."

"A force that size won't get near Tuur. The Con-jurah will intercept them."

"They'll camp outside the city limits," Sooka said. "They'd have to break up their party to get into Tuur. Maybe they'll send the mage by himself."

"Agreed," Kruush said. "He'll go to the inn where we were staying."

Sooka shaded his forehead from the sun with a hand and surveyed ahead. "Let's wait them out, and then make for Crest's Mark, there yon in the hills. That'll give us plenty of cover for tonight. I'm going back up. Stay here. If something's off, I'll let you know." He climbed back to the top of the hill and stretched out on his belly.

Petrah lost track of the minutes. He felt a slight tingle in his scalp but dismissed it as a phantom sensation, not a mind link from Master Joriah, and definitely not a probe from Anandawa, at least he hoped. Sooka eventually gave them an all-clear signal and came down to them. "They slowed just a little, and a couple looked my way—although they couldn't see me—and kept going. They could have easily spotted our horses, as we did theirs, but they didn't show it, or they didn't care. That's good for us, but we should move on."

They reached Crest's Mark by sundown. It was a small bluff amid the hills, topped with a diamond-shaped boulder the size of a small house. Petrah marveled at how such a colossal stone could have ended up on top of a hill, as if a giant had placed it there. They forewent a fire and shared a quiet meal of flatbread and cheese while the horses grazed freely. Petrah was glad for their provisions: warm and cold-weather attire, including cloaks and furs; cookery for boiling water and roasting meat; oat bars for the horses; hardtack, nuts, and jerked beef for the men; basic tools for digging; weapons for protecting against brigands; spare clothing; hooks and twine for fishing; an assortment of knickknacks that might help them in a pinch; even ink, quill, and parchment for whenever inspiration struck.

I would have never thought of these things. Thank the gods for Kruush and Tan's foresight.

And for sour Sooka too, who liked to complain, but knew what they needed to survive in the wild.

Petrah tucked into his bedroll as Sooka took the first watch. One minute Petrah was thinking about the An-jurahn procession and the phantom tingle across his scalp, the next he was asleep.

DORGAN, THE INNKEEPER OF the Chaka Inn, dusted the bottles behind the bar as his wife Arra swept the taproom. All the guests had gone to bed, and it was nigh time they did the same. The door to the inn creaked open, and Dorgan looked up from a bottle of Vergahl wine he was wiping down. A man with a green-trimmed black robe entered. His face was long, his hair a river of sable curls, his eyes hard like stone, and he was unusually tall for someone of Jurmehan descent.

Dorgan snorted. *Great. Another Ter-jurahn.* He was hoping to be done with their ilk after having had four of them stay at his inn for the better part of a week. He never cared for their kind or the way they prayed to their dark god. To see another after a hard day's work was more than annoying. It was downright vexing.

"We're closed for business, friend, and we just sold out our last room." Dorgan had three rooms available, but he'd be damned if he let this one stay the night.

The man with the black robe looked about the taproom before settling his stony eyes on the innkeeper. It made Dorgan uncomfortable. Dorgan fumbled around under the bar for the large knife he had hidden there. *Curses, where is it?*

"Didn't you hear my husband?" Arra said from across the room. "We're closed for the night."

The foreigner turned his attention to her. She took a step back and clutched her broom. The man addressed the innkeeper. "Apologies for the late intrusion, sir, but I don't need a room." He had a Terjurmehan accent, as Dorgan suspected he would. "I'm looking for some people who are staying here." He described the lad with the odd eyes.

Dorgan remembered the boy. How could he forget those eyes? The man also described the merchant named Kruush.

"Well, my friend, you're out of luck," Dorgan said. "They left first thing this morning. In a hurry too, if that's what you're wondering."

"They left?" A quizzical look ran across the Ter-jurahn's long face. "Where did they go?"

"Home, I assume, wherever that is."

The man walked up to the bar. He planted both hands on the wood top Dorgan had just buffed. His stare gave Dorgan the jitters, and he smelled like wet moss. "I think you know where they went."

"I said I don't know, didn't I? What business do you have with them, anyway?"

"That business is my own. Now." The stranger leaned forward menacingly. "It's time you told me the truth."

SOOKA LED HIS PARTY alongside the Tangeen the next day to put as much distance between them and Tuur as possible. By midmorning, they hit the first cataract in the river. It flowed like rapids, churning and bubbling and making a ruckus. There was no way a ship could have maneuvered against such roiling water without breaking apart against the jutting rocks. It explained why the region was devoid of human settlement.

The horses moved at a steady pace beneath scattered clouds. Sooka called the land Sky Country for its wide-open spaces. It was cool enough to warrant the woolen cloaks Sooka had procured for the trip. He told them they'd have to change their undergarments to warmer ones once they reached the foothills.

Petrah guided Pepper along. The gelding was finally cooperating, although Petrah veered north at times, which Tan pointed out.

"You're doing it again," Tan said. "Why do you keep pulling to the left? You're making my poor horse drag to the left too." He patted his mare.

"I'm not pulling," Petrah said. "And your horse is doing that on her own."

Sooka huffed. "You're pulling. You're developing a bad habit. I keep telling you not to pull, and still you pull."

"I'm not pulling." Petrah lavished Sooka with a broad grin, which only brought out a glower from the guide. "I'm drifting."

"Oh, he's drifting," Sooka said to Tan. "That explains everything."

Petrah pointed to his left. "There's something that makes me want to head north. A tug, if you will, like something drawing me toward it. I don't know what it is, but I've been feeling it since we left Hōvar."

Sooka's brow creased in annoyance. "Feeling what?"

Petrah gave it some thought. "It's like when the sun hits your face. You feel the warmth of it. You can close your eyes and know where the sun is, just from how it feels. The same thing with this. Something is drawing me north. At first, it was northeast, but the closer we came to Tuur, the more north it became. When we were in Tuur, it was true north. Now that we're heading east, it feels like I need to go northwest."

"Ridiculous," Sooka proclaimed. "Simply ridiculous!"

"That does seem odd," Tan said.

Kruush, who had been minding his own business, agreed. "Aye, maybe there's a lodestone we don't know about. Or a second sun." He smiled, baring his teeth.

"There's nothing but desert and barren wasteland to the north," Sooka said. "Some ruins perhaps, but that's all. After that comes the Northern Range, then the Prall Plateau on the other side, and the domain of the Northern Kingdom. And, if you're looking for the cold, you can go on to the tip of Acia."

"You forgot one place," Petrah said. "Kushan." Ever since he read about it with Ajoon, he'd been enthralled with the idea that the City of Night, as it was called, might exist out in the wastelands. The Malaji, the most powerful magi in the world, once ruled there. According to Ajoon, they still did, kept alive by the power of one of San's angels.

Sooka shot him a dark look. "Gods, why did you have to mention that cursed place?" He jabbed his heels into his horse's flank and trotted ahead.

Petrah looked at Tan, who shrugged and said, "Some people are superstitious. Guess he is too."

"Still," Kruush said, astride his gray mare, "mentioning that foul place does no one any good. The legends say it's a gateway to the Netherworld, and although San rules the night, I doubt he cares for such a place."

It made Petrah wonder if such a portal existed and whether the Watcher knew about it.

"You're drifting north again," Tan said. Petrah corrected his course.

Kruush chuckled. "Maybe we'll use Petrah here as a compass if we get lost, eh?"

Petrah chuckled as well, and Tan too. Sooka shook his head.

Although they'd joked about it, there had to be more to Kushan than it just being an abandoned city from ancient times. *Something's there, something powerful, and it's drawing me to it. Ajoon, you were right!*

Whether that power source was the Malaji or the city itself was anyone's guess. Petrah wished Ajoon were with them. His heart hurt, knowing he might never see her again.

Don't think that. You will *see her again, just as you will see Mina again.*

Petrah turned his head until he felt a warmth between his eyes, as if feeling the sun on his skin. Kushan waited to be discovered, with all its mysteries. On his last day at Maseah, Petrah had made a pinky promise with Ajoon to venture to the city together, a promise he intended to keep.

He guided his horse east, shoulders back and chin up, imagining the secrets he and Ajoon would uncover.

Chapter 12
The Eastern Gates

T HE FOLLOWING NIGHT BROUGHT a slight chill, a hint of what was to come in their easterly travels.

Petrah wrapped his cloak about him as they tended a fire in the nook of a depression along the bank of the Tangeen, sheltered from the wind. Some manner of bird screeched in one of the spindly makaria trees reaching up from the sandy ground behind them like scarecrows scraping at the sky. He also heard scuttling in the reeds, which Sooka suggested were either silver-tailed rats or claw-footed mongooses.

Dinner consisted of perch cooked over coals served with charbroiled makaria root Sooka had hacked with his machete, then peeled, sliced, and roasted over the open flame. The root was chewy, sweet, and filling. The horses grazed on coarse moat grass that sprang out of the embankment in clusters like weedy starbursts. Above, the stars congregated in brilliant constellations, reminding Petrah of a time when he dreamed of seeing such things while interred in the pits of Kanmar.

After supper, they rounded up the horses and tethered them to trees. "We should take turns posting watch," Sooka said, as everyone laid out their bedrolls in the hard-packed sand above the shoreline. A breeze swirled around them, foretelling a cool night ahead. "These lands are unoccupied mostly, but I've known cutthroats and brigands to wander the desert in exile after being chased from the cities. That's besides the Lowland Idarians, not a particularly friendly lot, but still a notch above the ones you'll find in Darkforth, who would slit your throat just to see the blood spray."

"What about predators?" Petrah asked. He was thinking of krell in particular.

"Not so much here," Sooka said. "Don't wade out into the shallows, though. There are water snakes and such."

"How about river beasts?" Something big was rooting around in the reed bank north of them, and although he could see each reed clearly in the dark, he couldn't tell what lurked among the stalks.

"Never seen one in this part of the world," Sooka said. "Could be a water hog. They like to eat at night. But they're harmless. They eat only plants."

"Thank the stars then," Petrah said. He was wide awake, much more energetic than he should have been. "I can take the first watch. I'm not sleepy, even though my body is wrung out from riding on horseback. In fact, I think I might do some writing."

"Suit yourself."

Petrah fetched pen and parchment from his travel sack he'd brought from Hōvar, which included a tablet with clamps for securing the parchment, and an inkwell.

The items piqued Sooka's interest. "Those don't come cheaply, I imagine. A scribe, are you?"

"More like a dabbler," Petrah said. "And you're right about the cost. The ink is made from pine resin. Luckily, a little goes a long way."

"And what, pray tell, are you going to write fireside?"

"Something private." Petrah didn't want anyone to know his business, least of all Sooka.

Sooka scowled. "Do as you like." He settled onto his bedroll. He had his machete and hunting knife by his side. "When you get sleepy, wake any of us and we'll take our turn. We leave at first light." With that, he closed his eyes.

"I'll keep you company for a bit," Kruush offered, retrieving the scimitar he'd borrowed from Montabijon.

Tan had a sword with a straight blade for protection, similar to the one Petrah had lost, and a bow and quiver stocked with arrows. After his archery sessions with Mina and Silas, Petrah felt he could make use of the bow and arrow as well. In truth, he wished he had Jayeem's sword for the wilderness. At least he had a dagger that Tan had lent him.

Kruush kept their fire going while Petrah considered what he might write.

Kruush added dried branches they had gathered earlier. The makaria wood gave off a spiced, sweet scent as it burned. They were nestled on a silty bank in a depression below an overhang that shielded their campfire from the wind.

Above, on level ground, Tan and Sooka snoozed away. Petrah loosened the clamps on the wood tablet and secured a precious sheet of parchment to it. He set the inkwell down on a flat patch of ground and got to work. He crafted the Jurmehan characters as he had practiced in school, smoothly and attentively, and drew inspiration from the books he'd studied, *Orumen's Phrases* and, especially, *Erun-lee's Diction for the Educated Mind*. When he was done, he blew on the parchment to dry the letters. He had four quatrains on paper, all written from the heart.

Kruush gestured at Petrah with a stick. "You're smiling like an ostrich."

"I've written a little something." Petrah lifted his chin with pride, although reservation tugged at him as he added, "Better than my last piece by leaps and bounds, I hope."

"Oh?"

"Perhaps not to the casual reader, but I profess it might catch the eye of the learned observer."

Kruush raised an eyebrow. "All right, I'll bite. What is this grandiose piece of literature?"

"It's poetry, not prose." Petrah pointed his quill at Kruush. When he saw Kruush's blank stare, he explained. "It's a poem."

"And what do we owe this transition from mage to bard?"

"Not so loud," Petrah said in a hushed tone, peeking to make sure the others were still asleep. "I wrote it for Mina."

"Ah." Kruush gave a thorough tug of his beard. "Of course you did."

"What is that supposed to mean?"

Kruush held up a hand of neutrality. "Take no offense, young master. I was just noting she seemed the obvious source of your muse."

"She *is* my muse. All of it."

"Exactly what I was surmising."

"So," Petrah said with a suspicious eye on his friend, "you're not making fun of me?"

Kruush laughed in a primitive way that sounded as if he'd never stepped foot in the cosmopolitan world. "Heavens no, boy! Come now, you're getting far too serious. I was merely pointing out that writing a poem for your beloved was the obvious choice. If I had an ounce of ability, I'd shower Ahleen in verse. Alas, I'm but a commoner." He gave a curt nod, like a sailor to his captain, admitting to his lesser station. With a gleam in his eye, he said, "Well now, let's hear this masterpiece."

Petrah colored from embarrassment. "Well, I hadn't intended for it to—"

"Oh yes, you did. You're practically pining for an audience. Enough deflecting. Spit it out!"

Petrah took a couple of breaths, reread the first line, and then acquiesced to his friend's demand, for better or worse. "Very well. I've named it, 'Flower of my Life.'" He expected Kruush to tip over laughing, but there was no mockery in his eyes or sign his intentions were anything but genuine. "Here it goes . . ."

"Oh, sweet nectar of flowering bloom
Your petals are fragrant as the dawn, your stem willowy and new

My chest beats aplenty, my wings flutter with delight
Like a hummingbird you are, dancing aloft in the gloaming's last light
O' precious blossom, velvety lavender, and fair
You draw me to your jasmine sweet scent, your honeysuckle-perfumed
snare
You've stolen the breath from my lungs and the tears from my eyes
I'm caught as a willing prisoner, like the moon in the night
O' fairest enchantress, thee above all I do desire
More than all the stars in the sky, and all the wants in the wild
Without you, I know only sweet-scented sorrow
And an ache in my soul, and the missing promise of tomorrow
O' my sweetest love, how you induce in me wondrous bliss
You inspire me to part such loving words, and capture the morn like a
kiss
For you are the warm glow on the horizon, the sun rising high
And the whole of my heart I gladly give, for you are the flower of my life"

Petrah finished reading and bobbed his left knee. He waited for the criticism to come crashing down. Instead, Kruush gave the tiniest of nods, his eyes glistening in the firelight. "That was . . ." Kruush stitched together a morsel of a smile.

"It was what?" Petrah tried not to bite his nails.

"Interesting."

"That's it? That's all you have to say?"

Kruush reached over to give Petrah a friendly shake. "Ease up, lad. I was only kidding. No, it wasn't just interesting. It was as if you fashioned the words like a mage weaving a spell."

"Technically, there are no such things as spells."

"You know what I mean."

"I do," Petrah said, wondering if his friend was mocking him or complimenting him. His heart beat like the hummingbird's wings from his poem. "Do you think . . . ?" He trailed off, not sure he had the courage to ask. He swallowed, rolled it around in his mind, and asked anyway. "Do you think she'd like it?"

"Do I think she'd like it?" Kruush chortled. Petrah was afraid Kruush might wake the dead with his laughter, but neither Tan nor Sooka peered over the ledge of earth to investigate the outburst. Kruush smiled genuinely. "Lad, she will shed tears of joy, enough to fill a lake. Trust me, if I can't understand half of what you said, it's a pretty darned good piece of literature."

"Poetry," Petrah amended, not taking kindly to Kruush's barbarous comment. He dismissed the subject altogether. "Never mind. It was a foolish thought."

He removed the parchment from the tablet and stuck it over the flame of the campfire.

Kruush snatched hold of his wrist and yanked it away. "Have you lost your mind, boy? Don't you dare burn that!"

"Why not? You said so yourself you couldn't understand any of it."

"Actually, I said half of it, but that's because I've got too much granite in my head for such finery. Ask Ahleen if you don't believe me."

Kruush let go of Petrah's wrist and sighed. He looked up at the stars. "If only I had that sort of talent, I'd woo my lady like a knighted suitor from the north. She'd melt in my arms." He fixed Petrah with a meaningful stare. "You better not burn that poem. In fact, I insist you memorize it. The next time you see Mina, you recite it to her, word for word, no matter how foolish you feel inside. You make her look you in the eyes, and you recite it all. I guarantee she'll weep for the ages."

"Not if her father has anything to do with it," Petrah said with resignation.

Kruush grimaced. "There you go again. The devil may care about her father! Even if he drags you away in chains, at least speak your heart to her."

Petrah responded only with silence, a craven version of affirmation. Kruush had a point. Petrah needed to be bold. He gave his friend a convincing smile of agreement.

"Good," Kruush said. "The matter's decided then." He added another branch of makaria to the fire and hummed an old sheepherder's tune.

Petrah reread the poem. Kruush had been too kind with his critique. It was too fancy and too flowery.

I'd recited a tavern ditty to Ajoon, and she liked it just fine.

But this poem wasn't for Ajoon. It was for Mina. And it would only be for Mina.

His thoughts steered in a more haunting direction. His face fell, and all appetites for romance burned away with the fire before him.

"What is it?" Kruush asked.

Petrah kept his voice low, aware of the sensitive nature of what he was about to disclose. "Master Joriah keeps trying to contact me. I've been avoiding him, but I'm scared to death of what might happen if I answer him. He'll be livid."

Kruush looked at Petrah, and then bobbed his head. "I don't pretend to understand how this whole mind link business works, but after what you showed me with those projections, I can relate to your dilemma."

"He'll skin me alive."

Kruush gave it some additional thought. "What if you don't answer him? Would he assume you're dead or missing? Would he know your whereabouts? Could he track you down?"

"That's the thing," Petrah said, poking a lump of coal with the tip of a stick. "I don't know."

"The Joriah I met is not a man who would allow your disappearance to go unanswered. I met him briefly, but I can say without question how direct, precise, and driven he is. And, if I had to make a wager, I'd add relentless. No, he will not stop until you answer him . . . or he finds you."

Petrah dug out a handful of earth from the ground and squeezed it into a clump. Master Joriah was as tenacious as Kruush suggested. *He knows I deserted my mission. Why else would he try to contact me?* Petrah tossed the clump and wiped the dirt from his hands. His best option was to keep heading east . . . and never go back to Terjurmeh.

Kruush gazed back up at the starry sky. "We're leaving familiar territory, venturing into the unknown. But that's not what frightens me. It's where we're going after that. I've seen it—well, through your eyes, I suppose. Deep in the jungle, in the middle of nowhere. A tear in the fabric of our world—as if San had ripped it open—leading to a land that's not of here, but far away, a place we may never return from." He cast his steely eyes upon Petrah. "I keep thinking that I should have hogtied you and dragged you back to Montabijon, kicking and screaming. Tan is a more reserved fellow, but he's thinking the same."

"It's not too late."

"Aye, we'll tie you up when you're asleep, then strap you to Pepper in the morn."

Petrah shifted the ash around as embers floated upward. "I'm sorry for getting you and Tan involved in this."

"Forget the apologies. We're in the thick of it now." Kruush massaged the knuckles of his left hand. "Let's go back to the subject of your master. What if he finds out you're missing? What will he do about it?"

Petrah hadn't thought it through. As with his escape from the pits in Kanmar, he had only focused on getting away, not on what was to happen afterward. "Master Joriah will have Anandawa search the city and the harbor to determine where I went."

"And then?"

"Who knows?"

"They've invested a lot of time and money into training you. Not something they'd just let go of."

"I don't know what's going to happen," Petrah admitted, frightened by the potential repercussions of his decision to cede his position as a journeyman. "All I know is that we need to keep going east. Anandawa and his party are supposed to head to Terjurmeh, so I can't imagine them backtracking, even if they found out from the city watch that a group of Ter-jurah had gone east. East where? Certainly not Darkforth. No, they'll stay a day, two at the most, and then carry on west."

Kruush nodded, but his brows drew together and his face tightened, indicating that he wasn't quite swayed by Petrah's argument. "Let's hope so."

ANANDAWA SLIPPED OUT OF Tuur where he had tied his horse among the trees and brambles. He rode to the encampment where the An-jurah waited. The innkeeper had been a difficult man to question, but he finally gave up some information of interest. He had overheard the oldest of the Terjurmehan guests two nights earlier talking about getting horses. If that were true, they weren't heading back to Hōvar aboard a ship. He checked with the harbormaster and confirmed no one bearing the physical descriptions of the three travelers had hired a ship west. That meant they were going to the Meerjurmehan capital on horseback, hiding out in the desert, or heading somewhere else. He contacted Joriah via mind link.

You're certain they're not in the city? Joriah asked.

I probed using the signature you gave me, Anandawa said. *It will take some time to cover the entire city. They didn't take a ship, so they're on foot or horseback. My guess is horseback.*

I need you to locate them. Uhtah-Pei and I are counting on you.

Of course, Joriah would say that. He assumed Anandawa could con-jure the boy out of thin air. *We can't stay camped outside Tuur's walls indefinitely. The Con-jurah have patrols. That's beside the point we're expected at the Shrine of San. The high priest has an audience with the Mighty One. If they're on horseback, we'll have to guess which way they went.*

Search inside the city again. If you can't find him, hire a tracker. You can let the An-jurah go after that. I want my Gray Robe back, do you understand?

THE WEEK PASSED, AND the terrain changed from desert to plains. Petrah had never seen such vast swaths of greens and browns. The grass was plentiful and stretched in all directions. There were mead-ows by the river speckled with a wondrous sea of color: purple clovers, yellow coneflowers, orange primroses, and red-and-white flowers with antenna-like stamen Sooka didn't know the name to, all fragrant and sweet. The horses grazed together like a small herd, chomping and chew-ing, shaking their manes and whinnying.

"They're magnificent beasts, aren't they?" Kruush asked Petrah while Sooka and Tan dressed a large trout they had netted on the river's edge.

"Stunning creatures," Petrah said. "You know, there are horses here in Acia and there are horses where I come from. The same goes for dogs, birds, and many other animals. But I've seen no gonatans, krell, or lope in my dreams. Odd, isn't it?"

Kruush scratched his face through his unruly beard. "A little odd, I agree. Perhaps Jah got bored when he made your world and took out a different paintbrush at the end. Or San came along and changed a few things just to be difficult. It's too much thinking for me, lad. I'd rather smell the sweet grass, lay out a blanket, and watch the sunset with my wife."

Petrah smiled. "I'm with you on that."

Two days later, they caught their first glimpse of Darkforth.

The mountains that formed the southern post of the Eastern Gates were visible, majestically tall, wide, and wooded. Their bases showed a shadowy green and their peaks a reddish-brown from the dawn's light, topped off with a splash of peach that would become white later in the day. The travelers gathered around their campsite to watch the sun's first rays illuminate the land.

"Will you look at that!" Kruush exclaimed, spreading his arms. "Have you ever seen anything so beautiful? My grandpapa used to tell us stories about his trip to the Fural Mountains in the west when we were young. Oh, those were some stories. But look at this. Look at it! There's forest everywhere. Have you ever imagined anything so big?"

The forest crossed the entire horizon. Petrah tried to imagine the woody scent of the trees, of hearing birds pecking at the trunks, of the branches swinging to and fro in the wind.

"How come we didn't notice that last night?" Tan asked.

"Because you were too tired, and it was dark," Petrah said.

Sooka cleared his throat. "We should eat something and get going. We have a long ride ahead."

"Fine, fine," Kruush said, folding his arms. "Ruin our moment, why don't ya?"

T HEY CROSSED FIELDS AND streams and land covered in brush. The air grew cooler.

The crooked course of the Tangeen pushed them north for a bit before turning east again. At one point, they saw a band of half-naked people walking along a brook away from them. A man with a spear turned and gestured toward the foreigners. Several men, women, and children watched Sooka lead his team across the water.

"Don't stare," Sooka cautioned. "Just keep going like you don't see them."

It was only when the land rose and then dipped again did the wild people fade from sight.

"Who do you suppose those people were?" Petrah asked during supper—a mix of dandelions, carrots, and some sort of large rodent Sooka had snared. The meat had an oily aftertaste that Petrah didn't care for, but he ate all of it, as the day's exertion had induced strong hunger pangs.

"Machoo," Sooka said. "They're related to Idarians, but a more primitive and reclusive people. They're able hunters and know every inch of these lands. Their tribes are scattered throughout Darkforth and as far south as the Green Unknown."

"I've heard stories about the Machoo," Tan said, tearing apart a stringy piece of meat. "Everything from ritual sacrifices to capturing and eating their enemies—savage stuff like that."

"Some of it is true," Sooka said. "I don't know the part about eating their enemies, although I wouldn't put it past them. They're watching us right now, I'm sure of it. As long as we don't bother them, they won't bother us. But if you cross their path and offend them in any way . . ." Sooka's voice trailed off.

Petrah looked at his friends, who seemed to share the same uncertainty and apprehension. "Well, let's not put it to the test then."

THEY JOURNEYED SOUTH, THEN east. The mountains soared like stone mammoths above them. Timber ran upward, changing from oak to pine. The closer to the top, the sparser the trees, until eventually there was only rock, and at the peak, a light dusting of snow. Petrah had heard stories of the remarkable substance: a powder cold to the touch that turned to water when melted. He had seen it fall from the skies in his dreams, flakes like ash that wafted to the ground.

The riders entered the woods.

The land climbed again, steep at one point, before leveling out. The scent of bark and mulch met them, accompanied by a gust of biting wind. Sooka took them along a wide, slow-moving river up to an abandoned Con-jurahn logging settlement, where they set up camp for the evening. It was like a giant, burned-out fort with remnants of a loading area and sawmill. Trees and saplings stood where a courtyard might have been, and decaying wood permeated the air. Sooka said they had officially entered the Eastern Gates, the northern and southern sets of mountains serving as the doorway into Darkforth. He had everyone gather around.

"From this point forward, the terrain gets more difficult as we enter a domain legendary for taking lives. The legend is well-founded. There are predators that will eat you, plants that will poison you, and natives that will kill you without a second thought."

Petrah glanced at his friends, who were engrossed in Sooka's dire talk. They didn't seem troubled that their journey was about to become far more perilous.

Sooka continued. "You've glimpsed the Machoo. They're not the only ones to be wary of. The Idarians have a nasty reputation for killing on a whim. And then there are the An-jurah. Although you share lineage with them, don't think for a moment they're your ally. They are skilled warriors, with little tolerance for outsiders."

Petrah didn't agree with that, considering Anandawa was traveling with an An-jurahn party. But Petrah kept his opinion to himself and let Sooka finish his speech.

"Their high priests pray to San and practice the dark arts. Their warlords rule their territories with vicious efficiency. I'll do everything I can to protect you and give you safe passage to Âhn. But you need to follow my lead and stay vigilant. We're all the help we have. Do you understand?"

Petrah gave a weary nod, as did his companions.

They ate in silence, with no fire this time. Sooka said the fire could attract attention, and that's the last thing they wanted out here in the wilderness.

Petrah volunteered for the first watch and sat against a tree stump. He shut his eyes and meditated, taking in the heartbeats of the animals around him while listening to the incessant calls of night birds and the chatter of insects. He tried not to let the forest swallow him, but he felt alone out here, more alone than he had in some time.

The buzz of Master Joriah's mind link grazed his scalp.

He wanted to answer, to hear his master's familiar voice, his assurance that everything was going to be all right, that he accepted Petrah's disappearance, and that there wouldn't be any consequences for his actions. Petrah clamped down before the link went through. The buzzing continued another minute, then ceased.

You'll have to answer him at some point.

Petrah slowed his breathing, which had quickened in his fit of panic.

He couldn't shake the guilt of betraying Master Joriah's trust. The mage had counted on him, had bestowed upon him the Gray, had told him he had won the favor of their party's leader, Uhtah-Pei, an Articulate of the Temple and not someone to be crossed. Yet Petrah was abandoning the very person who had believed in him, the man who had given him the opportunity of a lifetime when he was freshly escaped from Kanmar.

You've made your decision. You have to stick with it.

Petrah sank against the stump as the realization weighed down on him.

There's no going back now.

Chapter 13
Darkforth

JORIAH STOOD NEXT TO Baaka in his chambers, peering out onto the bustling streets of Elmar. For all his visits, Joriah never tired of the view from the rotunda in the Dome of San. It gave him a commanding perspective of Elmar's summit. He could see the faithful gathered in the square below. Or gaze across at the minarets jutting mightily toward the heavens. Or glance sidewise to take in the sharp angles of the black granite edifice that was the capitol building. The interior of Baaka's chambers offered an equally impressive view, with its many windows, curved walls, lush seating, domed ceiling, sconces of gold light, and niches filled with priceless artifacts, including Joriah's favorite: one-of-a-kind glassware imported from the Provinces of the South.

The mage had tried to get an audience with the Seer all week, but Baaka had been busy coordinating with the Temple on the recruitment of San-mahadi. Droves of mahadi were being sent out into the cities and throughout the deserts to the tribes in the name of San. Their purpose was to identify heretics plotting against the Temple—those opposing the will of the clergy leadership—and bring them to swift justice. The streets were full of Temple soldiers, and relations between the Temple and the ruling party, the Fist, were tenuous at best.

"These are trying times," Baaka said, not his usual pepped-up self, evident by the dark circles under his eyes. "We have enough tinder out there to spark a conflagration. The Fist and Black Arrow are on high alert, as one would expect from being turned inside out under Temple edict. The Great Act is afoot, and I imagine even the Iron Fist is shaking under that ridiculous three-pronged helm of his, wondering if a lowly Acolyte of the Temple might walk through his fortified gates and slit his throat in plain sight. Wouldn't that be a cause for a spectacle?"

"There are whispers of the Fist, Black Arrow, and Silver Blade colluding, with the goal of proclaiming the Temple in violation of the Codex," Joriah said.

"I've heard the whispers, too. It's conjecture—talks about sedition and insurrection by the Temple. Yet no formal decree has come. Do you know why? It's because the curs in charge know their heads will roll if they declare we're trying to overthrow the party system. We're not. We're simply setting order to the chaos."

Joriah caught a whiff of incense from just outside the window. "What if the rumors are true and the parties come together to put forth a declaration?"

"Then the times will get interesting indeed." The Seer sighed heavily. "But you're not here for small talk. You're fixated on your lost sheep."

Joriah bowed his head. "Holy One, I hope this matter isn't too much of an inconvenience."

"You mean the misplacement of the Great One's brother? Nisheppeh would be in an uproar if she learned about the loss of your sheep. Of course, our beloved Uhtah-Pei insisted your Gray Robe head east, so the blame is not entirely your own."

Yet Petrah was in Joriah's charge, even if their party leader had authorized the travel to Meerjurmeh. "Petrah performed tremendously for us. He did what he set out to achieve."

"But then he disappeared? Was Tuur that mesmerizing? That god-awful place is a blight in the world."

The incense smoke was visible now, rising from somewhere below in the Temple. Joriah watched as puffs of it drifted toward the sky. "We know he's headed toward the Eastern Gates, along with the merchant I paid to look after him and take him to Tuur to meet up with Anandawa."

"Anandawa is a capable mage. But the Eastern Gates? Are you sure?"

"The merchant hired a guide, and they took horses and provisions. You don't do that unless you're traveling away from the cities."

Baaka picked a loose fiber from the hem of his robe and tossed it out the window. "I agree, but it's an odd choice of travel. One doesn't venture into the wild unknown on a whim."

"With a guide, my Gray Robe and his companions have a slight advantage. As long as they steer clear of danger, they can survive, but the land is filled with savages. One unfortunate encounter, and then . . . " Joriah let the consequences speak for themselves. Even a capable channeler could end up with a poisoned arrow in the back.

"Then your mage must find them first."

"He will. Anandawa hired the best tracker to go after them."

A thin eyebrow lifted curiously on the Seer's face. "I assume your Gray Robe doesn't know he's being tracked."

"Correct."

"So why do you need my counsel? It sounds like you and Uhtah-Pei have the matter covered. I can't save the boy's life from here, nor can I make him appear. Have you tried a mind link with your lost sheep?"

"Many times. He won't answer."

"Dubious, wouldn't you say?"

Joriah had suffered an earful from Uhtah-Pei for the calamity, even though it was his insistence Petrah go to Meerjurmeh in the first place. That didn't nullify Joriah's responsibility for the youth.

"I'm seeking your insight into why he left and where he's going," Joriah said. "Something spooked my Gray Robe. I need to know what that is. Then I can communicate it to Anandawa to help him with his search. If Your Holiness will grant me this one small request?"

Baaka pointed at the throw of cushions. "Let us sit so I might meditate on it."

Once seated, Baaka closed his eyes. His lids fluttered as he chanted a mantra before settling into a quiet trance. Several minutes later, he opened his eyes and smiled as if he had discovered the deepest secret in the cosmos.

"It seems as if fate is playing a trick on all of us," the Seer said. "Your Gray Robe isn't running away from you. He's heading home to fulfill his destiny."

"Preposterous. How would he know where to go? Besides, he's not ready."

"Improbable perhaps, but not impossible. It appears our friend has shared important matters with the boy, including insight into his past and the glory of his brother's future. These visions must have moved him to act early."

Joriah picked at his seat cushion, trying to understand what Baaka was telling him. "I'd say prematurely, not early, and that's assuming Petrah's intention is to head into Darkforth. Why would he cut off communication with me? Is he afraid I'll have him flogged for disobeying me?"

"Wouldn't you?"

"It's certainly within my right, but I have no desire to punish him on the account of disobedience."

"He doesn't know that."

"He would if he opened a dialogue with me." Joriah was annoyed with the direction the conversation was taking him. Why wouldn't Petrah just answer his mind link? "Still, I'm not convinced he's journeying east for the sake of reuniting with his family."

"I believe you underestimate his ambition. Did he not strike down a rival? That boy you brought to me when they visited was quite capable. Your Gray Robe killed him, which sparked his potential. A hunger builds within him. I sense a darkness welling." Joriah started to say something, but Baaka held up a finger. "One doesn't travel to Darkforth to run away. There are plenty of other places in the world for that, almost all of them safer. This journey is deliberate and for a purpose that his companions could never comprehend. Only we can comprehend it. That said, the Machoo and Idarians will kill him if he crosses their territory unawares. They're called savages for a reason. I don't care how good this guide is that he hired. Anandawa must get to him first."

"And he will. When he does, he'll bring Petrah back to me. Then we will prepare the Great One's brother properly to fulfill his destiny."

T HE TRAVELERS CIRCLED NORTH of the southern post of the Eastern Gates and made it through the pass.

Sooka motioned to the trees beyond. "We're being watched. Idarian hunting party. See the lookout?" Petrah squinted, catching sight of a small smudge against the timberline. It moved slightly, showing a person, although it was hard to make out the details.

"What do we do?" Petrah asked.

"We do nothing. They're probably curious, and definitely territorial. Any more, and we'd have to flee on horseback. But as the saying goes, by the time you realize an Idarian hunter is after you, you're already dead."

"Thanks," Kruush said. "One more thing to worry about killing us."

At the higher elevation, the air was chilly in the evenings. Sooka made everyone don boots, breeches, and woolen cloaks. Petrah had never worn such garb. The heaviness of the boots and the restrictiveness of the breeches put his gait off-kilter.

Tan thought it hilarious. "It's as if you've aged three decades." He mimicked Petrah's slow movement.

"We'll see how funny it is when the Idarians decide to go after you instead of me," Petrah said.

Sooka frowned at them. "You shouldn't jest. You're putting energy out into the Netherworld that will come back to curse us."

Kruush harrumphed. "Now who's being superstitious?"

The day waned, and they found refuge along a giant, granite outcropping among the long shadows of the afternoon, cutting them off from the harsh wind that shook the trees and dropped pine needles atop their heads. Petrah breathed in the refreshing sap-laden air. He'd never seen so many trees clustered together, and certainly none as tall as these. They jutted into the sky like spears.

Sooka decided there was enough shelter under the outcropping to warrant a fire. Petrah took the first watch while the others bedded down, cocooned in their bedrolls. After some time, Kruush stirred and joined him.

Petrah added a handful of twigs to the fire and watched it crackle happily. He could taste the smoke on his tongue.

Kruush loosened his cloak. "If Ahleen could see us hunkered down like this . . . What I wouldn't do for her warm arms to be draped around me."

"I miss her too," Petrah said. "Don't worry, Kruush, you'll get back to her."

Petrah thought about the lock of hair Mina had given him, safely stowed away in his breast pocket, wrapped in the waxy folds of a broad leaf to protect it from the elements. He hadn't let anyone know about it, and he had only taken it out a few times, mostly when everyone was asleep, when he missed Mina the most. The lock still smelled faintly of j'boun flowers. Even now, his heart ached.

"My Ahleen is strong-willed," Kruush said. "Your Mina, too. If they were here right now, they'd tease us for complaining about our lot and tell us to toughen up."

"Then I guess we better survive and get back to them." Petrah stripped dead leaves from a branch he planned to use to stoke the fire.

A howl of wind tore through the trees, which shook, rustled, and creaked in response. Kruush rubbed his hands. "I've been doing some thinking about your brother. I've been wondering, what would drive a man to unite one people so he could destroy another? Why not unite all of mankind and let those who pray to one god live in peace alongside the other? Look how beautiful this wilderness is. Isn't there enough of this world for everyone?"

"Kruush, are you turning altruistic on me?"

"Seriously now, what's wrong with what I said?"

"Nothing's wrong, except the world doesn't run on fairness. As long as there is hate and envy, it will never exist."

"Doesn't the Great One give pause, even once, and question what his father is asking of him?"

"Everyone's faith is tested at one point or another," Petrah said. "But when a man becomes as powerful as a god, what is there to question anymore as you bend the world to your will? I've seen the darkness. I've felt its draw. I've heard his father's whisperings. They're my father's too." Petrah was still trying to grasp that San was his father. It didn't seem plausible. Why would a god beget a child with a mortal woman? Weren't there demons and fallen angels at San's disposal, worthier champions to exert his will and dominion? Or did such creatures not produce children?

"You paint a bleak picture," Kruush said.

"It's how the world works. You might be born an innocent babe, but forces beyond your control shape you, and eventually, you lean one way or the other."

"So there's no hope for us, is there?"

"There's always hope," Petrah said. "It's a matter of choosing to be-lieve in it."

Kruush grunted. "That's not what the priests preach about the Great Reckoning."

Petrah watched the fire sputter along the fringes, then flare up with a poke of the stick. He had studied the *Book of Prophecy* with Ajoon's help, teased apart the convoluted passages the best he could. He recited a verse that had stuck in his mind, white-hot.

"'The Mother shall give birth to the Dragon, and he will smother the light with smoke and fire and drive fear into the hearts of the Unbelievers. From the Dragon's birth will come Samath, the cycle that ends all things, and the Great One shall draw strength from the Dragon's shadow and unite the peoples of the world with the might of the Father, and those who oppose his might will despair and falter.' It's a foretelling of the Great Reckoning, plucked directly from the Scriptures, word for word."

"It sounds fantastic." Kruush gathered his knees to his chest as the wind changed direction and swept over them. The campfire guttered. "There are no such things as dragons, except in the storybooks. Serpent-like beasts who beat their ragged wings, breathing fire and ruin upon towns and villages and forests. Children love these tales. Dragons have no place in the real world."

Petrah pulled his cloak about him. "I agree. But assume for a moment everything I've recited is true. Assume my brother takes on this mantle of power, as prophesied in the Scriptures, and he enters Acia with an army at his back."

Petrah tried not to think of his dreams, but they were part of his memories, his waking thoughts—inseparable from his slumber. "This Dragon, whatever it is, casts the world in shadow and flame. My brother unites the believers of San under his banner as the Dragon spreads its shadow. They march upon Meerjurmeh first. They destroy the Church, burn the cities, and kill or enslave the entire population." He emphasized the destruction with an energetic sweep of his hands.

"Now the center for Jahism is gone, leaving the Prallites, Korinians, and the peoples from the Provinces of the South without an anchor for their faith. Assume my brother doesn't stop there. Where will he go? North to raze the kingdom to the ground? South to confront the Empire of Korin? How many soldiers will he have at his call? Will the peoples of the other domains of Acia bow to him as the sun is driven from the sky by shadow? Will they fall victim to despair? Or will they rise up, only to be cut down by his sword or burned by his fire?"

Petrah had seen the terrible possibilities in his nightmares. If he listened, if he shut out the wind, he could hear the cries, the moans, the yowls of horror of those cut down by Aman and his dreadful army.

Kruush rocked back and forward with his hands anchored firmly beneath his rump. His eyes searched the flames, prodding the cinders at the edge of the fire as if unfolding the imagery of Petrah's awful prediction. "This future you envision is filled with death. I don't like it. But I can't dismiss it either. In every tale, there is some manner of truth. The question is, how much truth is there in yours?"

"I wish there weren't any truth in it. Maybe there isn't. Maybe it's something the priests made up to scare their followers straight. A stray-to-the-light-and-you-will-die assurance to keep worshippers in fear of the consequences."

Kruush stopped his rocking. "And if the whole thing is true?"

"If you believe in Jah, your number is up. If you don't bow before the God of Shadows or convert from your religion, you will be chained up or slaughtered. It would be a massacre like the world has never seen. That's why we must stop it at the source."

"But you said so yourself, you're just one man. With me and Tan, that's three. Lucky number or not, three against thousands, perhaps tens of thousands, is senseless. Are we afflicted with such mania that we would so willingly throw our lives away, or is there a way to cut the head from the snake and watch the body wither and die?"

"The latter, I hope," Petrah said, allowing the glowing embers to blur in his field of vision.

"Which means you have no plan."

The blurred yellows and reds danced in front of him as if the entire land were aflame under the Dragon's fire. "I have a plan. A straightforward one, in fact." Petrah held a hand up to his left eye, making a circle so that he could see Kruush through it, and vice versa. Then he closed it into a tight fist. "We destroy the portal between worlds."

THE COMPANY OF FOUR resorted to lighter wear as they moved toward the forested lower elevation, where the weather warmed. The woods grew thick, filled with the scent of humus. Tall, deciduous trees, with trunks as wide as five men standing abreast, ran over a hundred feet into the air. Their crowns blocked out much of the sunlight, setting a dark, brooding atmosphere for the weary travelers.

Without preamble, it rained.

It started slowly, with a few sprinkles. Then it turned into a heavy downpour. Sooka ordered them to higher ground. They camped out in the hollow of a tree and munched on their dwindling rations: smoked fish Sooka had prepared several days prior with some root vegetables they had dug up. Petrah's stomach grumbled despite the food, as there wasn't enough to sate his hunger.

"Imagine if we had some lope on a spit," Kruush said, licking his fingers. "And a draught of ale."

"Or a piping-hot plate of grape leaves stuffed with rice and meat and lemon sauce on top," Tan said. "And a warm, dry bed. And a woman to fill it."

"Aye, wishful thinking. We're losing weight out here." Kruush pulled on the flab under his arm, which seemed leaner and less flabby to Petrah than when they'd first started out. Even Kruush's bearded face looked thinner, as did Tan's. He could only imagine his own.

"We'll hunt when the weather permits," Sooka said. He was skinnier than all of them, but hadn't dropped as much weight as Petrah or his friends. "We best get to grassland so the horses can graze. They need nourishment. They're getting too weak for us to ride them."

"How far away from Âhn do you think we are?" Petrah asked.

Sooka shrugged. "Hard to say, since I've never been that far north. I'd guess a week, maybe shorter, maybe longer."

Kruush's face darkened. "A whole week? We'll be driven mad with hunger by then."

"We'll manage," Sooka said. "We need to be mindful of our resources. If we have to set aside a day or two to forage and hunt or fish, so be it. Jah willing, we'll get lucky and make it to your destination in one piece."

"Jah can suck on my dead mom's tit, if that's who you are depending on."

Sooka gave Kruush a dirty look. "And what has your god done for you lately?"

Kruush turned away. Petrah spoke up for him. "He didn't mean to say that. We're all drenched and tired and worried, that's all."

The scowl on Sooka's brow remained. "Then we should hold our tongues. The only chance of survival remains with us. We need to work together, not against each other." He shriveled his nose in Kruush's direction.

"I know," Petrah said, "and we all understand what's at stake. Why don't we get some rest and start fresh in the morning?"

T HE RAIN DIDN'T LET up until the following afternoon. By then, the forest opened into a glade cleared out by a recent fire. Felled, blackened timbers lay in places while others stood where they were, torched to a crisp. The travelers navigated around the charred tangle of trunks, boughs, and bare branches. Tattered strips of clouds dotted the blue sky. A little while later, they came upon a roiling river where they refilled their water skins and let their horses drink and graze on meadow grass. It divided the land, about a quarter mile across, with a swift current running downstream. Mountains rose against a backdrop of timberland, the tallest painted white at their peaks.

Sooka waved Petrah over to where fresh tracks marked the soft alluvial soil along the water's edge. "We shouldn't tarry too long," the guide said. "These lands are occupied. See these boot prints? Less than a day old. I also found this." He showed Petrah a metal arrowhead, then handed it to him. Petrah hefted it. It was heavy for such a small thing. "Idarians typically use bone, horn, or stone for making their arrowheads. This is a three-bladed broadhead, cast from iron. Broadheads are made for hunting and warfare. The boot prints are clearly Idarian, but the arrowhead isn't."

"An-jurahn?" Petrah ventured.

"That would be my guess. Which means either a party of An-jurah came through here, or. . ."

"Or they're supplying the Idarians with arrows." Petrah realized the implications. If the An-jurah were arming the hillmen, it meant they had created a truce between their peoples, or an alliance. Perhaps the savage world of Darkforth wasn't as savage as everyone assumed.

Chapter 14
Chase

T HE MAGE CALLED ANANDAWA waited at the base of a copse, holding the reins of two horses, while the tracker he had hired, a short Tuur native named Jobe, scouted up a steep hillside that would give him a commanding view of the area. Jobe came rushing down the hill minutes later, breathless and flushed. "There's a band of Idarians on horseback coming this way. About a dozen strong, all armed."

Anandawa had spent weeks in the company of An-jurah, with just a few encounters with the tall hillmen, all civil and without conflict. Hillmen were wild by nature and a threat to the uninitiated. The war clans were the most dangerous, with both men and women being equally formidable warriors, especially those organized into hunting parties.

"We should hide," Jobe said. "There's sufficient cover downwind among those trees." He pointed at a line of trees bordering the forestland to the south. "But we have to hurry. They're a few minutes from here at the most."

They were standing on a well-trodden trail with their horses. If they didn't move, the Idarians would be upon them. Anandawa could feel the heartbeats of the warriors, powerful beats conditioned to their rugged way of life. "No, I will talk to them. They might have spotted the boy and his companions."

"What if they don't want to talk?" Jobe asked, a nervous twinge in his voice. "Idarians speak the guttural tongues, An-jek if you're lucky."

"Leave that to me. Here, take the reins of our horses."

A little over a minute later, the horsemen arrived at a gallop's pace across the steady, winding trail. They pulled up short, shouting and pointing at the mage and the tracker. The party was a mix of male and female warriors with reddish-brown skin and dark, wild hair poking out from leather headbands. Most had piercings in their noses, cheeks, and ears, and beaded necklaces or dangling trinkets of stone or bone, coarse outfits with colorful feathers or patches of hide, tribal-patterned tattoos on their faces, necks, or arms. They carried bows over their backs and held javelins.

Two had their bows out while a woman warrior with jagged, black-painted lines running horizontally across her cheeks broke away and approached the strangers. She brought her horse within a few feet of Anandawa and whiffed the air. It was a common Idarian practice to take in the scent of a stranger when appraising someone. She didn't make a face, which was a good sign. If an Idarian didn't like your smell, chances were you'd find an arrow in your throat shortly after.

"What are you doing on our land?" She spoke An-jek, her words a string of choppy syllables.

"We're tracking four men." Anandawa described the Ter-jurah, based on Joriah's descriptions and Jobe's knowledge of their Con-jurahn guide. "We know they passed through here a day or two ago. We need to find them quickly. Have you seen them and where they've gone?"

She sniffed a second time. Her face soured, and her hand went to the hilt of her sword. "Who are you?"

Anandawa remained calm. He could kill this woman if he had to with a single word. The rest of her party as well, although it would be a messy affair and not without risk. He doubted his companion would survive the encounter. He needed his tracker. Anandawa would rather deal with this woman in a civilized matter. He'd appeal to her Idarian sensibilities, the warrior part of her nature.

"I am Anandawa of the Ter-jurah, friend to the An-jurah and friend to the Idarians. I am a friend to the high priests of the night god."

The sourness on her tattooed face lessened, but the harshness in her eyes remained. "We saw these men two days ago. They head to Machoo territory. Bad for them."

It was as Anandawa feared. The Gray Robe was going to get himself killed. "I need to find them. Idarians are a friend to the Machoo. You can lead us there and save us time."

"The Machoo hunt as they want. Let them hunt."

"The young one is important to me. I can make it worth your while."

She sniffed again. The hardness of her eyes melded away to curiosity. "How?"

P ETRAH AND HIS COMPANIONS reached swampland the next day. The growth was dense, the ground soft, the air hot and humid. The men were forced to go on foot to maneuver the snaking, misshapen trunks and drooping boughs. Much of the time was spent swatting swarms of insects or trying not to trip on vines or roots. Sooka was in an abysmal mood as he cut through the choking greenery with his machete.

Petrah noticed his horse was slowing, becoming more difficult to lead. "What's the matter, Pepper? Why are you dragging?"

"The horses are getting weaker, that's why," Sooka snapped. "They can't forage in this muck. They can't drink in this muck. They can't maneuver in this muck. We're pushing them to their limits. Pah!"

They made camp on the edge of a bog that was free of growth. Every so often, something would flop into the stagnant, noxious water behind them, followed by a gurgling noise or rustle among the treetops. A steady buzz of insects pervaded the air, punctuated by yowls and a rush of movement among the branches. Tan, who had been calm most of the trip, started jerking his head at every strange sound, much the way he did when they escaped the pits in Kanmar.

"You're doing it again," Kruush said while helping Sooka build a campfire.

"I can't help it," Tan said. He prepared a kettle for boiling water. Petrah was busy clearing brush so they could have enough space to rest without worrying about being overrun with ants or other insects. The fire would also help.

Kruush added more kindling. "Then find a way."

Sooka got the fire started and had Kruush maintain it while fashioning a rack from branches for hanging their kettle. "We need to ration our water," Sooka said. "I don't know the next time we'll run across a fresh supply. I can get only so much out of those stinking vines, and this bog water is for piss. Take it easy with your consumption."

Kruush pinched his nostrils. "Speaking of stink, the smell of this place is getting to me. And if I have to swat one more bug, I'll turn back and head home."

A bubbling welled up from the stagnant pond, and one of the horses neighed and backed against the others. Sooka pointed at the poor beasts. "I don't know what we're going to do with them."

Kruush gave the guide an annoyed look. "What do you suggest? Let them go?"

Petrah looked over to Pepper, who huddled with Sooka's horse. He worried about them. This was no place for such animals. In fact, he concluded, this was no place for him or his friends either.

THE NEXT DAY, SOOKA guided the travelers along a narrow stretch of land between two bodies of swamp water. Mosquitoes swarmed the air above. When they arrived on firmer ground, Sooka used his machete to hack his way through the bordering brush. Petrah glimpsed snatches of blue and white between the crowded canopies above. As the day progressed, the white turned to gray. Thunderheads formed in the late afternoon. By evening, it started to rain.

They built a lean-to from long branches and positioned it against a tall tree over a bed of ivy. They fashioned one end of the ceiling to drape and funnel the rainwater. Pretty soon, their water skins were full again. Even the horses quenched their thirst by drinking from the many puddles forming on the flat, wide fallen leaves. At least this place didn't stink of bog water.

The four rested within the makeshift shelter, waiting out the storm. It was a dreary, wet situation. Petrah lay against the tree trunk and split his thoughts between Mina and home. Master Joriah had tried to reach him earlier, but he ignored the call.

He has to give up at some point, doesn't he?

Petrah hoped so, but he doubted the mage would give up so easily. Which prompted another question . . .

Could a mind link cross worlds?

If Petrah passed through the portal from Acia to his homeland, would he be cut off, or would the portal bridge the gap seamlessly, as if the worlds were conjoined as one? That meant testing his hypothesis with someone, and that someone was Master Joriah.

No, thank you.

It was getting dark when Petrah noticed a change in the wildlife. He had just slipped into a meditative state when he detected the heartbeats of men, faint at first, but growing in strength as they drew nearer. Petrah roused his companions. "We need to go. People are headed this way."

Kruush rubbed the sleep from his eyes. "Are you sure?"

A horse whinnied. Sooka sat bolt upright. "The horses!" He moved past them into the pouring rain. Petrah went after him, Tan and Kruush right behind.

Sooka tried to calm the spooked horses, who were tethered to a tree. They pulled against their restraints, eyes wide with fear. Sooka's horse reared and pawed the air. Kruush's mare bucked and thrashed her head. The rope holding her snapped, and she galloped off, vanishing into the dark.

Sooka slapped his breeches. "Damn it!" The other horses fought against their tethers.

Tan nudged Petrah. "Can you tell which way the people are coming from?"

"North," Petrah said, "and they're headed right toward us. We have to break camp. I can see my way around, so I'll guide us."

The horses continued to fight their restraints. Sooka motioned in the opposite direction from the source of the threat. "I'll go after the mare. See if you can get these horses under control. Then head south along the water. Hide our belongings for now. We'll circle back." Sooka handed Petrah his machete and took off after the escaped horse in the near dark.

Petrah and his friends disassembled the lean-to and tossed the pieces into the water. They hid their kettle and bedrolls among the nearby growth, along with a couple of water skins. Kruush grabbed a dagger while Tan got his sword. Petrah sensed the approach of men, as well as a new set of heartbeats he had failed to notice earlier.

"They've got dogs!"

"Gods. They're probably tracking our scent," Kruush said.

Tan turned in the threat's direction. "They can track us by scent in the rain?"

Kruush gave him a cross look. "Do you want to find out?"

"These horses are unmanageable," Petrah said. "They'll never make it. We have to cut them loose."

Tan objected. "Are you crazy? We'll never get them back."

"What other choice do we have?"

Tan cursed and severed the ropes. All but Pepper fled immediately. Pepper looked Petrah's way for a moment before charging after the other horses in the downpour. No sooner than the horses were gone did the sound of barking slice through the rain.

Petrah picked up a couple of lengths of cut rope. "Each of you grab on, and I'll lead. Let's go!"

Petrah led the way through the swampland. Tan and Kruush stumbled behind him, holding on to Petrah's rope. The three splashed through puddles, then knee-deep water, and finally a stretch of mud that sucked at each step. They tripped over roots and got caught in tangles of growth, but Petrah hacked and hurried them along as quickly as possible. The barking sounded closer now.

The rain lessened as the trio scrambled up one particularly nasty, muddy slope. At the top, Petrah spotted water through a cluster of spidery trees.

"There's a river about a quarter mile down," he told them. "If we can get into the water, they'll lose our scent."

The clouds broke apart, letting in shafts of moonlight that shimmered off the water. There was a change in the dogs' pitch. "They're loose. Run!"

They made a mad dash for the river. Petrah's lungs were afire, and his limbs burned from the exertion.

The barking grew louder.

When they reached the water, Petrah yelled, "Swim for the far shore!" He ditched his machete and dove in. He swam with all his might. He could hear his friends chop through the water just as frantically. The current carried them east at a swift pace.

Several dogs came yapping right up to the riverbank. Petrah paused to look behind and assess the threat. The dogs were large and scraggly and viciously snapping at the air. One tested the water with a paw while the others bounded over roots and plants and paralleled the swimmers. A hiss sounded, and the undergrowth erupted. One of the dogs yelped and was jerked to the side as something huge and reptilian clamped down on its hindquarters and dragged its squealing into the water. Just as Petrah turned back to swim, he glimpsed half-naked people with bows reaching the shoreline.

Arrows plunked into the river around Petrah, one striking the water right in front of him. By the next volley, Petrah and his friends were safely out of range, cleared by the rapid current.

Three soaked men climbed up onto a knot of slimy roots on the opposite shore. They gasped for air and struggled to drag their bodies over mossy decay and wet soil. A nearby hiss made them scramble for safety. They ran inland maybe fifty feet and stopped. The moonlight was gone, leaving the world dark.

Kruush caught his breath. "What the hell was that back there?"

"River beasts or their cousins," Petrah said, panting.

Tan cupped an ear with his hand. "Do either of you hear anything?"

"No," Kruush said, plopping down on a rotten log. "Nothing but frogs and insects."

Petrah slumped against the log. The ground was wet, the air rank. His shoulder muscles cramped, and he was a sweaty, thirsty mess.

"Do you think they'll come after us?" Tan asked.

Petrah concentrated. The heartbeats of his pursuers grew farther with each passing breath. "They're retreating. We're safe, for now."

"Gods, what a disaster," Kruush said, still laboring to catch his breath. "Weapons gone, food gone, water gone. The horses and Sooka, too. Now what do we do?"

"We're done for tonight," Petrah said. "Let's conserve our energy and regroup at first light. Then we can double back."

Petrah lowered his head against the soil. He was too tired to relieve his thirst, too debilitated to move to drier ground. He listened to the sounds of the night, wondering about the whereabouts of poor, irascible Sooka.

Chapter 15
Forced Apart

P ETRAH AWOKE TO FIND the tip of a spear poking into his cheek.

A copper-skinned man with dark, straight hair and a nose wide like a spade stood above him. At first, Petrah thought he was Mumooni. But he couldn't be Mumooni, not this far east of the Fural Mountains. The man wore only a loincloth with brightly colored feathers draped from his hips and a foot-long string of bone fragments dangling from drooping earlobes that jostled as he moved his head this way and that with intense curiosity. Petrah didn't know what to make of him or the lip plate that distended his lower lip as if he had tried to swallow a teacup saucer. His face and chest were scarified with serried rows of bumps that made him appear as if he had succumbed to the pox.

"*Ho chak-ra.*"

The man pressed the tip deeper into Petrah's cheek. Any more and the skin would puncture.

"*Ho chak-ra!*"

Someone else spoke. It came from behind them. The man with the spear withdrew his weapon and gestured for Petrah to get up.

Petrah pushed himself wearily to his feet. It smelled marshy like a bog. He stood wobbly and adjusted his eyes to the sunlight streaming through the branches. Kruush and Tan were already standing. They looked as filthy and disheveled as he did.

The man with the spear was not alone. He had eight dark-skinned companions, five men, two women, and a boy. The women were topless and also scarified in the same fashion as the men. The boy didn't have any scars, but he had painted designs of squiggles, dots, and dashes in black ink across his forehead and chest. Like the adults, he was armed with a spear, his shorter.

The eldest of the bunch, a short, skinny man with straight, silvered hair in a bowl cut, and wrinkled, weathered skin, stepped forward. A bone the width of his face ran through his nose. The man examined the prisoners one by one, jabbing midriffs with his fingers. He spent extra time feeling around Kruush's midsection. He said something to the others, and they laughed. Petrah couldn't take his eyes off the man's nubby, discolored teeth. They were brown like ground nuts and worn down from chewing on who-knew-what. The man spoke to Kruush.

"I don't understand you," Kruush said.

The elder arched a brow, his expression unpleasant. He spoke loudly to his group. Powerful hands seized Kruush and his friends and shoved them forward. Spears reinforced their intent.

Kruush stumbled, then caught himself. "This is ridiculous."

"Do what they want," Petrah said.

"Can't you do something about this, like knock them down or take away their spears?"

"I need to concentrate—"

A jab with the butt of a spear shut Petrah up.

"*Makk*," said the man behind him. "*Makk*."

After a tiring walk through increasingly dense jungle—pausing only to allow Petrah and his companions to drink from a streamlet—the group reached a small village. Thatched huts occupied a clearing littered with stumps where giant trees once climbed. A pot suspended over a smoldering campfire gave off the aroma of wild herbs and onions. Half-naked villagers moved about, mostly women and children. They stopped to observe the newcomers. A young boy jumped up and down and pointed excitedly. A girl standing next to him giggled, then hid behind a woman.

The captors led Kruush and company toward a large stone building in the center of the village, a relic from an age long gone with cracked steps rising two stories from the jungle floor to a tilting portico beset with moss. A pair of stone figures guarded the entrance, worn to where only their oblong shapes survived. Ivy covered the walls, and weeds sprouted from fissures. Petrah assumed the rudimentary triangle painted on the side was their version of a serak.

A man wearing a headdress with bright plumage stepped out from the shadows. Petrah saw a staff in his left hand, metal shod with a loop on top, just like the Watcher's. *Could this be a coincidence?* It gave him gooseflesh.

The party halted at the bottom of the steps. The old man with the nubby teeth moved to the front and called up to the man with the staff. They spoke in a staccato dialect. After a minute of choppy conversation, the man up top pointed east with his staff. Nubby Teeth nodded. He called to the boy from his group and the youth ran off into the jungle.

Nubby Teeth walked up to Kruush. He poked the merchant in the ribs and gestured up the steps.

"You want me to go up there?" Kruush asked.

Nubby Teeth said something unrecognizable. When Kruush started up the stairs, the native grabbed him by his ragged saba and pulled him back.

"Hey!" Kruush said. "I thought you said *up*."

The old man made a face and jerked his hand upward.

"I think he wants us to watch," Tan said.

Nubby Teeth gestured back to the top and crossed his arms. This time, the detainees kept their mouths shut and waited. The man with the feathered headdress held up his staff and spoke to them in his strange language. He shook his free hand to the cadence of his speech. He finished by pointing at Nubby Teeth, who said something to Kruush.

"I told you, I don't understand," Kruush said. "Speak Jurmehan, for San's sake."

A commotion stirred among the villagers. Petrah turned to see the boy who had been dispatched, proudly leading a procession of about a dozen warriors. They had reddish-brown complexions and were dressed in hides and matching animal-skin boots, brightly colored and adorned with strings of feathers and beads. Unlike the brown-skinned captors, who had straight hair, theirs was wild and wavy, held back by leather headbands or circlets of metal. They were armed with spears and were tall in stature.

A second, shorter group of soldiers of equal number marched alongside them. This group wore horned helms and had armor of red-on-black emblazoned breastplates, shin, and forearm guards. They carried swords sheathed in scabbards from leather belts. A shirtless man with a dark-red, stained scalp and ponytail trailed them.

Kruush's eyes met Petrah's. He was thinking the same thing: *I don't like this at all.*

One of the short warriors, a man wearing a large, horned helm, whose horns turned fire-red at the tips, raised a hand. The procession stopped. He went to Nubby Teeth and spoke to him in choppy bursts of his native tongue. The man responded accordingly, motioning to Petrah and his friends, then the man at the top of the stairs.

The red-horned warrior walked up to Petrah, smelling of the jungle. He gave the journeyman an appraising examination from head to foot and repeated the process with Kruush and Tan. He spoke to the trio in Jurmehan. It had the same jerky rhythm as the other language.

"Pichupa says you disrespected his priest. Machoon priests aren't forgiving. They tend to hold a grudge." The red-horned warrior spoke up to the priest. "Don't they, High One?"

The priest said nothing.

"You speak our language," Kruush said. "Are you An-jurahn?"

"I am," the warrior said. "Pichupa is Machoon. He speaks the tongue of his forefathers. It's not a civilized tongue, but the Machoo are jungle people, after all. Pichupa says he found you near the north shore of the Bankor River. He says you were sleeping in the mud and that you had nothing but the clothes on your back. Strange way to travel, don't you think?"

"We lost our belongings. The rain—"

The warrior quieted him with an upheld hand. "I already know everything that happened. I know what happened to your horses. With no possessions, how do you expect to bargain with Pichupa? You have nothing."

The red-horned warrior turned abruptly to Tan, leaving Kruush flushed. He shriveled his nose distastefully and moved on to Petrah.

He leaned close and sniffed.

"You smell different from your friends. Different sweat, different stink. Still foreign though. Where are you from?"

"Terjurmeh," Petrah said. "Just like them."

"Your friends might be Terjurmehan, but you're too tall, about the same height as one of my Idarian soldiers here." He pointed at the line of warriors with the wavy hair. "Your skin tone and eyes don't match your friends, either. Ter-jurah are built short and wide like us, not tall and narrow like you."

"That doesn't make me any less Terjurmehan," Petrah said.

"But it makes you a Westerner. We don't appreciate Westerners in this part of the world. What business do you have here on our lands?"

"We're just passing through. We mean no trouble."

"You're wrong about that," the red-horned warrior said. "You were sneaking about. Men who sneak about are spies, and spies consort with the enemy. Why were you spying on us? To what end?"

"If you're An-jurahn, then you know there's a bond between our peoples, and a common enemy," Petrah said. "We're not spies. Pichupa here would understand that if you explained it to him." *Why don't they get it?*

"You don't have to worry about what Pichupa thinks. You're in *my* charge now." The red-horned warrior pounded his breastplate. He turned to his men. "Put them in formation."

Soldiers grabbed Petrah and his friends and placed them at the front of the column.

The man with the ponytail looked at Petrah, his mouth disturbingly crooked.

And smiling.

I T TOOK AT LEAST an hour to thread through the jungle to the next Machoon village.

This village occupied about twice the land of the last village and had triple the population. The Machoo natives weren't all that interested in the newcomers. They went about their business, skinning and cleaning the kill of the day, sharpening blades, fashioning jewelry from stone beads, weaving baskets of straw, and working a millstone to grind grain into flour. Others busied themselves clearing a field of what looked like wheat or barley. Many had faded deltas painted on their foreheads, tributes of faith to their god.

And our god too, Petrah thought. *Except we're treated as foes, not friends.*

The red-horned warrior brought the captives to the far corner of the village, where three interconnected huts had been converted to cells. Stilts propped the retrofitted structures aboveground and wooden bars replaced walls.

One occupant lay slumped against the cell on the left, filthy, bloodied, and either unconscious or dead. He was unrecognizable at first.

Then Petrah put a hand over his mouth.

Sooka!

The red-horned warrior tapped the cell bars. "See your Con-jurahn friend over here? Ask yourselves if you want to look like him. Think about it. I'll return shortly."

He left the foreigners in the care of his men.

A soldier opened the cell to the right. Kruush, Tan, and Petrah mashed together into an area barely large enough to stand or sit in. The bars swung back into place with a loud click, and the soldiers dispersed.

The captives eyed the bucket made of lashed sections of bark in the corner.

"Would you look at that," Kruush said, shaking his head. "Ahleen would kill me if she saw this."

"What makes you think *they* won't kill you first?" Tan asked.

Petrah examined Sooka through the bars. Caked mud and blood completely masked the guide's face. When Petrah spoke to him, he failed to respond.

Come on, Sooka, wake up. Show us you're all right.

"How is he?" Kruush asked.

Petrah sensed a steady but weak heartbeat. "Not good."

"Poor Sooka," Tan said. "They really hurt him."

"Badly—those bastards," Kruush added. "And we're next."

Tan turned to Petrah. "We have to get out of here. Is there anything you can do?"

Petrah gripped the bars. They were sturdy and solid, more like metal than wood. "I don't know. There's some kind of locking mechanism under the floorboards. Let me see if I can figure out how to get to it."

Petrah sat cross-legged in the rear of the cell and tried his best to meditate.

It rained sometime later. The smell of wet earth rose thickly. The pitter-patter against the thatching reminded Petrah how thirsty he was.

He lost his concentration.

A palmful of water would be enough to keep his mind off his parched throat, but the eaves of the thatching ran well beyond the reach of his arm. He watched the rainwater cascade over the rooftop and licked his chapped lips.

The red-horned warrior returned, accompanied by the bare-chested man with the ponytail. He was now wearing a beaded necklace with a stone serak.

"Which one do you want, High One?" the warrior asked.

The ponytail man took his time choosing. When he got to Petrah, he closed his eyes. Petrah felt a prick at the base of his skull.

The ponytail man nudged with his chin and walked away.

"Looks like it's you," the warrior said to Petrah.

T HE HUT PETRAH WAS escorted to had a single room. Everything was thatched or woven—the walls, the roof, the door, even the chairs. A small, circular opening in the roof let in the daylight and rain.

It was drizzling now.

The water passed through a hole in the elevated floor, leaving the rest of the hut dry.

Petrah sat in a chair across from the ponytail man. The mist-laden light revealed faded tattoo symbols atop his stained scalp, strange geometric shapes with jagged edges.

The man stared at the journeyman with hard, bloodshot eyes that had witnessed much in life—unpleasant things, Petrah imagined.

He has the same ugly stare as Meska. Gods, what a look.

The man cracked his neck, tilted his head to one side, and wrung out the moisture from his ponytail. He said something to the red-horned warrior who was standing behind him.

"His Holiness asks if you need food or water."

"Water, please," Petrah said.

The red-horned warrior opened the door and called outside.

A moment later, an old man entered, carrying a wooden bucket with a ladle. He was short, had a Machoon bowl cut, mostly gray with streaks of brown, and a large wen bulging from a bony cheek like a third eye.

The man limped across the room, his grass-and-reed loincloth shaking to his lurching gait. He grabbed a ladleful of water and offered it to Petrah. "Master, drink."

Petrah was surprised to hear the Machoon speak Jurmehan. He drank. It went down in two gulps.

"More," Petrah said. He saw that the old man had one good eye, the other an empty socket with skin grown over.

The kindly man refilled his ladle.

"That's enough," the red-horned warrior said. He raised a hand to strike the skinny servant, but the old man ducked behind Petrah's chair. "Get out of here!"

The old man grabbed his bucket and scooted away on all fours.

The warrior turned his attention back to Petrah. "His Holiness has some questions for you. His Jurmehan isn't as good as his An-jek, so you and I will be talking."

The priest asked the first question, and the red-horned warrior translated. "Who do you work for?"

A SOLDIER SHOVED PETRAH into the cell with his friends. He landed face down, slimed with mud and bruised.

Tan helped him into a sitting position. "Are you all right?"

Petrah winced from where the red-horned warrior had punched him in the ribcage. "Like a new man." Petrah told them the bad news from his interrogation: he and his companions were branded spies and would be dealt with accordingly.

"What do you suppose they'll do with us?" Tan asked.

"What do you think, blockhead?" Kruush said. "They're going to cut us into pieces and eat us."

"Petrah," Tan said, "what if you contact Joriah? He might get through to that priest."

Petrah shook his head. "I can't do that."

"We're going to die, you realize that?"

"Even if I contacted him, he wouldn't know how to get hold of the priest. Mind links require unique signatures. Now leave me alone so I can see if I can get us out of here." But Tan's idea had merit. Master Joriah wouldn't be able to help directly, but he might know someone among the An-jurah who could. Or Uhtah-Pei might, considering his position within the Temple.

Or they might abandon Petrah altogether.

I've cut myself off from the people who could help me. How could I have been such a fool?

Petrah closed his eyes and lulled his mind into a trance. By the time he broke out of it, night had fallen and Sooka was still unconscious. Petrah wasn't any closer to figuring out the latching mechanism of their cell. Hunger pangs took over his thoughts, and he was thirsty again.

Kruush and Tan remained quiet.

The locals lit brands throughout the village. Villagers spoke among each other in the local dialect. They kept their distance from the prisoners.

"Pssst," came a sound from close by.

A head popped up outside the hut. Petrah saw the skinny shadow and recognized him. It was the short, older man who had given him water.

"What are you doing here?"

"Shh . . . mustn't speak so loud. Choola bring the masters water. Food, too." The villager lifted up a basket. He unfolded a palm leaf, which revealed a small pile of nuts. Next to them, he laid a handful of windy roots. Lastly, he squeezed a cup through a couple of the wider-spaced bars.

"Drink," he said, pushing the wooden cup forward.

Each of the prisoners took their turn drinking.

"Masters all right now?" Choola asked.

"Better," Tan said. "Thank you."

"Eat. I stay."

They ate. Within a few minutes, the food was gone. Petrah's head cleared again.

"I go now," Choola said.

"No, wait," Petrah said. "We need you to get us out of here."

The villager shook his head. "No, Master. Big trouble."

"Listen, they're going to kill us if we stay here. We have to get out." Then Petrah said, "What if we take you with us?"

The old man glanced at the neighboring huts skittishly and then stuck his face up against the bars. "Go where?"

"Far away from here," Petrah said. He made a movement with his fingers. "Escape."

The old man lifted his belongings and hobbled away. "No. Big trouble."

He ran off.

"Choola!" Petrah called. "Come back!" Choola disappeared behind a line of huts.

"You handled that just fine," Kruush said.

"Like you helped," Petrah said. "At least we're not dying of thirst and hunger anymore. We'll have to take care of this ourselves."

Petrah focused on the bars. No longer did his stomach grumble or throat feel like sandpaper. Now was the time—while he had the strength—to do something.

He concentrated on the wood and felt along the grain with his thoughts. There had to be a crack somewhere, something he could use.

He found one, a tiny vertical split.

Petrah formed a barrier of invisible energy. He thrust his hands forward and pushed out the barrier. It struck the cracked bar with no effect.

Petrah tried a second time.

This time, the bar jiggled. Still, it wasn't enough. A trickle of perspiration ran down his brow. "This is ridiculous. I know I could break these."

"Don't rush it," Tan said. "It'll come."

But it didn't, and the hours passed.

T HE DARKNESS LESSENED, SIGNALING the approach of morning.

Sooka snored steadily. Kruush gazed east, lost in whatever thoughts plagued him. Tan stared at his left palm, which he massaged with his right thumb. The humid air tasted heavy with rain. The only sound came from the buzz of insects or the occasional chirp of something up in the branches.

Petrah had tried a different tack the second half of the night. He discovered the winching mechanism below the floor of the hut and attempted to rotate it.

It wouldn't budge.

There was a rustle outside, followed by the clang of metal. The prison door swung up.

Kruush and Tan looked at Petrah, but the journeyman simply shrugged.

A head popped up, silhouetted by the dark.

"Masters," Choola called. "Come quick. Must go now."

The three squeezed through and dropped to the ground as quietly as they could.

"Come," Choola urged.

"Wait," Tan said. "We have to get Sooka." He pointed at the adjacent cell.

"No, Master. Must leave. No time."

Kruush ignored Choola and went to Sooka's cell. He found the lever at the base and depressed it. The door sprang ajar. Tan lifted it and tried to rouse Sooka. Sooka moaned but didn't wake up.

"We'll have to carry him," Kruush said.

They grabbed Sooka under the armpits and followed Choola, who was already moving away on all fours like a spider.

Choola hauled out a couple of straw sacks from the bordering undergrowth. "Supplies," he said, and handed them to Tan and Petrah. "Follow."

They moved as quickly as Kruush was able, with Sooka over his shoulders.

Kruush labored after them, staggering where the roots became congested. The jungle smelled like freshly dug earth with snatches of exotic plants and wildflowers and dung at other times, suffocatingly rich.

The dim of night faded by the step. The cloudless sky changed from dark to light blue.

An hour into their journey, they glimpsed sunshine in a clearing where several trees had fallen. Their first stop was by a trickling brook, where they drank their fill.

Petrah noticed their footprints on the soft earth. Anybody with tracking experience could find them.

We need to get well away from here.

"Where are we headed?" Petrah asked Choola. The smothering air made it hard to breathe.

"Away, Master. You'll see."

Petrah took his turn carrying Sooka. By midmorning, the jungle clamor settled down. Choola paused and sniffed the air several times. He babbled and scratched his head.

Tan was his usual paranoid self, which made Petrah even more uncomfortable.

Choola has no idea where he's going. He'll get us killed.

"This way, Masters," Choola said eventually.

He moved them in a different direction.

The ground rose. Then it split, exposing a hollow dug into the earth beneath one of the larger trees in the area. Clumpy strands of moss trailed down like a wig over something dark and reeking of death.

A den.

"Here," Choola said, parting the moss. "Get in. We wait until safe."

Tan peeked inside. "It's small. I don't think we can all fit in there."

Kruush whiffed the air. "It smells like a dead animal."

"Dead, yes. Good smell. Keep barks away."

"That may be true," Petrah said, "but the dogs will follow the scent of our trail here, won't they?"

Choola furrowed his brow and scratched the back of his head. "Maybe."

Petrah pointed at the narrow opening. "Kruush, get in there."

Kruush snorted. "There's no way I'm going—"

"Kruush!" Petrah said, irritated with his friend as much as he was with the stench. "Stop arguing and get your fat ass in there. So what if it stinks?

Here." Gingerly, he set Sooka onto the ground. "Help me get him in first."

Kruush and Petrah worked the unconscious guide through the den opening. The smell worsened and there was less space inside than Petrah had thought.

Tan and Kruush squeezed in after Sooka was in place. There was enough of a gap left for perhaps a child if they packed in or someone tiny, like Choola.

Choola looked at Petrah. "No room for us."

"But there's enough room for you," Petrah said.

Kruush poked his head through the opening and fanned the air with his hand. "Let's find another place. Somewhere less disgusting."

"There's no time," Petrah said. "Choola can squeeze in. I'll lead the scent trail away from here. We can meet up later. Stay put and I'll double back when we're in the clear, all right?"

"Are you mad, boy? You'll never—"

"I'm going. Wait for me." Petrah turned to walk off.

"Son of a krell," Kruush swore. He motioned to Choola. "Get in here, you!"

P ETRAH SEARCHED FOR A river or stream to wade into. If he did that, his pursuers might lose his scent. Perhaps they would parallel the course downstream or ford the waterway and continue their hunt on the other side. By then, they would be too far from his companions to be a threat.

Petrah thought he heard barking at one point. It grew distant, but now it was getting closer.

Dogs!

He ran.

He headed toward the roar of water up ahead. He leaped over branches, logs, and roots. The barking grew louder.

Faster! Run faster!

Hot air rushed into his heaving lungs. His legs hurt, but he couldn't stop to relieve the pain.

A glance over his shoulder confirmed his fear: the dogs were closing in. They were large hunting dogs with massive jaws and wild eyes.

Don't stop, don't stop!

Petrah pushed as quickly as his legs would allow.

He spotted a gush of water carving through the forest and followed its course toward a clearing where it disappeared from view. With all his strength, he sprinted. If he could get past the choke of ivy and roots, he might—

Petrah skidded to a halt when he discovered the clearing was the edge of a waterfall. He caught a loose vine to keep from tumbling over. Water surged past a jumble of rocks, burbling and misting as it dropped precariously straight down a hundred feet into a churning pool.

No, no, no!

He was stuck.

He started to reassess his situation when a dog took him down. Its teeth sank into his right clavicle.

Petrah screamed and thrashed.

He lost his footing and his grip on the vine.

The dog slipped, scraped at the slick ground with its claws, and then yelped as it went over the falls. Another dog knocked into Petrah, bowling him over the edge and yelping as the pair plummeted in a freefall.

Petrah flailed his arms. The roar of the falls cut the canine squeal short.

Petrah struck the water back-first, knocking the breath from his lungs.

Chapter 16
Beacon of Stone

F OR ALMOST A MINUTE, Petrah spun head over foot underwater, caught by the rotating current. Cascading water pushed down with constant pressure, preventing his escape. Every attempt to rise flipped him around and sucked him down.

Until he stopped fighting and started swimming.

Sideways.

Petrah emerged from the water and heaved air into his lungs. He clawed at tree roots, sputtering. With barely enough strength, he hauled his body onto the vegetation-choked bank and rolled onto his back. He begged himself to get up, to start running, but he didn't have the wherewithal. If he didn't start running, the dogs would find him. They would cut off his escape. They might rip him to pieces and leave his bloodied carcass for their masters to find.

Thankfully, the dogs didn't come.

In fact, there wasn't any sign of them. He thought he heard someone shouting at the top of the falls. When he squinted, he saw nothing but water and sky.

Petrah tried to lift his right arm, but the pain was too much. The dog had torn into the muscle above his collarbone. He touched the inflamed tissue through the hole in his saba, above the clavicle. He felt the gash and seeping blood. The bite had gone deeper than he first thought. He needed to wash and treat the wound before it became infected. But his friends . . .

Take care of yourself, then look for them.

Petrah tried to shake off the cloud of exhaustion. He needed to rally, to keep moving. His breath slowed, and he lost focus on the pain in his shoulder. He rested against the wet ground to clear the muddiness from his mind. One moment he was considering where to go, and the next—

—he fell asleep.

Petrah jolted awake in the early afternoon. Birds chattered in the surrounding trees. Water churned and branches sighed in the wind. By willpower alone, he shoved against the ground and set himself into a seated position. The waterfall pounded the water relentlessly ahead of him. He presumed the dogs had drowned.

I should have drowned too. I should be dead.

But he wasn't, so he pushed his fatigued and wounded body to his feet. He had to get back to the top of the falls.

Before he did so, he needed to tend to his injury.

Petrah found an alcove a short distance away where the bank formed a horseshoe indentation, blocking the ingress of the current. He took off his boots and removed his saba and bathed in the cool, fresh water, wary of potential predators and hunters. He washed debris from his hands and cleaned the wound. A flap of tissue hung below the semicircular avulsion where the dog had ripped into his flesh, tearing away some of the skin in the process and leaving the area pink, swollen and ugly. Honey could serve as an antiseptic, but now wasn't the time to find a beehive. Petrah used the sharp edge of a broken branch to tear the hem from his saba and then rinsed the strip of fabric and dressed his wound. He wrapped it over his shoulder and under his armpit, using his hand and teeth to secure a knot. He tested the snugness of the bandage and donned his saba.

Petrah spent the rest of the day searching for a way back. The more he searched, the more lost he got. By sundown, he was hungry, tired, sore, and smelly. He foraged until he found a man-high plant he thought he recognized from when he and Sooka went looking for tubers. It bore a crisscross-patterned stalk and an umbrella-shaped top. Petrah dug into the ground, brushed aside ants and beetles, and took hold of the heavy root. It was early evening by the time he wrestled the tubers from it.

He rested against the trunk of a moss-covered tree and bit into the wet, starchy lump and chewed. There wasn't any nausea or adverse reaction. If he didn't die in his sleep, he promised himself to find something better to eat tomorrow.

Now that he was no longer famished, he could think.

His priority was to locate his friends. Were they all right, or were they in terrible shape like him? He desperately needed their help. Without medicine or proper treatment of his wound, Petrah risked infection. Petrah had already come close to death when the snake in the desert bit him. He'd suffered chills, fever, and hallucinations. He didn't want to die from sepsis, nor did he want to get eaten by a predator or end up in the hands of hunters.

That meant finding his friends.

Or them finding me.

He could try to backtrack to where he left them, near the top of the falls. He had attempted to climb to the top earlier, which he thought was straightforward, until he realized there was no easy access up the sheer incline or the area surrounding it.

No, there had to be a better way.

What would a mage do in this situation?

Masters Nole and Maglo had instructed their students in various manipulations of the unseen—divine conduits that allowed the practitioner to alter the world about them with their thoughts or words of power. Petrah had communed with those around him, human and animal, and felt their life forces and spirits. He could see and navigate in the dark. He had started a fire, released a lock, survived a vaellra, levitated books, amplified voices through stone, moved objects without touching them, and communicated across vast distances. But none of that would help him find his friends. He needed to tap into aspects of the arcane arts he hadn't mastered yet.

If Master Maglo were here, lost in the jungle with nothing but his wits, what would the portly mage do?

Petrah pictured the old mage in his plentiful robes digging for tubers. It made him chuckle. The motion caused pain to flare up in his shoulder. He grimaced and tried to focus on the problem at hand.

Petrah thought back to how he had projected the images from his dreams into Kruush's mind. It was a mind link of sorts. He recalled the uniqueness of Kruush's thought patterns and how they differed from Master Maglo's and Master Joriah's.

Master Joriah's signature was always the same, like a heartbeat of the mind, with its own resonance. Master Maglo's was unique too.

Kruush's signature was different, a deeper tonal color that was rough and pitted. Since Petrah couldn't do an actual mind link with his friend, maybe he could project his thoughts. Maybe he could project his location, or better yet, signal a rendezvous point. Someplace that had a landmark unlike any other.

The falls!

Petrah shut his eyes and entered a trance.

ANANDAWA WAS INCENSED WHEN he learned Machoo hunters had captured his quarry. He was downright infuriated that Joriah's Gray Robe had been interrogated and even beaten at the hands of an An-jurahn red-horn, only to escape into the wilderness with his companions and get chased by dogs. The status and whereabouts of the four prisoners were unknown. If he had his druthers, Anandawa would have killed the red-horn.

He had bartered with the Idarians to gain the advantage of time and find the shortest route to his quarry. He'd handed over his tracker—much to Jobe's protests—in exchange for an escort through the jungle. He was still too late. Now, he was short a tracker, and Petrah was nowhere to be found.

I must be more resourceful.

But how?

Killing the An-jurahn might have brought temporary satisfaction, but it would do nothing to solve the bigger problem of finding Joriah's journeyman. The An-jurah in these parts served the warlord, Amal Dun, a vicious warrior and friend to the Ter-jurah.

But Amal Dun was not a friend of the Green Flame. That was despite Anandawa having met the warlord and the warlord having sent some of his best warriors to accompany Anandawa and his High Priest to the Shrine of San in Terjurmeh. Anandawa's influence was limited now that the priest was gone.

He needed help from the An-jurah to seek the Gray Robe and give the boy safe harbor. The Idarians in the area also served the warlord, so he couldn't go to them either. That left one avenue.

He mind linked Joriah. *I have a favor to ask of His Holiness.*

P ETRAH FOUND HIS WAY back to the waterfall in the morning and waited. It was late afternoon when he heard voices. Hunters. He sensed their approach, not from the top of the falls, but below.

Petrah cut into the jungle, away from the river. In his rush, Petrah lost his way.

When he tried to return to the river, he ended up someplace new. Evening arrived, and his wound ached and his belly rumbled. He was also thirsty. He sliced through a vine with a sharp stone he had found and drank water from it, as Sooka had shown him. Petrah forewent food, deciding to wait until morning to look for the crisscrossed plant with the tubers, after he rested. He had to conserve energy.

I can't afford to make any more mistakes.

If he couldn't get his bearings, he'd never escape this interminable jungle.

It rained at first light. Petrah drank by channeling the rainwater from a tree with wide, downward-pointing leaves. Food was his next concern, but he wasn't able to find any, except for a large beetle, which he smashed with the heel of his palm and ate. It had a nutty taste, but the mushy consistency almost made him retch.

Petrah couldn't tell how long or far he traveled.

He wandered in circles; other times, he covered what he thought to be great distances, only to discover the previous landmark still in sight.

Darkforth was vast and dense and unforgiving.

There was no one to guide him, no one to tell him where to go. He stopped often, marked his location—broken twig, bent leaf, rut in the soft earth—and started again. He hid when he sensed danger and sped up when he believed he was headed in the right direction. It was clear he was lost.

Not only that, he was getting sick.

The wound by his right shoulder was festering, and despite how often he cleaned it or exposed it to air, the puss continued to accumulate. Then there was the fever, which came and went. He eventually found a beehive, but when he tried to knock it down by poking at it with a long branch, the bees swarmed and stung him, and he had to run away.

Combined, his prospects looked bleak.

If he didn't end up getting eaten or eating something poisonous or dying from disease by the time he made it out of this mess, it would be a miracle.

I'm running out of options. I have to keep going, but where do I go?

He didn't know if Kruush had received his message, not that he had a viable rendezvous point anymore. For all he knew, Kruush and the others had found the falls and waited fruitlessly. Petrah thought of Ahleen, who most surely was worried to death over Kruush. He thought of Mina, too. He had pretend conversations with her in his mind to keep from going crazy from the isolation.

Petrah, I miss you, she told him in his thoughts.

I miss you too. Wait for me, my love. I'll come back to you, I swear it.

Her lock of hair was still in his pocket, and she would be with him until his parting breath.

Unless he fulfilled his promise.

Petrah hoped poor Sooka had regained consciousness with all his wits about him and that Choola had steered his friends away from danger. Then there were the horses. Petrah wished that Pepper at least had escaped the jungle and swampland.

One of us needs to make it out alive.

Darkforth was legendary for its lethality. There was a reason so few travelers returned to the civilized parts of the world.

You're smarter than this. You can either trudge aimlessly or pick a direction that makes sense.

Petrah sat with a handful of earthworms in his left palm, thinking about where to go. Their texture was atrocious, so he chewed quickly and sucked the squishy pulp down his throat. He needed something more substantial to sate his hunger and restore his strength. Worms and roots only went so far. He needed meat. It wasn't like he could hunt for food. He didn't have any weapons, so he was relegated to using his hands.

An hour of daylight remained.

Thick clouds mushroomed above. It would probably start raining in another hour or two.

I can think my way out of this.

No mind link, no mantras, just good old-fashioned contemplation.

He meditated. As he did, the first drops of rain thumped the waxy leaves around him. It turned into a downpour, and then steadied into a light rain. Nature's own mantra. It helped him concentrate.

Petrah took in the landscape and the surrounding area with his mind and then spread outward with his thoughts. Where was that beacon of stone the Watcher told him about? It had to be somewhere in the jungle. If he could find it, he could share its location with Kruush.

It was either that or die here, in the middle of nowhere.

I can't give up.

With his still-closed eyes, he turned his head north, then slowly moved it east a degree at a time. Petrah felt warmth in his forehead, starting on the right side. He turned his head left until the warmth hit center like it did when he sensed Kushan's presence. He ripped a stalk from a plant and set it on the ground, pointing to Hachaqua. At daybreak, he'd find his way to the pyramid.

T HE JUNGLE SPRAWLED ENDLESSLY in the clear morn.

Petrah maneuvered the riverbank, feverish with a persistent, dull throb in his infected wound. He stepped over convoluted roots that snaked their way from the mangroves into the water. Inland, they formed an impenetrable barrier so thick no person could get through, even with a machete. Twisting trunks climbed skyward, canopies high above the ground like green clouds. A symphony of hoots, shrieks, and squawks ran through the treetops as animals flew, hopped, or skittered from one branch to another.

This was the way. The right way.

Don't stop. Keep going.

Petrah paused every so many steps, felt for the warmth in the center of his forehead, and changed course, pushing deeper into the jungle.

His exposed skin was scraped, bruised, or bitten by mosquitoes or ants. His throat was parched from the humid heat and lack of fresh water. Still, he pushed onward, clawing his way through ferns and scrub, even crawling over knots of plants that rose from the jungle floor like hairs on his arms.

Petrah stopped often to rest—to lean against a tree or squat among the scattered, fallen leaves. He wrapped his arms around himself to stop the shivering, the chills that wracked his body, and to wait out the dizziness that had him stumbling over uneven terrain, lichen-stained rocks, and knobby shoots that sprang everywhere from the forest floor. Once the teeth chattering lessened and the fog lifted well enough, he resumed his trek.

After midday, when the sun reached its pinnacle, the jungle opened into a massive clearing several dozen acres in size. No trees, no brush, just ground and wild grass and . . .

A step pyramid rose into the bright blue sky.

Hachaqua. Beacon of stone.

Was this a mirage like the one he'd endured after the vaellra?

It can't be. It's too large, too real.

Petrah sank to his knees and cried. He'd found it! He'd found the pyramid.

The edifice was larger than his dreams revealed, larger than he wanted it to be, as he gazed upward. It was a mountain of giant stone blocks, easily a ton each. Sharp edges were weathered, smooth surfaces marred, and inscriptions all but faded. It had to be centuries, if not millennia, old. The only denizens now were a flock of black birds clustered atop a fallen section of stone. They cawed ceaselessly, a cacophonous welcoming to the newcomer.

Petrah closed his eyes and concentrated. The world spun around him, and he fell onto his side. He took in several breaths to let the wooziness fade, propped himself up, and tried again.

He projected the image of the pyramid in his mind to Kruush, along with the route he had traveled. If Kruush could describe what he saw to Sooka, they might piece together the means of getting here.

Petrah moved across the wild grass, then over the flagstones leading up to the pyramid's stairs. Giant stone urns, discolored and cracked with age, lined the ancient runway. He paused at the base of the stairs and looked up. The top was so far away.

He placed his foot on the first wide step and started upward. The stairs were grouped into sets of four, all steep. Petrah labored with each lift of his leg, each push with the opposite foot. He rested at step sixteen. Something was different. The black birds weren't cawing anymore. They sat together, maybe a hundred of them, watching him silently.

"What are you looking at?"

Some tilted their heads. Others wiped their beaks. They all watched him.

Petrah's head felt like it was on fire. Saddled with renewed chills that shook his frame and with teeth that rattled uncontrollably, he forced himself to continue.

The only sound now was his ragged breathing and that of soft-soled boots on stone. The higher he climbed, the more often he stopped. His joints hurt and his back ached. At one point, he slipped and caught himself on a jagged stair. He rested against the stone for several minutes, shivering. *Keep going*, he told himself. *You can't stop.* Groaning, he pushed away from the step and got to his feet.

Above, clouds drifted in. Each time he looked up, they seemed a little fuller, a little darker. By the halfway point, there was hardly a patch of clear sky. Two-thirds of the way, the sky had turned into a sheet of charcoal.

Like in my dream.

The last quarter of his ascent proved nigh impossible. His thighs and calves were cramped, his forearm muscles were strained, and he was juddering like a branch trapped in a violent windstorm. He kneeled and fell forward, pressing his head against the cool stone to gather himself. When he caught his breath, when he got his shivering under control, he reached up and clasped the next stair. He resumed his climb on all fours. Slow, grueling, and painful. Below, the birds were gone.

He crested the final step onto a rectangular platform and rolled onto his side, exhausted and soaked with perspiration. Broken stone plinths dotted the perimeter of the platform. Weeds sprouted from numerous seams from where the stone blocks came together. At the rear, a thirty-foot-high tetrahedron of stone formed the pyramidal capstone. One side was sheer, facing him with a narrow, recessed doorway shrouded in shadow.

Petrah detected a presence behind the doorway, different from a man's and definitely not an animal's. No heartbeat, but it was there—a palpable presence that gave him goosebumps.

Am I imagining this?

He squinted, trying to see if someone was there.

The air was still around him, oppressive with its smothering thickness. He felt outward with his mind, toward the presence. Spiritual energy radiated from the doorway, so strong that it seeped through the stone itself. The most powerful magi and priests of Terjurmeh emanated their spiritual energies, but this was greater than theirs, cold like iron in the dark and hot as the sun in the desert.

There was something else as well.

A barrier where the energy stopped, although it wasn't solid. Something lay beyond it, he could sense, cool and dry, and not of this world.

A portal.

The portal.

The gateway between worlds. It was here, and Hachaqua was the bridge.

A shadowed figure materialized from the doorway. It took a moment for Petrah's eyes to focus. By then, the figure had stepped forward into the light of day.

The Watcher.

He was seven feet at least, dressed in gray robes with a cowl drawn over his bare scalp and a metal staff grasped in his left hand with a loop of metal on top and runes running the length of the shaft, just as in Petrah's dream.

Lips parted to utter a single word that resonated with a metallic echo. "Immael."

How—? Petrah lost focus on what he was thinking. How was the Watcher here?

The Watcher moved toward the kneeling journeyman, dragging his robe behind him as if gliding over the stone. His uncanny height became more obvious the closer he got.

Petrah's vision blurred. He tried to shake it off, but it worsened the more he tried. The Watcher became an undefined blob, a backdrop of haze as he approached. Petrah was light-headed, his body heavy.

"What's happening to me?"

Petrah's sense of balance tilted and so did he. He landed on his left side, the dull ache of his right shoulder distant now.

The Watcher came up to him. He pulled back his cowl, revealing smooth, almost gray skin, hairless from chin to scalp, and eyes that glowed white.

"The sepsis runs deep," the Watcher said. His voice resonated like the slaver's gong in Kanmar. "You are fortunate to be alive."

"I tried—" Petrah started.

"I know," the Watcher said. "You have braved desert, hills, mountains, and jungle to get here. Despite your condition, despite being lost, despite being hunted, you have come to me. See how powerful destiny is?"

"My friends . . ." The world was spinning, growing dark. *How will they find me?*

"Rest now. Soon you will be ready to go home."

Chapter 17
Symorrah

TAN SCRATCHED HIS MOSQUITO-BITTEN brow while Choola prepped dinner. "We can't keep searching for him indefinitely."

They had found a cenote, a naturally occurring well hidden beneath the forest floor. Together, they sat on a dry landing of limestone beside a freshwater pool that ran clear to the bottom a dozen feet below. The air was cool and fresh, the water clean and invigorating. The cavern ceiling opened in a circle where it had caved in eons ago. They had already taken a dip in the water, cleansing the salt and grime from their bodies.

Kruush was mesmerized by the small, blind fish darting between flecks of white calcium deposits that floated atop the water while bats flapped around stalactites and soda straws made from limestone drippings.

When he heard Tan's comment, he fixed his friend with a heated glare. "Are you suggesting we give up?"

"I'm saying we can't last out here forever."

"We've lasted this long."

"So far."

"Aren't you the optimist."

"You're the grouch among us," Tan said. "Maybe a few bites of Choola's scrumptious feast will turn that scowl of yours into a smile."

Kruush sniffed with disdain at the roast snake Choola had prepared. It was wound around a spit like a corkscrew, its skin peeled away. The villager was very good at trapping all sorts of animals. But his choices, Kruush observed, were questionable.

Choola prompted with his skinny arms. "Eat, eat!"

"Choola's right," Sooka said, motioning with a weary hand. He was battered but able to walk, although their captors had broken his left wrist and done a number on his face. It was a mishmash of contusions. Choola had made a splint of wood strips and palm fibers for the wrist. "The meat is good for us."

"Yes," Choola said, bobbing his head up and down like a turtle. The wen on the side of his cheek looked as if it hurt.

Kruush appreciated Choola, even with his quirky mannerisms. He'd saved their lives.

It was Choola who had found the cenote, claiming it as a place where rituals were performed to honor the ancestors of his people. An old, wood offering vessel lay several feet away, along with evidence of powder burns on the limestone and bits of charred leaves. According to Choola, it allowed his people to see spirits and ancestors through a haze of smoke from burnt offerings.

Kruush sampled a piece of the meat. The snake was tough, sinewy, and tasted like bland fish. He had to pick out the small bones. "This is terrible."

"You're welcome to go fishing," Sooka said. "Jah knows there are plenty in the water around you. Judging by their bulging eyes and lack of pigment, I'm sure they're packed full of flavor. Go on and regale us with your culinary prowess."

Kruush snorted. "Thank you very much, master guide. You are delightful, as always. Any other helpful tips you care to add?"

Sooka flashed him an irritated look and went back to eating.

"We need to keep searching," Kruush said to all of them. "Petrah's out there, and he needs our help."

Tan flicked a small bone with his finger. "We have nothing to go on. Choola's not a tracker. You're not either. I'm certainly not good at it.

Sooka's the only one with a keen sense of direction, but he can't divine which way Petrah went, assuming Petrah's—" Tan stopped himself.

Kruush spat out a bone. If he would have known Petrah would disappear, he would have insisted they stick together and find an alternative place to hide. "He's alive. I feel it in my soul."

"Because you've seen images," Tan said.

"Yes. Remember in Tuur, when Petrah showed me his dreams? It's just like that. I wish he would have shown you, too. There's a pyramid among the ruins in an opening in the jungle. It's massive. Every four steps, there's a landing and then another four steps, and so on until it reaches a platform at the top of the pyramid with stubs of broken pillars marking the perimeter. In the center of the platform is a triangle of stone the size of a mudbrick house, with a shadowed entry that disappears into a short tunnel. He wants us to go there and climb to the top, to that very triangle."

"To do what?" Tan asked.

"To wait for him."

"And then?"

Kruush huffed. "And then we destroy that blasted portal. He was clear on that long ago."

"I don't remember any mention of a pyramid," Tan said. "Then again, you two were conspiring on several occasions, thinking I was asleep."

Kruush chuckled. "That we were. But you were awake."

Tan smooshed his lips in distaste. "Say what you want, but I still don't know why we need to climb some godforsaken pyramid. If it's anything like the monstrous pyramids the Korinians built, no thank you. I've heard they're so tall, they scrape the sky."

"They're tall," Sooka said, "but the largest is maybe five hundred feet. That doesn't take away from their massive size. The Machoo built pyramids as well, but theirs are shorter. They built them a couple of thousand years ago when they were at the height of their civilization.

They had kings who ruled chiefdoms, and each chiefdom had built cities of stone in the jungle and buildings where people lived and worshipped and even sacrificed."

Tan wiped the grease from his hands. "What was the purpose of these pyramids?"

"They served as cultural and spiritual centers," Sooka said, "where people would congregate for worship, mostly. The pyramids honored the old gods: wind, thunder, war, and fertility, to name a few. The pyramid Kruush described belonged to a particularly nasty Machoon king who liked to capture occupants of rival chiefdoms and sacrifice them to San, well before the other kingdoms gave up the old gods and converted to Sanism. They'd impale their captors at the top of the pyramid and let the blood gush down the steps."

Tan made a face. "That sounds wretched."

Sooka nodded. "It gets worse. The queen would partake in the rituals, adding to the display in front of her loyal subjects, piercing her tongue and drawing a twine with small barbs through the hole in her tongue as blood cascaded from her mouth." Sooka tugged with his hands as if pulling down on a rope. "Other members of the royal family would also take part in bloodletting, numbing themselves by smoking tíka leaves and then piercing their lips and genitals to gain favoritism from their gods over their rivals. Pretty barbaric, if you ask me, but it worked to maintain fealty and frighten their enemies."

Kruush shivered at the cruel image forming in his head.

Sooka went on. "The Machoo continue these traditions, but Choola said they avoid Kruush's pyramid in particular. It's forbidden. Trespassers supposedly suffer horrific deaths and have their spirits tormented in the afterlife. I think the superstition would work to a visitor's advantage, ensuring unchallenged passage."

"That's all well and good," Tan said, "but how does it matter to us?"

Kruush scrunched his forehead into a grimace. "Don't you see? What better place would you stick a hole in this world to another if you wanted to keep the locals and tourists away? You'd find the scariest place, that's what you'd do."

"And you got this all from these images Petrah shared?" Tan asked.

"Aye, I did."

Tan glanced at Sooka, who shrugged. "So what's the plan?"

Kruush rubbed his hands together. "The plan is simple. We show up, climb to the top, and wait."

P ETRAH STIRRED AWAKE TO the view of clouds and treetops passing by. He was on his back. Although the world was still spinning, he could tell he was moving through the forest. He craned his neck and saw a skinny man at the foot of the litter Petrah was on. His litter bearer had a bowl haircut and was garbed in a grass skirt with a tribal necklace of teeth over his bare chest. Where was the Watcher?

Before Petrah could turn his head to look over his shoulder, he passed out.

When he awoke again, he was shivering under a pile of blankets. Muted daylight revealed the inside of a hut thatched with dried palm fronds. The space smelled of mint and rot. The rattle of his teeth, his hoarse breathing, and his sniffling from a nose dripping with mucus—everything was amplified in here. A tattoo-faced man stood over him, examining his face.

"Who are you?" he asked the tattoo-faced man.

The man said things Petrah couldn't understand. The echo of his voice added to Petrah's dizziness. Petrah closed his eyes until the echoing disappeared.

When he opened his eyes again, an obese, dark-skinned woman had him drink from a hollowed gourd. She fed him. When he had to pee, she aided him. When he slipped, she caught him. The tattoo-faced man came and went. He inspected Petrah's wounds; prodded his ribs; made Petrah lift his right arm, then the left; and applied salves sweet with honey. Each time he spoke, his voice echoed loudly.

One morning, Petrah awoke with no one in the hut. He felt his forehead. It was cool. He waited for the spinning to return, but it didn't. When he pushed away the blankets and rose to his feet, he discovered he could stand on his own.

Petrah found his saba on the floor next to his cot, stitched and cleaned, although brown stains remained where his blood had set in. He poked the inside of the pocket with his fingers. Mina's lock of hair was pushed to the bottom, but it was still there, thankfully.

Petrah rotated his right arm and palpated his injury. The wound was tender but healing. He rubbed his side and felt the sharp relief of his ribs. He couldn't recall his hip bones protruding so much or his legs appearing so spindly.

This place . . .

Maybe I'm dreaming. Maybe the fever is still with me.

There was one way to find out.

Petrah slipped on his saba and stepped outside.

He emerged to a settlement in the middle of the woods. There were huts—primitive dwellings like he'd seen in the villages of the Machoo. He looked for signs of people. There weren't any, just pigs eating noisily from a trough in a pen by a patch of farmland that had gone fallow.

Across from the pigs was a small palapa with a wood altar underneath and bowls for offerings, one still smoldering. The sky was overcast, the air stale with a hint of sulfur, and the leaves not as verdant as they should have been. It was a strange setting. So still. So quiet. Almost surreal.

Petrah turned to find the Watcher standing silently behind him, his staff gripped in his left hand. Petrah startled and clutched his chest. "Where did you come from?"

The Watcher's voice hummed with its metallic tone. "I've been here, waiting. You look well enough." From this close, Petrah could see the unnatural grayish tone of the Watcher's skin, the lack of hair, wrinkles or blemishes, and his thin lips. His pupils were jet-black, no white glow as Petrah had seen while fevered atop Hachaqua. It was as if the Watcher were a statue chiseled from stone. The most disturbing thing was the lack of a heartbeat or drawing of breath. There was a strong spiritual presence, though, much more pronounced than the soul of an ordinary man, even a mage or priest.

Petrah pulled at his saba, which draped loosely off him. *I'm a skeleton.* "How long was I out?"

"Five days."

Five days? That's an eternity!

Even if Kruush had received his message, even if his friends had found the pyramid and waited, they would be gone by now. Either that or in serious trouble. The threats in Darkforth were too many to count. His heart sank like a stone in water.

"You're troubled," the Watcher said.

Petrah was more than troubled. His plan had gone terribly awry. "I've lost some people close to me."

"The companions who accompanied you to Darkforth."

Petrah looked up at the Watcher's pale face—porcelain gray in the light—and smooth head. He was impossibly tall. Did he age? Was there a soul behind his black eyes? Was he even a man? Or was he an immortal, a being from the elder days, from before humans graced the world? "You know about them?"

"Only that they escaped when you did."

That told Petrah nothing. "Do you know where they went, what happened to them, anything?"

"No. They are not my concern. You are."

Petrah's glimmer of hope vanished. He looked about the empty village, trying not to let the Watcher's callous response bother him. "Where is everyone?"

"The villagers have gone to Symorrah to pay homage to their god. Come, I will show you."

They traveled for some time through the forest. Petrah labored to keep up, after having been bedbound for days, but the Watcher was patient.

They climbed up an especially high incline to a promontory that gave way to a valley far below, as vast as the eye could see and as desolate as dry chalk. No vegetation. No lakes or rivers or streams. Nothing but an inhospitable stretch of land broken by small hills, a plateau to the east, and a mountain with smoke rising from the top in the center. The air was laden with sulfur. Hundreds of shapes were on the move, a military contingent on horseback and on foot, heading toward the mountain.

"I saw this place in a dream," Petrah said. "Except you were over there." Petrah pointed toward the mountainside in the distance.

"I was." The Watcher tipped his staff east toward a neighboring plateau. Its sheer walls dropped into the valley. "What do you see?"

"Rock."

"Look closer."

Petrah did. The indentations in the rock face were manmade. There were dozens of towers, columns, terraces, entranceways, and entire buildings carved from stone. A city within the bedrock. A more thorough inspection revealed hundreds of people milling about.

"This is Symorrah?" If it was, it put them well east of the pyramid and even farther from Âhn, where Petrah and his friends had been captured.

"This is the capital of the An-jurah," the Watcher said. "There's more to see beyond that ridge. The city spans dozens of miles in all directions. It was built almost three millennia ago, after the An-jurah sundered into two peoples in their fight against the Con-jurah. The Ter-jurah remained in modern-day Terjurmeh; the An-jurah settled here, then spread throughout Darkforth, splintering into factions. Slowly, they have come together over the past century, territory by territory. The North is already united while the South coalesces into one body. Soon, all of Darkforth will fall under one banner. We stand at the end of the world, a very special place."

"What's so special about it?"

"Her." The Watcher pointed at the smoking mountain with his staff. "The An-jurah call her *Vanya* in the ancient tongue. It translates to 'Mother.' She's in labor now." A plume of smoke rose high into the atmosphere from the cratered mountaintop, seemingly frozen, although Petrah could discern the slow churn of smoke near the mouth and a glimmer of red along the rim.

"Shouldn't those riders be going the other way?"

"Vanya's been in labor for centuries," the Watcher said. "There's still time before she gives birth. Until then, these people are safe. But after, only those with faith will survive."

Vanya reminded Petrah of the Holy Scriptures. "'The Mother shall give birth to the Dragon, and he will smother the light with smoke and fire and drive fear into the hearts of the Unbelievers.'"

"The verse you recite is from the *Book of Prophecy*. It speaks of smoke and fire, but do you know what the Dragon actually is?"

Petrah envisioned a scaly, fire-breathing winged serpent from a folk story. But if the Dragon from the Scriptures was to come to pass—

He would be worse. Far, far worse. "I don't."

"He's a great leviathan of molten fire, growing as we speak within his mother's womb, deep below the ground, the likes of a creature the world has never seen."

Gods help us!

The Watcher opened his arms, holding his staff aloft. "The Dragon shall be born of fire, spewed forth from this very mountain, and take flight over these lands. He will spread his wings as a mammoth shadow and rain down ruin upon the enemies of San. Can you imagine such a sight?"

Petrah didn't dare imagine it. He felt his mouth go dry and his skin turn cold. "This is certain? The Dragon's coming, that is?"

"Without a doubt. One need only dig deeper into the Scriptures to unearth the Prophecy of Darkness.

"A shadow destined to cover all
A fire to rage with endless hate
A darkness that will have no end
And seal the world in its fate

"The Great One's arrival will signal Vanya's birth. That birth will set into motion a cataclysm the world has never seen. From it will come eternal night. So it is written, so it will come to pass." The Watcher drew back his arms and set down the butt of his staff. He peered at Petrah with his black pupils.

"This place is not only the end of the world but also its beginning. It is here where the first people of Acia walked. Before that, only one other place in the heavens knew the heartbeat of mankind: your homeland, where you were born. Its people have renamed it Dagoth, the Dragon-lands, for much of it has been laid to waste, as if scoured by dragons. Before that, it was Aerth, the 'land of plenty.'"

Petrah's dreams were filled with wastelands and devastation. How could he have come from such a frigid, merciless place? Who could stand living there?

"Jah spawned your kind from the dust," the Watcher said, "where the rains mixed with the earth, and the mud took shape. The mud dried. Then it cracked, and out came the first man. Jah saw that man was good, and he begot the first woman, and your kind multiplied and prospered. But man became wicked, for in his heart, he harbored lust, greed, hate, vanity, and jealousy. From those desires, he warred and killed and even murdered."

The Watcher paused, black eyes dulled. Perhaps he was pondering the extent of humanity's failings. Or his own. "And Jah, angry with his creation, saved but a handful of the Chosen and flooded one end of your world to the other until all the evil was snuffed, or so he believed. But Jah never could understand the hearts of men—not as well as us Watchers or as well as San, the Father."

"But he didn't destroy my world," Petrah said.

"No, he let it destroy itself. The descendants of the Chosen multiplied, and again, they warred with each other. Jah deemed mankind wicked and without hope. When the generations that followed repeated the transgressions of the past, it brought him great sorrow. Your world could not forsake the corruption that marred the descendants of the Chosen. Jah's angels prayed to the Creator to start over, to find a place far away from us Watchers, the ones blamed—and punished—for man's downfall. So Jah took the ashes of the Chosen's bones and made man here in Acia millennia ago."

"How old are you?"

"Older than all of your ancestors."

No wonder you have no heartbeat, Petrah wanted to say. "Are you an angel?"

The Watcher's black pupils shimmered. "All the Watchers were angels. We were your guardians, your protectors, your teachers. We loved you like children."

"But something went wrong."

"We could only coexist with people so long before succumbing to desires of the flesh, and so we begot our own children. A whole race in fact, great and proud, like their fathers, but reviled by the Maker—and destroyed by the Great Flood." Petrah had not seen any emotion in the Watcher before, but now his dark pupils probed the horizon as if reliving the events of a painful past.

"Jah's wrath was mighty, his punishment swift. You don't know what it's like to see your children drowned, their lives erased. The Great Flood took them all. We were the only ones to survive—bound in chains, prisoners of the very earth we loved, forced to suffer until Kingdom Come." The Watcher's voice took on a harsh edge, like steel against stone.

"But you escaped," Petrah said.

"Your father freed me. I came here to teach the people of this world the secrets the heavens would not want them to know; to teach them the truth, as your father wanted it. And by doing so, the children of Acia have become independent and resourceful, strong and fearless. In the Creator's eyes, they've become tainted and befouled—all because my kind had opened their eyes. But we all know the hypocrisy of that. Jah's angels view us with contempt, but they are the ones who should be looked down upon."

Lightning flickered across the clouds, followed by a peal of thunder that rumbled across the rocky plains. The Watcher's skin took on a deep gray tone, like slate.

"The angels of Truth stand by your father's side, restless and eager to reclaim the heavens and snuff the light that has blinded humanity since the beginning. As your father knows, there's nothing but lies and judgment left in Heaven. It has become a shallow place."

Petrah's stomach knotted. It wasn't a mortal whose seed had begotten him.

But a god.

San, God of Shadows.

Bringer of darkness.

And, soon, the end of civilization.

Not for the Ter-jurah or the An-jurah or Idarians or Machoo, who all prayed to Petrah's father. They would be spared.

But Meerjurmeh, the Northern Kingdom, Korin, and the Provinces of the South; anyone who prayed to Jah and who was devoted as a Jahnist—their lives were in peril. That included the Con-jurah . . .

. . . and Mina!

The Dragon would spare no one in Hōvar. If it truly was a monster of fire, the city would be torched to cinders. Mokan-lee and his family would perish. Mina would die too.

The Watcher remained quiet as Petrah's worries raged in his mind. The once-angel leaned against his staff, his face an impassive gray, his expression unreadable. He reeked of fell power. He was a divine instrument for his master to wield upon Acia. If he was San's servant, what did that make Petrah?

San can't be my father. He can't be!

How could Petrah be the progeny of a god so bent on destruction?

I'm a son in name only. An orphan with no more godlike lineage or power than Ajoon or Miko. And yet the darkness that cloaked his sleep told him otherwise. Oma had seen it too. The demon within him, his demigod self. It groaned from the deep, calling, calling . . .

A rumble from the mountain made Petrah flinch.

"It's nothing," the Watcher said. "Vanya moans, her womb full. When the time comes, your brother will pluck the child from her, but that time is not at hand, not yet."

A chill rode up Petrah's neck at the thought of his brother setting the end of the world in motion. If he were truly Petrah's brother.

Another family tie I've accepted on faith alone.

"You need not fear your brother," the Watcher said, picking up on his trepidation. "He has grown to become loved by all. You'll see that when you meet him."

"In my dreams, they call him Aman." *And they chant his name endlessly.*

"It's his given name, just as yours is Immael."

Petrah heard his mother whisper from the shadow of his dreams. *Immael, come back to me.* He missed her, even if he couldn't remember knowing her. His time before slavery was still a mystery to him. Crossing from Dagoth to Acia had stolen more than his memory; it had taken his mother away from him too.

But there was a way to see her again . . .

"Tell me about the portal."

"It is a gateway between worlds," the Watcher said. "A special doorway, bridging Dagoth and Acia. I am its guardian, its Gatekeeper, and keeper of its secret. That is my purpose. You are the Key, the one to unlock the gate. That is your purpose."

Petrah had a question that had been on his mind since the Watcher first revealed Petrah's purpose in a dream after Miko's death. "When I asked you if the portal might allow my brother through, you said, 'Only if you guide him through.' What did you mean by that?"

"Jah has barred the way for him. Only you have the power to unlock the gate from the other side."

"Why is that?"

"Because you are a child of San and a child of the solstice, and the twain have imbued in you a special ability, written in the stars for all the angels to see. Jah might have barred the way for your brother, but even he can't stop you. The cosmos adheres to order, as do its angels. Fate guides us across its constellations and seas of stars, precisely and without wavering. We each serve a purpose, and we each have a part to play on this vast and intricate cosmic web. Try as we might disentangle ourselves, we can't, whether we are a lowly fish or an immortal god. We are all beholden to fate."

The heaviness of the Watcher's words pushed down on Petrah, making him wobbly in the knees. He'd known hopelessness as a slave, but this was much worse. The Watcher made it seem as if he didn't have any choice; that forces unseen were shaping his movements, pushing him forward to make him do things against his will.

Fumes of sulfur assaulted him. How could the An-jurah endure this vile place?

"It's not as calamitous as you believe," the Watcher said, again reading him like a page in a book. "You are the son of Truth. You walk upon a strand of stars in the great web of the cosmos. Look at all you have achieved, from escaping the bondage of slavery to learning the arcane arts to wending your way to me. Now, you stand at the barrier between worlds. On the other side, your brother marshals his army. Worry not about that. He will call upon you in due time. Of import is your mother. She's waiting for you. You've witnessed it in your dreams. She wants you to come home to her. I know you want it too."

Petrah had tried to find a word to describe how he felt about returning to his homeland. It wasn't until he'd left Maseah that he understood.

I'm homesick. That's what it is.

Even so, his purpose wasn't to see his mother. That wasn't the point of risking his life to come to Darkforth.

My purpose is to destroy the portal. I can't let my feelings about my mother get in the way of that.

He'd made a solemn oath to Tan and Kruush in Tuur to come here and sever the bridge between worlds. Petrah's mission was clear to him now, as it was then. By breaking the gateway, he'd end Aman's chance of coming to Acia. He'd prevent his brother from wreaking havoc upon the good people of Acia.

Petrah recommitted his vow as he breathed in the poisoned air.

I won't allow Aman to come here. He'll never set foot in Acia. And Vanya will never give birth.

Petrah couldn't allow the Watcher to know this. He needed to make the once-angel believe he would go willingly to Dagoth. The Watcher would believe him and take him to the portal. And then . . .

There was no *then*.

Petrah didn't have a plan.

That fact did not take away from his promise to destroy the portal. Once the Watcher brought him to the gateway, he'd have to figure out how to dismantle it and do so quickly. He'd used his wits to unlock his manacles aboard the slave galley and help the slaves escape a fiery death. If he could do that . . .

I won't fail. I'll do whatever it takes. I'll die if I have to.

With that, he turned to the Watcher. It was time to put his skills to the test. "I'm ready to go home."

The Watcher, as unreadable as the gray sky, lifted his staff. "Then I will take you there. But first," the Watcher said, "I have someone I want you to meet."

Chapter 18
Lesson

The Watcher guided Petrah through the jungles of Dark-forth, west toward Âhn. It took four days to reach their destination on foot. The Watcher never slept, never left his side. Blackened fingernails dug into the metal of his staff as if they were fused together. Even when Petrah had to relieve himself, his guardian was there, always a few strides away.

He treats me as a prisoner. Where could I possibly go?

Petrah wasn't like the Watcher: he needed rest and sustenance. When exhaustion overtook him, he piled leaves into a bed and slept. When hungry, he dined on rations taken from the village where he had convalesced: cakes made of ground corn, harvested yams, and salted pork that had been dried and smoked. He carried the foodstuffs in banana leaves tied with twine.

Petrah's one peace of mind came from the fact the Watcher could protect him against threats in the wild, human or animal. They encountered a band of Idarians on the third afternoon, men and women armed and on the hunt with spears at the ready. As soon as they saw the Watcher, they bowed their heads, murmuring prayers. The Watcher's spiritual energy hummed like his voice, emanating power unlike anything Petrah had known. No wonder the Idarians feared him. The longer Petrah spent with the Watcher, the more he realized this was no man at all.

Only a man can be killed. But an angel . . .

On the morning of the fourth day, with tattered clouds above and the smell of recent rain, the pair reached a fortification set in a clearing. Timbers at least twenty feet in height formed a wall of banded stakes, their sharpened points raking the sky. Within the walls were buildings made of wood, including an armory and soldier's barracks. An-jurahn warriors were busy training in the courtyard, practicing swordplay and hand-to-hand combat. It reminded Petrah of when his friend Taka would train with his garrisoned brethren at Maseah.

The Watcher led Petrah to the only stone structure in the compound, a round tower with a black metal serak mounted over the doorway. Two strangers were waiting for them, a female Terjurmehan priest with short dark hair and a tall mage who bore the robe of the Green Flame.

Petrah's heart thumped in his chest. Had the Watcher brought him here to return him to Master Joriah? Petrah's fingers tingled with cold sweat.

The Watcher greeted the priest. "Holy One."

"Gatekeeper," she said, bowing her head. Her voice was like iron and her deep brown eyes predatory. The hairs on Petrah's neck stood on end when she looked at him.

The Watcher introduced the woman priest. She exuded a confidence and brutality that made Petrah want to shrink away from her. "This is Her Holiness, Nisheppeh, Third Articulate of the Temple of Terjurmeh. She is the Terjurmehan Temple's official liaison to the An-jurahn Temple."

Nisheppeh regarded Petrah with cold eyes. "At last, I get to meet San-Jahad's little brother. I am honored to meet you, Petrah. Uhtah-Pei speaks highly of you."

The mention of Uhtah-Pei unsettled Petrah. *Now His Holiness will know what has become of me—and so will Master Joriah.* He remembered his manners and tipped his head forward. "Thank you, Holy One."

Next, the Watcher introduced the man who wore a gray cloak over a black robe and boots spattered with dried mud. He had dark, curly hair and a long face with deep frown lines. "This is Anandawa, a magus of the Green Flame."

Petrah stiffened at the mention of the mage's name. This was the mage he was supposed to meet in Tuur? And he was here, after everything Petrah had done to elude him? Petrah forced himself to incline his head. The mage barely dipped his chin in response.

How is this possible? How did he get here?

Petrah expected Master Joriah to step out from the shadows at any moment. His fingertips were now ice cold.

The Watcher said, "He has scoured forest and swamp to find you, haven't you, Anandawa?"

Anandawa gave the journeyman a hard look. "You were a difficult one to track down. If you would have waited another day in Tuur, we could have journeyed here together. It would have saved us both a lot of heartache." His words carried a strong edge of resentment.

If I had waited another day, we'd be back in Elmar, not here. "Apologies, but I was beset by a greater calling," Petrah said, hoping the brevity and loftiness of his answer would suffice. He also hoped the Watcher would step in on his behalf to corroborate his excuse, but he didn't.

"You could have at least let Master Joriah know your intentions. You owe him that."

"I know," Petrah said, lowering his brow in shame, "but I don't think he would have understood the purpose of my journey here." The whole point of leaving unannounced was so Master Joriah could never learn his intentions of going to Darkforth. Those intentions were foiled now that Anandawa was here. The mage would mind link Master Joriah and let him know he'd found Petrah.

But Petrah was in the Watcher's charge. No one would challenge the angel's authority. Certainly not Anandawa. If the Watcher was set on sending Petrah to Dagoth, neither Master Joriah nor Uhtah-Pei could do anything about it. That took the worry away that the Watcher had come here to hand Petrah over to Anandawa.

Anandawa went on. "I was informed your captors beat you, and you almost died from infection. You seem to have recovered. Are you well?"

"Better than I was before," Petrah said, still feeling a dull ache where the dog had torn into his flesh. He would have a scar for the rest of his life, adding to the tapestry on his back. *What is this mage getting at?* Petrah couldn't understand the purpose of their meeting. "I'm tougher than I look."

"So it seems." Anandawa's voice took on a bitter tone. "While it irks me to have chased after you through jungle and muck, and it rankles me to no end to know my efforts were for naught, there is a silver lining. We're both going to have our satisfaction today. We're going to mete out justice the old way. You see, our An-jurahn allies are our blood brothers and sisters, but even they forget their ties sometimes. Come. Let us remind them."

Petrah couldn't dissect the meaning behind the mage's words. His heart was beating too fast for him to think clearly.

The mage led the group over to the center of the courtyard, where a solitary wood post rose from a stone block. Bound and slumped against the post was the red-horned warrior who had ordered Petrah beaten. His helm was off, leaving untidy, brown hair tumbling over his face.

Petrah halted sharply, surprised to see his former captor. Had the man found his friends? Had he done something to Kruush, Tan, or Sooka, or even Choola?

Anandawa gestured to the bound man. "Is this him? Is this the man responsible?"

Petrah curled his fingers into fists. He wanted to punch the red-horned warrior in his already bruised face. The man's cheeks were swollen, and his left eye nearly shut, reminding Petrah of Meska on the day he'd gutted

Aggren. Just like Meska, this man had gotten a taste of his own medicine. That didn't make Petrah any less eager to blacken the other eye. The man even stunk as the Draadi had, a mix of sweat and rotten meat. "That's him."

"Did he know you were Ter-jurahn?"

"I told him, but he didn't believe me. Or he did, and he didn't care."

Anandawa grabbed a fistful of the man's hair and pulled back, forcing him to look at the mage with his one good eye. "Remember this young man?" He pointed at Petrah. "You do, don't you? Didn't expect to see him alive, did you? We've kept you alive so you could witness this moment, the moment your life came to its wretched end."

The man looked at Petrah, but Petrah had no pity in his heart for what this fiend had done. It was because of him that Sooka had almost died. It was because of him that Petrah and his friends had been forced to flee into the jungle. And it was because of him that Petrah had lost his friends, perhaps never to see them again.

The red-horned warrior spoke to Anandawa, although the fire was no longer in his voice. "The Machoo captured them. They lied to us!"

"But you're the one who imprisoned them."

"We had already caught their Con-jurahn guide. This one was different from the others, not like any Ter-jurahn I had seen before."

"And how many Ter-jurah have you seen before, exactly?"

"This one was different, I'm telling you! The priest chose him for questioning, not me. We thought he was a spy."

Anandawa yanked the warrior's head to the side. "Is that why you struck him? Is that why you sent dogs after him?"

The warrior's face creased in pain. "He escaped with the others. How could we have known he was one of yours?"

"You should have known." The mage let go and turned to Petrah, eyes blazing. "He's yours. Finish him." The mage stepped aside and folded his arms.

The An-jurah in the courtyard stopped what they were doing and congregated around to witness the spectacle. Nisheppeh had a hungry look, an eagerness Petrah found appalling. The Watcher stood off to the side, quiet and expressionless. Petrah chilled at the thought of what they were expecting of him. He needed to save face here. How?

The chill burned off when Petrah saw the leer on the red-horned warrior's lips. He had questions for his former captor.

"What happened to my friends? Where are they? What did you do to them?"

The warrior glared at Petrah, defiance set in his bloodshot eyes.

"Answer me!"

The man spat at Petrah's feet, then turned his head away.

Petrah clenched his fists again. *He knows! He has to.* How dare this animal deny him? He was another Miko, another heartless monster that needed to be put out of his misery.

But Petrah hadn't set out to take Miko's life. Miko had forced Petrah's hand. He'd given Petrah no choice. With this red-horned warrior, Petrah had a choice. He could walk away.

I can't just kill him.

Yet it was the only outcome that would be accepted.

I can feign his death, make him pass out. I'm not a killer. I'm not!

But he was. He'd thrust a sword through Miko's throat.

He'd also ended Meska's life, using a word of power to push the Draad into the clutches of desperate and furious slaves. A fitting end to such a hateful creature.

Now there was this red-horned warrior. Another mar upon the world. Another hateful creature.

Maybe I can give these people what they want without this man dying.

But if Petrah figured out a way to make the man go unconscious, Anandawa would know. The Watcher, too. And Her Holiness, Nisheppeh, would surely know. Her eagerness for bloodshed outshined them all, with her mouth open in wait like a krell slavering before a kill. Petrah didn't trust her to keep quiet. He suspected she'd turn on him, point a sharpened fingernail his way, and demand he rip the red-horned warrior's throat out until the man bled dry.

Which returned the argument to its original premise: the red-horned warrior would have put Petrah's friends to death. Didn't he deserve the same?

If Petrah took this man's life, then he'd be no better than a murderer. How could he face Mina again—someone who saw him as a compassionate human being, not a cold-blooded beast?

Everyone's eyes were on the former journeyman. Petrah had to act. He was out of time.

Forgive me, Mina. This isn't the man I wanted to become.

Petrah sensed the warrior's elevated heart rate and smelled the stink of unwashed hair and sweat. If their roles had been reversed, Petrah's life would have been forfeited by now.

The warrior regarded him with contempt. "Go on. What are you waiting for?"

Petrah probed along the man's throat with his mind. He felt the windpipe and arteries that carried life-sustaining blood. Petrah averted his gaze and clamped down with invisible fingers of pressure.

He squeezed, but couldn't watch.

The warrior choked. He flailed his legs. Petrah squeezed harder, praying the man would pass out first from the blood loss to the brain. The flailing intensified. Then there was a pop of cartilage, and Petrah let go. The man wheezed and bucked against the restraints.

Anandawa pointed. "Kill him already!"

Petrah froze. The warrior continued to choke and gasp.

The Watcher moved in.

With a whoosh, he swung his staff in a deadly arc. The loop struck the warrior atop his head with lethal force. The blow flattened the man to the ground, bludgeoning his skull in the process, the looped end of the staff lodging in the man's cranium. The Watcher yanked his staff free. Blood and brains erupted from the bloodied cavity in a revolting finality to the warrior's death.

"It is finished," the Watcher declared, bringing his staff upright.

Neither Nisheppeh nor Anandawa said anything. The entire An-ju-rahn congregation held their tongues in rapt silence. It was as if the world had come to a standstill.

The Watcher motioned to an outbuilding. No evidence of glee, anger, remorse, or satisfaction. Only the cold steadfastness of a being without a soul. "You will rest here tonight," he told Petrah. "Tomorrow, you journey home."

Chapter 19
Portal

Morning brought with it a crushing gloom. The stench of death and decay from the surrounding jungle invaded the warm, humid air as if the soil had been infused with the remains of the felled red-horned warrior.

The Watcher led Petrah away from the encampment in silence. Petrah felt a sense of relief when he'd crossed the threshold of the village and reentered the jungle. It was if he could breathe again.

Had the Watcher's point in taking Petrah to the encampment been to teach him a lesson? That the son of San must be ruthless if he was to gain the favor of his father?

Or his brother?

The Watcher has no desire for me to reunite with my mother. My sole purpose is to meet my brother. Then I'm to return here with Aman and his army. I'm but a tool to them.

Petrah had other designs. The Watcher believed Petrah was beholden to fate and prophecy, but Petrah wanted to believe he was the master of his own destiny.

I will destroy the portal, and Aman will be trapped in Dagoth. Then the Watcher will realize his folly.

But questions remained: How was the portal made? What was it made of? What could negate it?

And the most important question: Could it be destroyed?

Petrah's heart thumped in his chest. He didn't have the answers.

There was a second option. If he couldn't determine how to break the portal, what if he went through it and went after Aman? Could he stop his brother? Could he prevent a war?

If I can't, I'll end up stuck on the other side.

Then Petrah would never return to Acia, never see Mina again.

And what of his friends? Were they even alive? If so, could they trek through the unforgiving wilds of Darkforth to make it past the Eastern Gates into friendly territory? And journey home on foot with scant resources at their disposal?

They'll make it. I know they will.

Petrah revisited his dilemma: could he destroy the portal?

The individual who knew strode in front of him, cloaked in gray and with a staff in his left hand.

Why can't I find the solution?

The answer was an I-told-you-so directly from Kruush's lips: *It's because you didn't finish your training.*

Petrah trudged behind the Watcher between tall trees draped in moss, haunted by his inadequacies. Training aside, he was a channeler who had mastered the ability to sense objects with his mind; to levitate and listen through stone; to communicate vast distances; and to manipulate the mechanisms with just his thoughts. Surely he could devise a method to undo a portal between worlds.

Then there was the matter of location. In his dream, the portal had been on a field wide enough to allow three horses to pass at a time. An entire column of militia could make it through in several hours. The one at Hachaqua was narrow and prohibitively difficult to navigate. Could there be two portals, or did the first lead to one place and the second return him to another?

"I have a question," Petrah said, pushing through a jumble of leafy groundcover. Fresh rains brought out the scent of the forest floor. "When it's time to come back, how will I know where to go?"

"Your brother knows," the Watcher said succinctly, maneuvering the undergrowth with implausible ease.

"How does the portal work, then?"

"You step through. It's as simple as that. I have created the gateway for you."

"Are there others? Gateways, I mean?"

The Watcher turned, sweeping up leaves with the rapid motion of his robe. "Why are you so curious?"

Petrah stopped and stared up at the gray-skinned angel whose cold eyes bore into him like a draft in the mountains. "I have a right to know. After all, I'm the Key, aren't I?" Petrah hoped his resolve would hold up under the Watcher's scrutiny.

"Suffice it to say there can be a multitude of gateways at any time, but only those with the power to make them can control their existence." The reply was ambiguous and confusing, and Petrah didn't know how to untangle his thoughts well enough to get what he wanted out of the answer.

"Why can't my brother go through another portal, then?"

"Was I not clear in stating how Jah has barred the way?"

"But he hasn't barred me?"

"Is a key not a key? As long as there is a lock, it can be unlocked. You are the Key. That is your purpose."

The Watcher continued their march, and Petrah was left to mull over the angel's fatalistic words.

They arrived at the pyramid by early afternoon.

Hachaqua stood quietly, a mountain of immovable stone rising toward the angry sky where clouds gathered hungrily, ready to unleash a torrent of rain upon the land. The black birds were back, cawing atop a fallen section of stone. When the travelers reached the steps, the birds settled down and stared with unwelcome determination.

The Watcher paused at the bottom of the incline. "Someone's been here," he said, surveying the area with his black, gleaming pupils.

Could it be . . . ?

Petrah was afraid to finish the thought, as if doing so might jinx himself. Instead, he suggested something to keep the Watcher from suspecting otherwise. "An-jurah perhaps?"

"The An-jurah know better than to tread on these holy grounds. All are forbidden—the An-jurah, the Idarians, even the Machoo, whose ancestors sacrificed their enemies and cast the heads down the steps for all to behold." The Watcher sniffed the air. "No, someone else has been here."

Petrah grew hopeful. Had his friends come here in his absence? Were they all right and not harmed as the red-horned warrior led him to believe? Were they out in the forest, searching, or perhaps watching right now? Maybe they could distract the Watcher and give Petrah the time he needed to attack the portal.

"Does it really matter?"

The Watcher kept still for a moment, then said, "No, it doesn't," and led them up the stairs.

The Watcher seemed to glide while Petrah labored to keep pace. Unlike his last attempt up the colossal pyramid, Petrah didn't have to lie down or crawl. He was winded, and his leg muscles screamed from the exertion, but he made it to the top—all two hundred sixty stairs, which he counted to keep his mind off the burn in his thighs and calves. The Watcher waited for him by the tetrahedral capstone. The narrow doorway lay behind him, a blackened recess from which no light could penetrate. Once again, Petrah was aware of a presence in the dark, a barrier both impenetrable and permeable, a gateway to another plane, sealed by a means beyond his reckoning or comprehension.

"I promised to take you home. I have brought you here to fulfill that promise," the Watcher said, extending his staff toward the doorway. "You are brave, Immael, and strong. You have much to learn to unify your spirit with the divine, but I have confidence you will achieve greatness at your brother's side. Go to him. Complete your destiny."

Petrah's palms perspired in nervous anticipation as he peered at the doorway. It was so dark, a black rectangle leading into a passage. The Watcher's gateway was at the end of it. He wanted to run in the other direction, to disappear into the jungle and hide.

Petrah had no plan, no solution, no idea what to do next.

He was just a cog in the wheel of fate, as prophesied by the angel in front of him. If fate brought him here, then it governed every aspect of his life.

His slavery.

His mage training.

His mission to Hōvar.

Mina, too.

Here, he needed to take control of his fate . . . and outsmart the Watcher. Wasn't he the master of his own destiny?

He'd seen what the Watcher had done to the red-horned warrior with his staff. The angel's strength went beyond any mortal's. The Watcher exhibited no emotion, but he could kill at will. If Petrah defied him, would he take the same swift action?

There was only one way to find out.

Petrah took a hesitant lungful of air. "Where does this portal lead?"

"To the outskirts of an ancient city of iron. Fear not, you will find your way. Your brother's army controls the city and territories around it. All you have to do is come across one of his riders and show this." He reached into his robe and pulled out a medallion necklace and handed it to Petrah.

The necklace's supple chain formed links of gold. Suspended from it was a medallion with the thickness and shape of a coin, gold with a reddish hue. It was stamped on the front, bearing the relief of a serak as a perfect triangle with a lidless eye in the center. Along the circumference were runes, like markers along a sundial. The backside showed a serpent uncoiling from the center, wreathed in flame with different runes around the edge. The medallion was heavy and cold, unlike any metal Petrah had ever known.

"What is it?"

"A talisman of divine origin that may only be worn by the blood of the god of gods. It was cast from the molten rivers of the Netherworld and cooled in the darkness of the nether planes. No mortal has ever touched it, nor shall they. And while you are of the flesh—a mortal, by any definition—your father's ichor flows through your veins and will protect you from the necrotizing effects of the metal. It will also protect you from the dangers of beholding this device. If another were to peer into the Eye of Truth, they would go mad. You will wear it proudly and present it to your brother. Woe to any who seek to claim this talisman for themselves. Put it on."

Petrah's heartbeat quickened in his chest as he let the medallion hang from the finely wrought chain. It didn't spin or sway, but simply dropped earthward and went still. He lifted the chain and spread it with his fingers. He draped it over his head. The medallion slid down his breastbone until it came to rest.

When he released the chain, the metal sucked into his skin. In a panic, he tried to pry it off by its edge. "Why can't I lift it?"

"It has found its rightful owner. Go now, son of Truth. Find your mother. Let her see you grown and well. Seek your brother. Learn from him and become who you were born to be. You and I will meet again when the time is right."

Petrah dug his fingertips into the medallion's edge, but still, it didn't budge. He let go and peered over his shoulder at the dark passageway. He could see the stonework inside, pristine as if never touched by weather or human hands. At the rear stood the portal, shimmering like a pool of water.

He felt it with his mind, using the same feelers he'd used aboard the slave galley.

How do I destroy it?

Could he channel the right divine energy to cancel it? Could a word of power take it down? Perhaps a Kantaka move like Miko had used, employing his hands to shape arcane energy into a focused, destructive force?

"You tremble," the Watcher said.

Petrah noticed it too, although he couldn't stop the shaking. "Just nerves."

"Fear not, for the only way is forward, and the only destination is glory. Now go." The Watcher set his metal staff down with a hollow ringing that vibrated in Petrah's ears.

This was it.

I will step up to the portal, and before the Watcher can stop me, I'll destroy it.

And if the Watcher created another portal?

The thought unsettled Petrah. Could the Watcher really do that?

Petrah's mother had pushed him through a portal when he was eleven. Where was the one she'd used? Petrah had ended up in Terjurmeh. Surely there was another portal in Dagoth, one she knew about.

Petrah's feet moved on their own. He couldn't delay any longer.

He continued to use his mental feelers to test the surface of the shimmering pool. There was no sensation to it, no beginning or end. No edge and nothing to latch on to, just a fading off along its circumference. How did it function?

Petrah stepped up to the passageway and placed a hand on the hewn stone. It was worn with age and inscribed with weathered pictograms that showed animal symbols of a race long gone.

The Watcher remained behind, standing statue-like where Petrah had left him. The greater the distance between them, the more time Petrah had to act. In truth, it amounted to mere seconds.

Then I'd better act quickly.

The passageway wasn't deep, perhaps twenty feet, maybe less. But it was dark, oddly cold, and heavy, as if the stone walls rested their weight against him from all sides.

Petrah stopped about an arm's length from the shimmering oval that was the doorway between worlds. Behind him, the entrance to the passageway was gray and bright. Beyond, through the portal, he could make out the haze of another place. Not a jungle, but a dim hillside that seemed barren of foliage.

Petrah closed his eyes.

He dropped his mind into a meditative state as he'd practiced in Master Ecclesias's class, a technique magi used when on the battlefield and were about to engage an enemy in haste.

Petrah opened his mind.

Power flowed into him like a vessel receiving water.

Push, he told himself. *Sunder this portal from its bearings. Use your instinct and destroy it.*

Energy accumulated in his fingers, warm, then hot. He spread his arms to either side of the oval, mirroring the shape with his thoughts. He'd warp the portal, so it bowed outward, then he'd speak a word of power to thrust forward and dislodge the portal from its invisible hinges.

As he attempted the feat, another presence filled the stone passageway from behind.

The Watcher!

K RUUSH COULDN'T BELIEVE HIS misfortune. For three days, he'd waited atop the pyramid with Tan and Sooka while Choola kept watch from the jungle below. And for three days, he and his companions were prepared for Petrah to climb to the top and have Choola distract the Watcher so Petrah could destroy the portal. Once the portal was destroyed, they'd flee and return home.

As soon as the Watcher began his ascent up the pyramid, Kruush and his companions took to the sloping roof of the pyramidal capstone to lie in wait. The Watcher crested the top landing first, trailed by Petrah. Kruush expected Choola to come running out, to make lots of noise, but he was nowhere to be found. Choola needed to draw the Watcher away from the capstone and at least partway down the stairs for their plan to work.

But Petrah went inside the tunnel of the capstone, and the Watcher followed shortly after.

Curses and more curses!

This wasn't how it was supposed to go!

Tan helped Kruush slide down the capstone. Quietly as he could be, Kruush hugged the stone support that buttressed the passage entrance.

He poked his head inside.

His eyes adjusted to the dim. Petrah was about twenty feet away, standing in front of a shimmering oval that gave off its own light. The boy's back was to the giant Watcher who was closing in, staff and body taking up the entire height of the passageway.

Petrah, behind you!

Kruush gathered his voice to shout the words, to make the Watcher stop and turn around, to bait the giant to go after him.

But as his lips parted, the Watcher pressed the loop of his staff against Petrah and shoved him forward.

Petrah fell through the portal . . . and vanished.

Kruush caught his breath. Petrah was gone!

No, no, no!

The Watcher started to turn. Kruush pulled away, out of view. His heart pounded.

Tan helped Kruush climb back onto the capstone roof. He relayed Petrah's failure to Tan and Sooka with a defeated shake of the head, then motioned for them to flatten themselves. They lay perfectly still. The Watcher emerged seconds later. Kruush glimpsed the back of the giant, who went partway across the platform and stopped, about ten paces from the passage entrance. The Watcher set the butt of his staff against the stone. He faced away from the capstone, cowl drawn, and went still as a marble column.

Kruush's mind raced. *What to do? What to do?*

There was only one thing to do.

They would have to sneak down the side of the capstone, enter the passageway undetected, and go through the portal after Petrah.

And hope they'd find him on the other side.

Preview of the next book in the series

K EEP READING FOR A sneak peek of **Book 3**, *The Dark that Binds*

The Plunge

K RUUSH PEEKED OVER THE beveled edge of the capstone's sloping roof and cursed under his breath.

The Watcher hadn't moved, not one inch since he had taken up his post by the stairway running down the length of the giant pyramid. How long had he stood with his back to the capstone, cowl drawn over his head, black fingernails dug into the shaft of his looped staff? Mere minutes? Longer? It was as if he'd turned to bronze.

He's become a blasted statue, Kruush thought, clenching his jaw.

Kruush scanned the flagstone-laden grounds around the pyramid far below. They were dotted with grass, brush, and palm trees, along with the ruins of several ancient buildings of worn stone. Sprawling jungle surrounded the complex, thick as the humid air that clung to his skin.

Where was Choola? The strange, little man was supposed to emerge from the jungle, make a ruckus, and draw the Watcher away from Petrah to give the young mage the chance to destroy the portal. Had Choola misunderstood the plan? Or had he lost his nerve and left Kruush and his companions to fend for themselves?

He's a coward, that's what he is.

Kruush ducked his head beneath the one-foot lip of stone that edged the capstone and wiggled his body backward, flat on his belly. Tan and Sooka looked at him expectantly, also on their bellies.

"The Watcher's still there, same spot," Kruush whispered. "No sign of Choola, either."

Sooka, irascible to begin with, scowled so hard his eyebrows knitted together like a long caterpillar. "I told you that depending on him was a bad idea. Did you listen to me? Of course not."

"Did you now? And what glorious plan did you come up with instead?" The heavy stench of the jungle was getting to Kruush, a mix of moist earth, decaying leaves, and tropical gloom.

Sooka slicked back his ragged mop of reddish-brown hair, exposing the sheen on his forehead. "You hired me to take you this far, and I did. Is it my fault we're stuck up here? I'm a guide, not a magician."

Kruush swatted a mosquito. If he never stepped foot in this wretched place again, it would be a blessing. "Petrah needs us. We can't wait here indefinitely. What if the Watcher stays the rest of the day and through the night? We need a distraction to force him to leave."

Tan flicked sweat from his brow with his thumb. "We can't depend on Choola to distract him, now that he vanished."

"I know that," Kruush said, trying to keep his frustration from getting the better of him, as it had Sooka. "It's that confounded Watcher. He's—" Kruush didn't know how to describe him. "Inhuman."

Never had Kruush seen the likes of such a man: tall beyond conception and skin as smooth as a river rock, with a robe that matched the drab, gray patina of his complexion. There was no rise or fall of his chest, no shift of his fingers or feet, nothing but absolute stillness and an unnatural aura that made Kruush's blood run cold.

He's not a man at all.

If he wasn't a man, what was he?

"We can be stealthy," Tan said. "We climb down, nice and quiet, and sneak into the passage below us undetected. Twenty feet of passageway, and we're through the portal. As long as the Watcher keeps his back to us, we can make it."

"And if he turns around?" Kruush asked. "You've not seen how he moves. He's quick as the wind, like nothing you've witnessed. And he wields that staff of his like it's made of bamboo." Kruush shivered, remembering how swift and nimble the Watcher had been and how he'd pushed Petrah through the portal with the tip of his staff before Petrah had the opportunity to destroy it.

"Even so," Tan said. "We should take the chance."

A rumble of thunder cracked from the east as the wind picked up. It smelled like rain. Hiding on a slope of stone was no place to be if a deluge hit them.

Kruush swore, pulling on his matted beard. "Fine, let's take our *chance*. Sooka, you agree?"

The scowl remained on the guide's face. "I'm not going first, if that's what you think."

"Did anyone ask you to go first?"

Tan volunteered. "I'll do it."

"No," Kruush said, twisting his beard into a knot. "It should be me. Then you, then Sooka. And then we—"

A shout broke from the distance, distinctly human. Choola?

Kruush and his companions crawled to the edge of the roof. Kruush peered over the stone lip.

Choola appeared from the jungle, a tiny shape hopping across the field on all fours and waving his arms wildly like a baboon. He yelled up to the Watcher. "*Chakata!*"

The Watcher, still standing at the top of the long stairway running to the base of the pyramid, swiveled his cowl toward the Machoon intruder.

"*Hoomeni da chakata ma!*" Choola called.

The Watcher replied in the same language, his voice ringing out as if striking a temple bell. "*Na Hoomeni!*"

Choola beckoned the Watcher with excited hoops of his arms. "*Chakata ma!*"

The Watcher stepped down the first few steps.

That's it! Kruush thought. *Keep going.*

"*Chakata!*" Choola insisted.

The Watcher took several more steps, then stopped. Only the top of his cowl was visible from Kruush's vantage point.

Go on! Just a few more stairs.

But the Watcher remained where he was, even with Choola taunting him.

"Let's go," Kruush whispered to the others.

Carefully, he slid down the angular stone. Kruush dangled his legs over the eave and dropped as quietly as possible to the landing just below. He backed against the flat face of the tetrahedral capstone and waited for Tan.

Tan wasn't as graceful. His boots thudded the stone loudly.

You idiot! Kruush wanted to yell.

The Watcher climbed several steps and snapped his head toward them. Inky, gleaming eyes peeked out from his cowl.

Kruush froze, breath caught in his throat.

Then he shoved Tan through the narrow passageway. "Move!" He followed right after him. The blackened tunnel ended in a wall with a shimmering oval that floated in front of it.

The portal between worlds.

The oval emitted hazy daylight from the other side—an impossible illusion, considering there should have been a solid wall behind it. The shimmering reminded Kruush of swimming under the surface of a river and looking up through blurry, water-filled eyes. He could make out trees and sticklike towers beyond the rippling face of the wall.

Kruush pushed Tan forward. "Go!"

Tan stumbled and reached out with his hands. A second later, he disappeared.

Kruush turned. Where was Sooka? Just then, the wiry guide appeared at the mouth of the passageway. But as Sooka headed inside, he was flung backward as if he had been caught in a fisherman's net. A horrified look crossed the guide's face, followed by a piercing wail.

And then he was gone.

Gods help us!

Kruush plunged through the portal as if chased by a demon.

New World

THE FIRST THING PETRAH noticed after stumbling across the portal was the hazy sky—wisps of clouds strewn above, masking the afternoon sun—and that he was alone atop a hill with withered, brown grass, and not a soul in sight. Then the cold hit him, the thick jungle heat replaced by a gust of chilled air filled with the scent of tree sap that made his eyes water. With hands tucked into his armpits, he took in the downward-sloping hillside that led to a valley and a strange city beyond, or what remained of one. The jutting towers of metal and stone clustered together like a band of tall shadows. He could barely make out the shapes through the blur and sting of his tears.

This was the new world.

Dagoth.

His homeland and the wintry domain from his dreams.

And it was freezing.

He'd used his first few minutes on the unfamiliar landscape to search for a spot to shield himself from the unforgiving wind. A minute's walk from where the portal hovered unaffected by the drafts over the short, brown grass, he came upon the edge of a forest of birch and oak, stripped of their leaves. The branches shuddered in the wind and the boughs creaked hauntingly. Petrah found an oak with a wide trunk to block the gusts from scraping his face. Leaning against the sturdy tree, he slipped into a trance using Copper Still, the mantra he'd practiced as a mage journeyman. The world stilled, becoming quiet and distant. Drawing from his channeling skills, he summoned an invisible shield to block the crosswind that nipped at him. It was similar to the one he'd formed to protect against the sandstorm in the great Agobo Desert months earlier.

His teeth stopped chattering long enough for him to blink away the wetness in his eyes and take stock of his situation. He was woefully underdressed in his body-length saba, whose thin fabric did little to protect him. His heavier clothing had been lost when the Machoon hunters had pursued him and his friends in Darkforth. The saba had been plenty warm in the heat of Âhn. But here . . .

Here, it's frigid.

How could the Watcher allow him to come here so unprepared? He hugged his arms to his chest, still deathly cold.

"Allow" was the wrong word.

He pushed me.

The Watcher had shoved him through the portal, and Petrah's opportunity to destroy it from the Acian side was lost.

Petrah shook his head as an upshot of wind dug under his shield, drawing fresh tears. Could he have destroyed the portal, if given more time? When he'd finally made it to the portal, after so much agonizing effort, he'd realized his arcane skills were no match for the powerful magics that had created it. He might have studied the portal for centuries and still lacked the knowledge to undo it.

Petrah peered past the forest's edge, past the grassy slope and valley, to the ruined city of crumbling iron buildings far in the distance. Now that the wind wasn't blinding him, he saw the city was as large as Meerjurmeh's capital of Hōvar and was bordered by a wide river. If he left now, he might find shelter for the night inside the city. But from his vantage point, with trees in the way, he couldn't take in the details well enough to decide how to approach the enormous city. He needed to return to the clearing, to the top of the hill where the portal hung, suspended impossibly off the ground, an oval shape that reminded Petrah of a mirror he had seen in Mokan-lee's manor.

Comforting warmth lay behind the barrier, nagging at him, begging him to return to it, to cast aside caution and step through.

No, he couldn't chance it.

He'd seen what happened when he touched the portal's surface from the Dagothan side in his dreams. It had given Aman clear entry to Acia. Would touching it now, from this side, break the seal between worlds? Or had he already done so when the Watcher had shoved him through?

The right thing to do—the *only* thing to do—was to destroy the portal. But how?

Petrah projected mental feelers to probe the portal's shimmering surface.

He couldn't grasp the edges or find purchase. Was he too far away?

His invisible shield faltered, letting in more cold air. Numbness crept back into his toes, fingertips, and face.

Bracing against the biting chill, he reinforced his shield and strode toward the portal. The gateway between worlds defied the wind that swept across the brown, dead grass.

A few paces short of the shimmering oval, he stopped. The portal swirled at the edges, darkening at the center, hinting at the dark-gray stone of the pyramid passageway on the other side.

Not quite confident his shield would hold, he slipped back into a trance. Again, he extended his mental feelers, sending out tendrils of thought to probe the portal. The portal produced no surface tension, no resistance, nothing to latch on to. At least if he could grasp the edges using a tethering technique, he might be able to manipulate the shape of it, maybe collapse it. Was the portal more like smoke or mist rather than liquid or some type of membrane? If it was, why did the wind have no effect on it?

Petrah's shield faded again. He was losing precious strength—and energy. He gave up on the portal. The shield was more important. So was finding shelter.

Petrah turned his attention back to the city. Without the trees in the way, he was able to discern more details. Dozens of buildings spanned the skyline, taller than any he'd seen in Acia. Windswept clouds cast them in swaths of bronze and gray.

The structures appeared as a twisted system of chewed metal scaffolding, the same as he'd observed in his dreams. Many were stripped of their facades, leaving behind exposed latticework of beams, girders, struts, and columns. It was as if the gods had come down and battled among them. They were all different heights, the tallest higher even than the great stone pyramid, Hachaqua.

In his world of Acia, metal was rarely used in construction. The Ter-jurah and Con-jurah used stone, the Korinians too. The Prallites used lumber to erect their homes, and stone and timber to make fortifications. The artisans of the Provinces of the South, rich with forests, also crafted their abodes from wood.

It appeared the ancients of this world had used metal instead, and they'd clad their structures with stone and precious rectangles of glass. Petrah counted twenty rows of glass running up one of the taller towers. Twelve on another. Sixteen on a third. All the glassblowers of the Provinces in Acia, combined, couldn't produce glass on this scale.

Outside the city limits stood two bridges, also in shambles, spanning a river to an arid stretch of land that was as bleak as the Derel Wastelands in North Terjurmeh. A road carved through the desert, leading to a range of mountains beyond. As Petrah squinted to see down the distant road, he spotted what looked like settlements comprising a handful of smaller dwellings of stone, gray and beige in the light. They were too far away to tell whether people lived there or if they were abandoned by time.

The Watcher had called this place "the Dragonlands," the desolate remnants of a once-flourishing civilization, now laid to waste, as if a dragon had scoured and scorched everything.

But no dragon had done this. This was the result of time and decay. Dagoth was named for its emptiness, and emptiness Petrah felt.

He pulled his saba around him. He needed to find refuge from the wind. The woods offered none. The city was the obvious choice. If Petrah sought soldiers loyal to his brother's cause, he could show them the gold necklace with the medallion the Watcher had given him. They might grant him shelter. The necklace was oppressive in the way it stuck to his chest, like a lodestone against iron.

As Petrah battled to keep his shield intact, questions flooded his mind.

Why hadn't the Watcher warned him the weather would be so harsh? Why hadn't he provided Petrah with a cloak? Why hadn't he set the portal in the city itself?

Which begged another question: where was Petrah's brother?

Petrah had expected Aman to be waiting for him astride his coal-colored horse, surrounded by soldiers on horseback, like the ones in his dreams.

I'm all alone.

Not that he wanted to see his brother. That would just make Petrah his prisoner, and Aman would force Petrah to take him back through the portal.

Petrah trembled as the frost seeped into his skin. He was losing sensation in his cheeks, earlobes, the tip of his nose, toes, and fingertips. He wiggled his toes and flexed his fingers.

With his dwindling reserve of energy, he willed himself into a trance. Projecting his mental feelers once again, he felt outward, toward the city.

Find someone . . . anyone.

He did. Not just one person, but many.

He sensed human heartbeats, faint but present. From what he could tell, the majority of heartbeats were congregated in a tight knot along the eastern and western fringes of the city. Scattered throughout the rest of the city were pockets of people, some on the move.

He widened his search in all directions and noticed a strange shift behind him. Something was happening with the portal. His shield fell away as he lost his concentration. Petrah turned just in time to see two men stumble through the shimmering gateway, one after another.

"Tan! Kruush!"

Kruush ran over to him and grabbed his arm. "The Watcher's coming! Run!"

Tan veered in the forest's direction as if he hadn't seen Petrah, and Kruush ran after him. Petrah chased his friends, shouting, "Stop!" He pushed ahead, overtaking Kruush and then reaching Tan in time to grasp a handful of Tan's saba and yank him to a halt, colliding with him.

Tan tripped, then wheeled, wild-eyed, before recognizing Petrah. "Petrah!"

Petrah drew in hurtful swallows of cold air. He gave Tan a hug, then Kruush. "How did you find me?"

Tan spoke first, drawing his arms close to his body for warmth. "Kruush did. Tell him."

"It doesn't matter," Kruush said crossly, sucking in a mouthful of air. "Gods, it's freezing. Why is it freezing?"

"It's winter here," Petrah said. The brief chase had warmed him, but now he was shaking again, slurring his words from the numbness in his cheeks.

Tan darted his eyes through the trees and toward the portal. "You think the Watcher's coming?"

"I don't know," Petrah said, rubbing his hands together furiously. "But I think the more pressing concern is freezing to death."

"But he saw us!" Tan said.

"And he got Sooka, poor bastard," Kruush added. "But I agree. We'll freeze to death standing here."

Tan looked around, briskly running his hands over his arms. "Where do we go then?"

Icy wind stung Petrah's eyes. He pointed behind him, toward the city. "There. It's our best chance."

Kruush shook his head. "I heard what that Watcher said. He *wants* you to go to your brother. If we stumble into the wrong people—"

"I know that," Petrah said sharply, getting more annoyed by the frigid breath, which burst out in foggy plumes. "What choice do we have?"

"I thought the plan was to destroy the portal," Tan said between chattering teeth.

"I—I can't," Petrah said. "I tried."

"We're on the wrong side, anyway," Kruush said, shivering.

"Coming here was a mistake," Tan said. "We need to go back—" He stopped, looking at the portal. "Wait, something's happening."

The portal's surface rippled as if a storm raged across the surface of a lake. Then it began to dissolve. And shrink. Its edges collapsed in on the center. A few heartbeats later, the portal was gone.

Tan ran over and swiped his hand through the air where the portal was standing a moment earlier. "Where is it?"

Petrah's breathing turned shallow as dread stole the breath from his lungs. He'd intended to destroy the portal. But now that it was gone . . .

Tan raised his voice in alarm. "Where is it, Petrah?"

"I—" Petrah started. "I don't know."

"What do you mean, you don't know? How do we get back home?"

Petrah's jaw ached from his teeth rattling, and his eyes were a watery mess. His neck hurt from shivering so hard. "We have to find shelter before it gets dark." He pointed at the city. "We go there. Agreed?"

Tan, now a quivering, cold mess like Petrah, nodded reluctantly.

Kruush's face blanched as if he'd realized he might never see his wife again. He nodded as well. "Aye, let's get away from this wicked place."

Visit https://www.stevepantazis.com/lod3 to get **The Dark That Binds**, **Book 3** in the series, or scan the following QR code.

Acknowledgments for The Light of Darkness series

T HIS SERIES HAS BEEN decades in the making and has taken on many forms, culminating with the book you just read and the other books in the series.

As many an author can attest, writing is a lonely pursuit, but bringing a work of fiction to life and making it the best it can be requires a team. For those who've helped me along the way, I am truly grateful. What follows is a list of extraordinary human beings who have lent their sharp eyes, astute minds, and brilliant suggestions to me during my journey with this series.

Because *The Light of Darkness* started many moons ago—back when I thought my nine-book series would be a duology; then, a trilogy; and finally, the nine books it has become—I need to acknowledge three talented editors: First, there's Michael Wolf, who made all his amazing edits using a red pen and printout of the manuscript. Then there's Joshua Essoe, who tackled the beginning of the story. And, finally, Jonathan Miller, my current editor, who went above and beyond with his masterful edits and thoughtful suggestions, and pushed me to take my story to the next level.

Then there are my alpha and beta readers, starting with those who helped with the earlier version of my work (in no particular order): Daniel Piangerelli, Roy Hamilton, Janis Flax, and Andrew Alberti. My alpha (first) reader for this latest version of the series, Leslie Bridgwater, who dove into uncharted waters and offered indispensable feedback. And the beta readers who volunteered to read and comment on my work: Karen Harrison, Jerry White, Kate Julicher, Candice Lisle, and John Parus. A many thanks to you all.

Of course, we mustn't forget the gorgeous cover art and interior artwork.

The covers would not have been close to where they are if not for the critical eye of my good friend, Wulf Moon—an author and artist in his own right—who helped me choose the best color palettes, action poses, and lighting, and advised me on "guiding the eye of the reader on a journey."

For the cover design and creation, I want to thank my cover artist, Les (Germancreative), who worked tirelessly to make the eBook and print covers for all nine novels and the prequel novella. She created a brand for the series that offers an engaging and consistent look and feel. No matter how many revisions I requested, Les rose to the challenge to produce her best work.

While I can claim credit for creating the maps of my fantasy world, my artist, Sam (Samsul Hidayat), turned them into masterpieces, each with an engraved look that's both classical and timeless. He also made the background art you see at the start of each chapter. Ten custom pieces of art, one per book, based on the book's theme.

Because of my long voyage at sea with this series, which began as a watercolor map I painted in 1992, there will be those who helped me but whose names have slipped through the cracks of my ship. Know that your kindness and generosity are not forgotten and that your contribution is forever bound to this enduring work.

About the Author

S TEVE PANTAZIS IS AN award-winning author of fantasy and science fiction. He won the prestigious Writers of the Future award and has published short stories in leading anthologies and magazines, including *Nature*, *Galaxy's Edge*, and *IGMS*. He is the author of *The Light of Darkness* epic fantasy series. When not writing (a rare occasion!), Steve creates extraordinary cuisine, exercises with vigor, and shares marvelous adventures with the love of his life. Originally from the Big Apple, he now calls Southern California home. You can learn more about him at www.StevePantazis.com.

Connect with Steve

Get a **FREE eBook** just by signing up for Steve's newsletter: https://www.stevepantazis.com/subscribe

Support Steve at **Patreon** and receive early access to his short stories and novel chapters, along with cool swag: https://www.patreon.com/StevePantazis

To find out more about Steve and his happenings, check out these links:

Facebook page: http://facebook.com/SFFAuthor
Twitter: https://twitter.com/pantazis
Website: https://www.stevepantazis.com

Also by Steve Pantazis

Short stories and novellas:

A Matter of Time

A World Without Flowers

Aliens Anonymous

Apostate

Before I Let You Go

Between a Rock and a Fireball

C'est la vie, Humans

Chameleon

Cold as Space

Curse of the Goddess of Kaanapali

Cursed Magic

Daddy's Girl

Daughter of Time

Decadent Deception

Earth for Sale (Sold!)

Eternity's Traveler

Gods of War

Hex

Honor Bound

Humanity's Last Hope

I Dream of Stars

Illusions

In a Blink

In Darkness Lies

Infernally Yours

It's Only Skin Deep, Darling

Light in the Shadow of Worlds

Magic in the Land of Oppression

Murder on Moonbase 9

Odin's Daughter

Out of Print

Race to the Relic

Purple Orchid Eater

Reset

Surrogate

Switch

The Abernacle

The Daughter You've Always Wanted

The Devil Walks into a Bar

The Hunt

The Legacy

The Longest Mile

The Old Man and the Sea Siren

The Prize

The Sacrifice

To Be Human

Universal Problem

Unlucky

Untamed

Boxed sets:

Alien Worlds

Dragons & Magic

Human 2.0

Miscreants & Mayhem

Modern Magic

Robot Dreams

Space & Time

The Alien Within

The Light of Darkness epic fantasy series:

Prequel: The Dark That Ignites

Book 1. The Dark That Begins

Book 2. The Dark That Creates

Book 3. The Dark That Binds

Book 4. The Dark That Usurps

Book 5. The Dark That Defies

Book 6. The Dark That Burns

Book 7. The Dark That Destroys

Book 8. The Dark That Rules
Book 9. The Dark That Ends

Science fiction novels:

Blackout
Godnet